D0771446

WITHDRAWN

The Sheisty Saga:

Triple Crown Collection

The Sheisty Saga:

Triple Crown Collection

T.N. Baker

www.urbanbooks.net

Urban Books, LLC
300 Farmingdale Road, NY-Route 109
Farmingdale, NY 11735

The Sheisty Saga: Triple Crown Collection
Copyright © 2017 T.N. Baker

This title is published by Urban Books, LLC under a licensing
agreement with Triple Crown Publications, LLC.

*All rights reserved. No part of this book may be reproduced
in any form or by any means without prior consent of the
Publisher, except brief quotes used in reviews.*

ISBN 13: 978-1-62286-475-1
ISBN 10: 1-62286-475-1

First Trade Paperback Printing April 2017
Printed in the United States of America

10 9 8 7 6 5 4 3 2 1

*This is a work of fiction. Any references or similarities to ac-
tual events, real people, living or dead, or to real locales are
intended to give the novel a sense of reality. Any similarity
in other names, characters, places, and incidents is entirely
coincidental.*

Distributed by Kensington Publishing Corp.
Submit Orders to:
Customer Service
400 Hahn Road
Westminster, MD 21157-4627
Phone: 1-800-733-3000
Fax: 1-800-659-2436

Chapter 1

Epiphany

I didn't know who sang the old school song, but I turned up the radio volume and sang the hook as loud as I could. "Use what you got to get what you want." Ain't that the truth.

I was twenty-two years old, pushing a 325 BMW, living in a $700 a month apartment, all being funded by the power of the pussy. Shit, with beauty and a booty, who needed a job? I mean, let's not get it twisted. I wasn't no dummy. I did graduate from high school. I even thought about college briefly when Keisha went. Then I remembered how glad I was to finally be finished with high school. Me, with a job? Never! For one, I didn't like being told what to do. I hated getting up in the morning, and being on time was just something I wasn't good at.

Now sex—I could do that. And for money, I could do it all day. Don't get me wrong; I wasn't no street-corner ho or nothing like that. I just preferred to date guys with money that didn't mind paying to play, because after a good time, the bills still had to get paid.

It's like my mother always said: "If you want quality, you gotta pay for it," and Epiphany Janee Wright is top of the line quality.

I was excited about my date that night with Smitty, a potential "sponsor." Sponsor, buyer, or trick were just some of the little titles me and my girls liked to use to describe these niggas out here tricking, a.k.a. financially taking care of a woman's needs.

I met him at the club the night before, and from the looks of it, he had a lot of cash. But what impressed me was the bottle of Dom P he sent over to my table, along with his number. Now, that's class. Most guys will press hard for the digits but won't come up outta them pockets to buy a drink. Hmm, first impressions are the best impressions.

I glanced at the clock. It was 6:00 p.m. Smitty was picking me up in two hours, and knowing me, it was gonna take every bit of that two hours to get ready.

I hopped in the shower and was dressed, looking and smelling good, at exactly 8:00 p.m. I was so excited about possibly gaining a new sponsor that I forgot to call Malikai, my current trick, with an excuse for why I wouldn't be seeing him that night. I was surprised that I hadn't heard from him all day. There was no question about it: his ass was sprung, and I wanted to keep it that way. Whatever it took to keep his cash flowing my way, I'd do. I wasn't tryin'a mess that up, and the key was just keeping the nigga happy. Any real woman knows how to keep a man happy. You just fuck 'em when they wanna be fucked and tell 'em what they wanna hear.

Smitty showed up an hour late, blowing the horn of his Expedition truck like I was the one that kept him waiting. When I got in the truck, I could tell he was still pleased with my looks by the smile on his face. On the other hand, he didn't look as good as I thought—which was a slight disappointment—but he appeared to be paid, and that's what's up. Money does make a difference. I've seen it turn a frog into prince and a beast into a beauty queen on many occasions, especially in the entertainment industry. I won't name no names. They know who they are.

"So, where we going?" I asked.

"Yo, I gotta make a stop at my crib first and then we'll go get something to eat, a'ight?" he said.

I sucked my teeth and rolled my eyes at him as I thought, *I let him slide for being late, but now he's pushing it.*

Smitty had this cockiness about him. I wasn't feeling his personality at all, and my attitude was starting to show it. To top it off, he lived with his mother in the projects. Don't get me wrong, I don't have nothing against a nigga from the projects getting paper, but if you could splurge out thirty G's or more for a truck, your next move should be to come up outta the PJs.

"Yo, come on 'cause I'ma be a minute, and I ain't trying to leave your fine-ass out here around these niggas," Smitty said.

I wasn't sure if he meant they would be trying to push up on me or rob me, so I went with him into the three-story building. Upstairs, the apartment was a mess. His mother looked like she was his number one customer, assuming he had to be a drug dealer. I followed him to the back of the three-bedroom apartment, to a steel door with four locks on it.

When Smitty opened the door to his room, to my surprise, it didn't even look like a part of the dingy apartment. He had a nice bedroom set, stereo equipment, a DVD player, and all the CDs and DVD movies you could possibly think of. His shit was laced. Nevertheless, I wasn't impressed. It was still just a room at his mom's in the projects.

He locked the door, turned on his stereo, blasting Black Rob's "Like Whoa," and put a movie on also and muted the sound. Then he opened up a safe down by the side of the bed. It was filled with drugs, money, two guns, and some jewelry. He lifted his pant leg, pulled a stack of money tied in a rubber band out of his sock, counted it, and placed it in the safe.

As he shut the door to the safe, he quickly glanced over at me to see if I was looking. I pretended to be glued to the television.

Smitty came over to me and started to caress my leg, talking loudly over the music about how good I looked and how badly he wanted to fuck me. I laughed, because I found this nigga hilarious. Here it is, he hadn't even spend any real money yet and already he was pushing up on the pussy.

"Nigga, please. Look, you got shit twisted, Smitty. I don't know what you are used to, but this ass right here ain't free." I got straight to the point, since I already knew I wasn't gon' fuck with his ugly frontin'-like-he-stacking, still-livin'-with-his-momma ass.

The look on his face turned cold. What was I thinking? As a matter of fact, I wasn't thinking. I was locked in a room with this thug-ass nigga, and no one knew where I was or who I was with. No sooner than that thought crossed my mind, Smitty grabbed me by my throat and forcefully got on top off me.

"Bitch, do you know who the fuck I am? I ain't never had to pay fo' no pussy, and I ain't 'bout to start."

I felt helpless and almost breathless from the tight grip he had on my neck. Tears streamed down the sides of my face as he pulled my panties to the side with his free hand and rammed his dick inside me. It seemed like forever, although it was only a few strokes long. I couldn't believe that I was being violated like this, and all I could think about was what he might do next.

Suddenly, he pulled his dick out, bust his nut all over me and arrogantly said, "I took the pussy, you trick-ass bitch. Now what? Just fix your shit and get the fuck out!"

Chapter 2

KEISHA

Tucker was really starting to get on my nerves. It had to be my hormones tripping me out, because I loved the ground he walked on, but sometimes his excitement of having his first-born drove me nuts.

These last few months had been moving so slowly. I barely saw my friends anymore. Once in a while, Shana would call or stop by with gifts for the baby and small talk, but Epiphany had become so distant. I'd called and left several messages on her machine. I even asked Malikai to tell her to call me. To be honest, I didn't know what was up with her. She acted like pregnancy was contagious. Tucker and I had been engaged for over a month and I hadn't even been able to share the news with her. It hurt to feel like I was losing not only my best friend, but more like my sister.

Shit, I felt closer to her and her family than I did my own blood. Epiphany and I grew up together. I always admired the fact that she was raised in such a loving household by her mother and her father. Me, on the other hand, I was just the opposite. I don't even remember my father, and my mother being an alcoholic was all I seemed to remember.

I spent a lot of nights over Epiphany's house to get away from my mother. E's parents always treated me like family. Sometimes that girl didn't realize how lucky she was to have concerned parents that gave her the world.

Besides Epiphany, Tucker was the only other person I considered to be family. I had two younger sisters that lived in Atlanta with our grandmother, who always had her hand out for something. She thought since Tucker was high-rolling, it was our responsibility to help her support my sisters. And speaking of support, I hadn't heard from my so-called mother, Loretta, since I moved in with Tucker five years ago.

My childhood had made me a little bitter, but at the same time, I learned from it. I always felt as if I was ahead of my class. So, to get out faster, I dropped out of high school in the eleventh grade, got my G.E.D., and completed four years of college a year ahead of time. I was going back for my master's after my baby was born.

So you see, I did have a plan. I was not about to let life pass me by while I sat around feeling sorry for myself, just like my mother had. I would give my child the life I never had, no matter what it took.

I'd been with Tucker since I was sixteen. He was the only man I'd ever been with sexually. I loved him dearly. If something were to happen to him, I didn't think that I would make it. That was why I wished he would leave the drug game alone.

Tucker made a lot of money selling dope. Business for him was always good, so the money was definitely consistent, and you know what that means: more money, more problems. I knew he loved me, so I didn't worry about losing him to another woman . . . but the streets. Now, that was a different story.

Chapter 3

SHANA

It was Friday, and all I could think about was hitting the club that night. Since K.C., my abusive-ass man, got locked up two days before, I didn't have to worry about him running up on me in the clubs no more, trying to smack a bitch up 'cause I was out doing the same shit he was doing. K.C. was my nigga, no doubt, and he had some good dick, but he thought just because he spent his money on me, he owned my ass.

I remember one time, me and Epiphany was hanging out at Cheetah's on a Friday night, having the time of our lives, when here this nigga comes up from out of nowhere, making a scene, talking 'bout, "Go home."

I'm like, "What! Go home?" Yo, the way that nigga was acting threw me way off, 'cause I just started fucking around with him.

Right then and there I should've seen the "beat a bitch" signs written all over his ass, but you know how that goes. Instead, I just thought the nigga was really feeling me like that, 'cause I'm thinking, *Why else would he lose it and wanna beat the shit out of me if he ain't care?*

Most of the time it was my fault anyway. I was just the type of chick that was gonna do what the fuck I wanted to do and deal with the consequences later. Needless to say, getting my ass kicked was always the consequence for fucking with his ass. We stayed on some war of the roses type of shit, 'cause he wasn't gon' just be fucking me up without getting a few bumps and bruises too. I'll go hard for mines. But that was still my boo, and shit, y'all know what they say: Love is blinder than a muthafucka.

Epiphany couldn't stand K.C. One time she went as far as to say he tried to holla at her. Now, don't get me wrong; that was my homegirl. I'd known her for years, but most of the time I just wasn't feeling her whole attitude. She thought every nigga wanted to get with her.

When she told me that, I couldn't say the thought of it maybe being true didn't bother me, but he denied it, and I believed him. Shit, this nigga was taking care of me, and I loved how he took care of me. On top of that, did I mention the sex was the *bomb*?

I wasn't letting shit come in between us for nobody—until this nigga went and did some dumb shit and got locked the fuck up for a third felony charge. Three strikes and you're out, so there wasn't no need in trying to hold on, 'cause K.C. was finished, finito, outta here. He was locked up for the rest of his life. Shit, I wasn't that stand-by-your-man type of bitch—not if the nigga was doing a lifelong bid. I'll tell you this much though: that was a waste of some good dick, and I would damn sure miss his ass.

My skills weren't as tight as Epiphany's when it came to pulling a nigga that would spend his dough on me, so when I pulled K.C., I tried to hold onto his ass.

Epiphany had it good, 'cause she grew up in a house. It didn't matter what the neighborhood was like, as long as it was a house. With niggas, that played a big part in the amount of respect they gave you. On top of that, she was a pretty girl, plus all-the-way high maintenance. So, a nigga knew if he came at her, he had to come correct.

Me, I was a cutie, but I was from the PJs, so with that fact alone, it didn't matter what I looked like. Right off the bat, niggas didn't respect me. They stereotyped me hard, assuming I was a ho or I had three or four kids by different daddies.

One thing that did make me better than Epiphany, though, was that I could rock with a dude for his cash, but I also knew how to get out there and get my own paper. I was a hustler, any way it came—boosting, credit card scams, cell phone hookups, or transporting shit out of town for the cats around my way. You named it, along with the right price, and I was down.

Natural born hustler was in my blood, so with or without a trick-ass nigga, I was gonna get mine regardless, 'cause I loved the dough.

I had just started dancing at this strip club called Honey's. Yo! I made $500 in three short hours just off pussy-popping to some R&B and hip hop. Now, that's what's up. Shit, for some people, that's a month's rent and some food in the fridge, with a little pocket change left over for the club.

I was thinking about putting Epiphany on, 'cause she'd make a killing, and for that kind of easy cash, her money-hungry ass just might be down to do it. But knowing her, she'd only steal the spotlight and fuck up my shine, so on second thought, I'd keep my shit on the low.

Chapter 4

EPIPHANY

Shana had been calling me all day. I knew she wanted to hit the club that night. Lately I hadn't been in the mood to do anything. It had been a week since that muthafucka got me for some pussy. All I knew was I got the hell outta there as fast as I could. Anyway, fuck that nigga. He got that—for now.

That wasn't the first time the pussy had been taken, though, and that whole situation just brought back memories. When I was a kid, my father's brother lived with us, and I remembered him always sweating me. He would always be like, "C'mere," bragging to his boys about my cuteness, saying, "Yo, I got a fly-ass little niece. She gon' put a hurting on them cats when she get older."

Uncle Ramel was always buying me gifts and giving me money. Then, at the tender age of twelve, he took my virginity—only he ain't grab me by my neck and force himself inside of me. It wasn't nothing like what that stupid muthafucka Smitty did to me. It was a gentle kind of rape. He was my uncle, my father's baby bro, and I trusted him.

It was uncomfortable at first, but shit, it went on for so long that I started to enjoy it. He was eighteen at the time and out there slanging them thangs for my father, so his gifts always got better, and so did the amounts of cash he would give me. By the time I was fifteen and he was twenty-one, I was fucking and sucking his dick like a *professional*. Call it sick, but after a while, you adjust to a situation. That is, until the nigga started getting jealous when boys came around, acting as if I was his girlfriend or something.

His behavior made me realize how sick he really was. I started to feel disgusting, him carrying on like that. I would fuck with him by putting emphasis on *Uncle* when I called him. Every time he would look at me and I felt it was inappropriate, I would always threaten to tell my father, just to have control over him.

Guess he couldn't take the heat anymore, or the chance that I might one day tell, so he moved out. Now we tried to avoid each other as much as possible, but when I do see him at family functions, I got off on flaunting my cuteness in his face and calling him *Uncle* Ramel. He still looked at me like he wanted me, but what could he say? He created a monster.

I guess that's where I got my "get what I can get with the pussy" attitude from, huh? Shit, everything came with a price. Thinking back on all this was crazy, but the point I'm trying to make is even my uncle paid for the pussy, and so would Smitty, one way or another!

I picked up Shana a little after midnight. In New York, the parties were just getting started around 1:00 a.m. It was the weekend, so I knew the traffic would be a little crazy once we hit the city. Shit, you had to fight with the yellow cabs just to get to your destination.

The club was off the hook, as usual—except I needed to party with the very important people. Since I had the gift of gab to go along with my beauty, I was always able to talk a man into anything. After downing a straight shot of Hennessey, I knew working my gift on the big, ugly bouncer, who was guarding the VIP section like it was a meal, would be a piece of cake.

B.I.G.'s "Big Poppa" was playing. Dom P, Cristal, and bottles of water were all the bar was selling. Now, for those (like me) who didn't know, the water was for the ecstasy poppers. Shana let me in on that secret, because she got down too.

"Girl, what don't your project-ass do?" I laughed. "Shit, I don't need a pill to enhance my sex. If a nigga's pockets is stacking and he don't mind splurging, then I'm like Burger King, he can have it his way."

There were definitely a few hit record makers in the house, along with a couple of one-hit wonders still trying to floss from a hit they made five to ten years ago. I mingled away from Shana because she was being a real groupie. I kept telling her these niggas didn't respect groupies. If you wanted them to notice you, you had to act as if you were just as important as they were and not pay they asses no mind (You know, a discreet groupie, like myself).

By the end of the night, the champagne had me feeling real horny, and since my discretion wasn't working, I called Malikai on his cell and told him to meet me at my place. He didn't ask any questions before he agreed, and why should he? It was five o' clock in the morning, and the only thing I knew that opened up at that time was legs. He knew exactly what I wanted—to be buck naked, getting fucked, listening to some R. Kelly's "Bump and Grind" until the smell of boodussy filled the air (meaning booty, dick, and pussy). When the smell of sweat and sex hit the air, you knew that shit was good.

Malikai had spent the past two nights with me. I could tell he wanted to take our relationship to another level. He was such a sweetie, and we did have a lot of fun together, but if his pockets didn't run deep, he might've been history a long time ago. We'd been kicking it for maybe about a year now, and his dick game had always been kinda whack, plus it was smaller than your average penis.

I always wondered if a nigga with a little dick knew his shit was little. Somebody had to get pissed off or frustrated and tell his ass at some point in his life. It was always a catch-22 with these niggas. If he looked good, nine times out of ten the nigga was walking with deep pockets and a short reach (meaning he wasn't coming up off no dough). If he had some dough and freely gave it up, he was either ugly as hell, horrible in bed, or sometimes both.

Who knew if I'd ever settle down. Maybe one day I'd get lucky, maybe not, but if that was the case, I surely didn't have a problem with being single and having fun.

I guess everybody couldn't be lucky like Keisha, with a good-looking, faithful man who took care of her, stacked dough like crazy, and let her tell it, was a freak in bed too. Shit, fuck having the best of both worlds; she had the whole world in her hands.

Speaking of Keisha, I had to call and see how she was doing. I couldn't believe she was gonna be a baby's momma. Better her than me. I was a strong believer when it came to abortion. Shit, I'd already had seven, please believe it. I didn't have no time to be having nobody's baby.

Chapter 5

KEISHA

I got a call from Epiphany, and we actually made plans to check out a movie and grab a bite to eat that afternoon. I was upset with the way she'd been treating me since I got pregnant. Hanging out with Shana and E, reminiscing on old times, made it all better though. I laughed so much I almost peed in my pants three times. I hadn't seen Epiphany in about five months. To them, the past seven months went by fast; for me, it wasn't moving fast enough.

"I really miss you guys," I said, startin' to get teary-eyed. E laughed then reached over and gave me a tight hug, while Shana teased me for getting so emotional. I finally got to announce my engagement. Although Tucker and I hadn't set a date, I made both my girls promise to be there when we got married. We were having such a good time that I didn't want it to end.

So much was going on with them; it was hard playing catch up. Besides the baby and getting engaged, I didn't have anything to discuss that was as juicy as what was going on in their lives. All I knew was I couldn't wait to drop this load, not because I felt like I was missing out on what was in the streets, but because I was lonely and I missed times like these with my homegirls. For once, Epiphany didn't say anything to piss Shana off, which was good but rare.

Lately, Tucker had been back and forth out of town a lot. I was used to him being gone all the time, but he had promised to stay in town more toward the end of my pregnancy. His bullshit was really starting to bother me. Every time I said something, he said I was adding on to his stress, or I didn't have his back. So, I just keep quiet, but when his son got here, that nigga had better change his program.

I'd been spending a lot of time on the computer, meeting some interesting people online. I was logging into those kinky chat rooms, since I hadn't been getting much loving. What's wrong with living vicariously through others? Hell, I think I was addicted. I went by the name of BAPS, meaning bomb-ass pussy sweet. It was just innocent fun. Besides, it helped me keep my mind off my man's whereabouts.

Chapter 6

SHANA

I was glad that Epiphany finally got around to hanging with Keisha. The girl got on my nerves asking about her all the time. She had to realize that we were all grown up now and shit wasn't gon' be like it used to. Everybody was livin' their own life. It was cool getting together and chillin' like back in the days, but this wasn't back in the day, and that close shit was slowly fading.

I met this chick, Chasity, from Pomanock Projects in Flushing. She got her dance on out in Jersey, too. We took the Path train together. She was cool as hell. I didn't fuck with too many bitches, but we just clicked. One night, we were doing a gig out in Brooklyn with this other chick she was cool with from out there. I didn't really want to fuck with Brooklyn 'cause that shit was just too close to home. I wasn't ready to be on front street shaking my ass, but fuck it—$150 for three sets plus tips wasn't bad at all.

When we arrived at the spot, it looked sort of like a warehouse inside, but it was set up real nice. I noticed there was nothing but girls up in there. Now, I know how chicks like to pile up in the club when it's free before ten o'clock, but it was almost twelve.

"Yo, I know we ain't dancing for no girls," I said to Chasity, who didn't seem surprised at all.

"I didn't wanna tell you 'cause I knew you wouldn't be with it, but dancing for the women is where them dollars is at, girl."

It didn't take much to convince me. I'd done worse shit than that. Hell, these chicks liked what the niggas like, so how bad could it be? She still could've told me though.

Chasity's homegirl's stage name was Scar. I asked her, "Why Scar?" She said it was 'cause if she didn't leave a scar on a nigga's heart, she'd damn sure leave one on his pockets. Now, that was deep. I thought to myself that her and Epiphany would probably get along good.

I decided to call myself Cream, so I chose "Ice Cream" by Wu Tang Clan as my introduction song.

I couldn't believe how wild they went when I came out on stage. Those dollars was flying. The shit was a rush for me, because women are your worse critics, but these chicks liked what they saw. I even got a few numbers handed to me after my dance, but I wasn't with that carpet munching shit.

Chapter 7

EPIPHANY

Malikai was going out of town a lot more since his boy Tucker had to stay closer to home until his baby was born. Malikai was starting to bore me. He never wanted to do nothing but lay up when we were together. The money was still good, but he was out of town more than he was home. Shit, the nigga even had a crib down in North Carolina. He invited me to come chill with him, but I wasn't feeling him anymore, and the sooner he caught the hint the better.

It was comedy night at the Manhattan Proper. The spot was off the hook and always packed with niggas. A lot of Brooklyn cats were up in there too, I guess because they said Queens girls looked good. Should you expect anything less from a borough called Queens?

Shana's ass hadn't called me back yet, even after I paged her "911" about an hour before. Fuck her. It could've been important. She'd been on some different shit lately. I didn't know what, but I wasn't fucking with her.

I called up Tanya, this girl I went to high school with. We had run into each other about a week ago at the mall and exchanged numbers. She was cool enough to hang out with.

Tanya was with it and she could drive, so for once I didn't have to be the designated driver. She came to get me around 10:30 p.m. 'cause you gotta get there early if you want a good seat. We smoked a little weed to help us get silly, just in case the show wasn't funny.

It was exactly ten forty-five when we arrived. The only seats that were available were by the bar, which was cool, but the people talking around the bar made it hard to hear the jokes.

I ordered a Henny on the rocks and an Amaretto Sour for Tanya, while she went to the restroom. That girl was crazy. You should never go to the bathroom while the comedians are performing, 'cause you have to pass the stage, and they will crack on your ass. She got off easy this time though, 'cause the girl that walked behind her was comical—wearing some shit she knew her big ass shouldn't have had on. Somebody should have warned her, because the comedian lit her ass up.

"Girl, some guy was trying to talk to me just now by the pay phones. He said he'll be over to buy us some drinks," Tanya said, all excited. I just smiled. Besides her nice-ass shape and shoulder-length hair, homegirl was not cute at all, so good for her.

Then Corey, better known as C-God, walked over to the bar. I couldn't believe he was coming over to talk to Tanya. He could have pulled any girl he wanted. C-God was black and ugly, but he had money, confidence, and a cockiness about him that turned me on. He tried to get at me years ago, before the money, but a lot of things have changed since then. He was definitely looking kinda good.

Tanya passed him her number, but judging by the look on his face, I could tell he felt like he had just chosen cake but wanted hot apple pie. I was the pie. It wasn't like he expected me to be here chilling with her. I hadn't seen him in years.

C-God ordered our drinks. He was blinged out, diamonds everywhere—ears, neck, wrist, and pinky finger. I had my game face on. The eye contact between us was crazy. I wanted him just as bad as he wanted me.

"Damn, somebody must be treating you good, 'cause I remember when you was a toothpick, and you know they say love fattens you up," I said seductively as the alcohol started kicking in.

He flexed his muscles and said, "It ain't fat, baby. It ain't fat at all."

It was getting hot in there, and for every slick little comment I made, he came right back at me with one of his own. I wasn't sure if Tanya caught on or not, but she had to be slow or stupid not to see our chemistry. It was so obvious.

C-God was chilling with his boy Reggie, who must have known what time it was, 'cause he kept Tanya distracted with small talk, while C-God's eyes undressed me, and I loved every bit of it. I wanted his ass right then and there. It wasn't like he was a stranger or anything, I knew him for years in passing. Who cared if Tanya gave him her number? He could do better. He knew it, and so did I. All type of shit was going through my head, and the more I drank, the better he looked.

"Yo, y'all ladies wanna go grab a bite to eat with me and my man?" C-God said, looking in my direction. I smiled and said I was with it.

Since Tanya drove her car, they followed us to her house to park, so we could all ride together. I was hoping the bitch had to work early in the morning so I could roll solo, but Tanya walked right up to C-God's truck and sat up front with him.

Once we got to the diner, she still played him close. I knew what time it was, so I let her have her fifteen minutes of fame. We all laughed, cracked "yo' momma" jokes, and drank some more until the sun was starting to rise.

On the way out, I saw Smitty's punk-ass sitting at a table with some Spanish-looking chick, and there went my high. I hated that muthafucka.

This time Tanya and C-God sat in the back seats on the way home. I rode in the front with Reg. She was all over C-God, and I knew it was only because she felt our vibe. But after seeing Smitty's pussy-stealing-ass, I wasn't in the mood to play any more games. Tanya could have him for now.

Later that morning, I woke up on the wrong side of the bed with a banging-ass headache. I got up to get some Advil when the phone rang. It was Malikai, questioning me with the who, what, why, and where I was all night. He picked the wrong time of day to call and play daddy. I let his ass have it, and before I hung up the phone, I told him not to call me anymore because I was already fucking someone else. I lied, but that was all I could think of to get him mad enough to not want me anymore. Besides, I no longer wanted what was behind door number two. I had my eye on the grand prize.

C-God and I had some unfinished business to tend to. I didn't know how I was gon' make it happen since I didn't have his number, but where there's a will, there is a way.

***

A week had passed since we all hung out together, and Tanya couldn't wait to let it be known that she was fucking C-God. I was pissed about that whole situation. How the hell did he choose her over me? And I know she enjoyed rubbing that shit in my face. The bitch had the nerve to ask me to hang out with them that night because Reggie had been asking about me. Bullshit! I barely said two words to that nigga. Why would he ask about me?

"Cool, pick me up at ten. I'll roll, 'cause I ain't doing shit else," I said.

Tanya agreed and said she'd see me then. I had something for her ass though. The fat lady ain't sang yet! I pulled out a pair of jeans that hugged my beautiful, round-shaped ass so well that they looked like they was painted on, a black halter top that exposed just the right amount of cleavage, my stiletto boots . . . oh, and let's not forget my brand new Vicki's Secret thong (just in case).

The three of them rolled up to my crib about ten-fifteen, which was cool, because I had just finished touching up my hair and makeup, which was always an earth tone eye shadow and some lip gloss. My father always said real beauty needs no makeup. A man hates to go to bed with a beauty queen and wake up to a monster. Even though I couldn't look like a monster if I tried, I got what he was saying. If it ain't broke, why fix it? Anyway, I hopped in the back of C-God's Escalade and gave Reg a phony, "don't even think about it" smile.

"Hey, girl," I said to Tanya. "What's up, C-God? How you been?"

"Chillin', ma," he responded.

And looking even better than you did the last time, I thought to myself as he constantly watched me from the rearview mirror. C-God knew what was really good, so tonight, I was gonna play the game just to see how it all panned out.

He took us to Night of the Cookers in Brooklyn, which surprised me, because it was a nice, cozy, laid back spot. They had a live band, candlelight, and good food. Money wasn't an issue with C-God. He told us to order what we wanted. Even paid for his broke-ass friend—or should I say broke-ass boy? That's exactly what Reggie was.

Tanya was doing a lot of drinking, as if she was trying to be down or prove something. More power to her, because I wasn't about to get drunk, lose focus, and make a fool of myself.

C-God was so funny, and ain't nothing like a man with money that can make me laugh. Damn, I had to have him. The thought stayed in my head all night. When Tanya got up to go to the ladies room, I couldn't hold it in anymore.

"What's up?" I leaned in closer to C-God. "I know you want me, just 'cause of the way you keep looking at me. So let's stop the game playing and make it happen."

"Aggressive, ain't we? I like that," he said with a smile.

That was it! That was all he had to say, even if he was feeling Tanya. The way he looked at me, it was impossible. I ain't never had to work this hard for no nigga, and I wasn't 'bout to start.

Just then, Tanya came back to the table smelling like she'd been hanging with hurl (throwing up), so we decided to call it a night.

The seating arrangement was different on the way home. Instead of Tanya sitting in the front, C-God told her to take the back seat and Reg was going to sit in the front with him. I was curious to know why, but she didn't question it, and neither did I. Besides, Tanya was wasted and out cold within a matter of seconds.

When we reached my apartment, C-God told Reggie to take the car and make sure Tanya got home safe. I smiled, because I knew it was only a matter of time before he'd come to his senses.

"So, you coming with me?" I asked.

"No doubt." He followed me to my door.

Inside, I decided to set the mood by lighting some aroma-therapy candles and turning the radio on to Vaughn Harper's "The Quiet Storm" on WBLS. I swear the sound of that man's voice could get my panties moist any night of the week.

Before I could say a word, C-God was already undressing me. His body was so hard and muscular, and so was his dick. He worked his tongue from my breasts down to my wet and pulsating pussy and didn't stop working until I reached my climax. I returned the favor, because I had the dick-sucking skills to get a nigga hooked—and of course that was the plan. It wasn't because I was worried about him and Tanya, but because I wanted him all to myself. Besides, he couldn't be stupid enough to go back to burgers after havin' steak.

I gave him the pussy in every position possible: standing up, doggy style, legs up in the air, and even rodeo style. We went at it for hours, until we finally fell asleep. In the morning, I gave him some more.

He had it going on. I swear I had never been with a man that could make my coochie cream the way he did. The only thing that kept interrupting the flow was his cell phone and two-way. They were seriously competing with one another. I wondered if any of those calls were from Tanya, but I didn't ask.

After working up an appetite, we showered off the sex, got dressed, hopped in my car, and went to grab a bite to eat.

I asked him, "What's the status with you and Tanya?" His answer was that she was cool and he fucked her a couple of times, but outside of having a fat ass and nice set of tits, he really wasn't all that attracted to her. He felt that I, on the other hand, was the real deal, someone he wouldn't mind kickin' it with, spending a little dough on, or maybe even wifin' me up in a nice condo outside of the hood.

"As long as you good to me, I'm good to you," were his words.

Now, that's what I'm talkin' 'bout! I smiled and asked, "Wasn't I good to you last night?" Joking around with each other was something we both enjoyed doing. Then, he got a call that he couldn't put off and our brunch was cut short.

Chapter 8

KEISHA

"Oh, shit!" I screamed as the water started to run down my legs. "Tucker, get up. It's time!" I shouted, waking him out of his sleep with my bag packed and ready to go. I had felt light pains all night the night before, so I packed what I thought I might need to take with me to the hospital early that morning. The real pain hadn't kicked in yet, but all I knew was I was ready to get this little boy out of me and into my arms.

Tucker got up and started to panic more than I was.

"I'm fine. Calm down," I screamed. "Just take me to the hospital."

When we got to the hospital, I was only four centimeters, but they admitted me anyway because my water had already broken. I called up E and Shana because I wanted them to be there. I ended up having to leave messages for both of them.

My sweetie was by my side the whole time, anticipating the arrival of his son. I couldn't ask for a better man. As soon as I had this baby, I was gonna start putting the pressure on him about our wedding plans, before he even thought about taking his ass back out of town. My girls thought I had the perfect situation, but it's always nicer on the outside when you're looking in.

The pains were starting to hit me hard, real hard. I knew it would hurt, but I never imagined like this. Tears fell down the sides of my face, and the love of my life was now my enemy. I didn't want him to touch me; I didn't want him near me. His voice of support saying, "Push. It's okay," pissed me off even more. He couldn't begin to know what I was feeling.

***

Ten hours of excruciating pain was finally over, and I was holding the most beautiful baby I had ever seen. Now, all I needed was some sleep.

When I woke up, my room was filled with flowers, teddy bears, and balloons that said "It's a Boy" and "Congratulations." To my surprise, Epiphany and Shana were sitting there watching TV, waiting for me to wake up.

"Hey," I said, still feeling a little tired but excited to see my friends at the same time.

Epiphany smiled and bragged about how cute my baby was. She had jokes, talking about, "I wonder who he got his looks from. He is too cute." I was so glad that she came to see me. She looked so happy. It had to be a new man that had her smiling so much. Tucker told me that she wasn't fucking with Mali anymore.

Shana just stopped by to see me and the baby. She said she couldn't stay because she was working nights now.

"Shana, not *you* with a job. Doing what? It must be illegal," Epiphany said, laughing.

"Well, not everyone needs a man to take care of them," Shana said, not finding Epiphany's comment amusing at all. "I'll come check you when you get home, Keisha."

"What's wrong with her?" E said.

"I don't know, but she looks tired," I said, trying to make an excuse for her attitude.

"I ain't been feeling her," E said. "You know I paged that bitch nine-one-one a couple of times and she never called me back." I just shook my head because I knew how it felt to have a friend not return your calls. "I wonder what kinda job she got anyway. She's probably on the corner selling drugs or something," Epiphany said, being real snobbish.

"That's not nice. Maybe she has a real job, Epiphany. Besides, you guys are friends, so y'all need to stop trippin'," I said.

"I don't know, Keish. You see that little comment she made about me getting money from men? Sounds like jealousy to me. Anyway, speaking of men, girl, remember C-God?" she asked.

"From where?" I asked, not sure whether or not I knew who she was talking about.

"Corey, that used to hang with Walter and Stevie that lived around the corner from us," she said.

"Black-ass Corey Hinderson that used to try and talk to everybody back in the day? Where you see his ugly ass at? I thought he was locked up," I said, disgusted, making her not even want to tell me the rest of her story.

"Well, he's not ugly anymore, and he got money," she said, rolling her eyes at me. Just then, Tucker walked in—perfect timing. Epiphany congratulated him, said good-bye, and was out the door.

"What's up, Mommy? Thanks for my little man. He looks just like me," Tucker said.

"You're welcome. You know that was some painful shit, and I just wanted to apologize for being so mean to you."

"It's cool. I know you didn't mean it," Tucker said, accepting my apology.

I kissed his lips. "I love you, and I hope to spend the rest of my life with you, until death do us part." Hint, hint.

Chapter 9

SHANA

I swear, sometimes Epiphany could just irk the shit out of me, always thinking she was hot shit. Like she was really concerned about where I worked. Shit, now that I thought about it, she was the last person I wanted to know that I danced. I was glad I hadn't tried to plug her ass in, because if she wasn't with it, she was the kind of person that was gonna hate on me for doing it, with her trifling-ass. If I hadn't left when I did, it would've been a girl fight up in there. I was tired of her with that "I'm better then you attitude" and her slick "You from PJs," remarks. That shit was kinda played. On top of all that, I had a helluva hangover, too, so, oh hell yeah, it would've been on in that hospital.

I had gotten my head right at Scar's ladies only party the night before. She had a li'l of this, a li'l of that: cocaine, weed, and E pills. We called them the "freak-off drugs," 'cause they made you wanna get freaky and downright nasty. Shit, the theme was sex and a good time, and I'd had too much of both that night. I was supposed to be dancing at Honey's tonight, but I was not even in the mood. I called Chasity to see if she wanted to stay home and just chill with me, but she gave me the bullshit about how we needed to go make that money.

She was right, as a matter of fact. I could use the money since I had just spent $200 on a week's worth of Ecstasy. I couldn't dance without them, but I also started taking them just 'cause they made me feel good. Shit, I guess that was their purpose—to make you feel good.

***

Honey's was packed, but that didn't always mean you were gonna make a lot of money, 'cause fifty percent of the niggas wanted to see the pussy spit fire for a fucking dollar. About twenty percent would come up out their pockets, and the rest of the niggas was straight up trying to get some ass.

A couple of weekends before, this nigga threw beer in my face and demanded his money back. I told him just because he paid me ten dollars for a lap dance didn't mean he could bust off on my ass. I reached for my razor when, lucky for his ass, security came and tossed him out for making a scene. I was 'bout to give his ass a buck fifty slice, to cut him deep until the pink meat was exposed, right across his face.

Nasty bitches like Peaches were having these dudes getting shit twisted, thinking anything went for ten or fifteen dollars. Her anorexic-ass was over in the corner, up against the wall, pretending she was dancing when she was really selling pussy for twenty bucks. The ho knew that shit was against floor rules. That was why we had the champagne room. But niggas didn't be wanting to pay that hundred dollars for those kind of privileges, and the tricks didn't be wanting to give up that twenty percent to the club owner. Shit, I wasn't trying to knock nobody's hustle—and I ain't gon' front, I done sold pussy many a night to get by—but it wasn't what you did, it was how you did it, and these hoes was fucking up the game.

As I squeezed my way through the funky little changing room/bathroom to get dressed, or should I say undressed, I overheard two strippers named Mahogany and Diamond whispering that some baller was out there tricking off a knot of cash and buying out the bar. That shit was music to my ears.

"Chasity, hurry up. There's money out there, girl," I said.

"You ain't said nothin' but a word. Let's go." She smiled.

The deejay was playing my song, "There's Some Hoes in This House." It wasn't hard to figure out where the real money was, because the hoes flocked to him like he was Jay-Z shooting a video for "Girls, Girls, Girls." Only thing wrong with this video was that most of the bitches in here looked like "who done it and why." I mean, they were tore up from the floor up, so it wouldn't be hard to steal the nigga's attention.

Chasity's pretty-ass was a big flirt anyway, and a hustler, like me. Automatically, a scheme came into play, 'cause great minds do think alike. The plan was to get him to spend some money here, then hit a telli (motel) on some two-for-the-price-of-one type shit, fuck him to sleep, and rob his ass.

"Would you like a dance?" Chasity asked him.

"Nah, I'm good, but what up with you and your girl giving my man here a dance? It's his birthday."

After like five drinks, I lost count as far as how many dances we gave his boy. I also changed the plan about trying to rob dude. I was feeling him a li'l something. I was feeling him even more when he peeled off four hundred-dollar bills from the money stashed in his right pocket and gave me and Chass two hundred a piece.

"I didn't get your name," I said with a smile.

"That's because I didn't give it. What's yours?" he said, showing his pearly whites. "Sha—I mean, Cream," I said, almost giving up my government.

Chocolate boy wonder wasn't giving up nothing else but a smile. "I'll be back to check you, shorty," he said as he got up from the bar to leave.

I hit him back with a quick response. "I'll be waiting." It was only 1:00 a.m. I had a couple of hundreds in my pocket and still three hours left to dance my sets and make some more. Shit, I wasn't mad at all.

"Chasity, did you get dude's name?" I asked.

"Nah, but his boy's name is Mike. He gave me his number."

"Oh, really," I said with a li'l hate in my tone.

Chapter 10

EPIPHANY

I dozed off watching the amateur night part of the Apollo when the phone rang and woke me. I debated on whether or not I should answer or let my machine pick it up. I looked at the caller ID and decided to answer.

"Yo, what up, ma? What you doing?"

"Who's this?" I said, knowing exactly who it was.

"Damn, after all the good-ass pussy you been giving me, you still don't know who dis is?" he said.

"Oh, hey, C-God. What's up, baby?"

"I hope you and me, 'cause I'm in front of your crib."

"So what, you tryin' to come in?"

"Oh, no doubt, but for now why don't you throw on something and come take a ride with me?"

"All right. I'll be out in five minutes," I said. I jumped up and threw on a pair of Gap jeans, a baby tee, and a pair of Chanel shoes, then ran to the bathroom, took off my head scarf, and combed down my wrap. I brushed my teeth and put a little Oh Baby M·A·C gloss on my lips, with liner, of course.

When I got out to his truck, he was in the passenger's seat. I assumed he wanted me to drive.

"So, where we going?" I asked.

"Let's go get something to eat, 'cause a nigga starvin'."

I wasn't really hungry, but I could tell C had been drinking, so maybe a little food would sober him up. I suggested Georgia Peach, this diner on Queens Boulevard. He already had his eyes closed and seat leaning all the way back. I guess it was left up to me.

"Hey, wake up. I'm gonna just go place your order to go. What do you want?" I said.

"Order me some chicken fingers and fries."

After getting his food, I drove back to my place. He came in and fell out on my bed.

Two months had passed since I started fucking around exclusively with C, and to my surprise, I wasn't even tired of him yet. We had lots of fun together. He seemed to be doing all the right things. Not only did he give up that paper willingly, but he made me feel like I was the sexiest bitch to ever walk the planet. Sometimes, we would just take a late night ride, smoke some trees, and listen to slow jams. I felt safe with him.

Niggas knew not to fuck with him. He had a reputation for murdering niggas in a heartbeat, friend or foe. That was hard for me to believe because I hadn't seen that side of him yet, although I did hear him talking on his cell to his boy Mike about some cat that had the Carolinas and Virginia on lock and was selling his weight for cheap prices, so his clientele was large.

"Yo, I want you and Ness to keep an eye on that nigga. Find out who else he down with, 'cause that nigga trying to stop me from eating, yo, and it ain't gon' happen, son. What, yo! Just do what the fuck I said and holla back from a pay phone. A'ight, out!"

I walked in the room right as he slammed the hood down on his Nextel, feeling kind of turned on by his authority.

"What up, ma?" he asked.

"I'm about to show you," I said as I kneeled down on my knees and unzipped his pants. I began to deep throat his thick ten and a half inches of hardness.

"Um, damn, that's what's up. You tryin' to turn a nigga out or something? Don't stop," he moaned and moaned some more.

I knew I had him right where I wanted him. His body started to jerk as he clutched on to the edge of the bed and began to breathe heavy. "Oh, shit. I'm about to cum," he said. Normally at that point I would have stopped, but his excitement made my pussy start to cum as well, so instead of stopping, I drank them babies.

"C, next weekend my girl Keisha—you remember Keisha, right?"

"Yeah, she kinda short, brown skin, right?"

"Uh-huh, that's her."

"Who she fuck with?" he inquired.

"This guy named Tucker."

"From where?" he continued.

"He's from Brooklyn, but they live together out here in Jamaica. Anyway, listen. She's baptizing their son, and I'm gonna to be the godmother. You wanna come with me?"

"Nah, that ain't my type of party," he said.

I got a little attitude. Shit, after one of my best head jobs, "No" was not what I wanted to hear. As those thoughts ran through my mind, he must've noticed the disappointment on my face, because he started explaining his reason.

"Churches just make me feel uncomfortable, so don't be mad, a'ight." Then he said those magic words: "You need some money?"

"Yeah," I said with a smile.

"How much you need?" he asked.

"About five hundred."

"A'ight, I got you," he said, holding me tight. "So, what's good for the night? You wanna go out for a drink?"

This boy knew he could drink. Since I'd been fuckin' with him, I'd become a bit of a lush my damn self, I thought before I said, "Sounds like a plan to me."

Later that night we hit this spot on Merrick called Quiet Storm. I'd lived in south side Jamaica all my life, and I never knew Queens had so many local hangout spots.

C-God sat at the bar, and I went to the bathroom. The place was small but packed. On my way back to the bar, I heard the deejay say, "Free drinks for the first twenty-five ladies. Oh yeah, ladies, you got ten minutes to place your drink order."

You should've seen those thirsty bitches pushing each other as they ran over and bum-rushed the bar. The shit was crazy. It reminded me of the way them old ladies in my neighborhood be rushing to the church every Wednesday morning to get that free bag of food before it ran out. I wasn't even tryin' to take a chance getting back to the bar, 'cause if one of those thirsty hoes stepped on my $300 boots from Sacco's, it was gonna be on up in there. So I waited out the ten minutes.

Then the deejay stopped the music again and said, "Oh yeah, ladies, those drinks . . . compliments from my man C-God over there at the bar. Ha ha! I see ya, big baller. Y'all ladies thank him for quenching that thirst, a'ight. My man, this song's for you, player."

The deejay was giving C props. He threw on Jay-Z's "Big Pimpin'."

I was pissed. I couldn't believe this nigga was up in there spending money on those bitches, money that could've been spent on me. I squeezed my ass right through the crowd that had now loosened up a little. All I seen was girls up in his face smiling, and his ass enjoying every moment of it. Oh, he was really tryin'a play me.

"Excuse me," I said in a nasty tone.

"Oh, this my baby right here, ladies. Say hello," he said to the birds standing around him then turned to me. "You a'ight, ma? I got us a bottle of Mo. They ain't got the good stuff." I couldn't believe this nigga was on some real pimp shit, talking 'bout "This my baby, ladies. Say hello," like these skank-ass bitches really cared.

"To answer your question, no, I'm not a'ight. I'm ready to go."

"Come on, ma. I'm just having a little fun. Besides, ain't none of these hoes drinking what you drinking."

"Oh, so that makes it a'ight?"

"Yeah, it do. We came together, and we leaving together, so drink the champagne and stop trippin'."

I did what he said, while he continued to flirt and acknowledge my presence at the same time. I was so pissed off. Besides his money, I made him look good, so for him to sit there and play me was fucked up. I could have had any nigga I wanted, and I chose him. None of those hoes looked better than me. I repeated this in my head over and over again to build my shattered confidence back up. Then I spotted Shana and some girl on the dance floor. That was my cue to break away for a minute.

"C-God, I'll be back." I got up and walked over to say what's up. Shana was high as hell. She introduced me to her friend Chasity, who from the looks of it seemed to have straight attitude toward me, which I ignored. I didn't have much to say to Shana, and neither did she. You would have never guessed that we were—or should I say *used to be* best friends. I asked if she was going to Keisha's son's christening, and if so, I'd see her there. I felt kinda awkward, so I used that as my cue to move along.

Just as I was about to go look for Mr. Don Fuckin' Juan, he found me.

I noticed Shana's eyes light up from the sight of C-God, so I didn't even bother to introduce them to each other. I grabbed his hand and just walked off.

On the way back to my house, I let C-God have it. I told him he better not ever try to fuckin' play me like that again. He apologized too easily and promised to make it up to me.

When we pulled up in front of my place, he told me he couldn't stay because he had some business to take care of. He said he'd see me the next day. I planted a wet one on those thick lips of his, said good night, and went inside my house.

Maybe I was tripping just a little. Shit, what the fuck was a few six-dollar drinks compared to my rent, my car note, and the five or six hundred he kept in my pocket for me to spend? I thought as I lay in the bed and drifted off into a sound sleep.

Chapter 11

EPIPHANY

"Epiphany, pick up the phone. Hello? Hello." My mother's voice coming from the answering machine woke me up out of my sleep.

"Yeah, Ma!" I said as I picked up and glanced at the clock that read 12:00 p.m.

"Why are you still sleeping? Still hanging out until late night, huh?"

"Mommy, come on. Is that what you called me for?" I asked.

"No, I called because you're my only child and I don't think I need a reason to call you. Even though you're grown, I still worry about you, you know. I also worry about your choice of men."

"Huh." I let out a deep sigh, hoping she wasn't gon' take it there, but she did.

"Listen, Epee, your father and I worry about you, whether you like it or not. When we heard that you were running around with that loser, I couldn't believe that my daughter would settle for such trash. He ain't no good, and I got a bad feeling about you being with him.

"Now, listen, Epee, you know that I love me a thug too, but it will catch up to you. I've been through so much as a young girl dealing with your father, but he always put family first, and he kept us out of harm's way at all times. That's why I stayed with him. These li'l niggas out here nowadays ain't got that sense of family. All they know is shooting up shit and going back and forth to jail. Your father had a plan. He used the negative and turned it to a positive by taking his money, making investments, and turning his shit legit. He didn't run around killing and making babies all over the place. He took care of home."

"Mommy, I don't wanna hear it. Daddy hustled in the streets for years. I remember. So what, you tryin'a tell me he ain't never came across a life or death situation where it was either him or his enemy's life in jeopardy? If so, I don't believe it. Killing comes with the territory."

"Your father ain't no killer. Don't you ever come out your face to me about him like that. He's always been there for you and me both. He's still paying for your shit every month, young lady. You need to recognize when shit is too good. You're an adult now. He doesn't have to take care of you the way he does, Miss Thang, so think about that, okay?" she said in a nasty, like-she-just-let-me-have-it tone.

After that, I lost it, 'cause I felt like whatever they did for me, they owed me. No matter what they ever gave me, they couldn't give me back my virginity. I started to scream at her.

"Look, Daddy's there for you, Mommy. Yeah, he might put a check in the mail every month for me, but where was he when I really needed him? He was too busy wining and dining and taking you on trips, while Uncle Ramel was fuc—just forget it. I gotta go!" Almost in tears and ready to let the cat out the bag, I slammed the phone down.

Chapter 12

KEISHA

Tucker was not happy about me wanting Epiphany to be our son's godmother. For the past three months, all he had kept saying was, "You sure about that? 'Cause that trick ain't cut out for the job. The only person Epiphany thinks about is herself. Look how she played my man out. Matter of fact, look how she played you when you was pregnant."

"I know Epiphany ain't big on kids, but she's my best friend, and regardless of what you think, that girl was there for me when I didn't have you. What about Malikai's ass? He ain't no fucking angel, but you don't hear me tripping out. So what is this really about? What got you so salty toward my friend? Is it because she dropped your boy?" I said, defending my friend. Tucker just looked at me and didn't say a word.

The ceremony was beautiful, despite how Tucker or Mali might have felt about Epiphany. Everyone handled themselves like adults. Thank God!

Malikai had brought his new girl, or should I say one of them. Shana didn't even show up, and I didn't bother to ask Epiphany about Corey. I was sure she had her reasons for not bringing him.

After the baptism, we all decided to head out to Manhattan to celebrate over an early dinner. I was surprised but happy when E agreed to come along. I thought being around Malikai and his friend would've made her uncomfortable, but that wasn't the case. Actually, the way Mali kept watching Epiphany might have made his date feel a little out of place.

***

We reached home around eight o'clock. After bathing my li'l man, giving him a warm bottle, and finally getting him to sleep, the next thing I did was call Shana to make sure she was okay. I paged her three times before calling her house.

"Hi, Ms. Pat. Is Shana there?"

"No. Who's calling?"

"I'm sorry, Ms. Pat. This is Keisha."

"Oh, hi, sweetie. How's your little bundle of joy doing?"

"He's doing good. I just put him to bed."

"That's good. When you gon' bring him by to see me?" Ms. Pat asked.

"Soon, real soon. Can you please tell that girl to call me?"

"I will when I see her."

"What, she don't live there no more?" I asked.

"Barely. That child stay in them damn streets, and when she here, she got some nigga ringing my telephone all times of the night. I guess he her man or something. I don't know, 'cause I ain't never seen him. All I do know is when he call, she's out the door like a bat out of hell."

"Well, what about her night job?" I asked, 'cause Ms. Pat will tell it all.

"What job? Shaking her naked tail for them perverts. Shit, that ain't no job."

"Ms. Pat, she's dancing now?"

"Now? She's been doing that for a while. She didn't tell you?"

"No!" I said, surprised.

"Yeah, she's been dancing with some new girlfriend of hers."

"What girl?"

"I don't know, but she ain't from around here. I think her name is Cassidy," Ms. Pat answered. "What, y'all ain't friends no more?"

"Of course we're friends. I've just been tied up with the baby, that's all."

"Well, that's good you ain't out in them streets, 'cause ain't nothing out there but trouble. I'm through talking. I done washed my hands with Shana. She just gon' have to find out what's out there the hard way."

"Okay, Ms. Pat, just tell her I called, please."

"Like I said, when I see her, I'll tell her. You take care now. Bye."

Whew, that lady knew she could do some talking! Damn, talking to Shana's mother made me really start to worry about her. I just prayed my friend was okay.

Tucker came out of the bathroom smelling so fresh and so clean. He must have been feeling the family thing, 'cause he laid his head on my lap and said, "Keish, you know I love you, right, baby?" I nodded. "We got us a fly li'l man. He looks just like his pops. So, let's just do the damn thing. Be my wife. That's all I want from you. We gon' do it up big, too," he said proudly. I was speechless and trying to hold back my tears.

"Keish, I'm getting tired of this lifestyle I'm living. I got enough money stashed to take us up outta here, anywhere you want to go, and to hold us over for a while. So, think about it, Keish. I'm serious. I promise you after I make these last couple of moves this hustling shit is a wrap."

I couldn't hold back my tears of joy any longer. I'd been praying for that moment. I kissed his lips and made love to him like never before. Everything was falling right into place, I thought in silence, and before I closed my eyes I thanked God for answering my prayers. I asked Him to look after my two best friends.

Chapter 13

EPIPHANY

On the bright side of things, I thought I might be in love with C-God. That shit was crazy. When we were together, I swear the nigga gave me butterflies. He was definitely the first out of many. I'd never had a man that took pleasure in stimulating my body the way he did. I mean, I never had a nigga that just concentrated on satisfying the pussy without just trying to get a nut. You feel me?

One night, I had a dream that I was having his seed, and I woke up happy thinking about the possibilities. Now, you know his shit was good if I woke up hoping to become baby momma number six. Yep, six babies and five mommas. Now, that's five times the drama for your ass. That was part of the not-so-bright side of what I'm talking 'bout, 'cause when there is a bright side of any relationship, there is a dark side that follows, and everybody has one.

Lately, everything had been, "Yo, I gotta go take care of some business, so I can't stay long," or "I might be back, I might not." What type of shit was that? I'll tell you exactly what it was: it was some man-shit for your ass. You see, before they get you, they gotta have you no matter what it takes. But once they get you, the thrill is gone and you become just another piece of pussy.

One night, I got a call from Bay, this older Jamaican cat who was still in the game. He hustled weed. We got up every now and then on the low . . . no public appearances, because he looks like a monster—a monster with money coming out his ass. Bay would trick off hundreds just to eat my pussy and that's all. I would let him, but it didn't turn me on at all. I mean literally, he really did look scary, and on top of that, his uncircumcised dick looked like a fucking oversized anteater.

On the real, though, Bay was the kind of trick that you'd want to keep around, because there were times when all I had to do was call him up, kick some "I miss you" bullshit for some cash, and he'd give it up.

In his strong Jamaican accent, he ran his game. "Baby girl, where ya been? I miss yer sweet stuff. Come, let me see you and take you shopping."

"Oh, yeah? When would you like to do all of that?" I asked.

"Tomorrow, baby," he responded.

Of course my answer was yes, 'cause I didn't turn down money or shopping. We set up a date to meet around 1:00 p.m. at the Cheesecake Factory on Long Island. Yeah, yeah, yeah, I know I said I didn't like being seen with him, but it was either that or meeting up at his house. Besides, I already had it planned out: after we grabbed a bite, he'd give me some cash, and I'd tell the nigga that I was on my period or something, 'cause Jamaicans don't run those kind of red lights.

I woke up that morning, checking my caller ID. I fell asleep the night before waiting on C to call me back after paging and calling his ass around three or four times. There were no calls from him, so I paged him again. That was the bullshit I hated: that inconsiderate shit that came with fucking with a drug dealer. You never knew what was going on in the streets when a nigga didn't call you back. Three things came to mind: *I hope he ain't somewhere shot the fuck up, locked up, or out fucking some other bitch.* Shit, I know it sounds fucked up, but I'd rather his ass be dead or locked up than for him to be out somewhere screwing some other ho.

I called Keisha to push back the time that I was coming to scoop my godson for a couple of hours, while she went to enroll in school. Things had been so cool between us, and I was surprisingly loving the god-mommy thing more and more.

"Hold on, Keisha. Somebody's on my other line," I told her. It was C calling with some bullshit excuse about how he was so busy last night that he forgot to call, and his battery was dead on his cell phone. Yeah, whatever. I'd heard it all before, I said to myself, while he kept going on and on with excuses.

"Okay, C, let me go, 'cause I'm on my way to Keisha's," I said with an attitude. He didn't know he just gave me a reason to go see Bay and not feel guilty about it.

"Yo, where she live at again?" C-God inquired.

"What you mean, where she live at again? I never told you before where she lived at in the first place, and what's with all the questions lately about my girl and her man? You checking for her or something?" I asked heatedly.

"Nah, boo, I was just gonna stop by her crib and hit you with some of this dough I was busy getting last night, that's all."

"Well, when I get home, I'll call you, then you can come over and we can both hit each other off. Okay, daddy?" He liked when I called him daddy.

"Yeah, a'ight then. See you later. Be good. One."

I wasn't trying to be on no jealous shit, but C had been asking me a lot of fucking questions about Keisha and Tucker. If it wasn't Keisha he was interested in, then it must have had something to do with her man. Whatever it was, I didn't want no parts of it.

Speaking of Keisha, I clicked back over to her holding on my other line and made sure she was cool with the time change. "Girl, don't be late," she yelled as we were hanging up.

I took a quick shower, threw on my Juicy jeans and match-ing jacket and some Timbs, and put my hair in a ponytail. I didn't want to look too good for Bay's ass, which was hard to do even when I dressed down, but who's complaining?

I arrived at the restaurant around 1:15, which was cool since I didn't want to seem anxious anyway. The wait was always long at this restaurant, but the food was good.

There was no sign of Bay, so I decided to give my name to the hostess. She said there was a twenty minute wait.

At one-thirty, I called Bay's cell phone but got no answer. I kept calling until some Jamaican woman, who sounded like she was crying, answered his cell. She gave me the third degree before she told me he was dead. She said she found her brother this morning. He was shot in the head, and whoever did this didn't know who they was messing with. Her other brothers were on their way from Kingston, Jamaica, and they were gonna "lick up every bomboclot until they find the one who did this."

"Epiphany, table for two, your table is ready," the hostess announced over the loudspeaker. I told Bay's sister I was sorry for her loss and that he was a good friend to me and I hoped they found the bastards that did it.

"Last call for Epiphany, table for two," was all I heard as I walked out of the restaurant.

Damn, I couldn't believe Bay was dead. I really wanted those Prada shoes and matching bag. I guess C was gonna have to buy them for me now.

I felt bad, so I went and bought myself a Louis Vuitton bag and a bottle of Donna Karen's Cashmere Mist perfume to make myself feel better. I hope I don't sound too shallow. I just do what works for me.

Chapter 14

KEISHA

Epiphany had been such a big help to me with my son. She was my sista for life. Now, as far as Shana went, I didn't know what was up with that girl. After leaving several messages with her mom, I still hadn't heard from her. All I knew was that she was still alive, and Ms. Pat said if that should change, she'd let me know. In other words, I guess that meant stop calling so much.

I finally got around to enrolling back in school for my master's. Tucker thought I should wait until we moved, but why put off for later what could be done now? Besides, I was hoping maybe he'd hold off on moving until I finished. I honestly didn't know why we had to move anyway.

Tucker had been in and out of town like a madman. I knew these were the final moves before his retirement, so as long as he kept the lines of communication open, I tried not to complain. Now that I was back in school, I'd have more to do with my time. I was still planning my wedding.

Even though Shana had been M.I.A. I still had faith in her and our friendship; however, I had already asked Lea, a good friend of mine that I met in college, to take her place if I should need a Plan B. I had no choice; the bridal shop needed everyone's measurements as soon as possible. I also made arrangements for my younger sisters to be in my wedding.

This was going to be a very special day, because not only was I marrying my man, but I hadn't seen my sisters in about six years. They were nine and eleven the last time I saw them. I had to bribe my Nana with a couple of dollars for her to agree to it, but what the hell . . .? Money makes the world go 'round.

I was so excited. Tucker and I had already come up with 150 people on our guest list and counting. Once again, Epiphany and Malikai had to put up with each other, because he was the best man and she was my maid of honor. I told her jokingly that she should have stayed with him, because she saw him more now than when they were together!

The catering hall that I chose was beautiful, and once everything was set, I knew it'd be a day to remember.

Ring, ring.

My cell phone snapped me right out of my wedding plans. It was Tucker calling. There had to be some drama, 'cause that was the only time he called my cell. Tucker never discussed the game on the home phone.

"Hello," I answered, hoping everything was okay.

"Hey, Keish," he said on the other end, sounding a little stressed out.

"What's wrong? And when are you coming home? We miss you."

"Keish, I miss you guys too. I can't wait to hold you in my arms. I wanted to send for you and little man, but some kids that I fuck with down here just got knocked, so shit is a little crazy right now. I gotta hit his people off with a little bail money, and then I should be back up that way by Saturday night. I love you. Gotta go." He hung up before I could respond.

I swear I couldn't wait until this shit was over so we could live a normal life. I spent so much time worrying and praying to God to keep my man safe that it was starting to drive me nuts. I even started a trust fund for the baby and stashed away over fifty G's in a safety deposit box, and let's not mention the million dollar life insurance policy just in case, God forbid, something happened to Tucker. Lord only knows. I hated to think like that, but this shit scared me.

Chapter 15

EPIPHANY

It was the first time I'd seen C-God sniff coke. "Yo, boo, you want some? It'll make the sex a lot better," he said.

"Nah. I don't fuck with that shit."

Then he had the nerve to say I wasn't no fun. Shit, I didn't think my sex needed any improvement. This nigga was trippin'. For one, I barely saw him anymore and then his wife had the nerve to call my house the other night talking 'bout I better leave her man alone. That's right, his so-called wife. I didn't even know he had one of those.

Unfortunately for her, he was eating my pussy when she called; therefore, I even didn't trip. I just passed him the phone. The only reason I was certain that it was over between them was because of what he said and the hateful way he screamed at her when he said, "Yo, ain't nothin' wrong with my seeds, right? Then what the fuck I tell you? If they a'ight, then don't be fuckin' calling me for no bullshit, and don't call my girl's house no fuckin' more either, understand?"

I asked him how she got my number. He didn't know the answer to that question. Then I asked him why he didn't tell me he was married.

"'Cause the bitch is crazy." He explained that she only called herself his wife because she had two kids by him, so the bitch felt special.

I let the shit go, 'cause she couldn't possibly be that stupid to let him talk to her like that and still be fuckin' with him. I gave them both the benefit of the doubt. Plus, I knew he'd been stressed out lately, and I wasn't trying to add on to it.

A lot of C's stress was because the nigga didn't believe in using condoms, and now half his baby's mommas wanted to take him to court for child support. As far as him hustling, his product must not have been moving too well, 'cause lately he hadn't been spending money like he used to. Now he was breaking the number one rule of the drug game: Getting high on his own supply.

"C, what's up? Is everything okay?" I asked.

"I'm good," he said.

"You sure? 'Cause I didn't know you was getting high."

"What the fuck is you talking 'bout, getting high? Shit, every muthafucka out there hustling fuck with li'l girl every now and then. You don't be complaining when you getting this stiff dick up in you, huh, thanks to this shit right here," he said, sounding very irritated.

"Listen, calm down, I just didn't know, C-God. I barely see you anymore," I said, feeling a little intimidated by his tone.

"Well, I can't fuck with you all the time. A nigga gotta make money, especially since you be in my fucking pockets all the time. So don't start beating me in my fuckin' head 'bout what the fuck I do with my time, 'cause I'ma start dismissing bitches and niggas, whoever trying to stop me from getting that paper. That's my word, niggas don't know. I want it all, and if I gotta start killing muthafuckas for it, then that's what it's gon' be. These niggas is out here pushing fly-ass whips, bouncing in and out of town and shit like they the kings of fucking New York. They 'bout to get it, and they ain't even gonna see it coming. On that note, yo, I'm out. I got moves to make." C-God grabbed his pint of Remy V.S.O.P. and headed out my front door.

I started to assume shit. Could he be talking about Malikai and Tucker? They were out of town a lot, and Tucker did push a 745LI BMW, SL500 Mercedes, and a Range Rover. Mali just had his Navigator truck. With all the questions C was asking me about Keisha, it was possible.

I didn't know what to do. If I told Tucker and Mali to watch their backs, then C might fuck me up, and I wasn't trying to have that happen. Besides, what if I was wrong? I was sure there were other niggas out there getting money in and out of town. I was just gonna mind my business.

***

It had been two weeks since C-God walked out talking shit that night. He hadn't called me, and I hadn't called him. Part of me missed him and his money. The other part just didn't want to fuck with him anymore because of the way he acted.

I'd been over Keisha's crib a lot lately, helping her get the wedding together, and neither she nor Tucker mentioned any possible beef with C-God. Keisha knew I was fucking with him, so believe me, if there was some drama involving Tucker, she would have said something to me about it by now.

Watching Keisha and Tucker all over each other, kissing and laughing, made me miss C-God more and more. We had good times, too, and maybe I should've been easy, knowing the stress he'd been going through.

When I got in my car to head home, the first thing I did was call him. I didn't want to call the cell, so I just left a message on his two-way, telling him how much I missed him. That way if he felt the same, he'd hit me back.

In less than two minutes after leaving that message, my cell was ringing. It was C calling me back. He apologized for the way he'd acted. He said the only reason he didn't call me was because he felt like maybe he might have turned me off when I seen him sniff coke. He assured me that it wasn't a habit, and if I was uncomfortable with it, he promised to not even fuck around with it.

Then he said, "You know I love you, baby girl."

A big Kool-Aid smile grew across my face as I said, "I love you back. Now, can you meet me at my house and give me some of that stiff dick?"

"I'm on my way," he replied.

Chapter 16

SHANA

I knew it had to be Epiphany that called and had him flying outta there. If it was one of his babies' mommas or business, he would've talked in front of me. He told me about their argument, but I guess all that talk about him not fucking with her boring-ass anymore was just a bunch of bullshit. I wasn't stressing it, 'cause I was the one laying up in his crib, making runs with him, counting his money, moving 500 X pills a week at Honey's for his ass, and fucking him any way he wanted it. I was that down-ass bitch that a thug-ass nigga needed by his side.

So, if he wanted to fuck with Epiphany still, I was't gon' sweat it, 'cause he dropped her ass off for a reason and came back to Quiet Storm that night to holla at me. When I seen him with Epiphany, I was just gonna fall back, but her nigga chose me, so like Snoop Dog said, "It ain't no fun if my homie can't have none." Let the games begin; for once the shoe was on the other foot.

The shit I had put up with from Epiphany all these years, she had better be glad all I was doing was fucking her man. I should've beat her ass on several occasions a long time ago. Like that time when we were seventeen and she fucked Curtis Jacobson just to get back at his boy Dre for doing her dirty. She knew I was crazy about Curtis. I used to love the ground that boy walked on, and even though he wasn't feeling me, she still violated our friendship rule. Talk about being hurt; I was crushed, but I let it slide.

Then there were times where she used to try and play me around a bunch of niggas 'cause I ain't have as much as she did, so the bitch would give me clothes—nice shit she didn't want and Keisha couldn't fit. Around guys, Epiphany always got a lot of the attention, but that wasn't enough. She'd say shit like, "Girl, them jeans I gave you fit nice. Did the other things fit good too?" Like the ho ain't seen me all fucking day to ask me that shit in private. I would get so embarrassed, until I got used to it. Keisha would always do what Epiphany told her to do, but I wasn't having that bullshit, and she couldn't stand it.

The girl had something against people who lived in the projects, too. She thought she was better, but if her father hadn't hustled hard to get that house in a neighborhood that was still the hood, she probably would have been my next-door neighbor.

What it all boiled down to was this: I'd had enough of her, and even though Keisha never did anything but look out for me, she was Epiphany's friend first. The bitch barely came to see her when she was knocked up, but who did she ask to be the godmother and maid of honor? Not me. It was best that I just kept my distance from both of them bitches for a while.

I picked up the phone to call Chasity. I'd been so caught up with C-God that I hadn't really been fucking with her. I knew she was mad.

"Hello," Chasity answered.

"What's up, Chass? I miss you."

"Oh yeah, you miss me now? So is this how it's gonna be every time you get a little dick in your life? What, you just gon' push me off to the side?" she asked.

"Listen, C-God and my relationship is not just about sex, and you need to stop trippin' 'cause it ain't like I don't put you down. You enjoy getting high for free and his dick too. Me and you is me and you, but I told you from the door, dick and hustling is something I ain't never giving up," I said, setting the record straight.

"So he be paying you?" Chasity asked.

"Hell yeah. That's the only reason why I ain't been coming to Honey's to dance. I be in the bathroom pushing that Dr. Feelgood hard, 'bout three hundred or more Ecstasy pills at thirty dollars a pop in less than a week. That's nine G's, and out of that I get a bullshit li'l fifteen hundred. But I need his ass right now, 'cause I'm trying to get my own hustle going through his connect. I'm stacking my dough, too, so I can get a whip and come pick you up from the club sometimes. But anyway, what's up for tonight? Let's go hang out," I suggested, knowing that would increase the peace between us.

"A'ight, there's this nice all-girl spot on the west side of Manhattan," Chasity said.

"That's what's up. I'll meet you there at eleven."

Chapter 17

EPIPHANY

If I had known a couple of weeks apart would have made shit this good between me and C-God, I would have started a fight with him when he first started to fuck up. We were hanging out in the city that night. I was gonna rock my leather jumpsuit because it hugged the hell out of my curves, and with the chinchilla fur jacket that C just bought me, that shit just added more fuel to my fire.

Business must have picked up for him, because he was definitely splurging again. Since we had been back together, he'd been handling a lot of business over the phone and spending every night in my bed. I hadn't picked up my phones or checked my answering machine that read "full" in days. There had been no need to. I had what I wanted right there.

I grabbed the phone and called up Walk That Walk Salon to speak to Ardie (girlfriend knew he could do some hair) to see if he would squeeze me in his morning schedule, which I was sure was already tight. After he cursed me out for missing my last appointment three months ago, he agreed by saying, "You better not be late."

I hated driving all the way to Harlem to get my hair done, but it was worth it. I got up, threw on some clothes, and set off the automatic starter on my car so it could warm up because it was cold outside. I walked into the bedroom and woke up C-God to let him know I was on my way to my hair appointment. I knew he probably would use that as an opportunity to go take care of some business. I kissed his lips and told him I'd see him later.

When I arrived at the salon, Ardie snatched me up as soon as I signed in, and started my wash. I told him I wanted something a little different than my usual.

"Miss Thing, I know you ain't trying to cut all this pretty hair."

"No, I don't want to cut it, but maybe add some color."

"Oh, 'cause I was fixin' to say, girl, I'll cut the hell out of it. Humph, you'll still be a diva either way, but don't worry, girl. I got you," he said.

I wasn't worried, because Ardie was the best, and three hours later, a few shades lighter, and a couple of streaks, I was definitely feeling fierce. I even tipped girlfriend fifty dollars, which was a stretch from the usual fifteen. I felt too cute to go home just yet, so I headed to Macy's on Thirty-fourth to do a little shopping.

I reached home a little after six and called C on his cell to let him know that I was home. Then I decided to check the messages on my cell and answering machine. Most of my calls were from Keisha. She was calling to see if I was okay, because she hadn't heard from me. There were also two messages from my dad, calling to tell me and remind me about the big bash he was throwing for my Mom's fortieth birthday, which was the next day.

Oh, shit! I had forgotten all about her birthday. I spoke to her after we had that argument, but that was over a month ago. I quickly dialed my father's cell phone and gave him a song and dance about how I was working as a customer service rep for a cellular phone company and my hours had been hectic. That was why I took so long to get back to him, but I would be there, and if he needed me to bring anything, he should just let me know.

Daddy always seemed to fall for whatever I told him, but not this time. I sensed some real anger in his voice.

"I know you're grown, but your mother and I feel you should come around or call more often than you do. I've been calling you for damn near three weeks and you're just getting back to me. Anything could have been wrong, Epee. This shit has to stop. The only time we hear from you is when you need something, and since that job is keeping you so busy, let him pay your car note and your rent from now on. I'll see you at the party." *Click*. A dial tone was all I heard.

I couldn't believe he'd just said that to me. Shit, I didn't need him or his money, and what he didn't know was any job I was fucking with was paying my bills. Daddy's check went straight to the bank. Shit, that was one thing Mommy did do right. She ain't raise no fool. She always told me to get it while the getting was good, so when it stopped, I'd have. And that's exactly what I did. I deposited the check Daddy gave me every month in the bank. Then, when it cleared, I withdrew it and put it in my safety deposit box. Keisha put me on to the safety deposits, because if you have more than $10,000 in the bank, they will report it to the IRS, and then they'll be all up in your business. So to avoid that, a deposit box was better. I ain't gonna say how much I had saved up, but let's just say if it ever rained or poured, I was good!

C-God rolled up in front of my place just before midnight with his boy Mike, who hated me for whatever reason. From the look on his face, he wasn't too happy about me hanging out with the fellas tonight. I could tell, 'cause the nigga even hesitated like he had some shit to think about before he gave up the front seat.

Let me tell you about this nigga Mike. He was one of them arrogant-ass niggas, mad at the world, but especially at women.

"Man, them chicks is all the same, only good for fucking, or getting fucked up for fucking up. I'll beat a bitch ass in a minute. I don't give a fuck. Them ho-bitches know not to fuck with me." That's the type of shit that came out of Mike's mouth.

Unfortunately, he was C-God's right-hand man, basically just another "do boy." He was a hot-headed li'l twenty-year-old with a happy trigger finger. He would go all out for C, 'cause C-God had been looking out for Mike since he was a li'l nigga. Nevertheless, the feelings were mutual, because I couldn't stand his ass either.

When we got to the club, the place was pretty small. It must have been an exclusive spot, because from the outside it didn't even look like a club. The music was hot to death, and you had to be on balla status just to get in the spot. I mean, you could only sit at a table if you were popping bubbly at $350 a cork.

We sat in a cozy li'l corner and C ordered three bottles of the good stuff. Cristal is a li'l overrated to me, 'cause the shit's nasty, but I'll drink and order it if a nigga's buying it.

After a couple of glasses, I got up to go to the ladies' room. As I walked through the croweded little club, I felt someone grab my hand. It was Smitty, with a devilish smile. I snatched my hand away from him and proceeded to the bathroom. My heart started racing. I felt nothing but pure hatred toward that boy.

I took my time in the restroom, hoping he would go away. At the same time, I had to get it together and walk back out there before C-God started to wonder where I was.

"Yo, come here!" Smitty said as he grabbed me again when I walked back passed him. This time his grip was much stronger around my wrist.

"Get off of me!" I screamed, trying to yank away from him, but his grip just got tighter as he pulled me closer.

Smitty put his hand on my ass. "You stuck-up li'l bitch, why you acting like that? I just wanted to say what's up to you. It ain't like I ain't already had the pussy. Stupid li'l bitch. Matter of fact, how's the pussy doing since I beat it up?"

"Get the fuck off of me, you fucking rapist," I screamed. I could tell I embarrassed him with that, 'cause his friends started to laugh.

Then one of them said, "Yo, son, you took the ass?"

"Nah, this bitch just think her shit is gold, and she mad 'cause a nigga ain't pay for that puss. Shit, she bleeds once a month like any other ho."

"Let me go," I shouted once again.

The next thing I knew, Smitty was knocked the fuck out, while C-God and Mike commenced to stomp Timb prints all over that nigga. His boys just stood there and watched, until security came and broke it up. Since the club catered to the big money spenders, the bouncers bounced Smitty's ass right up outta there, and we went back to our table to finish our drinks.

My mother's party was packed. Everybody from the neighborhood came out to show love.

I watched Keisha and Tucker out on the dance floor. They always seemed so happy. Tucker reminded me of my father, because he treated Keisha just as good as my dad treated my mom. I remembered when I was a little girl, watching the two of them together in their own little world. It used to make me sick. She'd always had him sprung, and he'd always had her attention.

Mommy did look good as ever. She was rocking a leather skirt and top. No doubt about it, I got my body and looks from my momma. She had it going on with her light-skinned complexion, short honey-blonde-streaked haircut, beautiful almond-shaped eyes, and high cheekbones. Tiara Wright was her name, and Daddy had been hooked on her since she was in high school.

"Happy birthday, Ma," I said.

"Thank you, baby. I'm so glad you're here. Do you see what your father's done? Girl, I swear I knew nothing about this party. He had me thinking we were going out to eat," she said, smiling from ear to ear.

I didn't have time to get her a gift. Besides, what do you get a woman that has everything? Dad owned six laundromats and brought his money home to her.

My father was still pretty upset with me, so neither one of us had much to say to each other. He made a few comments before sarcastically asking me where my boyfriend was. I didn't bother to answer him, because I knew he wasn't really concerned. It was just his way of saying that if he was a real man, he would've showed his face out of respect for not only my parents, but for me. Maybe my dad did know something I didn't, but I loved C-God, and I knew he wouldn't play me.

Chapter 18

KEISHA

"Baby, don't go out and do something stupid. You know I need you, but most of all, your son needs you." Those were the words that ended the argument between Tucker and me; before he stormed out of here wearing a bulletproof vest and carrying a gun. He was convinced that C-God was still fucking with Epiphany, but I knew Epiphany was through with that troublemaker.

I couldn't argue with my man when it came down to his life and our safety, so I respected and supported any and all drastic measures he might have to go through to keep us safe.

I'd been calling E for days, but couldn't seem to get in contact with her. I prayed she was okay. The sooner that loser C-God was out of the picture the better off we all would be.

Every day there was different drama going on in our life. I swear, at first I didn't want to move out of New York because it was my home. But my wedding date was not that far away, and as soon as we were married, I'd be ready to kiss this city goodbye. The time had come. Here in the hood, the jealous ones would always envy; especially when they knew what you came from. They didn't want to see you come up, and trust me, it wouldn't be long before they started scheming to take what you got.

The money didn't really matter to me; my family did. But in this fucked up society, you have to have both to be happy, and do what you have to do just to get by. Niggas didn't want to bust their ass to get it. They wanted the easy way out. To them, that was either someone giving it to them or them taking it.

I knew Tucker wasn't no angel. He chose street pharmaceu-ticals over a legit way of living—that fast money. One thing was for sure: He worked hard to get where he was without robbing or stealing from the competition. Shit, I spent many nights alone, worried sick about where my man was, while he was out grinding for this comfort zone he provided for us. Now, some sheisty-ass nigga that grew up around my way (who just happened to be fucking my best friend) wanted to take that away. Oh, hell no! It wasn't happening.

Chapter 19

EPIPHANY

Today was a good day for shopping, since that seemed to be the only thing that kept me happy. A week had passed since me and my so-called man spent some real quality time together. I mean, I understood his hustle, but he had to lay his head down sometime. My question was, where?

Lately, all he seemed to do was pull these fucking disappearing acts. Now my dad's comments about C at my mom's party the week before had me wondering what was really good. Maybe C-God didn't respect me.

Fuck it. I was too pretty for this shit, and if he didn't realize what he had, then fuck him. It was time for me to do me.

No sooner than that "I'ma do me" thought had crossed my mind, my cell phone started to ring, and guess who it was? C-God, telling me how much he'd been missing me and that he freed up his schedule that night just for me. He let it be known that his working so hard was because of me. He wanted to give me the world. Now, who could argue with that?

Shit, those words were like sweet music to my ears. All those thoughts about "doing me" were out the window. Still, I decided to go to the mall. Who knew? Maybe Vicki's Secret had some new shit in—something sexy for that night.

On my way from the mall, I noticed Tanya walking toward her car, and her belly was big. I wasn't sure whether or not I should speak; you know, with how everything went down with me and her over C, but what could it hurt? Either she spoke or she didn't. Besides, I wanted to know who knocked her funny-looking ass up anyway!

"Hi, Tanya. How you doing? Wow, look at you," I said, congratulating her on her pregnancy.

She thanked me with an intimidated smirk on her face. She probably read right through my phoniness—like I cared. I didn't want to ask, but I assumed she was probably due any day 'cause homegirl was huge. Pregnancy didn't agree with her looks at all. It made a bad situation worse.

She seemed very happy, so good for her. I was so curious to know who her baby daddy was, but again I decided not to pry. Shit, as long as the bitch moved on, why should I care?

"Okay, well, take care and good luck," I said as I was leaving.

"Epiphany, if you're really sincere, thanks for not having any hard feelings. I know you were really feeling C-God," she said.

My heart dropped. I threw my bags down and charged at her, ready to catch a case for beating this pregnant ho's ass. She had to be lying. How the fuck could he do this to me . . . and with her?

Tanya jumped in her car, locked the door, and screamed, fumbling with her keys as I tried to kick a hole in her door. Then it dawned on me: The motherfucker never told her about us, nor did he stop seeing her.

I calmed down and stopped to hear what she was yelling from inside the car, but she pulled off.

I was furious, and I knew she was gonna get to him before I did. Lord only knew I had to calm down, because I wanted to murder the bastard.

Still sitting in my parked car in front of the mall, I called Keisha, and the minute I started to tell her, tears flooded my eyes. For some reason, however, I wasn't getting the support I was expecting from my so-called best friend. She was cold and distant.

"Listen, before you continue," Keisha interrupted, "I need to know if you knew anything about your li'l boyfriend having serious beef with Tucker."

"What? How could you ask me something like that? Of course I didn't know, and that's what I'm trying to tell you. I obviously didn't know a lot about that motherfucker." Not even caring about what went down with C and Tucker, I went on about what he did to me.

***

Days went by without me answering my phone. I just wanted to shut the world out, and all I could do was feel sorry for myself. Why me? When was my chance at happiness gonna come? Shit, I did everything he wanted me to. I never cheated. I gave him the pussy whenever he wanted it. I went out and got drunk with him, even put up with his baby momma drama, and now Tanya was gonna be number six.

All these thoughts ran through my head as I listened to "Why Does it Hurt so Bad?" by Whitney Houston on the *Waiting to Exhale* soundtrack, over and over again. I couldn't understand why he'd want to give her a baby and not me. I was twenty times better looking than her. What did she have that I didn't?

For instance, she stayed in her mom's basement and I lived in an apartment. She leased a Honda Civic and I owned a BMW. She was more of a Filene's Basement, T.J. Maxx, and Marshall's type of shopper, while I was Bloomingdale's, Saks, and Nordstrom. Now, that was a big fucking difference. The more I compared myself to Tanya, the more frustrated I became. It felt like I was putting a puzzle together but didn't have all the pieces.

Chapter 20

SHANA

I finally moved into my first apartment. It was a small one-bedroom in a basement, but it was mine. I still had a few things at my mom's that I needed to get.

While packing my stuff, I ran across several unopened letters from K.C. I didn't even know he had written to me since he'd been locked up. The first letter said:

> *Sha,*
> *By the time this letter reaches you I hope it finds you and your family in the best of health.*
> *As for myself, I'm doing the best I can considering my circumstances. Listen, I know I'm facing a lot of time in here because the man has got me on some bogus conspiracy charges, but I am innocent and I'm gonna fight these bastards for my life. I have a lot of time to think in here, and I could not let another day go by without writing to tell you how much I love you, and I apologize for not treating you like the Nubian Queen that you are.*
> *You stuck by me during all the bullshit, and I'll always love you for that. I hope you can find it in your heart to forgive me. A nigga needs you to drop me a line or come see me. I'll be waiting.*
>
> *Love always,*
> *Kalub Cright*

Something melted inside of me. My insides got all hot and shit, because deep down inside I had mad love for him.

As hard as K.C. tried not to show it when he was out on the streets, I knew he loved me too. I had to see him and drop a few dollars on his books. By the time I got to the last letter, his words were slightly different:

> *Sha,*
> *Yo, shorty, you really shitting on a muthafucka. I guess you ain't really give a fuck about me 'cause now a nigga fucked up and I can't even get a few words on some fucking paper from you. Yo, that shit hurts, word up. I took care of your bum-ass when your people ain't do shit. I ain't never asked you for nothin'. It's all good though. A nigga see what's really good. U take care. Breathe easy, baby girl.*
> *ONE*

I wasn't even gonna trip 'cause these letters were dated back three and four months before. He was only speaking out of anger 'cause a nigga thought I shitted on him.

After making a call to the house where at least 75 percent of our black men reside, Riker's Island, I was told that he had been transferred Upstate. It took me a week to find out his exact location and information, but I had to see him.

Chapter 21

EPIPHANY

Listening to him beg and plead on my answering machine several times a day didn't help much. It only made me weaker and more eager to hear what he had to say, even though it wouldn't matter now after all the bullshit that went down. I wanted to talk to him and needed to hear what he had to say, his side of the story. As much as I tried to fight the feeling of missing his no-good-ass, I couldn't. It's a difficult situation when your heart won't feel what your mind needs it to.

It had been twenty-four hours since my phone stopped ringing, and the thought of C just giving up on me made my heart hurt. I checked my caller ID to make sure I didn't sleep through any of his calls, even though I really hadn't slept much. I just needed to make sure. I would rewind and replay every message over and over again, until I finally stopped fighting it and called him up.

The first ring had my heart pounding. Second ring, it pounded even harder. Third ring and then his voicemail, my heart dropped into the bottom of my stomach. I hung up the phone wishing I had never called him at all. Damn, I should've just picked up the phone. Maybe he was with Tanya, I thought, feeling partly to blame for him saying fuck it.

Ring!

Oh, shit. That was my phone. I jumped up and ran to the caller ID to see if it was him, 'cause that would determine if I would answer or not. It was him. My heart started pounding again.

I picked up, speaking in a tone that showed no pain. "Hello?"

"Epiphany?" he hesitated, unsure that it was me.

"Hey," I said.

"Did you just call me?" he asked.

That's some bullshit. He put the ball in my court to start off the conversation. I threw it right back in his.

"Well, I was out of town a couple of days, and I got your messages, so I was just returning your call." Yeah, I lied about being out of town, but I wasn't about to let this nigga know that I was in the house all week, fucked up and losing sleep over him. "So, what's up, C-God? What you gotta say?" I said, giving him and myself the benefit of the doubt to at least hear what he had to say.

"I need to talk to you face to face," he said. Face to face was too easy. He was probably thinking if I saw him I'd get weak. That's what that was all about, and I wasn't going for it.

"Listen C, whatever you have to say can be said over the phone, 'cause I don't wanna see you. Oh, and no more lies, please." I threw that in to let him know that I was fed up with his bullshit.

After an hour of listening to what he had to say, I learned that he just found out Tanya was pregnant, and it happened before we grew close. He also said he wasn't sure if it was even his. Although she said it was, he heard she was fucking with someone else. C also said he was gonna tell me once he knew whether or not he was the kid's daddy. He said I needed to know she meant nothing to him.

I was somewhat convinced, but I didn't want to make getting back with me too easy, so I brought up his beef with Tucker.

"Yo, that was just a small beef over some nonsense. That shit has been squashed. So when can I see you?"

"Whenever you want to," I replied eagerly, as excitement started to take away the pain.

Chapter 22

SHANA

K.C. and I kicked it, and everything was all good. Seeing him made me realize how much I really loved that nigga, and he needed me to be in his corner. Since he'd been locked up, his peoples had been shitting on him, so he'd been on some fuck-the-world type shit. He said I was his first visit since he was shipped Upstate, and seeing me made a nigga feel like he had something to fight for.

He was waiting on an appeal, 'cause there was some foul play on the state's part, which meant he might be coming home. But his lawyer needed ten G's to proceed with the appeal. Three visits later, collect calls, some sneakers, underclothes, lawyer's fees, and about six hundred dollars in commissary, he asked me to marry him.

K.C. always knew the right shit to say to me, but being in jail made him more sensitive, respectful, and loving. With all that in mind, I said yes. I had a lot of shit going on in my life that he knew nothing about, and I didn't need him to know. His freedom card had been revoked. He was in there, and I was out here tackling life every day, doing what I had to do to survive.

It was funny how life took its turns. When he was on the streets, he took care of me, but he also did his dirt. Now it was my turn to take care of him, not because I owed him, but because I loved him and I was a rider for mine.

I no longer needed to fuck with C-God, now that I had my own connect with his supplier. I was making twice as much as I did when I was working for him, but he served his purpose. Once he put me on, we ain't fuck around that much. It became mostly business, but we remained cool. You never burn bridges with a nigga like him. I liked them thugs, but on the real, that nigga was a li'l too self-destructive for me. He was either gonna end up dead or in jail. I didn't want to be caught up in that shit when it happened.

Chasity was on some new shit, so I stopped fucking with her altogether. That licky-licky shit wasn't my thing anyway. Them fucking chicks wasn't nothing but a headache, worse than a man. Shit, trying to keep up with that kinky threesome shit was wearing me the fuck out. Not to mention her jealousy when it came to me and C having sex and not including her. The bitch would start getting all emotional and wanna fight me. I wasn't with that. I was making moves now, and I ain't had no time for headaches.

I had rings to buy. I never put that much thought into getting married, but I knew one thing: if I wasn't paying for my own ring, it would have been a much better one. Shit, they say that diamonds are forever, and looking at how much they cost, they should be. Picking out K.C.'s band wasn't hard at all, but every ring that I liked cost three thousand dollars and up. I settled for a nice little diamond chip cluster that cost me six hundred bucks. I didn't need people asking questions about no big-ass rock on my finger.

As I was leaving the jewelry store, I ran right into Keisha. She was the last person I wanted to see. Her expression was cold, and I knew she had every reason to be salty. I hugged her and tried to play shit off, but she wasn't falling for it. She hit me with every question that she could think of. I told her I was going through a tough time and just needed my space. It wasn't personal.

I did miss Keisha. She was always a sweetheart. I knew I could have at least returned her phone calls. My problem wasn't really with her. I started to feel bad for cutting the only true friend I'd known for half my life. With all that said, I saw a look of true friendship in that girl's eyes, more that what I probably deserved.

Keisha forgave me, and even though it was too late to be in her wedding, I was going to make it my business to at least be there. I owed our friendship that much.

Chapter 23

EPIPHANY

There wasn't a lot of talking going on between C-God and me last night. When I opened up the door and seen my man standing there, I forgot why I was even mad at him in the first place. As a matter of fact, I was mad at myself for staying away from him so long. From the time he walked in the door up until the moment he left, there was nothing but straight fucking—I mean lovemaking—going on. His lovin' was definitely what Epiphany Janee Wright needed to get back on track.

The way he sucked my pussy took me to a world of fucking ecstasy. As my legs started to tremble, the need to feel him inside of me grew stronger. I pulled him up from my drenched pussy so I could taste it from his lips, and as usual his thick ten and a half inches of hardness knew how to find its way home. I missed being fucked so good. It was long overdue.

My pussy started to throb every time I thought about my sweet chocolate boy wonder. I gave it to him any way he wanted it and in every hole he wanted in. C had always been crazy about my head job, and that night I almost sucked the skin off it and gargled his babies before I swallowed them.

I was really feeling myself after he screamed out, "Damn, I love you!" I wanted him open off of me, so I gave him all I had to give. God, if loving him was wrong, I didn't want to be right. And if loving him meant keeping it from Keisha, so be it.

Speaking of Keisha, that afternoon was the first wedding rehearsal brunch, and I swore if I didn't have to be there, I wouldn't. Two wedding rehearsals for a wedding that was less then two weeks away. Who the hell needs two lessons on how to walk down a damn aisle and carry flowers?

C-God left me drained of all energy, so sleep was what I needed to recharge my batteries. Unfortunately, I had to drag myself up out of bed and into the shower 'cause Lord only knows if I was late, I wouldn't hear the end of it.

The rehearsal was longer than I anticipated and a li'l boring, but very well organized. Keisha always wanted everything perfect, especially that day. Shit, if I didn't know better, I would've thought today was the real deal 'cause my girl was on cloud nine. I wasn't mad at her, though, 'cause I'd be too if I was marrying the love of my life.

I had yet again come face to face with Malikai, who had barely said hello to me or paid me any mind, and I was looking so good. I remember the last time we all got together for the baby's christening. The nigga couldn't keep his eyes off me, and he was with a bitch. I felt a li'l awkward because we had to be partnered up side by side for a while during rehearsal, and while everyone was laughing and joking with their assigned partners, he wanted to be bitter. But for the most part, I ain't really give a fuck. My mind was on C and getting out of there to be with him.

On my way home I blasted "Love's House" with Eddie Love on WBLS. I was definitely in the mood for love. I even did his "take a deep breath and exhale" routine. Shortly after that, he took it there when he played SWV's "Weak." Damn, that was my shit back in the day. I was loving this song even more now that I could relate. A nigga damn sure had me feeling weak and outta control. Shit, I was ready to propose marriage to his ass and become Mrs. Corey Hinderson.

When I got home, there were two messages flashing on my answering machine. I pressed play and began listening while I undressed. The first one was from C. I wondered why he didn't try me on my cell, until I heard him canceling our plans because of unexpected business. That answered my question: He didn't want to hear my mouth. That was why he chose to just leave a message on my home phone.

He ended his message with, "I'm sorry. Don't be mad. I'm glad you're back in my life. You know I love your pretty ass, girl. I promise I'll make it up to you. Keep it warm. I'll call you later." With all that said, how could I possibly trip or be mad?

I'd been dealing with him long enough to know that business came first.

Message number two made it rain on my whole fucking parade. At first I couldn't make out the voices because there was a lot of giggling, kissing, and moaning going on, and then loud and clear I heard the muthafucka say, "Mmmm, Tanya."

My mouth dropped as my machine went, "Beep! You have no more messages in your mailbox." I ran over to my caller ID box to check the number. I clicked back to the first call to make sure I wasn't bugging the fuck out. Both calls came from C's cell phone. I ran over to my phone book to compare the numbers, hoping that maybe it was the wrong number, even though I knew there was no way possible. Ain't it funny how fast shit changes? Just a minute before, I was on top of world, and just that quick this muthafucka done knocked me down. I couldn't understand it. Why?

How could he do this to me again, and with that bitch Tanya? I screamed. My pussy was still fresh on his breath, and here he was doing God only knows what with the next bitch. Oooh . . . I couldn't stand her, and I hated his black ass.

I played the message again just to analyze the whole shit, then I saved it to use against his ass before he could even think up a lie. I figured it out. You see, his first message about "Oh, I can't make it 'cause of some unexpected business" message was left at 7:32 p.m. By 8:05, when the next call came, he was taking care of business, all right. I must have been the last call he made, and somehow his cell phone dialed me back.

Well, that was it. I wouldn't be falling for the okey-doke no more. If he wanted to be with that skank, fine. I was through crying. Besides, I could do much better in the looks department.

I felt sorry for their kid, 'cause Tanya wasn't much to look at and neither was he. Tears filled my eyes as I asked myself one question; *Why can't I be happy?*

As much as I didn't want to feel it, I couldn't help it. I was hurting inside. I dropped to my knees, once again with emptiness in my heart. Trying to hold back my tears, I did something I hadn't done since I was little. I got on my knees and asked God to please help me through this.

Chapter 24

SHANA

I hadn't missed a visit since me and K.C. decided to work on this jailbird love affair. Especially now that I was officially his Mrs., and needless to say, when we had our first conjugal visit, we fucked like bunny rabbits. It wasn't nothing like being the first piece of pussy a nigga had in a while. We also talked about the streets, my hustle, and our future plans.

Things were looking up for him. That's right, my man might be coming home sooner than we expected. His lawyer discovered that there was some hidden evidence and foul play on the arresting police officer's part, so his request for an appeal had been granted. He also got some connects in house, so the papers were processed faster.

I saw K.C. really wasn't ready to change though. Just like most of the niggas doing time, always talking shit about how when they get out they gon' come home and do the right thing, and as soon as they get out . . . bam, right back to doing the same shit that cost them their freedom the first time. K.C. hadn't even smelled freedom's air yet and here he went. He was already asking me to help him set up C-God for fucking up this kid Smitty that he's supposedly real cool with.

Smitty got a baby by K.C.'s li'l sister, and he looked out for K.C. from time to time, hitting him off with a li'l dough for his books before I came back on the scene. I didn't want to get involved in that shit at all. Nope, I didn't want no parts of it. That nigga C had a lot of enemies, but I ain't wanna be one of them. He looked out for me, and if it wasn't for his connect, I wouldn't have been on now, or able to keep paper on K.C.'s books like I'd been doing.

I told him that I worked for C for a while, pushing E pills, and how he respected my gangsta so much that he put me on to his li'l hideout spot where he kept all his pharmaceutical supplies and money. Even how he threatened to kill me if I ever crossed him. Yeah I told him everything, except for how often we used to get our fuck on, or about Chasity, for that matter. His homophobic-ass might've killed me or himself if he found out about that. Still, I didn't wanna burn that bridge with betrayal. C-God ain't never did me dirty, and I never knew when I might need him again.

Although I hadn't heard from the nigga, I didn't think there was any bad blood between us. Hopefully he wouldn't suspect I dropped dime and come looking for me. If he did, I hoped K.C. had my back, 'cause now and forever my loyalty was with my man—but I would do what I had to do to protect myself if it came down to it.

On a lighter note, that night was Keisha's bachelorette party, her last weekend as a free women. Well, shit, she wasn't ever free, so let's just say her last weekend with the last name Moore. She had no idea that I was now a married woman, so I had some celebrating to do myself, and I was ready to get my party on.

Chapter 25

EPIPHANY

I woke up that morning feeling like the Lord was probably gonna work on me slow, because I still felt like shit. I knew if I stayed in this house it would only get worse, so instead of canceling my 10:00 a.m. appointment with Ardie, I decided to get my ass up. First things first, I had all my numbers changed, because I didn't want no parts of C-God or his lies. I had to start somewhere, and that somewhere meant avoiding his ass by any means necessary. On my way out the house, I grabbed two CDs that I knew would help ease my depression: Mary J's *My Life* and *No More Drama*, because I damn sure couldn't take any more drama in my life.

As soon as I arrived at the shop, Ardie rushed me to the back and got started on my wash as usual.

"Girl, where you been at? I ain't seen you in a month of Sundays. I know you ain't seeing a new stylist, 'cause, girl, your hair is a hot mess."

I gave into his prying and started telling him all the shit that C was putting me through. Ardie was a straight drama queen, so if anyone could give me some advice, he could. The only thing he kept saying was "What?," "Uh-uh, girl," and "Oh, no he didn't."

When he finished up with my hair, Ardie spun my chair around toward the mirror. "*Voila!* A star is born. Girl, look at you. Besides the fact that I do know how to work a miracle, you are too pretty to be going through this kind of bullshit. Now, suck it up and go find you a winner. Forget that loser, honey. Humph! Life is too short," he said, sucking his teeth. "Shoot, girl, let me tell you something. You are lucky I love me some dick, 'cause I would've been after you, Ms. Thing." I fell out laughing. "Don't laugh, girlfriend. That's a compliment," Ardie said, placing his hands on his hips.

Now it was definitely time for me to go. Ardie's words did make me feel better, but that was a little too much information for me.

My new style was looking tight. I exhaled and left there feeling like I could breathe again, work it out, and feel unfoolish about it all. That's right; JLo, Béyonce, and Ashanti put together ain't have nothing on me.

I hopped in my car and continued to blast Mary. Singing along with "Rainy Days," I decided to go see my parents.

When I pulled up to the house, my father looked like he was on his way out, and my mother's car wasn't there. He greeted me with a smile and, of course, some sarcasm. "Hello, stranger. Long time, no see." I wasn't gonna stay, but he told me to come inside.

"Where is Mommy?" I asked, still calling her Mommy like I did when I was little.

"She got a new gig working at Citibank as a financial consultant, and if nobody else knows, I know she can stash away some cash," he said, laughing.

Wow, I wondered what made Mommy want to start working after all those years. Even though she held down every one of Daddy's laundromats, it never took her long to hire help. She liked being the boss, giving orders, and collecting the dough.

Daddy always had a way of knowing when something was wrong, especially when I didn't want him to know. He looked at me and said, "Epee, what's going on with you?"

"Nothing, Daddy. I'm good," I answered back, trying to avoid direct eye contact.

"So, what do you plan to do with your life, Epee?"

"Daddy, I really don't want to get into this."

"Well, Epee, it's time we do. I'm your father, and I really don't get into your business as much as I should. I know I let you get away with a lot as a child, but you're an adult now, so it's time you start making better choices for yourself . . . first, with the niggas you choose to run around with. You know what they say: sometimes we choose our own poison, and that Hinderson boy is gonna take you out slow."

I rolled my eyes and folded my arms like I always did when I didn't get my way, which wasn't often. Today, I could tell it wasn't going to work.

"Look, Daddy, I don't see him anymore, and I know you love me, but I don't understand how the same kind of people you want me to stay away from is the same kind of person you used to be. Have you ever thought that maybe I'm attracted to that lifestyle because that's the way you made me? I want someone to take care of me financially so I don't have to work. I want to be able to get up and catch a plane to the Bahamas or cruise the islands whenever I want. I wanna do all the things you and Mommy did when you guys were neglecting my needs."

My father's facial expression changed. His face became full of hurt when I said that last part, but it was true. All those years, I never told my parents how I really felt. Since he was the one that wanted to talk, I felt it was time I told him how I was feeling.

"Epee," he said, "look, I always tried to give you everything, and if I could do it all over again, I wouldn't change that. I tell you to stay away from my kind 'cause I know shit you don't. And I also know that it's not the life I want you to have.

"Besides, shit is different since when I was in the game. In my days, if you were fine, a brother would do anything just to have you as a trophy on his arm. Now niggas don't care how fine you are no more. It's about what's upstairs. It ain't about the looks no more, because don't no man wanna take care of a woman that can't take care of herself, especially a cat out there hustling in them streets.

"They're looking for a woman that's about something, meaning going to school and getting that education, getting good jobs, and let's not forget establishing good credit. You see, they're going for the corporate type. The strong ones that'll hold 'em down, Epee. It's like an investment 'cause if they gotta do some time for doing a crime, a nigga expect his lady to hold it down until he gets out.

"Let's say he wants to buy a car, house, or whatever. He gon' look for her to sign for it because her credit's good.

"Epee, listen to me. I ain't gon' tell you nothing wrong. I've seen, done, and been through it all. I was just one of the lucky ones who had a good woman that put up with a lot of bullshit and stuck by me when I was out there doing shit to her and had no business doing it. You see, I had that mind frame that a lot of men out here have when they taking care of everything: You do what you want. A lot of the shit I did for your mother, I did it out of guilt because I was fucking up.

"I'm glad I'm still here to tell you all these things, because as long as I was out in those streets, hustling and doing fucked-up shit, I should've been locked up somewhere or dead a long time ago. That's how it usually ends up. Niggas don't care 'bout you, your family, or none of that. They'll kill you just because of your affiliation. I've seen it happen. So, trust and believe me when I tell you how lucky I am to be here. God kept me here for a reason, and I believe that reason is to make sure my baby girl is all right."

With all that my father just said, I started getting emotional when I thought that maybe that was C-God's reason for holding onto Tanya. Everything my father said made a lot of sense. She was not cute, but she had a degree, a decent job, and probably good credit, and all I had were good looks and material things. I couldn't hold it back any longer. I started to cry.

My father came closer to comfort me. It reminded me of when I was a little girl, how I used to cry and throw tantrums thinking that it would keep him from hitting the streets, because I didn't want him to leave. He would hold me tight and say, "Epee, Daddy loves you, and it's gonna be all right. Daddy'll be back."

I couldn't tell him that the nigga he loved to hate got me on this fucking emotional rollercoaster. My father squeezed me tighter and apologized for all the times I might've needed him and Mom and they weren't there. I guess now I understood that they were young, and they showed me love the best way they knew how.

Chapter 26

KEISHA

The Bachelorette Party

Shana insisted on picking me up. I wasn't too sure I trusted her driving, but I agreed because after I got my drink on, I didn't think I'd trust myself behind the wheel either. Lea and Simone, my two friends from school who had shared the same major as me, went all out putting this li'l shindig together for me with the intention of getting me pissy drunk. I would have preferred just having a girls' night out at the club. Lord knows I hadn't been to a club in a while. But Lea wasn't having it. Her exact words were, "Girl, this is your last chance to live a little. You can go to the club anytime, but you might not ever get another chance to see some beautiful black men slinging big dicks in your face. You just remember to thank me when it's over, girl."

Shana arrived at my house a little early, looking real cute. She handed me a medium-sized box wrapped in silver and white wrapping paper with a big, pretty white bow. "Here. This is for after the wedding," she said, giving me her best strip tease dance while singing "Nasty Girl" by Apolonia 6. We both started laughing, then I noticed she was wearing a nice li'l ring filled with small diamonds on her left ring finger. I grabbed her hand.

"Oooh, what's this all about?"

She smiled and said, "Oh, I ain't tell you I was married?"

"No, bitch!" I screamed at her like we always did back in the day when one of us was holding out on some juicy information. Then I proceeded to ask details like who, when, and for how long?

"Congratulations, girl. Now when is K.C. coming home?" I said, chasing her around for a hug.

On the way to the hotel, I asked Shana to please be cordial to Epiphany and told her that she has to tell her how she feels one day, just not tonight. We had been friends for a long time. We'd seen each other go through some heartaches, pain, good times, embarrassments, and struggles.

"Shana, we both know that Epiphany is full of herself. She's conceited, self-centered, and self-righteous; just plain self-absorbed. She can't help it. That's just the way she is, and that's the way she's been since we've known her, so don't end a long-term friendship over something she can't change. We all got personality issues, maybe not as bad as Epiphany, but we love each other, and I know we'll always have each other's backs, so try to forgive her, 'cause she knows not what she does." We both busted out in laughs. With all that said, Shana agreed and even admitted to missing her a little bit.

It was party time! A room filled with about seven of my closest friends and associates yelled out when I arrived to room 202 at the fairly new JFK Sheraton right off of 150th Avenue. The girls had a connecting two-room suite decorated with mini brown dicks hanging from streamers, chocolate dick-shaped lollipops, and a cake with a big dick on it.

"This is ridiculous," I said with a smile. "You guys done went dick crazy."

"Well, enjoy," Lea said, "'cause the best is yet to come."

I was surprised to see Epiphany there so early, and she was surprised and happy to see Shana. She ran over and gave her a big hug, and everything seemed to be fine, for now. Simone was playing deejay, and her li'l boom box packed a lot of bass. She played some of the hottest songs from way back in the days, while we all tried to remember all the old dances like the whop, cabbage patch, and the Smurf.

The party really started to jump off when the entertainment came, which was right on time. Although I couldn't speak for anybody else, I was feeling a li'l hot and a lot tipsy.

Since Lea was the host, she stood up over by the door of the connecting room and introduced three of the finest shades of chocolate men I had ever seen in my life (at least that was how the alcohol made me feel).

"Let me present Mr. Goodnight. He'll put that ass to sleep. Chocolate Ty will take you on a natural high, and oh, yes . . . last but not least, The Damager will put a hurting on the pussy."

I almost dropped my drink when he stepped out of the other room. He had a caramel complexion that could just melt in my mouth. Standing about six feet three with a baldy, his chest was covered with a fine texture of hair, and the bulge in his pants was unbelievable.

They gave Simone a tape to pop in the cassette with songs like Ginuwine's "Pony," Jodeci's "Freakin' U" remix, and R. Kelly's "Sex Me." All three of them immediately came over to me and got the party started. Chocolate Ty picked me up and the chair I was sitting in, while Mr. Goodbar—I mean Mr. Goodnight—laid down on the floor what appeared to be a clear shower curtain, and then me. I closed my eyes, feeling a little nervous about what was about to happen next. Then all three of them participated in covering my body with saran wrap, whipped cream, chocolate syrup, and a variety of fruits, then one by one, starting from my toes, they licked me off. The best was saved for last.

When I opened my eyes, The Damager was on top of me. I wanted him so bad; the way he touched me made my heartbeat jump between my legs. While the other two were keeping the girls preoccupied, The Damager gently tugged on my shirt, leading me into the other room. I didn't try to stop him.

He closed and locked the door then grabbed me by my hair, stuck his long tongue in my mouth, and started caressing my body. His touch felt so good my knees started to buckle; bad enough I only stood five feet two inches against his very large frame. He picked me up and slowly, still working his tongue, walked me over to the bed. I didn't know what came over me, but I knew what was about to happen, and not one bone in my body wanted to stop it.

My heart pounded as he began to undress me, and with no hesitation he stuck at least twelve inches of hard dick inside my pulsating, wet pussy and fucked me until my legs started to shake uncontrollably. Then, just as it felt like my insides were going to explode, he snatched his hardness out of me, making me feel like a dope fiend without his dope as my pussy throbbed so hard.

He made me beg for more as he whispered, "Tell me how bad you want me."

"I want you. I want you so bad," I moaned as he bit on my neck and breast.

Then he demanded I turn over on my hands and knees so he could toss my salad. After he finished licking and sucking on every inch of my ass, he inserted his dick again and pounded me out from behind, shifting all twelve inches or more up in my guts, giving me a feeling that I had never felt before in my life.

As soon as I started to cum and thought it couldn't get any better, he put his face between my legs and slowly drank my pussy's juices. It was so amazing.

When I woke up, the clock read 4:00 a.m., and the other room was quiet. The Damager had left. I had a hangover and a sore, swollen pussy. I got up to put my clothes on and noticed he left a business card with his home number on the back. It said *Next round is on me*. I thought to myself I couldn't possibly fuck him again. I was about to be a married woman.

Then the guilt started to hit me hard. I shouldn't have fucked him in the first place. What the fuck was wrong with me? I waited all these years, right before my wedding, with a bunch of my friends in the next room, to cheat on the only man I had ever slept with and loved, with a stripper who probably ran around laying pipe to every woman that booked him.

The thought of him fucking other women the way he fucked me made me feel nasty. I tossed his card right in the garbage. When I opened the door to the other room, Epiphany, Shana, and Lea were still there passed out on the couch and king-sized bed. I didn't wake them. I just tip-toed over to the bed and lay down in an open space, as if I had crashed there the whole night.

Chapter 27

SHANA

I had a migraine from all the mixes of alcohol I drank the night before. I shouldn't have gotten so fucked up knowing I had to be at the prison at 9:00 a.m. sharp in order to be able to have our conjugal visit. I was running late. There was no way I would make it there in twenty minutes, so I decided not to even try. I went home and got in the bed, hoping to sleep off the headache I had. Five minutes into a doze, the phone rang.

"You have a collect call from K.C. Do you accept the charges?"

"Yes," I said to the operator. Before I could get a word in, this nigga just started going crazy with twenty questions.

"Why the fuck you ain't here? You fucking around on me? Who's there with you, and where the fuck you been at anyway?"

"Hold up, K.C. It's too early in the fucking morning for your bullshit. Damn, I miss one visit and you flipping out on me. I'm your wife now, not one of your li'l girlfriends, so you gon' have to start trusting me," I said, feeling like I just put him in his place.

"Yo, Sha, you the only one out there on them streets really looking out for a nigga, and for that I love you more every day, but always remember this one thing about me, I trust no one, not even my momma. You feel me? Now, check it out. I need you to make it to my next visit, which is tomorrow. You got that, Shana? Tomorrow at one o'clock. I got some shit I need to run by you about that thing we talked about. Yeah, I came up with a plan."

"All right, I'll be there."

"Cool," he said, ending the conversation without an "I miss you," "love you," or even "I can't wait to see you." Boy, I tell you, unnecessary drama. It was a bad move on my part telling K.C. about my business dealings with C-God. His only concerns were commissary money, visits, and his plans to move in on that nigga C. Was that all I was to him—the missing fucking link to help him get payback? I'd been loyal and he knew that. How could he call me and say some bullshit about trust and in the same breath ask me, someone he didn't trust, to help him commit murder?

The phone rang again. I answered it, screaming, "Yes, operator, I'll accept the charges." Thinking it was K.C. again, I was ready to give him a piece of my mind.

"Damn, baby, who made you so mad this early in the morning and got the nerve to be calling you collect?"

"Who's this?"

"Oh, so now you don't know who this is? What, you got some other chick calling you baby now?"

"Chasity, what do you want?" I said, sounding annoyed.

"I want you," she said.

"Look, ain't nothing happening. I told you the last time I saw you that it ain't going down like that no more. I ain't feeling it. Besides, I got a man now, so don't call my numbers no more." I hung up and unplugged the phone.

My migraine had just gotten worse.

Chapter 28

KEISHA

As soon as I got home, I ran straight to the bathroom to run me some water for a nice hot bath. Besides me needing one, that was the only thing I could think of that would soothe the soreness my coochie was feeling. Tucker and the baby were still asleep, and I didn't want to wake them, at least not until I got cleaned up. After my bath, I grabbed my towel and began drying myself off.

Then I remembered the gift that Shana brought over and decided to open it. I wrapped the towel around my body, still dripping a little, snuck into the bedroom and removed the pretty wrapped box from my night table. Once I tippy-toed back into the bathroom, I closed the door and tried tearing the sturdy wrapping paper open as neatly as possible, but at the same time I was anxious to see what was inside the box. It was a beautiful sheer white negligee with embroidered satin roses on it.

I slipped it on and saw that it complemented my body's curves so nicely. I admired myself in the full-length mirror behind the bathroom door and got excited from the thought of Tucker getting excited once he saw me in it. I exotically started to twist my hips to the sound of "Drop It Like It's Hot" as it played in my head, but then I couldn't believe what I saw on my left booty cheek: a big, purple passion mark.

I freaked out. How was I going to explain this and how was I going to hide it? I looked in the medicine cabinet in search of all the high school remedies I could remember for removing a hickey. The comb didn't work, or toothpaste, and neither did the frozen spoon.

Knock, knock.

Tucker knocked on the door, and my nerves started to go crazy. I threw on my sweatpants quickly and opened the locked door.

"Hey, Keish," he said, planting his juicy lips on mine. "Why you got the door locked?"

I stalled a little before I answered, trying to think of a reason why I would lock the door when I usually didn't. With my heartbeat racing, I told him the truth.

"I was trying on a little surprise from Shana that I planned to wear for you on our wedding night. If you don't mind."

Damn, that was close, I thought, until Tucker took my hand and placed it on his morning hardness.

"You feel big poppa? I woke up hard as hell thinking about that pussy."

"Tucker, you always wake up hard. Just go to the bathroom. I gotta go check on the baby anyway."

"Come on, Keish. The baby's all right. I'm horny as hell. Let me get a li'l bit. Just lean over the sink and let me hit it from the back."

"No, T. What part of no don't you understand?" I snapped at him, but really I was angry with myself for having to tell him no.

"Oh, we about to get married and it's like that. You holding out on the goodies already. Yo, what the fuck is up with that? What time did you bring your ass in here this morning anyway? You out there fucking around with Epiphany's grimey-ass, ain't no telling," he said, getting angry with me.

"Are you accusing me of something, Tucker? Because if you are, you need to ask yourself should we even be getting married," I said, flipping my wrongdoings on him. But fuck it—men do it all the time.

"I don't know. Should I be? I mean, you was out all night, and now I can't get no pussy. You ain't never told me no before. Now all of a sudden I can't have none, so what I'm supposed to think?"

"You ain't supposed to think nothing. You supposed to just trust me," I said.

This heated discussion seemed as if it was gonna last forever, and my conscience was starting to wear me down with guilt. Over and over again in my head, one side was saying I shouldn't have done it, and the other side was saying, "Fuck it. You only live once, and at least it was good." All I knew was at that very moment, I just wished the night before had never happened, the hickey was gone, and this discussion was over.

Beep, beep, beep, beep.

Somebody upstairs must have been listening, because that's the way Tucker's cell phone rang when there was drama. He called it "the warning," biting off of the way Biggie's pager went off in the beginning of his song "Warning." That meant two things: some shit just went down, or it was about to go down.

Tucker ran out of the bathroom to catch his cell before the ringing stopped. His frustration was no longer toward me but to whoever he was on the cell with, because all I heard him yell was, "What? Where the fuck was y'all at? Man, y'all some damn asses. Where's Mali at? A'ight, yo, I'm on my way." And out the door he went without saying another word to me.

Chapter 29

EPIPHANY

I was the last one to leave the hotel room. Since I had no one to go home to, there wasn't any rush. I ordered the deluxe breakfast from room service and went back to sleep until checkout.

I had a good time the night before, 'cause it gave me a chance to get my mind off of you-know-who and to hang out with my girls like we used to.

I couldn't believe Keisha had given up her goody-twoshoes crown that night. All that moaning she was doing in the other room made me want to form a line at the door and go next. I knew she had some bad girl up in her somewhere.

That was my girl. Shit, niggas had been doing it for years and still were. Look at C's cheating-ass, telling me he loved me and then when he left me to go and take care of so-called business, he was laying up with the next bitch, playing house and picking out baby names. I hated that lying bastard.

Speaking of the devil, I approached my street and noticed C-God's truck parked in front of my apartment. I got weak from the sight of his truck, I knew mentally I wasn't ready to see him face to face, so I just kept driving.

Once again the pain took over. Trying to fight depression, thoughts of encouragement stroked my ego. *Epiphany Janee Wright, snap out of it. You're the one in control. You're strong, tough, the one who gets what she wants and then breaks away. A certified heartbreaker . . . with a broken heart.*

No matter how hard I tried to convince myself, it wasn't working. It's so hard to get out of the situation when your heart won't do what you want it to do. It felt like I had fallen and couldn't get up.

I ended up at the mall on Sunrise Highway. Shopping always made me feel better. Unfortunately, I saw nothing I wanted, so I only purchased a bottle of a new fragrance by BCB Girls called Nature and headed back to the car. I assumed the coast would be clear by now, 'cause that nigga C ain't had no time to be staking out in front my crib like that—not for long anyway. The streets were always calling him.

As I was driving, I noticed this hooptie speeding up alongside me. At first I wasn't sure who it was, but as Smitty was passing, he pointed his finger at me as if it were a gun and he was busting off shots. My heart pounded in fear, because there was no telling what that crazy muthafucka would do.

Chapter 30

C-GOD

"Yo, what up, Mike?"

"Yo, C, that shit was a piece of fucking cake last night. We got them niggas shook, son. Took all their shit, yo. Where you at, man? 'Cause I know you don't want the details over the phone," Mike said, thinking like a lieutenant was supposed to.

"Naw, you right. I'm out here in front of this bitch E crib. Yo, I ain't heard from her in a minute. Shorty done changed numbers on me and all that, son. I don't know what's up with her. I'm 'bout to file a missing persons report out on her ass or something," I said, a li'l stressed.

"Yo, fuck that high-price ho, man. It's something about her I ain't feeling anyway," Mike said, girl-hating as usual.

"Nah, yo, watch your mouth, dawg. Chill with that. She a'ight. Anyway, yo, meet me on the block in twenty," I said, getting a li'l pissed over Mike's comment about Epiphany.

I got off the phone, happy to hear that niggas made out all right running up in one of Tucker's spots. I already knew that Tucker was soft from their last run-in. That nigga was about to be put out of business, I thought as I drove off to go get the details.

Chapter 31

KEISHA

My wedding was a week away, and there had been nothing but chaos in my household. Tucker and I hadn't said too much to one another. It had been a week, and he still wanted to be mad. On top of that, one of his spots got robbed for over ninety G's and a couple of keys. I didn't think anyone was hurt, but I heard the words "murder that nigga."

At first I wasn't sure who he and Malikai were talking about when I overheard them talking in the basement. I put two and two together and came up with C-God when I heard Tucker say, "We fucked up by letting that nigga slide when he was mouthing off with that bullshit 'bout putting me out of business before. He was testing me. We should've took care of that nigga then, 'cause now he's a problem that has to be handled."

With all that said, he and Mali bounced out of town early that morning, for what or how long I didn't know. All I did know was some serious shit was about to go down, and I didn't know what that could mean for our future. It seemed like the closer he got to the exit in this game, the further the exit became.

Now, here was some more shit, more drama in our lives. I mean, I wanted my shit to blow over peacefully, no more arguing between us, but now he was caught up in some danger that had his focus, and it didn't look good. The shit that was going on with him now sure took away from my shit. We hadn't talked about it, let alone had sex, and now that the hickey was gone, where was my man? Out of town a week before our wedding. Next time I would have to be careful with what I asked for, because the man upstairs damn sure took Tucker's focus off me. Only God knew what kind of drama He replaced it with.

Leaving the house, I noticed a package wrapped in gold paper in front of my door. It didn't have a return address on it, and the mailman had left already. Someone must have hand-delivered it.

Attached was a card with no name that read: *I hope you enjoy this as much as I did. Best wishes.* I wasn't sure if I should open it, especially with all that was going on. It might have been a bomb or something.

I examined it closely. First I listened to see if it was ticking. I shook it and threw it in the street, but nothing happened. Not too many people knew where we lived, so it had to be a wedding gift from one of the neighbors.They were very hospitable around there.

I took the package inside and opened it. It wasn't a bomb, of course. It was a videotape with no writing on it. I popped it in the player, but nothing happened. I hoped the machine still worked because we hadn't used the VCR since DVDs came out.

I looked in the back of the big screen and discovered the wires weren't hooked up.

Damn, look at the time. I was running late. I was supposed to be at the airport to pick up my sisters at 1:00 p.m. and it was already ten minutes to. I couldn't fool with this now. I grabbed my sleeping son from the couch and headed out the door to the airport.

Their flight had already landed by the time I parked the car and finally made it inside. I wasn't sure I would remember what they looked like, since they were no longer nine and twelve but fifteen and eighteen, teenagers now.

I spotted them at the baggage claim talking to some lady they'd probably befriended on the plane. They were so pretty and still had those same faces. I decided to slightly roll my son's stroller toward them first, since he was the surprise I had for them. I then walked up right behind him, just as they were smiling at him and talking about how cute he was in their Southern accents.

"Surprise!" I yelled out, and they both jumped on me and formed a group hug. Then my sister Kelly asked whose li'l boy that was. I laughed, of course, because I wasn't used to the country accent, and said, "He belongs to me. This is your nephew, li'l T." Not only were they surprised, but I was too when the lady they were talking to turned around.

"That's my grandson?" she asked.

I had to take a deep breath for this one. So many emotions flashed through me the moment she turned around and I realized it was my mother, or should I say the lady that birthed me. I didn't know if I should hug her or slug her. To be honest, I felt like slugging her for being absent from my life for so many years, but at the same time, part of me was happy to see her. So, I went with the hug.

We all agreed on getting a bite to eat, which was a good idea because it would give us all a chance to catch up on what had been going on in each other's lives.

I learned that Loretta (my mother) lived in Atlanta now, working as a home health aide, and had been sober for 186 days. I watched her as she bonded with my son. Just like most men with food, French fries was the way to his heart.

My sister Kelly attended Clark University on a full scholarship, and my younger sister hated school, was hanging out late, and just doing all the wrong things.

If you've been listening to me up until now, you should know how good I felt then, because family was so important to me. Although I still had issues that needed to be worked out between my mom and me, I was glad she was trying. It was better late then never, and no matter what she did, I could never change the fact that I was here because of her, and she would always be my mother.

Chapter 32

TUCKER

"Yo, Mali, take Corn and Peewee to that motel off Rockaway Boulevard. I gotta go take care of some things right quick. Oh, and Mali, I want you to give Epiphany a call. See how she doing. Keish said she don't fuck with that nigga no more, but get back on her good side. See what she knows. She might be just the person to lead us right to that C-God."

Peewee and Corn was from the Dirty South, the thoroughest niggas you'd ever want to meet. Those niggas would rob, beat, or kill you in broad daylight. They wasn't never scared; especially when it came to doing dirt for me and Malikai. Those li'l fellas believed in loyalty to the extreme.

I had met them about three years ago. They lived in the first apartment complex I moved to down South when I started slanging dope down there. They used to sweat us because we was from New York and locking shit down. That shit was funny, because those li'l country niggas thought 'cause we was from N.Y. we had to know all the rappers out. I would send them to the store for me—and if you know anything about certain parts of the South, where it's mostly roads, you know the stores are usually far as hell—but they never complained.

Anyway, there was this kid from the other side of town. I think his name might have been Otis or something like that. He was a li'l older, and he had my li'l men scared shitless. One day, he was fucking with 'em to the point where, I kid you not, those li'l niggas wanted to cry. Me and my man Mali peeped it. We let him have his fun and get his li'l laughs off and whatnot. Then we grabbed him up, made his li'l ass strip butt-ass naked and stand still while them li'l niggas Corn and Pee beat the shit outta him. Ever since then, them li'l dudes had been straight gangsta.

That was why I had to drive all the way the fuck to North Carolina to scoop them up. They were both on parole and wasn't s'posed to leave town, so I ain't wanted them trying to catch no planes or shit like that. I didn't even think they owned IDs anyway, but I did know they'd get shit done.

We scouted all over town, from the blocks he would be at to the fucking clubs. That nigga C-God and his whole crew was M.I.A. He must have knew we was coming for him.

Chapter 33

SHANA

"In regards to Kalub Cright, due to a tremendous amount of foul play in this case, the court finds him not guilty of the charges brought against him on January 9, 2004. However, after completing a total of fourteen days for a parole violations, he will be released. All drug charges will be dropped. Court is adjourned."

Now, that's what's up! I thought as I jumped up and ran over to give him a hug before those rude-ass court officers pulled him away. That shit wasn't cool, but it was all good because, "My man is coming home," I sang in a little tune to them as if to say, "In your face."

His visiting hours started at three o'clock. I had just enough time to get me something to eat and then head over to Riker's Island to congratulate him on his get-out-of-jail-free card.

I was happy that he was coming home, although deep down inside I was worried about him flipping on me. I wasn't stupid. I knew a nigga in jail would tell you anything if he thought it would benefit him in some kind of way. I also knew K.C. loved me, but that wouldn't stop him from kicking my ass and fucking around with other bitches when he was in the streets. I felt fucked up for feeling that way, but I liked having control while he was behind bars; there wasn't much he could do, and I knew where he was at.

From the moment he sat down to the moment the visit was over, all we discussed was the plan—his plan to set up C-God. He had it all mapped out. He even made arrangements for me to meet up with that kid Smitty the next afternoon.

I agreed to meet with his homeboy. I told him I'd give up the location of C's hideout spot where he stashed his shit, but I wasn't participating in shit, and I wasn't feeling his plan.

K.C. looked at me like I had better be glad we were where we were, or else he would've slapped the shit out of me. But I wasn't going for that bullshit no more, and I told him that.

Then, of course, he hit me with some guilt shit. "Why you gotta act like that?" He frowned.

"Like what?"

"Like you ain't happy a nigga coming home or something. What's up? You don't love me anymore?"

"Yeah, I do, and I am happy," I said.

"So, knock it off and let's just do the damn thing, Sha. I told you I ain't gon' never do nothing to hurt you. You've been holding a nigga down for real, and I ain't gon' do you dirty. Believe that. Meet with dude tomorrow, handle your business, and let's get this nigga's paper, a'ight."

"Cright, your time's up," yelled the correction officer.

Before I could respond, K.C. got up and threw his tongue down my throat then slapped me on my ass.

"Daddy'll be home soon. I love you, ma," he said as the C.O. escorted him down the hall and through the steel door.

Chapter 34

EPIPHANY

A nauseating feeling, sharp pains in my stomach, and vomiting had me up all morning. At first I thought it might have been from that nasty-ass Chinese food I had the night before, but laying there feeling the way I was feeling made me think back to the last time me and C had sex and lots of it. I knew sooner or later one of his balls was gonna make the basket. On top of that, I wasn't no stranger to the feeling. I'd been down this road too many times, but this time seemed like the worst. Instead of lying there hoping it wasn't so, I decided to get up and go buy a pregnancy test. The sooner I confirmed it the faster I could get rid of it.

On my way out the door, you'll never guess who called me. Malikai. Ain't that funny? My first question was a dumb one. I asked him how did he get my number, and before he could answer, I already knew it was Keisha. He started kicking the game about how much he missed me, and that he not only wanted me back, but needed me back in his life.

His timing couldn't have been worse. I had enough drama in my life, so I shut him down by telling him I wasn't interested. Although I did miss him a little bit, I wasn't about to make his comeback an easy one. If his ass was serious, he'd call again.

Ever since I saw C parked in front of my apartment, I'd been parking my car on the next block over. The walking distance was a pain in my ass, especially since I picked up this laziness. I was in and out of CVS in about five seconds flat. I then stopped at the bodega on the next corner, because I had a taste for a turkey and cheese hero with a lot of mayo. The way I was creeping, you would have thought someone had a hit out on my life or something, but I just didn't want C-God rolling up on me.

On my way back to the crib, it started to drizzle a little bit, so I decided to park in front of my apartment. It was bad enough I didn't feel like walking anyway, and I damn sure wasn't about to walk in no rain for nobody.

First thing I did when I got inside was lock the door. Second, I ran to the bathroom, squatted over the toilet, and peed in the plastic cup that came with the First Response pregnancy test. In exactly one minute, it was confirmed. I was pregnant and once again smacked in the face with the unexpected.

Chapter 35

KEISHA

I was out all afternoon running errands, something I usually didn't get to do alone. Most of time I was lugging the baby around with me.

My family had been a big help. It felt good to have them around. The past couples of days had been a blessing, because it gave me a chance to have a heart to heart with my mom and finally hear and understand her side of the story. She explained to me what her weakness was, which at the time was my father, a man that had full control of her—until he left her. She told me she felt like giving up, and alcohol became her savior. No other man could walk in the shoes my father walked in—not the fathers of my sisters, no one except a bottle of booze.

She stayed drunk all the time, hanging out 'til the wee hours of the morning, and sometimes she ain't even come home. I never knew which one of her two alcoholic boyfriends fathered my sisters, and neither did she. They used to all get drunk together and try to figure out who looked like who.

That shit was sad, but I now understood that she had a sickness and all that mattered was that she was fighting it. I also felt her pain as far as my father was concerned, because I know I would definitely lose myself if Tucker ever left me or something tragic happened.

Speaking of Tucker, he was back in town but not staying at the house. He decided it would be best if he stayed away because there was too much heat around. I was not a happy camper, but he felt it was for our safety, so I decided not to argue with that. All I knew was he had five days, three hours, and twenty-two minutes to turn down the heat before our wedding.

Back at the house, I called ahead to have the girls meet me outside to help with the groceries. As much as they liked to get their eat on, I knew it wouldn't be a problem. When I walked in the house, my mother pulled me to the side.

"I think you should take a look at this in private. The girls hooked up the VCR to play a tape for the baby and this came on. I don't think they saw that much because I was only in the kitchen for a minute, but I made them turn it off and give it to me as soon as I seen it. After you watch it, if you feel you want to talk about it, I'm right here. You hear me? If not, that's okay, but either way, I suggest you get rid of that tape."

I didn't understand the seriousness coming from my mother. What could be on this tape that was so vital? There was only one way to find out. I unplugged the VCR in the living room and carried it up to my bedroom. My heart pounded and my hands shook as I connected the wires to the back of the television. I inserted the tape, pressed play, and there I was having the best sex I ever had in my life . . . with the stripper. I jumped up and stopped the tape in disbelief.

What the fuck? This can't be?

All kinds of thoughts were going through my head. I ejected the tape and put it in the small lock box I kept in my panties drawer. I started to tremble all over as I paced back and forth, racking my brain, trying to figure out who could hate me that much to do something like this and drop it off on my doorstep in hopes that . . . what? Tucker and I would watch this shit together?

The funny thing was, I couldn't think of any one of the girls there that night that would want to destroy my happiness. Even though Lea kept on insisting we have some dick in our face for entertainment, what would she have to gain? She only dated Spanish guys and had a man, so I didn't think she'd do this. Epiphany and Shana, they wouldn't, so that was not even a question. The stripper guy didn't even know where I lived at. Simone and I were cool, and doing something like that wasn't even her style. Now, Tawanna and Dana, those two were suspect, 'cause I didn't know too much about them, nor had I known them long.

No matter how many excuses I tried to come up with for my so-called friends, what it all boiled down to was somebody there in that room that night wanted to break up my happy home, and I was gonna find out who.

"Who is it?" I said, responding to a knock at the door.

"Is everything okay?" my mother said, talking quietly through the door.

"It will be if you can look after the baby for me just a little while longer, because I need to be alone for a while." She agreed. Out of embarrassment and all the mixed emotions beating me in my head, I stayed locked in my room for the rest of the night.

Chapter 36

SHANA

Chasity had been calling me all morning with straight drama. Who knew this chick would have turned out to be a psycho bitch? I didn't even have caller ID so I could screen my calls. I decided not to answer the phone anymore. I just hoped K.C. didn't try to call me, 'cause he'd be trippin'. I had already spoken to his boy Smitty and confirmed our meeting. We decided to hook up at the food court in Queens Center Mall, somewhere crowded and noisy.

When I got to the mall, the nigga wasn't there. He told me that he would be wearing a Philly 76ers Allen Iverson jersey, blue jeans, and some all-white Air Force Ones. I ordered some KFC and waited. Twenty minutes later, this nigga had the nerve to come strolling in to the food court with bags in his hand. I couldn't believe I was here to do his ass a favor and he had me waiting while he shopped. That was some bullshit, I didn't even know his ass, and already I wasn't feeling him.

I raised my hand to catch his attention. He walked over to the table on some real hard shit, like he had just won an award for thug of the year. I wanted to laugh, 'cause if it was that serious, we wouldn't be there now trying to plot his payback for C-God whipping his ass.

"Yo, what up, ma?" he said as he sat down.

"What up?" I responded back.

"Yo, ma, you look mad familiar. I seen you before?" he asked, staring me in the face.

"Yeah, that's possible. You're from my projects."

"Oh, word," he said, acting like he didn't know.

"Listen, what's really good?" I said, trying to cut all the small talk and get down to the topic at hand.

"Yo, I wanna murder the nigga C-God. Him and that pussy-ass nigga Mike that roll with him," he said in a hostile tone.

"Well, K.C. ain't say all that. He just said y'all was gonna rob him."

"Come on, ma. You from the hood, so I know you ain't no dummy. How the fuck you gon' rob a nigga like him and not split his wig, unless you ready to die? You feel what I'm saying, ma?"

"Yeah, I feel you, but if you don't mind me asking, what is y'all beef over?"

"Man, some bitch I fucked got that nigga open off her ass or something. So I'm out chilling by myself and shit at this little spot, you know what I'm saying, and I sees the bitch, right? So I said hi to her. Next thing I know, that punk-ass nigga and his boy done snuff me out and shit for speaking to the ho.

"Yo, all I got to say is them niggas is lucky I wasn't strapped that night and ain't seen them since, 'cause that's my word, niggas would've been a memory by now. That bitch too. Matter of fact, I rolled up on her ass a while back, wishing I had the gat." He started to get real hype as he spoke.

"Who's the girl?" I said, not really caring, just being nosey.

"Some bitch, man. I can't even remember the bitch's name. She a light-skin chick. She drive a fucking silver three-twenty-five."

"Epiphany!" I blurted out. Actually, I wasn't surprised at all. I should've put that shit together a long time ago, when he first said some girl who was out with C, but then again, everybody knew that nigga C-God be running around with different chicks.

"Yeah. How you know her?" Smitty sounded really curious.

"Let's just say she's like my family, and if you want me to give you the info you need, you gotta leave her out of it."

"Man, fuck that ho," he said like he had to put some thought into to it. "A'ight, a'ight, I ain't gon' fuck with her."

I knew most of the time E got on my nerves, but Keish was right when she said Epiphany was the way she was and had been ever since we'd known her. I wasn't trying to go out like that, letting something happen to her that I could prevent.

To make a long story short, I gave up the location to C's Long Island apartment in West Hempstead. The only thing about his spot was you gotta be buzzed in to get inside. To my knowledge, only Mike knew about that spot. Oh, and of course me. I also knew where Mike's baby momma lived at in Brooklyn, right off of Atlantic Avenue on, I think, Carlton Place or Fulton, one or the other. I told Smitty that Mike was always resting his head at her house.

Just as we were getting ready to go our separate ways, this psycho bitch Chasity came from out of nowhere, blowing up my spot with all her yelling and screaming.

"Oh, this is the muthafucka you left me for? This scrawny, dusty-ass li'l nigga right here?"

"Bitch, who the fuck you calling scrawny and dusty, you dyke bitch?" Smitty said, ready to scrap.

"If I'm a dyke, then your bitch is one too, 'cause she eats pussy just like I do," Chasity screamed, putting me on blast and embarrassing the shit out of me.

"Yo, ma, you get down like that?" Smitty asked me.

"Hell, no. She's just mad 'cause I don't."

All I could do was deny every word that came out of her mouth by saying, "You need to stop it. Don't be mad 'cause I ain't no fucking carpet muncher, bitch."

Boy, why did I say the B-word? She charged at me like a raging bull and started swinging. Look, I wasn't no punk bitch; I just didn't want to fight the girl. What happened next, she brought on herself.

She was still running off with the mouth and trying to fight me, so Smitty grabbed her up off of me and punched her right in her mouth. She hit the floor, and we hit the door just before security came.

Smitty walked me to my car, but ended up having to drive me home because my tires were slashed and windshield was smashed. He was amused by the bullshit.

"Damn, yo, that was some crazy shit. Yo, why she acting like that? I'm saying, you sure you ain't never licked on that girl's pussy? 'Cause that bitch is fuckin' looney, yo," he said, full of laughter.

I didn't open my mouth. Besides, it was none of his fucking business, asking twenty-one questions and don't even know me. I knew he couldn't wait to tell K.C., and that was the only nigga I had to answer to.

Chapter 37

KEISHA

I tossed and turned, trying to get some sleep. It was only 11:00 p.m. and I could not stop thinking about that tape. It also dawned on me that I hadn't spoken to Tucker all day, so I picked up the cordless and called him on his cell. The phone rang about six times then went to voice mail. As I was leaving a message, he beeped in on the other line. I clicked over.

"Hello?"

"What's up, Keish?" he said nonchalantly.

"Nothing. Where are you?"

"Come on, Keish. You know I can't discuss that over the phone," he said.

"Well, I want you to come home tonight. I need you," I said.

"Listen, Keish. We already talked about this shit. I told you what's going on, and you guys don't need to be around it."

"Yeah, yeah, yeah. So how are we supposed to be getting married in four days if you won't even come home?" I said, rudely interrupting what he was saying.

"We won't be if you don't let me handle my business. Night. I gotta go." *Click*. He hung up on me.

I dialed him back, but my call went straight to voice mail this time. I waited for about five seconds and dialed him again and got the same results—his voice mail. This was not good. How could something that had been so good for more than five years turn bad in two weeks?

I got up from the bed and went over to my panty drawer, where I had stashed the tape. Maybe there was something on it besides me that might help me figure out who was behind it.

Within the first two minutes, a weakness fell over me as I watched the tape. I tried to ignore that pounding feeling, along with the wetness I felt between my legs, but I couldn't fight it any longer. I masturbated to the fast and slow strokes he laid upon me that night, the biting, the sucking, the licking, and kissing. That night I experienced pure ecstasy, coming close but not close enough to the phenomenal feeling of pleasure he had given me. Compared to his, my touch was a tease. I wanted more. I wanted him, but I couldn't. I couldn't do it again.

"Damn, I should've stuck to dirty chats on the Internet."

That morning, I awoke to wet kisses from my little man, while my big one watched, before he kissed me. *Maybe it was all dream*, I thought, actually hoping it was, until I sat up in the bed and noticed that the VCR light was still on and the TV screen was fuzzy. I jumped up in a panic and turned both of them off.

"Well, good morning to you too," Tucker said.

"Good morning," I replied, remembering him abruptly hanging up on me and turning off his phone last night. Before I could address it, he did, with an apology and flowers he had sitting on the nightstand. He said he needed me to understand that he was dealing with a life or death situation, and in the game, just surviving alone was an everyday struggle.

"I don't always tell you how serious shit is because I don't want you to worry any more than you already do. Just know, no matter what happens, nothing will ever change how much I love you, and hopefully my business will be straight in the next forty-eight hours so we can move on to the happy times."

With all that said, he kissed me and the baby and was gone again. At least he left me with the reassurance I needed to help get rid of all those tainted thoughts from last night: the tape and the memories.

Chapter 38

EPIPHANY

Malikai had proven how persistent he could be. All week he'd been calling me to say hi, check on me, or just for small talk. Sometimes small talk was helpful. Last night, we'd spent about three hours on the phone reminiscing on some of the good times. I'd actually forgotten we shared so many. We got along really good, come to think about it. Talking to him made me realize I missed him more than just a little. I even agreed to let him come over, but now I was not so sure that was a good idea, because this pregnancy hadn't been agreeing with me at all.

I was sick all the time. I hadn't been able to hold any food down, so I just stopped eating. I had gone to the clinic the other day to put an end to this misery, but they told me that I needed to be at least six weeks, and I was only four.

I knew that if this was Mali's baby, things would be a lot different; especially since this would have been his first kid. We probably would have had a double wedding—Keisha and Tucker and me and him. That would've been fly. *Shit, I should just give him some pussy,* I thought, *wait two weeks, and then tell him I'm pregnant by him. Just my luck I'd have a li'l tar baby, black as hell, looking just like C-God. Nah, that wouldn't work.*

I really needed to talk to someone about what I was going through. Usually, Keisha would be the one I confided in, but ever since that incident between C and Tucker, I couldn't go and tell her I was pregnant by her man's enemy. She wouldn't understand. What kind of friend was I? If I was a good friend, I wouldn't be in this situation right now.

My hormones had me feeling real emotional and down on myself. I hated the person I was. I hated the fact that my friends had become so distant. How did we go from talking every day to only on special occasions? Oh my God, I was starting to sound like Keisha now. I hated that. I also hated not having a man to love me like I needed to be loved, but more than anything, I hated C-God's trifling-ass and this baby. That last thought of hate did it for me. I busted out into an uncontrollable cry.

The doorbell rang. I wasn't expecting Malikai for another half hour. Damn, I fucked up when I told him he didn't have to call before he came.

"Just a minute." I ran to the bathroom to fix my face, but with puffy red eyes, there wasn't much I could do to hide the fact that I had been crying.

My doorbell rang again, only this time it was more of an impatient, hurry-up-and-open-the-door ring. I ran to the door, yelling, "Okay, I'm coming."

When I opened it, it wasn't Malikai. I tried to close it back quickly, but it was too late. C-God forced his way in.

"Yo, what the fuck is up with you? You got a nigga coming by your fucking crib every day and shit looking for you. I don't do that shit for no bitch, but yet a nigga doing that shit for you. What the fuck? You thought you was gon' just play me like that? Why the fuck you change your number, huh? What, you fucking with some crab-ass nigga now or something? I should fuck you up!"

C started to get real angry when I refused to answer him. He started calling me every bitch and ho word you could possibly think of. I didn't want to show any signs of weakness, but I couldn't help it as the tears started to roll down my face again.

C-God really started to scare me with his threats. He said if he caught me fucking with anybody, he was gonna kill 'em and cut my face up bad. That threat caught my attention fast.

I looked up at him, and I could tell he was high. I could always tell, because his nose would sweat and get so wide it was scary. I had to get him out of my house, because if Mali came while he was there, ain't no telling what might have gone down. I walked over to my answering machine and played the message I had been saving for him to hear.

"Our shit is over and done with, C-God. You're busted. There's no need to explain anything, the message explained it all for you. With Tanya is obviously where you wanna be, since you supposedly ain't her baby's daddy, but yet you're still fucking her.

"You know what, though? It's cool. Y'all can have each other. I have nothing else to say, so if you'd excuse me, I got shit to do," I said, hoping he'd just leave without making the situation worse.

"Yo, E, don't give me that you-the-victim bullshit. It ain't like you ain't know shit. You wanted me to beat on that pussy from day one, and you knew I was fucking with ol' girl then. Now all of sudden you wanna act like the Virgin Mary and shit, like you got fucking morals now. Bitch, please!

"You right about one thing, though. Tanya's pussy is where I wanna be. You know why? 'Cause she got a fucking brain. All you wanna do is spend a nigga's dough and look cute all fucking day, but it's all good. You know what? Fuck you, Epiphany." On his way out the door, he grabbed something from my hallway table. "I'm going home to wifey and my new son now. Have a nice life, bitch."

I didn't know what he took, and at that point I didn't care. I slammed the door and locked both locks, relieved that he left, 'cause he was about to find out that I was the wrong bitch to fuck with. Still, my feelings were hurt from all the mean shit he said. I lay on the couch and continued to cry as his painful words repeated over in my head.

Minutes later, my doorbell rang again, but this time I got up and ran to my closet for my nine. I wanted to kill that muthafucka.

My daddy didn't raise a soft bitch; he taught me how to shoot. When I was eighteen, he started me off with a .22, but he said those small-ass guns were only made to wound a nigga, slow 'em down but not kill 'em. Then when I turned twenty-one, he gave me my nine, something that packed a punch, and it would kill a nigga. So, if that nigga thought he was gon' come up in here again talking shit to me like I was some weak-ass bitch, then I was gonna have to show him a real bitch.

I rushed to the front door in a rage. This time, instead of just opening it, I peeked out the window first and saw Malikai walking back toward his truck.

Chapter 39

KEISHA

It was just one of those days. Tucker called that morning and dropped a bomb on me.

"Keish, look, this ain't got shit to do with us, so don't even think that, all right? It's just bad timing right now, that's all. Too much shit is going on for me to even focus on getting married, so just call everybody and tell 'em that the shit ain't canceled, just postponed until further notice."

What kind of shit is that, three days before? How the hell . . .? I mean, what did he expect me to tell them? "We're still getting married, I just don't know when." Unbelievable! First he couldn't stay home 'cause it was too dangerous, and now he was postponing the wedding. What next? Leaving me for another woman?

This was just too much for me. I tell you, when it rains it pours. I needed some serious pampering—a nice massage, manicure, pedicure, facial, and waxing. That's what we did, the four of us. My mom and sisters seemed to enjoy it the most, because it was their first time. Me, I was a regular.

The massage was good, but it didn't change the fact that I was still upset, and on top of all that, I was horny as hell. The masseur's big, strong hands and Kenny G's "Songbird" playing softly in the background gave me a chill up my spine. I didn't know what was wrong with me lately, except for the fact that I hadn't had sex since . . . well, you know.

I was past that now. I needed some dick from my man—the man who was supposed to become my husband in three days. Now sex with Tucker seemed too far-fetched. Ever since I told him no, he hadn't touched me. I knew he had shit going on, but that had never kept him from wanting it before.

I had tried to get a quickie when he came by to check on us the last time. I even offered to meet him at a hotel, and the answer was no. So, if this was his idea of payback, he got me.

I opened up my wallet and pulled out my credit card to pay for our day at the spa. There it was, temptation staring me in the face once again—The Damager's card, the card that I should've left in the garbage but hadn't. I'd forgotten all about it, but this time, as soon as I got home I was gonna tear it up and throw it away.

I tried to get rid of it; I swear. I actually thought I could, especially since the tape was so easy to destroy and discard . . . after watching it a couple of times. I needed to do the right thing for all the right reasons, I kept telling myself. I was getting married one day. Tucker was just going through some drama that had nothing to do with us. How could I even think about another man? Where was my loyalty?

My conscience was telling me to do the right thing . . . but my hormones were more influential. I started thinking about the way Tucker had been acting toward me lately, how he hung up on me, his conversations were always short now, he practically lived in a hotel, and all of a sudden he postponed our wedding. I stared at The Damager's card as I thought about Tucker's behavior. I couldn't destroy it. The devil was definitely working overtime. Using every ounce of will in me to fight the temptation, I just couldn't. My body craved him and another round of his sexual pleasure one last time. Only this time, I would do it right. Wouldn't be no tapes being made.

I waited for The Damager in the lobby of the motel. I had already paid for the room under the name Lisa Smith. That should explain what type of motel it was: no ID required, check in, do what you gotta do, and check out, no questions asked. When he walked in and spotted me, he smiled as he headed toward me. My heart started to pound as it usually did whenever I was nervous or doing wrong. In this case I was guilty of both. I thought maybe my memory of him would have been a little off, because looks can be deceiving under the influence of alcohol. Thank God, not in his case. This brother was gorgeous, better looking than I remembered.

"Hi. Kelly, is it?" he said, looking down at me with that Colgate smile of his.

"Yes," I said, smiling back at him and wondering why I gave him my sister's name.

"You're beautiful. And by the way, my name is Julius," he said.

"Okay, but if you don't mind, I'd rather call you Damager."

Julius, what kind of name is that? I thought. Besides, the name Damager was more suitable for the situation. My being here could cause a lot of damage to my relationship if Tucker ever found out. If you asked me, there was really no need for us to get personal. I just wanted some dick, and then we could forever go our separate ways.

I told him that I would also prefer no conversation. The less we knew about each other the better, and just so we could keep this on a business basis, I offered him two hundred dollars.

He looked at me and said, "You can't be serious. Look, I don't know much about you and can't say that I want to, but I do know you're getting married, and believe me when I tell you that I'm not trying to stop that from happening. Yes, I think you're attractive, but it is not that serious, so you need to relax with all the do's and the don'ts, baby girl. I assume we're both adults, correct?" I nodded.

"So, let's handle our business like adults and have a good time. And put your money away. Last time was a service. This time I want to make you feel good for free. Did you read what I wrote on the back of my card?" I nodded again. "So let's just get our fuck on . . . no strings attached."

Round two: It was on and poppin'!

Chapter 40

SHANA

The past weekend's conjugal visit was definitely what was up. K.C. was so into me. We discussed everything from his release in six days to building our future together, and even one day having some kids. There was no talk about the plan or any other criminal activity. He didn't even mention my meeting with Smitty. And speaking of that nigga, I was guessing maybe he'd chilled on running back and reporting the recent beatdown of Chasity. Well, at least I hoped he had. I knew he didn't forget about it, because he enjoyed that shit too much.

Maybe Smitty was a real nigga and he wouldn't snitch me out. All I needed was for K.C. to hear that I was pussy-bumping it for a while. He hated gay people. When he was growing up, before his moms died from a drug overdose, she was one of them hard-boy type lesbians, and she was very open about it. Kids used to tease him, making jokes, calling his moms names like she-man, shim, and dyke. So he didn't want that nowhere around him. He didn't play that. Smitty couldn't have said anything about it, 'cause even though I was the only one out there keeping his bread buttered right now, K.C. wouldn't even care. He'd probably fuck me up first and then tell me to go fuck myself.

Speaking of dykes, I hadn't heard from that bitch Chasity since she got knocked the fuck out, and I wanted to keep it like that. I needed for her psycho ass to stay as far away from me as possible, and just to make sure of that, I wouldn't even be going up in Honey's anymore. I put these two girls that I'm cool with on to help me out, push my supply and get that li'l side dough outside of shaking they asses.

Raina and Silk, they was both some thorough-ass Brooklyn chicks. They didn't take no shit from them females or the niggas up in Honey's. When I met them we just clicked for some reason. Another thing I liked about them was that weed was their choice of get-high, so there shouldn't be no shorts, no getting high off the supply-type shit going on, 'cause that was bad for business.

I told them about the incident I'd had with that crazy bitch Chasity, and they were ready to beat her ass for me just on GP.

"Now, that's what's up, but nah, it's cool. Don't even fuck with her," I told them. I didn't want to take it to the extreme unless I had to. In a way, shit worked out for the best, 'cause I needed some rest. Besides, my man was coming home.

Chapter 41

EPIPHANY

I was glad Mali was there with me. I told him that I was going through a stressful time. He could tell I'd been crying, and the last thing I needed him to think was that a nigga made me cry, but his company made me feel a lot better. I didn't want to get into details, but I touched on my situation with C-God and Tanya just a little. Mali said he knew Tanya. Don't ask me how, but I wouldn't have been surprised if the bitch had been around the block a few times, you know what I mean?

He was interested in what I had to say about C, until I asked about their beef. I guess it was too soon for him to trust me again, 'cause after I asked him about that, he told me that shit was cool and he ain't wanna talk about the nigga no more. Before, he used to tell me everything—well, I won't say everything, but a lot. Now he was on some hush-hush bullshit, which was cool. I knew I just had to spend a li'l time with him and shit would be all good.

Instead of talking, we could play a few hands of cards, order Chinese food, and watch *Love Jones*. I didn't care how many times I saw that movie, I'd never get tired of it, maybe because I wished so bad that I had a love like Nina and Darius. I think I had love for Mali when we were together. I was not sure. I thought I loved C-God, but please, now that I thought about it, maybe I didn't know shit about love.

I got up to go to the bathroom. "You all right? 'Cause your ass is looking kind of thick in them shorts, girl," Mali questioned.

"I'm fine. That's just good living, that's all." I laughed.

"Yeah, I hear that," he said.

On my way back from the bathroom, I decided to spice things up a bit. It was only six p.m., and I wasn't ready for him to leave yet. I was feeling kinda horny and wouldn't mind giving him a sample of some of this pregnant pussy (and you know what they say: it's the best). I walked over and stood in front of him, wearing some Spandex boy-cut shorts that hugged my ass nicely, and a tank top. My pussy was dead smack in his face.

He looked up at me. "What's up?" He was playing stupid.

"Don't you miss this?" I asked.

"I'm here, right?" he said.

I sucked my teeth and sat back down on the couch. He wasn't stroking my ego the way I wanted him to. I knew he wanted me.

"Yo, you mad?" he asked, puzzled.

"Should I be?" I answered back sarcastically.

"Nah, I don't even know why you trippin', 'cause you know I missed you. What, you need to hear a nigga say it?" he said, cracking a smile. Mali always had a nice smile to go with that sweet caramel complexion of his.

His smile made me smile. "Yes."

"Okay, cool. Epiphany, I miss the shit out of you . . . and that, too," he said, pointing toward what was between my legs.

We both laughed. I moved in closer, kissed his lips, and asked him to stay with me for the rest of the night.

Chapter 42

SHANA

Smitty called me in the morning with some good news. He said K.C. was being released that evening, but he wasn't sure what time yet, and he was gonna pick him up.

"I thought he had to do a few more days. Not that I'm disappointed or anything, but how did he get out of doing those days?" I asked.

Smitty said somebody K.C. was cool with pulled some strings in the right places and got him released a couple days early.

"Somebody like who?" I asked. I didn't trust those C.O. bitches up in them jails, 'cause I heard they be letting the inmates hit it on the low and shit. "And why he ask you to pick him up?"

"Yo, 'cause we got some shit—we got some matters to discuss. That's why." He laughed. "Any further questions, ask ya man when he get there, a'ight?"

"A'ight, Smitty. Bye."

"Hold up. One more thing, Sha, before I go. Let's just say he did fuck one of them C.O. bitches in jail. Why would you even trip if it got the nigga home early to be with you? You feel what I'm saying?" His grimey-ass started to laugh.

"Bye, Smitty." I ain't even respond to that shit, 'cause four or five days was nothing. Now, years, that was some different shit. Smitty was a'ight, but I could tell that nigga loved some drama.

When I got off the phone, I took a good look at the crib, and it was a mess. It was a good thing Smitty was picking him up, 'cause I had work to do.

I put on Ashanti's CD and got busy. That was the first time I had listened to her whole CD, and it was hot. I must've played that song "Baby When You Call I'll Come Running" like four times in a row. By the time I finished cleaning, it looked like Mr. Clean ran up in that muthafucka. Shit, I surprised myself. That nigga had better come home and appreciate what he had, 'cause he had me running around trying to be all domesticated and shit. I even went out and got a bucket of fried chicken and a Pepsi to feed his ass when he got home. If that ain't no wifey shit, then what is? I was that nigga's wife for real.

"Yo, open up, Sha. Where you at? I know you got a key made for a nigga to get up in this muthafucka," K.C. yelled through the locked screen door.

I rushed to the door, opened it, and jumped right up in his arms.

"What up, nugga?" I said all hard and shit, 'cause I knew that tough talk turned him on.

He palmed my ass and shoved that wet, fat-ass tongue of his in my mouth. We must've swapped spit for about a good two minutes, until Smitty interrupted the flow, opening his mouth with his hating ass, talking 'bout, "Y'all niggas cut all the mushy shit out. Wait 'til a nigga leave. Damn, dawg, it ain't like you was locked up and wasn't getting no pussy, 'cause yo, Sha's ass ain't miss them conjugals."

"Yo, nigga, stop with all the hating. She ain't supposed to miss none!" K.C. said.

"Nah, dawg, that's what's up. Yo, Sha, what up with that chicken?" Smitty asked midway through what he was saying. "Oh, shit. That's New York Fried. Yo, man, they got the best chicken; that's my word.

"Anyway, as I was saying, Shana's a good girl, man. Ain't too many broads out there that's gonna hold a nigga down. When you on the streets, maybe, but let a nigga get locked up, a bitch'll be out. Sha, you a'ight with me though, word," Smitty said with chicken grease all over his lips.

"Yo, Sha's my ride or die chick for life. I ain't never gon' leave her fucked up. She good, believe that." K.C. smiled and patted me on the ass.

"A'ight, y'all, can we talk about something else?" I said. Even though assurance was all good, I didn't want to be the topic of discussion anymore.

"Yo, Sha, you got some liquor or something so we can welcome my man home the right way?" Smitty asked.

Let me find out this nigga was a freeloader, I thought. "Yeah, I got some Henny in the kitchen."

"Oh, that what's up, baby girl. Yo, go hook us up," K.C. said.

I went into the kitchen to fix them a drink. I glanced at the time on the microwave. It was only seven o'clock. *It's gonna be a long night,* I thought. When I walked back in the living room, I knew it was gon' be an even longer night, 'cause these niggas done started playing Madden on the PlayStation, and you know how a nigga forget about time when they fucking with that game shit.

"Ay, yo, Sha, we got 50's new shit?" asked K.C.

"Nah," I said.

"Yo, how you from south side and you don't have that nigga's shit, man?"

Before I could respond, Smitty paused the game. "Yo, I got a bootleg copy in the car. I'ma go get it."

"Yeah, nigga, 'cause I need to hear it. That shit is hot, yo," K.C. said, getting hyped.

When Smitty came back inside, he put on 50, sparked some hydro, and we all played puff, puff, pass. I started to relax as my high took effect, and even though I was kinda heated that this nigga Smitty ain't knew when to take his ass home, eventually it became all good. An hour later and all was high—drinking, smoking, bopping our heads to the music, and of course them niggas was still playing the game.

Knock knock.

"Sha, who that?" K.C. asked.

"Who? What?" I said, not able to hear the door through the loud music.

"Somebody knocked at your door. You ain't got no niggas coming over here to check you, 'cause if so, tell them mutha-fuckas Daddy's home, word up."

I laughed, trying to play it off, 'cause I had no clue who the fuck was at my door. When I looked through the screen, my high was blown.

"Can I talk to you for a minute?" Chasity asked. Something was up, 'cause this bitch was too calm.

"Nah, I can't talk right now. It ain't a good time," I said, brushing her off.

"Just open the door and let me talk to you, Cream."

Damn. Now, why the bitch wanna go there? "Yo, you bugging out. Just get the fuck away from my door please." I just gave it to her bluntly, 'cause she done made me mad calling me by my stripper name.

Then the devil surfaced, and she started banging and kicking on the thin-ass aluminum door. "You stupid bitch! Don't make me fuck you up. Open the fucking door. I just wanna talk."

K.C. and Smitty came running to the door to see what the chaos was all about. Before I could think of an explanation, Smitty had my back, taking charge of the situation. He pushed me out the way and opened the door.

"What the fuck did I tell you before, huh? Stop following me, yo, you broke-down bitch. I ain't feeling you. It ain't gon' happen, so beat it, 'cause I'ma fuck around and catch a case for whipping ya ass, yo. I'm telling you. I should fuck you up right now for knocking on my girl's door and blowing my muthafuckin' high. Get outta here!" Smitty really got a good look at her this time, and then it dawned on him where he recognized her from. As a matter of fact, he remembered where he knew both of us from—Honey's.

Chasity was yelling so much that after a while I couldn't even understand what the fuck she was saying, and on top of that, she was walking away pretty fast. I guess Smitty's crazy-ass put that fear in her the last time.

"Nigga, what up with that? Keep fucking around with them crazy-ass hoes," K.C. joked.

"Nah, man, them hoes don't be crazy until I give 'em the magic stick. That's when they lose their muthafuckin' minds," Smitty said, laughing and giving K.C. a pound.

"So, how the fuck the bitch know you was here?" K.C. asked, trying to make sense of what just happened.

"Yo, she gotta be following me."

"Nigga, you been here for how long, and she just now coming?" K.C. said.

"Maybe she spotted my car. How the fuck I'm supposed to know? That bitch a nut," Smitty said.

"Yo, nigga, that's bad business, and the shit still don't make sense, 'cause if she spotted your car, how the fuck she know to come to this house and to the side door, at that? What the fuck the bitch do—eenie, meenie, miny, mo? Come on, dawg. I'ma leave that shit alone, though, 'cause you think a nigga stupid," K.C. said, becoming annoyed.

"Yo, man, it's that hydro making your ass paranoid and shit. That's all, nigga. Chill the fuck out. It ain't what you thinking," Smitty said as he started to laugh, trying to ease K.C.'s mind.

I laughed along with him, 'cause I couldn't understand why he was going through all this bullshit just to cover for me. I barely knew his ass. Shit, he could have easily just said, "Yo, your girl was fucking with that bitch, so take that shit up with her." But he didn't, and I was glad he didn't, but why didn't he?

"Yo, I'm out, son. I'ma go take care of that thing we talked about earlier," Smitty said to K.C.

"A'ight, nigga. Hit me later," K.C. said.

"Yo, Shana, come lock up," he said as he walked to the door.

I followed behind him, and on his way out the door he turned to me, cracked a devious smirk, and said, "You owe me, nigga. Big time!" And from that, I knew I was in for the bullshit.

Chapter 43

KEISHA

Time sure does fly when you're having fun, and I was having too much fun. Julius was such a nice guy, and he made me laugh, too. I didn't want to leave, but I knew I had to, and oh my God, the sex . . . The sex was so damn good, you better believe we fucked each other like it was our last time—and it was for real this time. I did give him my cell phone number, though, just so we could keep in touch as "friends" because we had a lot in common.

For my comfort, I inspected the room to make sure there weren't any hidden video cameras or anything while Julius showered.

I didn't shower, because I didn't want to leave him alone in the room. Not to say I didn't trust him, but the video tape thing was still a mystery, therefore everyone was still a suspect.

We departed the room at the same time. After I turned in the room key, Julius walked me to my car and kissed my forehead. (You see there, I got the forehead kiss. That definitely meant it was over.)

I reached in my purse for my cell phone and noticed I had three missed calls, all from home, and no messages. The first call had come nearly two hours earlier. To me that was strange. Why not leave a message?

I called home to see if every thing was okay. My sister answered on the first ring.

"Hello."

"Hey, who's this? Keely?" I asked, not able to tell the difference between the two because of their strong southern accents.

"Nah, dis ain't Keely. Dis Kelly. Girl, where you at? Big T was looking for you. I think he was mad 'cause nobody ain't know where you was. Ma told him to call you. He said he did but you ain't answer your phone."

"Is he there now?" I asked.

"I don't know. He mighter left."

"Well, where's my son?" I said, getting a little aggravated because she didn't know the answers to any of my questions.

"Oh, li'l T sleeping. You fixin' to come home soon?" she asked.

"Yeah, I'm on my way now." I hung up the phone, thinking of a good excuse to come up with.

My nerves were starting to act up. How could I go home and face him knowing I just finished letting another man fuck my pussy? Maybe I should call him, I thought. No, I wasn't gonna call him. I was gonna go to the mall and grab a couple of things for the baby. That way I could say I was depressed about the wedding, so I went shopping. Yeah, that was a good idea. Plus, he knew my piece of shit phone didn't hold a good signal in the mall.

I was confident that my excuse would work, so I rushed to the mall and hit Baby Gap. I even grabbed a few items for myself, 'cause the regular Gap was attached. After spending three hundred dollars, I was ready to go home.

When I got there, I didn't see Tucker's car. I pulled into the driveway, and guess who was waiting to greet me at the front door? Tucker.

"Hey, baby," I said, not wanting to get too close because I wasn't sure whether or not I smelled like sex or had dick on my breath. I could tell he was furious before he even opened his mouth.

"Where you been at, Keish?" he asked in a mild mannered tone as if he wasn't upset.

"What?" I replied. Might as well see the ugly come out and get it over with.

"What? Oh, now you don't understand English. Where the fuck was you at all day, Keish? You couldn't even call to check on our son or answer your motherfucking cell phone? Huh? Answer the question."

See, didn't I say it was about to get ugly? "Tucker, if you stop yelling and calm down, I'll answer your question."

"I'm listening," he said.

"I was at the mall." I hoped I didn't look like I was lying.

"Keisha, you wasn't at the mall for no six hours," he said, giving me that "I ain't buying it" look, but that was my story, and I was sticking to it.

"Look, Tucker, I've been out shopping all day, and I just wanna take a shower and go to bed. Besides, what are you doing here? I thought it wasn't safe for us if you were here," I said sarcastically.

"Just hurry up and take your shower, 'cause I got something I want you to see," Tucker said, flashing a fake smile.

You know what? l don't even wanna know, I thought as I rushed into the bathroom, relieved that he didn't push the mall issue that much. All I wanted to do was freshen up and get through the night without Tucker asking me for any coochie, because two dicks in one day ain't cool, and if I said no again, he might really get suspicious.

When I got out of the shower, I dried off, threw on some sweats, a tee, and no body perfume or nothing. I wanted to look as unattractive as possible. I wrapped my hair, threw on a scarf, and went downstairs to make sure all the doors were locked. My sisters had the spare set of keys, so no one had to worry about listening out for them when they got home from the movies that night. Then I took a peek into the guest bedroom, where my mom and the baby were knocked out asleep. The last stop was my bedroom. I opened the door, and instantly tears started to fill my eyes when I saw Tucker sitting on the edge of the bed, watching the videotape of me giving my body to another man.

Chapter 44

C-GOD

It was a quarter after ten and I sat in my Hempstead apartment fucked up, my nose buried in a pile of coke to numb the pain after receiving a call from Reggie about Mike, his girl, their son, and his girl's moms all getting murdered not even an hour before. Reg said he just had spoke to the nigga and they was gon' get up and go shoot a game of pool up on Flatbush Ave, but when he swung by the crib to get the nigga, the door was half open. He went inside, but before he could get far, he spotted Mike's baby moms, Angie, lying less than four feet away from the door, with her son in her arms, both dead. Her moms caught one sitting in the chair by the window. Bullet went throw the right lens of her eyeglasses, and Mike must've been taking a shit when niggas ran up on him, 'cause he was sitting on the toilet in the bathroom, lit up with bullets holes.

"Yo, son, the TV was up mad loud, so if they screamed, the nigga probably thought that shit was coming from the fucking tube. Man, I ain't call no cops or nothing. I just broke out, 'cause yo, shit was ugly, son. Mike's gone, and whoever did it, did my man and his fam dirty."

Those words hurt me to my heart as I hung up the phone, needing a minute to make sense of what the fuck I just heard.

Mike was my li'l brother, my soldier, the head nigga in charge under me. Out of all the niggas I put on, I had love for that nigga big time. The one thing I couldn't figure out was how niggas knew where he was resting his head at in Brooklyn. Mike was too fuckin' paranoid, and at the same time too smart, to let a muthafucka follow his ass. He stayed with his guards up at all times.

My mind was boggled. I opened a bottle of Hennessey and poured a little out on my hardwood floor, reminiscing about the fun and the drama me and Mike shared together. "To my nigga, my muthafuckin' Lieutenant Ike," I said, letting go a smile as a tear trickled down my face. Niggas used to call Mike's ass Lieutenant Ike 'cause that nigga ain't have no problems with beating a bitch's ass. He ain't care where they was. If the bitch pissed him off, he was fucking her up Ike-on-Tina style, no doubt about it.

I laughed at that thought then took a swig from the bottle and said, "I got you. I'ma kill that muthafucka Tucker, his mans, and whoever hang with them faggots. That's my word, son."

I then made a call to Ness, another li'l crazy-ass nigga on some 'bout-it, 'bout-it shit. I put him on a while ago. I liked dude, but he couldn't take the place of Mike. Still, he was thorough. Besides, I knew what niggas in my camp to call when it was time to get at muthafuckas—the ones with heart, 'cause some of them was straight pussy. Like, for instance, Reggie. He was good for making runs and a couple of dollars doing the hand to hand thing on the block, and even playing chauffeur when I entertained the bitches, but when it came to his murder game, the nigga just wasn't cut out for it.

"Yo, nigga, I know you heard about Mike, right?" I asked.

"Yeah, man. That shit is fucked up, yo. What up?" said Ness.

"That muthafucka executed my man and his fam, yo."

"So, how you wanna handle shit?" Ness asked, already down for whatever.

"Yo, just tell niggas it's time to get on they grind, 'cause we need to find them niggas tonight. I don't really give a fuck how y'all handle his mans, but that nigga Tucker, I wanna deal with his ass personally, starting with his bitch and the nigga's kid. I'ma do him like they did Mike, only worse. So yo, after you kick it to the fellas, I want you to meet me over on 137th and Guy R. Brewer, a'ight. And come strapped."

"Cool. Yo, is that where that nigga rest at?"

"Nah, this bitch I used to fuck with live over there, but she cool with his peoples, so she the bitch that's gon' give up his information."

"Yo, a'ight, I got you. I'm on it," Ness said, quickly hanging up the phone.

***

Ness was on point. He did exactly what he was told. When he arrived on 137th, he spotted me chilling in a beat up li'l white Ford Taurus that I usually used to take runs in. He parked his car behind me, walked to the passenger side, and got in.

I was zoning out, listening to Biggie and 112 singing "Missing You." We sat in silence until the song was over, then I snapped back into rare form, and the plan was murder.

I made a right onto 137th Street and crept down to the middle of the block. Making a complete stop, I spotted a red Navigator parked in front of Epiphany's crib with the license plates that read LIVELIFE. Right away I knew that was Tucker's right hand man.

I was heated, because even though I had done my dirt to Epiphany, I still felt like she belonged to me, and the fact that she was fucking with that nigga made matters worse.

I started thinking back to the night that Mike, Epiphany, and me hung out, and whether I dropped the nigga off in Brooklyn at his baby moms' crib, or possibly to one of his other chicks. I couldn't remember.

Well fuck it. That's two birds with one stone. She better be ready to die with this clown-ass nigga, I thought.

"Yo, Ness, look under the seat and give me that thing."

Ness reached under the seat, pulled out a Smith and Wesson, and passed it to me. Then he checked the clip on his shit to make sure he was fully loaded.

"Yo, you ready, son?" Ness asked.

"Yeah, just hold up a minute. I got that bitch keys somewhere in this car."

"Yo, how that happen?" Ness asked.

"I was at her crib earlier, arguing with her stupid ass, so I took them shits just to be spiteful, and now look. These shits came in handy."

"Word, yo, that's what's up," Ness said, impress- ed.

"Got 'em, yo. Let's do this," I said. I stuck the key in the door, unlocked it, and opened it slowly.

I heard laughing and talking while Prince's "Do Me Baby" played. I was gon' do them, a'ight. Ness followed behind as I quietly crept down the small hall leading to the living room.

Chapter 45

EPIPHANY

Great. This was what it boiled down to, me having to give Mali a lap dance off Prince just to get some. Damn, see what a girl had to do just to get a li'l dick—and I do mean little. I ain't mind, though, because just like old times, we were having fun. I had him for the whole night. Just like he was putting me to work, payback was gon' sure be a pain in his back when I got him in my bed, I thought as I turned around toward him. I froze in shock because of what—I mean who—I saw standing behind Mali.

Before I could react or say anything, they shot him in the head. His blood and parts of his brains splashed all over me. I covered my face with my hand, afraid and hurting at the same time. I didn't scream. As a matter of fact, I was in complete shock. My body trembled all over. I just stood there while C-God ordered his boy to check my bedroom and the bathroom.

Peeking through my fingers, I saw Malikai's lifeless body slumped over on the couch as blood seeped from the hole in his head. I couldn't believe what was happening. The pain I was feeling for Mali was much greater than all the pain I had ever felt before in my life.

C-God started kicking my stereo system, trying to shut Prince up, while calling me every name in the book. I was a stink bitch, a trifling ho, and then a chickenhead. Every disrespectful word you can think of, I was. I just stood there thinking about how bad I wanted to kill his muthafuckin' ass.

Then he grabbed me by my hair and forced me to my knees. He had the nerve to call me a sheisty-ass bitch for fucking around on him, and I wasn't even with his ass. He went on, saying I helped Tucker and Mali kill his boy. He then put his gun to my head. Tears poured down my face as I cried like a baby. I wasn't ready to die. I tried to release the words from my mouth, but couldn't find my voice. I tried again, and this time I was able to speak. I had to if I wanted to live.

"I swear I don't know who or what you're talking about, and I didn't have nothing to do with nothing. Please don't do this C."

"Bitch, shut the fuck up!" he yelled, knocking me completely down to the floor and kicking me so hard in my pussy. He demanded to know whether or not I slept with Malikai.

"Ouch!" I cried out in agony as I placed my hands between my legs, trying to ease the pain. I turned to my side and lay in a fetal position, crying and screaming, "Please don't hurt me! Please."

Thoughts of me fucking Malikai sent C-God into a rage. He started to lose focus on the real reason he was there. "Did you fuck him? Huh, did you?" He wanted an answer right away.

"No, I swear I didn't," I cried out.

"Shut up, you fucking lying-ass, trick-ass bitch! If I ain't come in here when I did, that dead muthafucka would've been up in that ass. You wasn't up in here dropping it like it's hot for nothing. Now tell me I'm wrong. Huh? Tell me I'm wrong." C-God didn't wait for me to answer his question. He just started kicking and punching on me like he was crazy.

I lay there with my eyes shut, balled up, trying to shield myself, wishing I could just make it over to the sofa cushion where my piece was stashed, so I could kill this bitch-ass nigga.

Out of nowhere, I heard his boy say, "Damn, son, you fuckin' that ho up. She's prettier than a muthafucka too. Word. Yo, son, you should let me hit that before you kill her," Ness suggested, knowing the only way he could ever get close to even smelling my pussy was if my life depended on it.

I could tell C didn't like that proposition very much by the look on his face, and I guess Ness could too, 'cause he quickly excused himself. "Yo, I'ma be in the front if you need me, dawg, a'ight."

C-God didn't respond. I was relieved that he left, but afraid that C was gonna continue kicking my ass. I knew I had to act fast before this nigga fucked around and killed me for real.

"Yo, E, listen. If you tell me where your friend Keisha live at, I promise I won't hit you no more." I guess that was his idea of playing fair.

I took a minute to think. I thought about how important my life was to me. I didn't wanna die. I probably hadn't been the best person or friend I could've been, but I would never be able to live with myself if something happened to Keisha, my godson, or Tucker because of something I did. I just couldn't. *Oh, God, please help me out with this one!*

"I don't know where she lives," I said, tightly shutting my eyes, shielding my face with my hands and waiting to die. He grew furious, but he didn't hit me.

I knew he didn't really want to kill me, but that didn't mean that he wouldn't. It was obvious that this nigga still had feelings for me. If I was right, then hopefully my plan would work, I thought as I grabbed my stomach and screamed like I was in excruciating pain. At first he wasn't buying it.

"You think I give a fuck about your pain? My boy and his family is gone because of that dead nigga right there"—C-God pointed his gun at Mali's body—"and his punk-ass man. So either you gon' tell me what I wanna know or yo, you gon' wish we never fucking met. The choice is yours," C-God said as if he was through negotiating.

"I don't know!" I cried. "Please, baby, just listen to me. I swear I don't know. Keisha ain't spoke to me in over a month. She kicked me out of her wedding, moved, and changed her numbers because of you, because I chose loving you over my friendship with her. Then you hurt me. You hurt me bad, choosing Tanya over me.

"And the only reason I had Malikai over here was to see if I could butter him up for her information. That's the truth. I just wanted to find out where Keisha is, because I need her. She's the only one I can talk to, and I knew she would convince me to keep it. Aaahh," I moaned in an over-exaggerated tone of agony.

Clutching my stomach, I kneeled down and whispered, "I don't wanna lose our baby."

"Baby? What baby?" C-God inquired.

"Oh, God, it hurts," I cried before I told him that I was four weeks pregnant with his child. Like most niggas, his first response was, "How you know it's mines?"

"I know it's yours 'cause I ain't been with nobody but you since I started fucking with you. If you don't believe me, just look at my papers from the clinic, there in my purse over on the table. I'm four weeks. Do the math, C-God."

I was hoping I'd get the opportunity to get to the cushion, but he didn't go for my purse. He just stood there looking in my face to see if he could tell whether or not I was sincere, and I did my best to convince him, 'cause I was sincere all right; sincere about making the bastard pay. I was gonna act my ass off if it meant saving my life, and that's what I did.

C-God finally broke his silence. "So why you ain't tell me about the baby before now?"

"I just found out about it a week ago. I wanted to tell you, but I also wanted us to be together. Then you came over here calling me names and talking about Tanya being better than me, so after all that, how could I tell you? C-God, I'm so sorry to hear about Mike. I really . . . I am, even though I didn't care much for him. I would never wish bad on him, because he's your friend and I love you so much," I said as I started to boo-hoo like crazy.

It worked! *The award for best actress of the year goes to me, Epiphany Wright, for playing on a nigga's emotions,* I thought as he fell for the okey doke.

"Yo, shit is fucked up right now. I'm fucked up. Mike's gone, and I gotta make shit right for my nigga. Word . . . I got to. I didn't want to hurt you, yo. I really didn't! I just snapped when I seen that nigga up in here.

"I ain't even gon' front, ma. I got mad love for you. Now you telling me you got my baby inside you after I done put my hands on you and shit. How you think that's supposed to make me feel, huh? Damn, E, why you ain't tell me? What if you lose my seed?"

C-God was touching, but not enough. I let out another agonizing moan and cried out, "Please, I need to go to the hospital. I think I'm losing the baby."

C-God started to pace back and forth. "Okay, wait a minute. Let me think for a minute. I can't take you to the hospital. Them muthafuckas gon' think I beat you up like that and call the police, and if I call a ambulance, they gon' see this dead nigga's body lying here and call the police."

He finally said, "Fuck! A'ight, this is the plan. I'ma have the nigga Ness drop you off at the hospital," like he was doing me a favor or something. Still pacing back and forth, he said, "Damn I gotta do something with this nigga's body. I'ma dump that shit in Baisley Pond or some shit like that, then call one of my boys to come get the nigga truck and take it to the chop shop. Yeah, a'ight, that's the plan," he said, having his shit all figured out.

"Aahhhhh," I screamed again to remind him that I was still in pain and needed help.

"A'ight, ma, let me see where the fuck this nigga Ness at." Leaving the living room, he headed toward the front door. On his way, he stopped and checked out the papers that were in my purse to see if I was telling the truth about being knocked up. He looked back at me and continued toward the door.

I jumped up and limped over toward the couch. I paused for a moment and just stared at Malikai's body lying there lifeless on the couch. I wanted to check his pulse, but I didn't have time for that. Besides, I was wearing some of his brains on my clothes, so I knew he was gone.

I pulled my nine out from under the cushion and stood up straight, just as C-God came back in the room.

"Drop your fucking gun and push it over here, you dumb muthafucka. Do it now!" I screamed.

"A'ight, you got that. Just don't shoot me," he said, dropping and kicking his gun toward me.

"Don't shoot you, what? Muthafucka, you got the nerve to tell me don't shoot you. You should've thought about all that shit when you was kicking my ass." Tears poured down my stinging face as I thought about how badly he beat me. "You bastard, my daddy ain't never put his hands on me, and since you did, I can't wait to kill you.

"I just want you to know one thing: I fucking hate you. You black muthafucka, I started wishing long before tonight that I never fucked with you. Now you gon' wish the same. You took this shit too far, C-God, and you fucked with the wrong one!" I yelled as my anger took control.

C-God just stood there in silence. He knew the seriousness of the situation from my tone. He knew that it was over and I'd had enough.

I glanced at Malikai's dead body one last time, and with the hate and anger I had floating inside me, I didn't think twice before I aimed my gun toward C-God's head, closed my eyes, and squeezed the trigger. Just as I did, I could hear Ness entering the living room, but before I could open my eyes, he blasted off a bullet from his .38.

"Oooooh!" Not knowing whether my shot was a successful one, I screamed from the burning sensation I felt as the heat pierced through my chest. I cried out "Noooo!" as I was thrown to the floor from the strong impact. Instantly, I could feel the warmth of my blood leaking from the stinging opening in my chest and my eyes getting real heavy.

The pain was too much to bear.

Chapter 46

"Oh God, please noooooo," were the last words Epiphany whispered as tears fell down the sides of her face and she lost consciousness after the shooting. C-God damn near pissed himself. His heart was pounding rapidly. For a moment he thought *he* was shot. Fortunately for him, Epiphany's aim was way off because she had closed her eyes when she squeezed the trigger.

"Yo, man, c'mon. We gotta get the fuck up out of here," Ness screamed. C kneeled down beside Epiphany and felt remorseful. Finally, he felt her pain. In any other situation, he wouldn't have given a fuck, especially when it came down to his life, but this wasn't just any situation. As much as he tried to front on Epiphany, he really did care for her. He'd had no intention of killing her. He'd just wanted to shake her up enough to get her to talk.

C-God looked down at the papers still clutched in his hand, confirming Epiphany's pregnancy, and he felt even more fucked up.

"Yo, fuck that bitch. Lets roll, dawg!" Ness yelled in a panic.

Finally, C snapped out of it, grabbed both guns, and together they fled the scene doing eighty down South Jamaica's residential back streets.

"Nigga, you must have been soft on that chick, but yo, it was either you or her, nigga. Look at it that way." Ness was the type of nigga with a big ass mouth that didn't know how to leave well enough alone. "If I ain't come up in there when I did, your shorty might of murked you dawg, for real, but I had your back though."

C-God just sat there wearing a screw-faced look on his face, thinking about the 'what ifs' as he listened to Ness in silence.

Deep down, C-God knew Epiphany would have kept shooting at him until she killed him. So, yes, he felt Ness reacted the way he was supposed to when he shot her, but C didn't want to hear him boasting about it.

Obviously the look on his face wasn't enough, because Ness didn't catch the hint; he just continued to go on and on about the incident until suddenly C snapped.

"Shut the fuck up! Damn! A nigga can't even think straight with you running the fuck off at the mouth. Just don't say shit else to me until I ask you to, and pull this muthafucka over at that payphone right there."

Ness did what he was told. He shut the fuck up and pulled over. It was C-God's duty to live his life coldheartedly. He never cared too much about anybody except his parents. Outside of them, the rest of his family was cool, but if they crossed him, they could easily be killed for doing so.

On the real, he was all bark with no bite, only nobody knew it because they never put him to the test. It was his older brothers that were the truth back in the days. Nigga's ain't fuck with his three brothers or whoever they considered to be family. Pop, Black Russ, and Lloyd were well known and now legendary gangstas, ranking with some of the best that ever terrorized Queens. They were ruthless, with no respect for a person's life. Killers without a cause. If they weren't feeling you for whatever reason, then they didn't give a fuck about you or your family, and in their presence you had better not show fear.

Unfortunately, living that life came back to haunt them, leading to the brutal deaths of Pop and Black Russ, and landing Lloyd in prison for life with no chance of parole. Still, C-God felt since he was the last breed of the notorious Hinderson brothers, he had something to prove. He had to own up to his family name and the reputation they paved.

For some reason, his conscience was eating away at him tonight, and that wasn't supposed to happen to no Hinderson.

C-God picked up the receiver on the payphone, using the papers he had taken from Epiphany's purse. With a piece of tissue covering his fingertip, he dialed the police. He always thought

with a criminal's mind. Disguising his voice in an unrecognizable high-pitched tone, he called for an ambulance in hopes
that Epiphany might still be alive.

Epiphany briefly regained consciousness, oblivious to the
sounds of the loud sirens as she lay still in a pool of her own
blood. An ambulance and three police cars arrived at the
scene shortly after the call was made. The cops entered first
and took a look around, then signaled the paramedics with an
"Okay, the coast is clear."

When the paramedics entered, the police suggested they
tend to the girl first. Besides, from the looks of things, Malikai
was already deceased.

The EMS workers ran over to Epiphany and checked her vital signs.

"She's still alive," one of them shouted. "Start an IV. Her
pulse is weak. This is not good. She's losing a lot of blood.
Let's get a move on it!" Lifting Epiphany onto the stretcher,
he continued, "We're losing her. Let's get her to the hospital now!"

Chapter 47

Keisha stood in the bedroom doorway, completely appalled. Her heart fell into the pit of her stomach and tears instantly fell down her face. As she stood there, her fiancé watched her give herself to another man, performing and receiving sexual pleasures on camera as if her name were Janet Jackme. She froze; stuck on stupid, puzzled as to how the videotape she had destroyed managed to resurface again. She searched for the right words to say. She wanted to say something, but what? "I'm sorry." No, that wasn't gonna cut it. There was nothing to be said. She fucked up and she knew it. She felt like she had just slid down a razor blade, right into a pool of alcohol.

Tucker's face was filled with a rage that she had never seen before, and it put fear in Keisha's heart. She was afraid to say or do anything, so she continued to watch him watch her fuck and suck on another man in ways she had never done with him.

He had never, ever thought about putting his hands on any woman, let alone Keisha, until now. Fuming, he was to the point were he really wanted to hurt her. Tucker jumped up, snatched the VCR from the top of the 52-inch screen TV, and tossed it into to the wall close to where Keisha was standing.

Keisha jumped out of the way and into the hallway as the VCR crashed into the wall and then hit the floor.

Water flooded his eyes, and his heart was filled with pain. This was the ultimate feeling of betrayal, but he would never give her the satisfaction of seeing him cry. No one, for that matter. His militant father had instilled in him as a boy that a man ain't supposed to cry. A strong man sucks it all up and keeps it moving.

By now, all types of distasteful thoughts were running through Tucker's mind, but he never said a word. He simply looked at Keisha with such anger and disgust. If looks could kill, she would have suffered a painful death. Keisha was still standing in the hall, afraid to move or say a word. She wasn't sure what to expect from this furious side of Tucker.

Keisha's mother, Loretta, and her son, Li'l T, were awakened and startled when they heard the crashing sound. She jumped out of bed, grabbed the baby, and rushed from the bedroom to see what was going on. Right outside her door, she spotted Keisha near the doorway of her bedroom, crying.

"Keisha, is everything okay?" asked her concerned mother.

Keisha didn't respond. Instead, she took it as an opportunity to get out of Tucker's sight. Making a run for the bathroom, she locked herself inside and cried like a baby.

Loretta was curious as to what was going on. She assumed that maybe it was just a heated discussion about the wedding postponement. Since there wasn't any sign of domestic violence, she felt no need to get involved, so she headed back to her room.

Tucker had no sympathy for Keisha or her tears, and at this point, all he felt for her was pure hatred, but he would never hurt her because of his son.

"Let me just get the fuck up out of here," he said to himself as he quickly gathered up some of his belongings and breaking out in a hurry. He wasn't sure if his anger would allow him to honor the fact that she was his baby's mother.

Once the sound of Tucker's truck sped off, confirming that the coast was now clear, Loretta laid Li'l T in the bed and came back out of her room. She knocked gently on the bathroom door.

"Keisha, is everything all right?" she whispered again.

Keisha wasn't all right. Her life was over. She opened the door and fell into her mother's arms for comfort.

"He's gone, and I don't think he's coming back," Keisha stuttered as she cried.

"What happened?"

"The tape. He saw the tape."

"No! Keisha, how? I thought you got rid of it."

"I did, I did. And there's no way possible that could be the same tape. Somebody had to set me up. One of the girls at my bachelorette party, posing to be my friend, set this whole thing up, and my stupid ass fell for it. Now he's gone, and what am I gonna do, huh? How am I ever gonna get Tucker to forgive me?" she asked her mother, hoping and wishing she could give her all the right answers.

"Keisha, you know Tucker loves you. Just give him some time. He'll come around so you guys can at least talk and try to work things out. In the meantime, you need to be strong and try to keep it together, not only for you, but for that baby boy in the next room. Don't make the same mistakes that I did.

"You know what you did was wrong, but we all make mistakes. I know you love him, and he knows it too. Understand that that was a pretty big bomb you dropped on him, so he's gotta be devastated and full of hurt right now. You' re the mother of his son, a son that he loves more than anything in this world, and nothing will ever change that. Just give it some time. He'll come around. You just have to pray for the best and prepare for the worst, just in case he can't find it in his heart to forgive you. If he can't, then you just got to find a way to move on," Loretta said, stroking her daughter's head while she cried in her arms.

Keisha listened to her mother's words, but at the same time, she didn't feel like she could manage life without Tucker. She went and got her son from her mother's bed. Holding him close, she reminisced on how happy Tucker was when she told him she was pregnant. Their son, Li'l T, was the bond that she and Tucker shared, a bond created out of love. It was a bond that, because of her stupidity, might be the only thing she had left of Tucker.

Before shutting her puffy red eyes to get some sleep, she made a promise to herself to find out which one of those bitches was responsible for causing this misery.

Chapter 48

Epiphany's father had a terrible ringing in his left ear all evening. Old folks used to say that when you heard a ringing sound in your ear, that was the sound of death bells and someone close to you was gonna die. Jay Wright didn't believe that ol' superstitious shit, but for some reason tonight's feeling just wasn't right.

Those feelings were confirmed when he was awakened in the middle of the night by the doorbell. He jumped up out of bed and rushed down the stairs to see who it was. It had to be some bad news, because nobody rang his bell that time of morning ever since he left the drug game three years ago.

When he reached the door, he opened it slightly and peeked out to find two police officers, one black and one white, standing there. He assumed something might have happened to his brother, Ramel, who took over his position when he retired from the game.

Before he could speak, one of the officers addressed him. "Good morning, sir. I'm Officer Johnson, and this is Officer Riley. We're sorry to bother you at this time of morning, but are you Jay Wright?"

Epiphany's dad hated the police, but he kept his composure, because finding out their reason for being at his front door was more important.

"Yes, officer, I am. What's going on?"

"Mr. Wright, I'm sorry to have to be the bearer of bad news, but your daughter, Epiphany, and a young man were found shot in her apartment around midnight. The man was pronounced dead at the scene. Your daughter was severely wounded and rushed to the nearest hospital. We don't know the status of her condition, but she was still alive when she was admitted to the hospital."

"Aww, fuck! Fuck! Hell, nah! Nah, not Epee!" Jay Wright punched his fist through the wooden door.

His wife awakened from her sound sleep when she heard his loud outburst. She threw on her robe and came running down the stairs. Hearing her husband yell out like that could only mean that something terrible had happened.

"Baby, what is it? What's wrong? Oh my God, baby, what happened?" she questioned with fear. Jay's face said it all. She knew something was terribly wrong, and her gut instincts told her it was Epiphany. She started to cry. "Where is she, Jay? What happened to Epee? Jay, answer me. Please say she's all right!" she demanded frantically.

"Baby, listen. We gotta go to the hospital. Epee's been hurt," he said, grabbing her close, trying to comfort her. He knew that any second she was about to lose it.

"No, no, no, not my child. Where is she, Jay? What happened? What fucking hospital, huh?" she cried out and tussled to break from his arm lock.

"Stop it, Tiara. You gotta calm down. She's been shot. Now, either you gon' sit here and go crazy, or go get your shit so we can go see about her," he said, putting the situation in a better perspective.

The police offered to take them to the hospital, but Jay refused. Before he could slam the door shut, the officer handed him his card and informed him that he might have to answer some questions later. They wanted to know if he had any idea who might have wanted to harm his daughter or the young man that was with her.

"Yo, I'on know nothing right now, but whoever did this better hope you guys find 'em before I do. Now, will that be all?" Jay said, fuming.

"Mr. Wright, I know you're upset, but trust that we'll do the best we can to find the shooter or shooters. I can only imagine how you must be feeling, because if that was my little girl lying up in some hospital bed with a gunshot wound to the chest, badly beaten and barely holding on, I'd want to take matters into my own hands too. But you take it easy, you hear?" said the Uncle Tom Officer Johnson.

Both police officers turned to walk away. Once they reached the squad car, Riley looked at his partner with a devilish smirk on his face.

"Hey, Johnson, what was that about? You damn near told the man to take the law into his own hands."

"That's exactly what I did. I could tell you some stories about that man. Mr. J. 'Smooth Criminal' Wright, a.k.a. 'The *Untouchable.*' He was big time, some years ago. The state and the feds had him under investigation for years, but we could never get any hard evidence on that nigger to arrest or convict him, not even a petty crime. He knew the game too well, so I was just giving the brother a little rope to hang himself with, if you know what I mean. A little encouragement never hurt nobody. Besides, knowing that scum like him is behind bars would help a lot of us sleep better at night." He laughed.

"Maybe what happened to his daughter was someone settling the score, or having a vendetta against him," said Riley.

"Yeah, could be, unless the apple doesn't fall far from the tree and she got herself caught up in her own mess. We'll just sit on this one, push it to the side, and let the animals do what they do best–*kill each other off,*" said Smith.

Jay Wright wasted no time getting to the hospital, doing 110 miles per hour on the Van Wyck Expressway. Under any other circumstances, Epiphany's mom would have been car sick from that type of speed, but this time was different.

"Hurry, Jay, hurry," she hollered.

They arrived at the hospital in five minutes flat. Jay pulled up to the front of the emergency entrance. Both of them hopped out of car and rushed through the double door entrance of the emergency waiting room.

"Sir, excuse me. You can't park there," said the flashlight security guard.

Jay pushed past the guard. Right now, his only concern was his daughter and finding out her condition. Then, he wanted the bastards responsible for trying to kill her, even if he had to take shit back to the old school way of handling beef.

"Excuse me, miss. We're looking for our daughter, Epiphany Wright. She was shot and brought in by an ambulance a couple of hours ago. Can you tell me where we can find her, please?" Tiara said to the lady behind the information desk.

The lady punched Epiphany's name into the keyboard and directed them to the intensive care unit. Once they reached the ICU, they still had to follow the same procedure again.

"Excuse me. I was told that we could find our daughter here. Her name is Epiphany Wright. She's twenty-two years old and she was shot," said her father, this time getting even more impatient and hoping that she could assist them. Before the nurse could answer any questions, the doctor walked up.

"Excuse me. I'm Doctor Frye. Did I over hear you asking about a young woman that was shot? Are you her parents?"

"Yes, we are. Is she okay, doctor?" Tiara asked.

"Come with me, please," the doctor said. "It's been a long morning." Doctor Frye let out a sigh as the three of them began walking down the corridor. "Your daughter was shot with a .38, which is a very powerful gun, in the chest. When she was brought in, she had already lost an enormous amount of blood. We had to rush her into surgery right away. Her heart rate was fading fast, and we were without a doubt going to losing her.

"I had no choice but to authorize an emergency transfusion to get her heart to start pumping again. It was successful. She also has a ruptured lung that I was able to save. That's the good news. The bad news is the baby your daughter was carrying did not make it."

"Baby! Wait a minute, what baby?" Her mother was shocked.

"Yes, your daughter was in the very, very early stage of her first trimester. Unfortunately, she lost a lot blood, so the oxygen supply to the baby was cut off. Your daughter apparently miscarried before she even got to the hospital."

Tiara's jaw dropped. Jay Wright wrapped his arm around his wife but couldn't bear to look at her.

"Also, I noticed a lot of bruises on her body, which leads me to believe that whoever shot her had beaten her first. That could've been the initial cause of the miscarriage. Either way, the child would not have survived. As of now, your daughter's condition is still critical. She's in a coma, and due to her injuries, she's on a respirator. Your daughter is definitely a fighter, and I strongly believe she will pull through this."

Chapter 49

On his way to the hotel he'd been staying at for the past week or so, Tucker tried calling Malikai's cell phone several times, but didn't get an answer. He figured Malikai probably got caught up with Epiphany all over again. Even though Mali never told him, Tucker knew his boy was still sprung the fuck out over her conceited ass.

Right now, he could've used some of his boy's advice. Malikai had been there for him from day one, before the money, cars, and even Keisha. So, his feedback about what Tucker should do about the situation with Keisha, the videotape, and the nigga she was fucking on it, was needed. There was no doubt that he still loved Keisha with all his heart, but at that moment, he wished her dead.

Mali would understand and never sugarcoat anything just to spare his best friend's feelings. He would give it to him raw and be honest about it.

Once he got to his room, he plopped down on the bed and stared at the ceiling until he finally fell asleep. At about six in the morning, Tucker's cell phone and two-way started going off like crazy. He ignored the first few rings, assuming it was Keisha ready to plead her case, but after tossing and turning to the vibrating sound of his two-way and the constant ringing of his cell, he became annoyed and finally went to answer his phone. The caller ID displayed Momma D.

Maybe the nigga stayed at his mother's house last night, he thought as he picked up the cell. He heard the unbearable sounds of a mother's cry. His heart ached instantly. Afraid of the possibilities, he hesitated for a moment.

"Momma D, what is it? What's wrong?"

"O lawd, lawd, lawd, my son is gone. He's dead, Tucker. Malikai is dead. The police came and wanted me to go identify his body, but I just can't. Tucker, what I'ma do now? My only boy is gone. What I'ma do?" she asked.

Tucker was crushed. *This can't be,* he thought. There was nothing he could say or do that would ease her pain.

"Momma D, get dressed! I'm on my way to get you," was all he said before ending the call. In disbelief, he called Mali's cell repeatedly and got the voice mail each time, just like he had when he tried to reach him last night.

"Nah, Mali, not you, dawg," Tucker mumbled.

Malikai wasn't only a business partner to Tucker. He was like his own flesh and blood, the only nigga he could trust with his life, money, girl, and his kid. Mali trusted him just the same. He was a genuine dude. Tucker knew this for a fact, because he had tested his loyalty on several occasions, and Malikai passed every time with flying colors. He was alone in this world for real now.

He got up out of the hotel bed, got dressed, and headed over to Momma D's house. She opened the door wearing a wrinkled dress, mismatched shoes, and her wig was on crooked. She was an emotional wreck. Tucker didn't know what else to do besides wrap his arms tightly around Momma D to console her.

"Momma D, come on. We gotta go do this. Maybe it ain't him," Tucker said, trying to be hopeful for both of them.

"No, Tucker. I . . . I can't go see my son lying dead on some cold metal table with his brains all over the place. I just can't and I won't. The police already showed me his picture anyway. I know it's him. The streets done took my son from me. This cruel world done killed him. All I had left is gone. I just buried my husband two years ago, and now I gotta bury my son. No, you go for me, Tucker. You were like a brother to him, and I can't see my boy looking like that. I just can't."

Mrs. Delores had always been like a mother to Tucker, especially ever since his moms passed away when he was eleven. She never treated him as anything less than a son, and he depended on her for the motherly love she gave to him. She was such a sweet old lady, the type that would feed you a good hot meal if you were hungry and give you half of her last dollar if you needed it. Tucker had mad love and respect for her.

He even gave her the nicknames Momma D and Mom Dukes, both short for Delores, her first name. So, to see her suffering caused Tucker a great deal of pain.

He planted a kiss on her forehead and headed for the morgue. On his way there, it was so ironic that Puffy's tribute to Biggie, "I'll Be Missing You," was playing on the radio. Tucker refused to believe it until he saw him. He phoned his boys from the Dirty South, Peewee and Cornell, to tell them the news.

Everything became a reality when he stepped into the morgue. Tucker's body caught an instant chill from the cool temperature in the place, and the smell of dead people gave him a nauseated feeling. The coroner asked him what his relationship was to the deceased.

"I'm his brother." Tucker followed the man to another room, where he saw his best friend lying dead with a head the size of a basketball and his brains oozing out on the table.

His stomach felt very weak from the sight of Malikai, and his emotions were mixed with pain, anger, and sorrow. Mali was the closest thing to a brother he had, and his loss was too great to ignore. Tucker disregarded the words of his father and shed a few tears. Then he started to beat up on himself, feeling responsible for not being there to protect Malikai. He had failed as his brother's keeper. To him, he was just as much to blame as the nigga that had pulled the trigger.

Looking at Malikai lying there like that was hard on his eyes. Tucker leaned over Mali's corpse and thought about all the good times they had shared. There were so many memories to hold on to. Malikai, twenty-five, was too young to die. He was just starting to live life and just like that, it was over.

"Damn, Mali, we should have left this drug game alone a long time ago. It's over for me now. This shit is so played out. I'm done! I don't want to do this shit no more." Tucker spoke to Malikai as if he could hear him.

The shine was no longer worth the headache, heartache, or losses that came along with the territory. Tucker was eighteen when he started selling drugs, and it had taken him every bit of the ten years he'd spent hustling to realize that this game wasn't fair. There was a lot of money to be made, but it would never make you rich, nor would it let you go without paying a price. Either you lost yourself, your freedom, or your soul at the end of either road. It wasn't worth it. Tucker would never gain anything from hustling that could replace his loss, so for him this *was* the end of the road. Malikai's death was surely his wakeup call, while he still had half a soul left. The game, as he knew it, was over.

Chapter 50

Shana couldn't help but wonder what Smitty's "You owe me" comment meant as he walked out the door, but she didn't spend too much time dwelling on it, 'cause more than anything else, she was happy he had finally left her and K.C. alone. Shana wasted no time taking advantage of her "alone at last" thoughts as soon as she closed the door behind Smitty. Her man was home from jail, and it was time to put some good ol' freedom pussy on his ass. For the past couple of months, she'd been giving it to him with restrictions, due to the rules of their conjugal visits.

Shana fucked K.C. until his nut sack started running on empty, putting him into a comatose sleep for the rest of the night. That was a good move on her part, because shortly after that, the phone started to ring off the hook. It was Chasity calling just to harass her. Shana decided to pick up and hear her out, but all she would say was, "Bitch," and then hang up, so Shana turned off the ringer. Still, she couldn't sleep, thinking about the stunt Chasity had pulled earlier, the crank calls, and wondering how much further she was gonna take things.

I swear if I would've known the girl was a psycho, I would've never fucked around with her. She also thought about Smitty coming to her rescue with the quick cover-up. That was real suspect to her, because her vibes for Smitty weren't right from day one. She could tell he was a sheisty individual. Being from the streets, where game recognizes game, it wasn't hard to tell who was grimey off of one sit-down conversation. Smitty fit the bill in every sense of the word, so when he said she owed him, he meant it, because it wasn't in his character to look out for her for nothing. Without any doubt, Shana knew he had some shit up his sleeve. She just didn't know what to expect.

Maybe I should have just been straight up with K.C. about what went down while he was locked up. Shana never thought his life sentence would really get thrown out, so she kept her secret to herself. Now, she had to make sure Smitty kept it.

K.C. had issues with the fact that his mom was a lesbian. It was because of that, she knew it would matter that she had been with Chasity, especially since she was his wife. In no way did Shana feel she was a lesbian, or even bi-sexual, for that matter. In her eyes, it was just a little bi-curious experience that got out of hand.

Now Chasity is trying to fuck up everything, but I won't let it go down like that. First thing in the morning, she decided she would change their phone number and begin her search for a new apartment.

Chapter 51

C-God felt it would be best to stay at a motel for a couple of days, at least until he got his head right. He figured if niggas knew where Mike was resting on the low, they more than likely knew about his spot.

As Ness dropped him off, he gave him direct orders. "Yo, go to my crib, get the yayo, the guns, and here, this is the combination to the safe. Bring my money too," he said, handing him a small piece of paper with six digits on it.

Money, Ness thought to himself as jackpot bells went off in his head. "How much money?" he asked C-God out of curiosity.

"Shit, I don't know. It's enough, though. What the fuck you worried about it for? Just bring it to me." C-God knew exactly how much money he had, but this was a test to see if he could trust Ness. "Oh, and don't forget the scale, a'ight. Can you handle that? 'Cause yo, y'all li'l niggas don't be on top of shit like my man Mike. A nigga gotta get all specific, breaking shit down for y'all slow-ass muthafuckas. So, I'm trusting you to get my shit and bring it to me. Don't fuck up! A'ight, one!" C-God said, giving Ness a pound and then getting out of the hooptie.

Ness quickly agreed and sped off. Wasting no time, he pulled out his cell phone and called Smitty.

"Yo, what up, Smit?"

"What up, nigga? How's it going down?"

"Yo, man, this nigga don't have a clue. He thinks it was that kid Tucker."

"Oh, word. That's a good thing."

"I know, but yo, he's sending me over to his spot right now to get his shit—all of it, yo!"

"Yo, you for real, dawg?"

"Hell yeah, nigga. I got the combination to his safe. I'm heading over there right now!"

"So yo, fuck all that other bullshit we talked about and let's get his ass now. How much shit he working with?"

"Yo, he ain't say, but that's his spot, so everything is probably up in there. I just ain't wanna straight gank his ass like that, 'cause then he gon' know I did it."

"Man, fuck that punk-ass muthafucka. He handing his shit right to us, and with Mike gone, that nigga ain't shit, dude. Besides, niggas ain't feeling him like that no more in the hood. I'm telling you, if we come around and start showing these niggas mad love, they gon' flip on that nigga C, son. Word up!"

Ness pulled up into a parking spot in front of C-God's building. He turned off the car and sat in silence for a moment, thinking about how C had treated him like some punk-ass chump. Never once did C say "Good looking out," or "Thanks, man. You saved my fucking life."

"Yo, you still there?" Smitty asked, breaking the silence.

"Yeah."

"So what, muthafucka? You need me to come hold your hand or something?" Smitty sensed some hesitation in Ness.

"Nah, dawg. I got this. I'll hit you when I'm done."

"You sure, nigga? 'Cause I'm sensing some nervousness in your blood."

"Nigga, I got this. I'ma hit you back!"

"A'ight!" said Smitty.

Ness entered C-God's Hempstead apartment, and greed took over instantly. Inside were ten kilos of uncut cocaine wrapped tightly in clear plastic, about 200 G's in the safe, and three guns. He thought about what Smitty had said: C-God did hand everything to them, but he hadn't expected it to be on a silver platter.

All types of come-up schemes ran through his mind as he placed the keys in a plastic garbage bag, poured a bottle of fabric softener on top to conceal the scent, and then packed it all inside a duffel bag filled with dirty clothes. There was no way Ness could take everything down to the car all at once, so he figured he'd take the drugs first and then come back for the money. He planned to leave the guns behind.

Ness entered the elevator with the duffel bag strapped across his shoulder. When the elevator doors opened, he headed toward the double doors and spotted the FBI everywhere. Starting to panic, his instincts told him to run like hell, but where was he going to run to? The best thing for him to do was play it cool and proceed with the plan.

Exiting the building, Ness walked past them as calmly as possible. He'd been arrested enough times to know that a reaction or the slightest sign of discomfort is what they looked for. Just as he had reached nearly twenty feet from the car, a voice called out to him.

"Hey, boy, where you coming from?" an officer asked.

Ness, shitting bricks, managed to remain calm and speak without showing any signs of nervousness.

"I'm coming from my girlfriend's house. Is there a problem, sir?"

"Well, I don't know. Is there? It's pretty early in the morning, boy. Where are you heading to? Did your girlfriend and you have a fight? 'Cause that's a big ol' bag you got there."

"It's just some dirty clothes I'm taking over to the laundromat. You know, underwears, socks, and tees.Would you like to take a look, sir?" he said, unzipping the bag just enough to expose the dirty clothes he had lying on top of the coke. Ness was scared shitless, but he had to take his chances, hoping it would throw him off.

"No, that's okay, son. By the way, what did you say your name was again?" asked the officer just as he was headed back toward the building.

"It's Calvin. Calvin Greene, sir," he said, smiling and lying his ass off. He knew damn well he had never asked his name in the first place.

"Would you happen to know a fellow in this building that goes by the name C-God?" the officer asked.

"No, officer. I don't. Why? Did he do something bad, sir?" Ness pressed for info.

"Let's just say he's one of the bad guys."

"No way, officer. I stay away from them bad guys." He was really laying it on thick. "Far away! I'm a good guy, you know.

I have a nine-to-five. As a matter of fact, I was just promoted to supervisor at my job."

"Really, and where is that?" asked the officer.

"McDonald's, and one day I hope to open a franchise of my own." Ness couldn't believe the bullshit coming from his own mouth.

"All right, kid. Good for you. Just stay out of trouble," the officer said, heading toward the building as he spotted the K-9 unit pulling up.

Oh, shit, Ness thought as he opened his car door in a hurry, jumped in, and pulled off immediately before the dogs caught a whiff of what was really in the bag. Sweating bullets, he knew how close he had come to getting knocked. He started to laugh, thinking about how well he played that pig.

"Ahhh, fuck!" Ness yelled, remembering what he had left behind. "Damn, why I ain't take the fucking money?" Pulling his cell phone from his pocket, he dialed C's cell.

C-God saw Ness's number come up on the phone and picked up, beefing, "You's a stupid muthafucka. Why the fuck is you calling me from your cell, nigga?"

"Yo, C, I know, but—"

"No, nigga, obviously you don't know! Go find a fucking payphone and—nah, you know what? Fuck all that. Just bring my shit to me," he said with such authority in his disrespectful tone before hanging up.

"Fuck you, nigga! You ain't got your shit," Ness yelled as he threw his phone in the passenger's seat.

"I ain't giving that nigga shit." He had a plan, and C-God was going to have no choice but to step down for Ness's take-over or else he would die.

Ness's plan was simple: set up shop with the bricks and flip the profit. It would take some careful planning, but Ness had the overall scheme ready. He didn't really know much about pushing weight, but Smitty did. Now all he needed was a few soldiers behind him, just in case C-God tried to get at him. Ness remembered the wild stories from back in the days about the fear C-God pumped into nigga's hearts, but for the past few years, he'd been rolling with him, and all he had witnessed was his sharp-ass tongue. It was Mike who always pulled the trigger for him, and he had been dismissed.

So, what next? Ness thought. After watching C-God get weak over a broad, Ness no longer respected his gangsta. Of course, he wasn't gon' straight sleep on the nigga neither, because it was always better to be safe than sorry. Establishing a squad that was ready for war was first on his list of things to do, you know, just to be on the safe side of the fence.

Ness stopped at a payphone and called C back.

"Yo, who this?" C answered his cell on the third ring.

"Yo, man, it's Ness. Listen, I ain't got your shit, dawg. I went to the crib and the feds was all over the place. They had dogs and all types of shit, so a nigga just kept going."

"Yo, what the fuck? Did they get in my crib?" C-God asked.

"They was running up in the building, I ain't even get out the car. All I seen was police rolling deep and I got the fuck up out the area."

"So, yo, wait a little while, go scoop up Reg, then go back over there and check that shit out. It might not even be my spot they hit," C-God ordered.

"Nah, dawg. I ain't going back over there," Ness said.

"What the fuck you mean, you ain't going back over there?"

"Yo, son, check this out. If they ran up in your shit, then nine times out of ten they still there, or they watching it, and I ain't getting caught up in that, dawg," Ness said standing his ground and refusing to let C-God punk him.

"Yo, you bitch-ass nigga, what the fu—" Before C-God could finish his verbal lashing, the payphone operator asked for five more cents for the next two minutes, and Ness hung up.

He was excited about his chance to finally make some real dough. Finding a tape, he popped it in and turned up the volume.

Ness had one more important phone call to make.

"Yo, we on, nigga. We working with ten of them things, nigga, and shit look sweet too!" Ness didn't need to go into details. His partner knew exactly how it was going down.

"That's what's up! So, yo, let's get up in a little while and get this shit popping, a'ight?" asked Smitty.

"Sounds like a plan,"

Chapter 52

It was shortly after seven a.m. when Mrs. Wright got over the initial shock of someone trying to murder her daughter. She didn't feel up to it, but she knew it was necessary to call the family and Epiphany's closest friends. Of course, as far as friends went, Keisha was number one, and then came Shana, who she was unable to reach.

When Mrs. Wright broke the news to Keisha, she was devastated. After some encouraging words about Epiphany's condition and the doctor's reassurance that she would pull through this, Keisha managed to calm down long enough to get the details on what they believed had happened. Mrs. Wright questioned her about the guy who was murdered while visiting Epiphany, but she couldn't remember his name, and Keisha couldn't offer much help.

"Keisha, you are the closest friend Epiphany has. You two are like sisters. I am her mother, so she tells me nothing, and if I do hear anything, I hear it from the streets. I know she talks to you, so I need to ask you something, and I want you to be straight with me, okay?" she asked Keisha in all seriousness.

"Okay, I'll do my best," Keisha replied in a soft voice.

"Was she still messing around with that Hinderson boy?"

"Mrs. Wright, in all honesty, I don't know. I wanna say no 'cause the last time we talked about him, she told me it was over. She found out about some girl he had gotten pregnant, and supposedly she ended it with him."

"Keisha, I just have one more question. Do you think he had something to do with this?" she asked as tears formed and her voice started to crack.

"Mrs. Wright, you know C-God stepped to Tucker over some nonsense a while ago. He's made threats, and as a matter of fact, he's the reason why Tucker doesn't feel it's safe to stay at home with me and the baby. So, to answer your question, yes, I do think he had something to do with this. I don't like him, nor do I trust him, and I strongly believe he's absolutely capable of doing something like this." Keisha was starting to get angry.

"Even though she was pregnant?" Mrs. Wright questioned in disbelief. *How could he be so coldhearted?* she wondered.

"Wait a minute. Epiphany is pregnant?" Keisha couldn't believe her ears.

"She was," Mrs. Wright said sadly.

"That bastard! How could he? Mrs. Wright, I gotta go. I have to call Tucker, but I'll be at the hospital as soon as I reach him, okay?" Keisha's eyes flooded with tears all over again.

Keisha arrived at the hospital alone, carrying "Get Well Soon" balloons and some flowers. She had only half an hour left before morning visiting hours were over. Seeing Epiphany was something she had to do, but her mind couldn't stop wondering about Tucker. He'd been ignoring her calls all morning.

He really might not forgive me, she thought. Regardless of the circumstances, she felt she was still the mother of his child, and there was no excuse for his behavior.

She ran into Epiphany's dad, who was standing at the elevator when she got off. Jay Wright looked like an exhausted madman. He showed her to the room and thanked her for coming before he headed out.

As Keisha entered the room, she felt sick. She hated the smell of hospitals. To her, they represented sickness and death.

Epiphany's mom greeted her with a tight hug.

"Where is Tucker?"

Keisha's heart dropped into the pit of her stomach. She didn't have an answer, so she thought up a quick lie.

"Loretta and my sisters weren't able to make it back in time to watch the baby, so he stayed home with him," she said, looking down at the floor.

"Oh, okay. How is that handsome little boy of yours?" Epiphany's mom smiled, but her eyes were still puffy and her voice was rather hoarse from her lack of sleep and the crying she'd been doing all night.

Mrs. Wright was trying to make light of the situation, but Keisha knew she was having a hard time dealing with everything. Epiphany was her pride and joy even though she didn't always approve of the life she was living.

"He's doing great," Keisha answered back.

"Good! Well, I'll give you a little time alone with Epee. I'll be back shortly. Okay, sweetie?"

"Okay." Keisha walked closer to Epiphany's bedside. Seeing Epiphany lying there like that brought Keisha to tears. Epiphany's face was bruised up pretty badly. Keisha pulled up a chair and moved in as close as she could to the side of the bed. Taking Epiphany's hand into hers, she began to talk to her.

"Hey, E, it's me, Keisha. I know you're in bad shape right now, but you're gonna pull through this. I know you will, because you know the world can't make it without Epiphany J. Wright." She let out a little laugh. "We just can't do it without you, girl, so you better hurry up and get better before I go crazy. You're my best friend and I love you, plus I need you to help me fix this mess with Tucker.

"I'm in the dog house, and he'll probably never take me back, let alone trust me. I should have never let Lea talk me into having strippers at my bachelorette party. I know it's nobody's fault that I fucked Damager, but if his ass wasn't there in the first place, doing all them freaky things to me while I was drunk, none of this would have happened. And that damn tape . . ." She drifted off into a distasteful thought.

"Anyway, I won't get into that right now." Keisha quickly snapped out of her daydream and changed the subject.

"Girl, your godson is getting so big. He's trying to walk now, and he's got eight teeth. Ain't that something? He's a real cutie, though. I know all mothers think their kids are cute, but my son is just gorgeous, and I'm not just saying that 'cause he's mines, neither. Seriously, girl." She laughed.

She looked at Epiphany's swollen face and felt terrible for not calling and keeping in touch more. She really missed talking and spending time with her friends.

"I tried calling Shana, but her phone has been discon-
nected. Her cell ain't working either. It's like she ain't part of
the crew no more. We're all moving in different directions, but
when I leave here, I think I'm just gonna stop by her house to
see what's up with her." Keisha had more to say to her friend,
but the announcements came on, saying that visiting hours
were now over.

"I gotta go now, but I'll be back tomorrow," Keisha said as
she kissed Epiphany on the forehead and headed toward the
door.

"Keisha, wait," Mrs. Wright called out as she spotted her
walking down the hallway. Keisha stopped and turned around.

"I just wanted to thank you once again for coming and remind you to tell Tucker to please keep his ears open in the
streets. Oh, and remember I was telling you about the guy
they found dead at Epee's apartment? You knew him. I found
out that he was one of her old boyfriends. His name was . . .
something like Mahkai."

"Oh, no. Mrs. Wright, please tell me you don't mean
Malikai."

"Yeah, that's him. Wasn't he a friend of Tucker's?"

"Oh God, I gotta go." Keisha bareley made it out of the hospital before she dialed Tucker's cell. Again, she got no answer,
so she waited for the beep. "Why aren't you picking up your
cell phone?" she screamed into the receiver. "Mali is dead, and
Epiphany is lying up in the fucking hospital. Damn, T, I know
you hate me right now, but they're our friends. Please call me
back." Keisha hung up.

Seconds later, her cell rang. Keisha answered before the
first ring even finished, and she cried out Tucker's name.

The voice on the other end wasn't him. It was Julius a.k.a.
the Damager. Her crying kind of threw him off.He paused for
a moment before he spoke.

"Ahhh, is this Keisha?" he asked hesitantly.

"Who is this?" she cried.

"It's Julius. Are you all right?"

"No, I'm not all right, and please don't call me anymore!"
Keisha screamed, taking her anger out on him and abruptly
ending his call. She dialed Tucker again, expecting the voice
mail, but was thrown off when he answered.

"What, Keish?" Tucker was short with her.

"H—hello," she stuttered into the mouth phone.

"Yeah, what?" he replied.

"Did you get my message?" Keisha asked nervously.

"Which one?"

"The one I just left about Malikai and Epiphany."

"Nah, but Momma D already told me about Mali. She's fucked up over this shit. I just came from identifying his body, and I'm just as fucked up. Everything is fucked up. I gotta bury my best friend. I gotta take care of his funeral arrangements. Damn! I can't believe this shit." For a moment there was complete silence. "What's up with Epiphany, though?"

Keisha could hear the sadness in Tucker's voice, although he was trying hard to act like everything was under control. She knew he was going through hell right now. She added her deepest regards first before telling him about the condition Epiphany was in.

"Hmmm, so she gon' be a'ight, right?"

"Well, the doctors are hopeful. You know she was pregnant?"

"By who? That nigga C?" he said, answering his own question.

"I don't know."

"She probably had Mali set up. She told that nigga C-God that Mali was going to be there." Tucker jumped to conclusions about what he thought had happened that night.

"Oh, come on, Tucker. That's ridiculous, and if that was the case, why is she lying up in the ICU?"

"Maybe the nigga was just using her, got what he wanted, then tried to kill two birds with one stone. Or maybe she was shot as part of the plan to look innocent. Who knows?"

"What! Epiphany would never do something like that," said Keisha, speaking in her friend's defense. "Besides, she really cared about Malikai."

"Cared! What's that supposed to mean? You supposedly *loved* me, but that ain't stop you from getting it on with the next nigga, did it? I ain't putting nothing past a bitch no more."

Keisha realized that Tucker was no longer talking about Epiphany and Mali. He was talking about her. "Bitch! You know what? I'ma let that go because you just lost your best friend. Yes, I played myself, but you better not ever fix your face to call me out my name again. I am your son's mother, just in case you forgot, and regardless of what you might think of me right now, that part won't ever change. So, while you try your best to make me feel worse than I already do, you need to ask yourself why I did what I did, Mr. Get-money-and-never-have-time-for-anything-else," Keisha said sarcastically.

"Yeah, getting money for what, though, Keisha? Could it be that six hundred thousand–dollar house we living in and the expensive-ass cars we got? Is that the money you talking about? It gotta be."

"No, I'm talking about the money that keeps you out of town all time, my needs neglected, and your black ass in troub—"

"Yeah, the money that I was out there busting my ass for just to keep shit comfortable for us, while you go out and get fucked, right?"

Keisha didn't say a word. How could she? He was right.

"Yeah, yeah, yeah, I didn't think you wanted to go there. Where's my son at anyway?"

"He's home."

"Well, listen, after the funeral, I want you, your moms, the baby, and your sisters to go on vacation or something. At least until shit blows over. Go back to Atlanta with them if you want. Your family came all the way up here for a wedding, and since you fucked that up, maybe you should just take them somewhere. Miami, Mexico, or even Disneyland. Wherever. I don't care, just go somewhere until things calm down a bit. And, Keisha, I ain't asking you; I'm telling you. I already lost my boy, and I ain't trying to take no more losses, so make it happen, a'ight? I gotta go." Tucker abruptly ended the call.

"Tucker, hello?" Keisha repeated his name, hoping he was still on the line, but there was nothing but silence. She was pissed off, but at this point, she didn't feel the need to call him back just to argue. Keisha knew exactly what he was going through, 'cause she was going through it too. Because of her mistakes, they couldn't be there for each other.

Chapter 53

Shana arrived home late in the afternoon, exhausted and in a not so pleasant mood. Not only did she lose sleep worrying about Chasity's craziness and Smitty's motives, but she was up and out early searching for a new place. Out of the six apartments she viewed that day, not one of them was to her liking. To make matters worse, when she opened the door to her small basement apartment, there was no "hello," "how you doing?" or "how's your day?" but instead beefing.

"Yo, how the fuck you gonna go change numbers without telling a nigga? I got muthafuckas calling me for some important shit, and they can't even get in touch with me 'cause your stupid ass done went and changed the number. Then I tried to get in touch with you on your cell, and you done changed that, too. And why you had the ringer turned off on the phone, Shana? Huh? What the fuck is up with that? I told your sneaky ass to tie up all them loose ends with whatever crab-ass niggas you was fucking with before I came the fuck home. Smitty said he tried calling me 'bout four times last night, and the phone just rang and rang. Shit, you even heard me tell the nigga to call, and you still went and did some stupid shit like that."

Shana wasn't in the mood to argue, which was rare, because normally she would have been all up in K.C.'s shit. She never backed down from an argument with him, even when it got physical.

K.C. lived for drama, so he made it hard for Shana to ignore him. He would go on and on until he got a response, and that's exactly what he got. Shana listened quietly to him bitch about changing her number to her phones until her head felt like it was going to explode.

"Shut the fuck up, nigga. So what I changed the numbers? They're my fucking numbers anyway. You only been home what, a day and a half, and already you starting to get on a bitch nerves," she yelled.

"Oh, why am I getting on ya nerves? 'Cause a nigga fucked up, huh? Fresh out the joint and I ain't got shit. Now, all of a sudden I'm getting on your nerves? That's what it is, huh? But when a nigga was getting paper, it was a whole other story. Right, Sha?"

K.C. paused the game he was playing and walked over to Shana. "I remember when my shit was all good. You wouldn't let a nigga breathe then. Now you wanna come at me with my phone, my this and my that. You got it twisted, for real. Just 'cause you laid a few dollars on a nigga's books and bought a few funky-ass outfits for me to come home in don't mean shit. You need to stop tripping the fuck out, acting like you forgot some of the shit I did for you. I see how a bitch change up when she think a nigga need her muthafucking ass, though. But I'ma be back on soon, real soon," said K.C. His face was now less than an inch from hers.

"Yeah, well, I see how quick a nigga can change up from all that sweet shit you was kicking when you was locked the fuck up. So what, you don't need a bitch no more 'cause you free?" Shana said, taking a step back.

"Yo, Sha, just shut up!" K.C. turned around, sat back on the couch, and reached for the remote.

"Whatever." Shana went into the bedroom, closing the door behind her. The argument was over, but her headache was just beginning.

"Yo, Sha, you still ain't give me the number," K.C. yelled out loud enough for her to hear from behind the closed door.

Shana had left the new numbers big and bold on the refrigerator for K.C. to spot before she left this morning. She figured he would notice it at some point during the day, but obviously not. Avoiding any further conflict, she wrote both numbers down on a piece of paper, opened the bedroom door, handed it to him, walked back to the room, and shut the door.

She woke up about two hours later to find K.C. in the same spot, still playing video games. On her way to the kitchen, K.C. told her the horrible news.

"Yo, Sha," he said. "What's that broad's name you used to run around with all the time?"

Shana started to get a little nervous, afraid he might have heard something about Chasity.

"What broad, K.C?" she replied snobbishly.

"You know. That stuck-up, light-skinned bitch with the long hair."

"Oh, Epiphany!" Shana said as her nerves began to settle down.

"Yeah, her."

"What about her?"

"I heard niggas ran up in her crib and let off some lead in that ass, that's what!"

"And who told you that?" Shana almost dropped her glass of juice.

"Yo, that's your friend, right?" K.C. sarcastically asked.

"Yeah," Shana responded with a sarcastic look on her face.

"A'ight then, don't worry about who told me. Just be glad they did," K.C. arrogantly replied.

Shana rushed back to the bedroom to call Keisha and find out if it was true, because she would be the first to hear anything about Epiphany.

"Hello?" Keisha sounded like she was sleeping.

"Hey, Keish, it's me, Shana."

"I know. I've been trying to get in touch with you. Epiphany's in the hospital. She got shot."

"I just heard that. Is she all right? What happened?" Even though they had their share of differences, Shana still cared for Epiphany more than she showed.

"I don't really know exactly what happened, but whoever's responsible killed Malikai too," Keisha said.

"Wait a minute. Malikai is dead?" Shana was in shock.

"Yeah, and my guess is that black motherfucker, C-God had something to do with it," Keisha fumed.

"You think he would—never mind." Shana put some thought into who they were talking about. She knew damn well C-God was capable of a stunt like this. "So how's Epiphany doing?" she asked.

"She's alive but hooked up to all kinds of tubes. I went to see her today, and seeing her lying there broke my heart. That bastard really did my girl dirty." Keisha began to sob.

"Well, is she gon' be a'ight?"

"The doctors said she will," Keisha whispered.

"Damn, I know Tucker must be taking Malikai's murder hard."

"Girl, hard ain't the word. There's so much other shit going on right now. It's crazy." Keisha felt so distant from Shana, so she wasn't going to tell her everything.

"When are you going to visit Epiphany again?"

"Every day until she comes home. Why?"

"Because I wanna go with you tomorrow," Shana answered.

"That's cool. I'll call you in the morning."

"Yeah, but wait. First let me give you my new numbers," Shana said.

Chapter 54

Shana and Keisha had been spending a lot of time together, mainly back and forth to the hospital visiting Epiphany, which gave them a lot of time to talk. Keisha finally poured out her guts to Shana about the tape, the canceling of the wedding, and the drama with Tucker. Shana was vexed that one of those jealous bitches at the party could play Keisha like that. She wanted to help Keisha find out who was responsible.

The two of them arrived at Malikai's funeral a little early. It was Keisha's idea. She hoped to see Tucker and maybe get a moment of his time—not to bring up their situation, but to be an extra shoulder if he needed it. Of course it didn't work out that way. Tucker took one look at her, turned up his face, and walked right past her. Shana noticed his look of disgust.

"Keisha, maybe now is not the best time to approach him," she advised.

"It might not be, but I have to." Keisha was really desperate.

"You sure? 'Cause I ain't never seen him look at you like that before, Keisha."

"That's because you haven't seen him lately. What's the worst that could happen? He's not gonna make a scene and embarrass me. Not here anyway."

"A'ight, Keish, but if he does, I got your back."

"He won't," Keisha said as she slowly walked over to Tucker. This was the first time in a long she'd seen him in a suit, and although he hated her guts, she wanted nothing more than to tell him how good he looked and make sweet love to him.

"Hey, T, how you holding up?"

Tucker slightly rolled his eyes and shook his head. "I'm good. Where's my son at?" he asked.

"Is that all you got to say to me? Where's your son at?"

"Yep," Tucker said coldly.

"Well, he's at home with my mother."

"Did you make those arrangements we talked about?"

"What arrangements?"

"Keisha, I told you to book a flight somewhere for you and your family until shit calms down a bit. What, you forgot?" Tucker, forgetting where he was, began to raise his voice.

"Oh, yeah, I did that already. I just had to pay my last respects to Mali before we left." Keisha was lying, but she knew that was what Tucker wanted to hear. She did plan on getting around to it.

"Good," Tucker said, turning to walk away. People had started to arrive, and the self-appointed host had to go shake hands.

"T, do you plan on talking to me before I leave?" Keisha grabbed his arm and spoke softly.

"About what, Keish? There ain't really nothing to talk about." Tucker lowered his voice so the guests couldn't hear him.

"Tucker, I'm sorry. I was so drunk. I didn't mean to do it. Please just—"

"Look, Keisha, not now." Tucker took her by the hand and pulled her into the hallway. "I don't know if I'll ever be ready to talk about it. You can cry and say you're sorry until you turn blue in the face, but it don't mean nothing to me. Keisha, you should've thought about all that before you let dude run up in my pussy. You fucked up, but I just hope it was worth it." His voice started to crack. Tucker walked away, leaving Keisha right were she stood.

Shana rushed over to comfort her. "Come on, Keish, stop crying. If he wants to act like that, then fuck him. You tried."

Keisha couldn't stop crying though. The thought of Tucker not wanting her anymore pained her so bad. She loved him so much, but the way he was acting toward her made her question his love for her. He could've at least heard her out. Yeah, she fucked up really bad, and no, it wasn't worth it, but she was truly sorry.

"Come on, Keisha. The service is about to start." Shana put her arms around Keisha and walked her over to the seats she was holding for them.

Flowers were everywhere, and on both ends of the platinum-colored casket stood bleeding hearts made out of fresh red and white roses. Tucker had taken care of all the arrangements.

People came out of the woodwork to say their final goodbyes, and of course a few haters popped in as well.

It's just sad that it takes a death to bring so many people together, Tucker thought as he stood near Pee and Corn, who acted as armed security at the door, just in case niggas wanted to act up. Tucker personally greeted most of the mourners that entered the funeral home. A couple of them even pulled him to the side to share different versions of hearsay from the streets about what had happened.

Pictures of Mali were all over the place. Due to his disfigurement, the casket was closed, and Tucker preferred it that way. He wanted today to be more of a remembrance than a farewell. He wanted the pictures of Malikai to remind people of the life he lived, the fun he had, and what a loving person he was. Momma D was the only one allowed a final viewing of her only son before the service started. She managed to keep her composure during the viewing and service, but she broke down at the burial.

"It's so Hard to Say Goodbye to Yesterday" played softly as loved ones and friends dropped red roses onto Malikai's casket as it was being lowered into the ground. Tucker stayed by Momma D's side the whole time. While trying his best to stay strong for her, he was torn apart on the inside and needed Momma D to lean on just as much as she needed him.

Chapter 55

C-God was furious. He found out that Ness had betrayed him. The feds did run up in his spot, but no drugs were reportedly found, and only fifty G's out of two hundred thousand, a scale, and a few minor items were confiscated. Also, word on the street was that Ness was the one responsible for Mikes' murder. C-God tried for days to get at his workers, but none of them returned his calls. Finally he got in touch with Reggie, one of his regular runners.

"Yo, Reg, what up with y'all niggas? Don't nobody answer their cell phones no more? Just 'cause a nigga go on a hiatus for a week or so to get his head right, niggas fall off track and forget what's good?" C-God said.

"Yo, C, man, niggas ain't running with you no more. They done got down with that kid Ness. He be showing us mad love in the hood, making sure we all eat."

"Oh, so you down with the nigga too?" C-God asked as he sniffed a long line of cocaine from the glass plate in front of him.

"Yo, I'm saying, dude do look out, and you know what I'm up against. I just wanted to give you a heads up, man, 'cause shit is real out here," Reg said.

C-God was outraged. He jumped up and smashed the glass plate.

"You muthafuckas think I'm gonna sit back and eat shit. I'll kill all y'all niggas. Y'all ma'fuckers gon' do me like this, turn around and betray me, the hand that fed y'all niggas for years. Y'all some dead ma'fuckas, ya heard! Fucking dead!"

Just as C-God was about to hang up, Ness walked over and snatched the phone from Reg. "Yo, is that that bitch-ass nigga C?" he questioned. Reggie nodded his head, and Ness put the phone to his ear.

"Yo, man, save all that bullshit you talking, nigga. If your heart was as big as that fucking mouth of yours, your punk ass might not be in this situation now, would you, huh, nigga? You soft, dukes. I should've let that ho kill your bitch ass.

"It's over for you now, son. You had your turn. Now I'm running this. See, I'm being a nice guy about it, letting your punk ass live. I know Mike wished I was nice enough to let him and his family live, but it be like that sometimes." Ness laughed. "So, yo, man to bitch, I suggest you break out. Go hide up under a rock or something, 'cause ya nobody, dawg. Ya nobody 'til somebody splits that fucking wig of yours. So bring your bitch ass back around, thinking shit's sweet, and I promise you I'ma make you famous. One!"

Talking greasy to C-God like that got Ness's adrenaline pumping. He was hyped and ready for whatever came his way.

C-God was fuming. Normally he'd call Mike to kill a nigga that crossed him the way Ness had, but Mike was gone. Everyone on his team was gone. There was nothing else for him to do but get skidded. Locked up in his hotel room, C-God sniffed so much coke his nose started to bleed.

He only had access to about five grand, and that was gonna have to hold him down until he came up with a plan. He knew it would be hard to go up against those niggas as a one-man band.

Another problem was the feds. They were hot on his trail, so C-God decided the best thing for him to do was skip town and lay low for a while. Team or no team, they hadn't heard the last from Corey Hinderson.

Chapter 56

As she walked down what appeared to be a very long tunnel, Epiphany heard a voice calling her name. It was coming from behind her. The voice was male and sounded familiar. Afraid, she paused for a moment as the voice continued to call out to her. It was as if they were in some sort of danger.

Epiphany hesitantly turned around. Something inside of her forced her to follow the voice. As she followed the voice, she could see a beaming ray of light, and the further she walked, the brighter the light got. The light was her guide. Suddenly, she could see images of her life posted up on the tunnel's walls. The good, the bad, and the ugly had all been caught on film. She felt like she was trapped in a projection room that featured The Life and Times of Epiphany Janee Wright.

There were moments she'd spent as a child with her parents, moments with friends, and even X-rated moments she'd shared with many men, including her uncle, who had molested her.

This is some weird shit, Epiphany thought , but being vain, she found this experience to be fascinating, watching her life, her memories, and her personal moments. All of it, from adolescence to adulthood, surrounded her. This was either her journey to heaven or hell, the weighing of her good deeds and her sins.

As she continued down the long tunnel, the sound of her name became louder. When she finally reached the end, she saw Malikai smiling at her. He was dressed in an all-white suit, with a pimp daddy hat slightly cocked to the side. He looked like a gift heaven sent to her. He had been calling out to her all along.

Once she approached him, no words were exchanged, and although he was smiling, she could see that there was some sadness in his eyes. He wrapped his arms around her tightly, as if he would never see her again. His body temperature was so cold. Epiphany tried to speak to him, but her words could not escape her mouth. She felt numb.

Suddenly, darkness filled the hall. Everything had faded right before her eyes—Malikai, the images, and the light. Epiphany stood alone at the end of the tunnel. Malikai had just saved her from eternal darkness, and it was time for her to go home.

Epiphany's Mom noticed slight movement from Epiphany for the first time. Her eyelids were shut, but her eyeballs moved as if she was trying to open them.

"It's been two weeks. Wake up out of that misery, Epee," her mom whispered as she reached for her daughter's hand. "I know you're a fighter. Your father knows you're a fighter. Your friends know, and even these doctors know. So fight, baby. Make your way back. You're too strong to be lying up in this damn hospital bed like this. Do you hear me?"

Epiphany didn't respond with words, but she squeezed her mother's hand just enough to let her know she heard her. That was all the assurance Mrs. Wright needed. She knew Epiphany would pull through for sure now. She walked over toward the window and dialed her husband immediately to share the news, but wasn't able to reach him. Mrs. Wright just stared out of the window, wondering where her husband could be that he wasn't answering his phone.

Jay Wright had been on a mission since the incident happened. He felt he owed it to his baby girl to find the bastards responsible and see to it that they suffered the same way his family had. He didn't give a fuck about the police; they had yet to be of any help. Besides, he felt jail would be too easy for the punk.

Mrs. Wright definitely wanted whoever was to blame to suffer as well, but just not at the hands of her husband. She had waited a long time for Jay to give up that gangsta shit, and there was no way she was going back to living that kind of life-style with him.

Epiphany had been lying in a coma for two weeks, but to her it seemed more like months or years, and every day was a struggle. Mrs. Wright looked toward the Lord to pull her through.

She had always believed in Him, although she never appreciated how good He'd been to her and her family over the years. It took a tragedy to open her eyes and make her realize that she had a lot to be grateful for. Jay had been in the drug game for over twenty-five years and somehow he never been locked up, shot, robbed, or killed. Harm had never crossed the Wrights' path, nor had they ever hit any financial hardships. That had to have been the work of the Lord, she thought. She was finally ready to give thanks and praise to Him. *God only knows, it's long overdue, but never too late.* Tiara Wright had joined the Born Again Baptist Community Church, and the changes within her had been miraculous.

"Mommy," Epiphany said, looking around the hospital room.

Mrs. Wright froze in disbelief. That word sounded like a sweet melody, music to her ears.

"Praise the Lord, thank you Jesus," Mrs. Wright closed her eyes and said a little prayer before rushing to Epiphany's bedside.

Right away, Epiphany started to panic as she looked around at her unfamiliar surroundings. She began to forcefully pull at the IV tubes in her arm and question about her whereabouts over and over again. Her mom tried her best to calm her down but decided it would be best to call in the nurse.

Two nurses rushed in and immediately tried to relax Epiphany, but she continued to struggle. One of the nurses, a heavy-set older woman, used her weight to restrain Epiphany long enough for the other nurse to inject her with a sedative. She explained to Epiphany's mom that the sedative was a mild one, just enough to help Epiphany relax a bit. She also explained that it was likely for a patient to react this way when awakening from a coma with no recollection of what had happened to her.

The medication worked instantly. Epiphany began to settle down. Mrs. Wright reached for her cell phone and called Jay again. This time he answered.

"Hello?"

"Baby, where were you? Didn't I tell you? I told you she was gon' pull through." Mrs. Wright couldn't control her excitement.

"Epee's awake?" asked Jay.

"Yes, honey, she woke up swinging."

"Get the fuck out of here! Baby, are you serious?" Finally Jay started to believe his wife. He was cheesing from ear to ear.

"Yes! Wait, baby. Hold on for a minute." Tiara placed her cell to Epiphany's ear.

Epiphany softly mumbled, "Hello?"

There was nothing more to say. Jay Wright was on his way.

Chapter 57

The feds had all operations shut down for a minute. They ran up in every spot possibly linked to C-God. They offered "get out of jail free" cards and all kind of plea bargains to the small-time hustlers that got caught up in the sweeps if, in return, they could give up any helpful information that could lead them straight to C-God or link him to Malikai's murder. The feds wanted C-God, and niggas were ready to snitch him out, but no one knew his whereabouts.

C-God had never really showed his workers no love on the streets, so they ain't have none for him. While he was driving his tricked-out Cadillac Escalade, peeling off hundreds for bottles at the clubs, and flossing, his workers were barely getting by. After making the minimum—enough dough for an outfit but not enough for the footwear, or vice versa—for so long, niggas was ready for him to fall. The heat was coming from all angles. C-God had the feds after his freedom, a mob of niggas trying to take his life, plus Ness and Smitty taking over his business.

Peewee and Cornell made a trip to New York to person-ally do C-God some harm. They ran up in his parents' home, guns exposed, and scared Mrs. Hinderson so bad she suf-fered a massive heart attack and died on the spot. Poppa Hinderson watched helplessly right before Peewee shot him in his head. On their way out of C-God's parents' house, Peewee and Cornell joked about how easy a job it was.

Since Tucker left strict orders to leave C-God's kids out of their beef, the two knew that the death of his parents would definitely get a rise out of him. They assumed that aside from his kids, his folks were probably the only other people he held dear, because everybody knew he treated all his baby mommas like shit. He ain't give a fuck about none of them, and two of them was smoked-out on crack, so getting rid of those bitches wouldn't phase C-God. It would've been a favor to him, and it made no sense to waste the lead. Tucker knew the deaths of C's parents would get him to surface sooner or later, but for right now it was best for him to lay low and just wait.

Peewee and Cornell headed back to the Dirty South until further notice. Once they got home, they established their business, 'cause with the start-up tools Tucker gave them, it was on and popping. Tucker hit them off with five keys and put them on to his Colombian connect as a token of his appreciation for their latest endeavor. Peewee and Cornell were about to get it crunk down in the Carolinas.

Chapter 58

"Finally something good happened." A smile spread across Keisha's face when she received the news from Mrs. Wright that Epiphany had regained consciousness that night. Morning couldn't have come fast enough for Keisha, who wanted to rush to her best friend's side. She also couldn't wait to hear Epiphany's details on what had happened and who was responsible.

Keisha had been spending so much of her time at the hospital that she had almost forgotten that her own life was still in shambles. Keisha became very depressed because of all the bad that had been surrounding her life lately, and she wondered how she was gonna weather this terrible storm.

On several occasions, she had tried to see Tucker so they could sit down and discuss her affair and their future, but he was avoiding her. Sure, he'd call, but only to ask about his son. Keisha didn't push the issue, because she was the one that had fucked things up between them. Tucker did his best to remind her that she was to blame every chance he got. At the same time, she needed to understand what was going on with him. Could they work it out, or should she do the unthinkable and just let him go?

"Maybe he's just not ready to forgive me, but he will. He's just playing hardball, acting like he could care less about us." She tried to rationalize the reason for his behavior. Sometimes he was almost convincing, but Keisha knew better. Deep down past the hurt, she knew he still loved her. That was her motivation to keep trying.

She even decided to take his advice—well, part of it anyway—by sending Loretta and her sisters on a real vacation to wherever her budget could afford. Unfortunately, her mom declined because the girls' spring break from school was just about over and she had no more vacation time at work, so they were headed back to Atlanta soon. Loretta could sense that her daughter needed her to stay around a little longer to help out with the baby; however, she also knew that her daughter's pride would never allow her to come out and say it.

"Look, Keisha, I know you're up under a lot of stress right now, so why don't I take the baby back with me, just for a couple of weeks, to give you and Tucker a little time to try and work things out a bit? And Nana would love to see her great-grandson," said Loretta.

"Umm . . ." Keisha hesitated. *What kind of mom would I be if I just shipped my son off with her?* she thought.

Loretta noticed her daughter's uneasiness and spoke in her own defense. "Listen, Keisha, I'm not the same person I was when you were growing up. I was a drunk who cared about nothing but getting drunk, but I've changed my life around completely, not just for the moment. I love my grandchild as much as I love you and your sisters, and I want to be a part of his life. I can't change the past, honey, but at least let me be here for you now. If you don't want him to go, then that's fine with me. As long as it's not because you feel he won't be in good hands. Okay, sweetie?"

The resentment Keisha still had toward her mom did pop into her head. She thought back to her childhood, when Loretta would get drunk, pass out, and sleep for days without moving. Keisha would get so hysterical thinking that her mother was dead.

The "new" Loretta had already proven she'd changed. She was such a big help with the baby, especially since the whole fallout with Tucker. Keisha had been having a hard time trying to deal with the stress and take care of her son and her responsibilities at the same time. Half the time when she was home, she'd lock herself in her bedroom.

I know I haven't been the best Mommy lately. What will Tucker say if I let the baby go without me? It doesn't sound like a bad idea after all, she thought.

So much was going on at once that she didn't even have the time to get down to the bottom of the whole sex tape mystery, but please believe she didn't forget. Keisha was going to get her life back in order. With all that in mind, she agreed to let Li'l T go to Atlanta, but only for a couple of weeks. Keisha also let Loretta know how much she appreciated all that she was doing.

"You don't have to thank me, because you already have, just by allowing me into you and my grandson's life," Loretta said.

Tears ran down both of their faces as they embraced each other. Soon everything was a go. The flights were booked, and in two days, Keisha would have the house to herself, and her plans would be set.

Chapter 59

"Hey, Daddy," Epiphany said as she opened her eyes. It was the second day she'd been awake.

"Hey, baby girl," Jay Wright answered back as he leaned over and planted a kiss on her forehead. "You had me scared for a minute, Epee."

"I did? What happened to me? How did I end up here?" Epiphany was still unsure about what had happened to her.

"Baby girl, let's not talk about it right now. I'ma take care of—"

Tiara walked in, giving Jay the eye.

"Yes, Lord, praise God."

Jay tightened his lips and shook his head. She was taking this church thing a little too seriously. She cried as she hugged Epiphany tight and whispered a prayer of thanks. Epiphany was a bit shocked by all the praising her mother was doing.

Damn, I know I gave everybody a bit of a scare, but what got into her while I was sleeping? Epiphany thought.

Just then the doctor came in to check Epiphany's vital signs and informed her and her parents that the nurse would be in shortly to check the healing of her gunshot wound. He then asked to speak to Jay Wright and Tiara in private. They agreed and stepped outside of Epiphany's room.

"You are aware that we ran a few tests on Epiphany yesterday, right?"

"Yes, we are," both parents answered.

"Good. Now, for the most part, Epiphany is going to be okay, so I don't want anyone to panic, all right?" Dr. Frye said, directing his attention toward Mrs. Wright.

"Okay," she answered.

"Good! Now, we did discover a bit of a problem in her right lung. It seems to be healing, just slowly. It's still very weak at this time; therefore, she will be experiencing some difficulty with her breathing. Now, it's not as bad as it sounds.

"I will be prescribing her an inhaler, which will be useful to her if she should have any trouble breathing. She must carry the pump with her at all times.

"Now, the results from the other test we took confirmed that Epiphany is suffering from partial amnesia, meaning she's not likely to have any recollection of any person, place, or thing that has occurred in the previous hours or months leading up to the shooting."

"So, doctor, does that mean that she might not ever remember who did this to her?" Tiara asked.

"Well, it's probable that she will regain her memory in spurts. It will be kind of like putting a puzzle together piece by piece. Epiphany's memory could start coming back to her tomorrow, or a year from now. That part I can't say, but I will be discharging her at the end of the week. Now, if you'll excuse me," said Dr. Frye as he walked off to speak to a passing nurse.

"Jay, we might not ever find out who did this to Epee," said Tiara.

"Woman, you know just as well as I do that punk bastard C-God did it. I'm gonna kill him dead, I swear."

"Baby, we don't know that."

"Has he been up here to see her yet, huh?"

"No, but—"

"Ain't no buts about it. That's guilt right there, and now the nigga's hiding out. He can't even be a man about it." Jay Wright slightly raised his voice.

"Shhhh. Okay, honey, please, just let God handle it. What's important is that Epiphany is going to be fine. She's coming home with us, and we can look after her. I don't need my husband going to jail because of some low-life. Are you listening to me, Jay? It's not worth it."

"Not worth it to who, Tiara? Epee is our daughter, and as her father, it is my job to protect her by all means, and that's what I'm gonna do. All that shit about God handling it is for the birds, 'cause if He was handling it, why did it happen, huh? Answer that."

"I'm sure He had his reasons, but I'm not gonna question His will," said Tiara. "We have a lot to be thankful for. Epiphany is still here with us, and we are a family, and that's what you need to be focusing on."

"You and this holier than thou act is really starting to get on my nerves."

"Okay, well, let me just say this, Jay: We ain't getting any younger, and if you want to convert back to the thug life, go right ahead, but I don't want it around me. So put that bullet in your gun and shoot it, gangsta!" Tiara might have been a changed woman, but she still had a sharp tongue.

Just as Epiphany's mom headed back to the room, she bumped into Keisha and Shana at the doorway.

"Hi, girls," she said.

"Hey, Mrs. Wright. Is Epiphany awake?" asked Keisha.

"Yeah, she is, and I know she's gonna be happy to see you guys, but I must warn you: she has amnesia. She's not going to remember anything about the shooting or her friend's death. Please don't mention it to her, because I don't want her getting upset. Okay, ladies?"

"Wait a minute, Mrs. T. If she has amnesia, how's she gonna remember us?" asked Shana with a puzzled look on her face.

"She'll remember you guys because it's only part of her memory of the last couple of months that she seems to have lost."

"That's crazy. She won't remember C-God, her pregnancy, or Malikai's murder?" Keisha asked.

"Well, I hope she never remembers that no-good Hinderson boy," said Mrs. Wright.

"But what if he is the one that tried to kill her?"

"Shana, come on. He did it. I know he did." Keisha had no evidence, but she felt it in her gut.

"Keisha, you sound like my husband. Y'all need to come to church with me and get some Jesus in your life. Anyway, go ahead in. I know she'll be happy to see you two. Just remember what I said."

The girls' eyes widened when Mrs. Wright mentioned going to church and needing Jesus. They both turned to each other with the *I don't know, girl* look on their faces.

Keisha and Shana slowly pushed open Epiphany's room door, not sure what to expect. They smiled when they saw her cursing out the nurses over the intercom about how cold and nasty her breakfast was.

"She's back," said Shana.

Keisha ran toward Epiphany with open arms and hugged her carefully, so as not to pull on her IV tubes.

"Hey, y'all, what's up? Finally, my girls. Now, which one of y'all is gonna tell me what the hell happened to me? Shana, you ain't shoot me, did you?" Epiphany cracked a smile.

"Oh, I see you got jokes, right," Shana responded.

"Epiphany, me and Shana been coming up here to see you every day. I'm so glad you're back. You just don't know," Keisha said.

"Yes, I do. I know y'all can't live without me, but I gotta get the fuck up out of this hospital. Look at this cold-ass oatmeal they trying to feed me, and who the fuck still eats oatmeal anyway?" Epiphany was already back to her silly self.

"I don't know, girl," Keisha agreed.

"No, but seriously, who did this to me?" Tears began to fill Epiphany's eyes, and her humor turned into sadness.

"Honestly, E, we don't know," answered Shana.

Keisha decided it was best to keep her mouth shut, because she was ready to fill in all the blanks for Epiphany.

"Keisha, where's Mali at? I know he's trying find out who did this to me, right? Does he know I'm out of a coma? Where's his ass at?" Epiphany's questions started to wear Keisha down. She burst into tears and started spilling the truth.

"Epiphany, Mali is dead. Whoever did this to you killed him. He's gone."

"What! No, not Malikai. Why him? Why did he have to die?" Epiphany cried.

"We think C-God had something to do with it," Keisha added.

"C-God?"

"Yeah, Corey. Corey Hinderson. Ring any bells?" asked Keisha.

"Ahhhh, yeah, black Corey that used to live around our way, right?"

"Bingo!"

"But why, Keish?" Epiphany was puzzled.

"Because, you was fucking him, that's why," Shana replied.

"I was? So Mali is dead 'cause of me?" Epiphany cried.

"Epiphany, don't start blaming yourself, because we don't know what Corey's reason was. He's been hating on Tucker and Mali for a while. I honestly don't think it was you that caused of any of this," Keisha explained.

"Why can't I remember any of this?" asked Epiphany.

"Epiphany, maybe once you get better you'll remember. Besides we ain't a hundred percent sure it was C-God. And, Keisha, you make sure to tell Mrs. Wright that it was you that opened your big mouth. E, I'm glad you're okay, but just concentrate on getting better, all right?"

"Keisha, I'm about to be out. I got a few things I gotta take care of, but I might be back later, a'ight," said Shana.

"Okay, I'm gonna stay for the afternoon visit, since I ain't got the baby or no man to run home to," Keisha replied.

The afternoon quickly turned into evening, and Keisha ended up staying until visiting hours were over. Playing catch-up, she filled Epiphany in on all the drama that was going on in her life and answered whatever questions Epiphany had for her.

Chapter 60

Shana had to drive out to her supplier's house in Staten Island to re-up, which was something she dreaded. She always traveled alone and made sure her transactions were quick. She let it be known that she was always on the move, so her time was limited. Once she safely made it back around the way, she'd arrange to meet with Raina at various locations, so she could hit her off with work for the week.

This time the meeting was at Applebee's. Shana waited in a booth, watching the entrance and her surroundings at the same time. Finally, Raina came walking in, looking like Babs from Da Band. She was wearing a Rocawear baby tee, a short jean skirt, and some crispy clean tan Timbs.

Representing BK to the fullest, Shana thought as she watched her approach.

"What up, Cream?" Raina was the only person who still called Shana by her hustlin' name.

"Chillin'. Excuse me, waitress, we ready for some drinks or something," Shana said, flagging down one of the uniformed girls as she walked past.

"Okay, your server will be with you in a minute," the girl replied.

"Hey, there's five hundred of them things in the backpack under this table, a'ight," Shana whispered softly to Raina, getting the business part of their meeting out of the way first.

"A'ight, I'ma handle that." Raina knew the routine.

"So, what's good, Raina?" Shana was ready for the gossip.

"Ain't shit, really. You know me. I'm mostly business, but some baller niggas been coming through the spot lately, and they from out here in Queens. One of them niggas be acting like he checking for me too."

"Yo, word, they be up in Honey's like that?" Shana asked.

"Like that, kid. For the past couple of nights or so," answered Raina.

"I hear that! Get that money. Just make sure it don't interfere with getting mine," Shana said, flipping it back to business.

"Yo, I got you, kid. I'm handling my shit."

"What's up with Silk? Where she been hiding at?"

"Man, that bitch done fucked around and got her ass pregnant again. She was still doing her thing up in Honey's until she started showing too much. She home chilling now, out of commission for a while," said Raina.

"So, what's up with Chasity? You seen her lately?" Shana questioned out of curiosity.

"Nah, I ain't really seen her that much, but I heard she still be coming through."

"Oh, that's cool," Shana said, relieved.

"Excuse me. Are you ladies ready to order?" asked the waiter.

Knock . . . Knock . . . Knock . . .

Shana woke up out of her sleep when she heard the knocking at her door. She glanced over at the clock. It read 2:00 a.m.

"I hope K.C. ain't lose his damn key," she mumbled as she got out of the bed.

"Yo, Sha, it's Smitty. Open up," he yelled.

"I'm coming. Stop knocking on my fucking door like you crazy," Shana yelled back as she cracked open the door.

"Yo, what up, what up, Sha?" said Smitty in a playful tone.

"K.C. ain't here, Smitty," Shana snobbishly responded.

"I ain't here for him."

"Then what do you want?"

"Yo, Sha, what's up? 'Cause I'm saying, you been throwing me a lot of shade lately."

"Ain't nothing up." Shana stepped back to let Smitty come inside.

"Oh, so I'm bugging out then, right?"

"Look, Smitty, I don't know what you talking about."

"I'm saying, Shana, every time I come through, you start rolling your eyes, huffing and puffing and shit, like a nigga did something to you. All I wanna know is, what the fuck is up with all that?" Smitty carried on.

"Whatever, Smitty. Look, it's late and I'm tired, so uhh—"

"Nah, ain't no 'so ahhh.' Just let me finish."

"What do you want, Smitty?" Shana rolled her eyes and let out a hard sigh, making sure he knew how annoyed she was getting.

"Yo, how's what's her face doing?" Smitty said, skirting around the real reason for his visit.

Shana was getting defensive and stared Smitty down. She ignored his question for a few moments, assuming he was asking about Chasity to be sarcastic.

"Yo, I don't know who you're talking about, and honestly I don't give a fuck, so why are you wasting my time?"

"Epiphany, that's her name," said Smitty.

Shana was relieved that it wasn't Chasity he was talking about, but she still decided not to give up any information.

"What is it to you?" she questioned.

"Nothing really, but since she's your friend, I just thought I'd ask. Either way, that's neither here nor there, 'cause that ain't why I'm here," said Smitty.

"Then what is the reason?"

"Business, of course," Smitty replied.

"What business you got to discuss with me?" Shana asked with a puzzled look on her face.

"Your little business down at Honey's."

"And what about it?" Shana snapped.

"I hear you're doing well for yourself down there."

"Oh, yeah, that's what you heard?"

"Yeah, that's what I'm hearing. I hear you done stepped up your game. You saw a little gold mine and handled your business. Instead of lap dancing for that bullshit-ass money you was making, you charging them bitches thirty dollars a pop for E. I'm really impressed."

"So what you saying, Smitty?"

"I'm *saying,* I'm trying to be on your team."

"What team? I ain't making team money," Shana argued.

"Oh, really? 'Cause I fucked this stripper bitch a little while ago from Honey's who said you be making at least ten to fifteen G's a week. Now, that's a nice little piece of change. So, since I know your man hates dikes and you're into girls, you should be looking out for a brother. Say forty percent and I'll keep your secret."

"Forty percent of what? You bugging the fuck out if you think I'm giving you my money," Shana yelled.

"A'ight then, I guess I'ma have to tell K.C., and you know how that nigga feel about that shit."

"Yo, I can't believe you, Smitty. If it wasn't for me, you wouldn't be making the money you making now. I helped you out, and now you trying to play me. It's all good, though, nigga. You do dirt, you gon' get dirt."

"Oh, I'm so scared. Just see me with that when you collect from Raina on Sunday, a'ight."

"You'll get your forty percent. Just go, a'ight. Get out my house."

Smitty slowly walked out the door past Shana, who was holding it open. She slammed it right behind him. He was kind of surprised at how easy it was to get Shana to agree to his terms.

"You muthafucka!" She stormed into the bedroom and grabbed her cell phone. Her heart raced with anger as she dialed Raina's phone.

"What's up, Cream?" Raina answered.

"Yo, what's up with you putting my fucking business out there like that, and to a nigga you don't even fucking know?"

"Yo, Cream, hold up. Pump your brakes for a minute, 'cause I don't know what you talking about," said Raina.

"Oh, you don't know what I'm talking about, huh?"

"Nah, and you shouldn't even be coming at me like this with bullshit," Raina replied.

"So, you ain't fuck this kid named Smitty?" Shana asked.

"Yeah, I fucked him, but I ain't tell him shit. That's my word. This what happened: The nigga got a lap dance from me a couple of nights ago, right? Then he starts asking me questions, like, do I sell E and who I work for. So I got a little paranoid, and I backs off from the nigga. Then I start asking some of the girls some questions about him. They told me he hustled and shit was gravy with the nigga, so I'm like, cool.

"Now I'm more relaxed around the nigga the next time I seen him, which was tonight. The vibe was good, so I went to the hotel with him; but I swear I ain't mention your name. That's my word on everything I love, my son all that. Did that nigga tell you some bogus shit?"

"Yep, but it's all good." Shana was pissed.

"Yo, that's my word, Cream. I wouldn't do no sheisty shit like that to you, and if you got that nigga's number, we can straighten this shit out now."

How you fuck a nigga and don't get his number? Shana wondered.

"Nah, don't even worry about it. I'll check you on Sunday."

"A'ight, see you then." Raina hung up.

Now Shana was furious, and at this point she didn't know what or who to believe. She knew somebody was ratting her out.

Chapter 61

Keisha spotted Tucker's BMW parked in the driveway as she pulled up to the house. She knew he was probably still pissed off at her, but just seeing his car put a smile on her face. She thought that maybe now she would have a chance to finally get some things off her chest. Keisha quickly unlocked the door, put down her keys, and ran upstairs.

"Tucker," she called out, but he was nowhere in sight, nor did he answer. She ran back downstairs to the living room and walked toward the kitchen. Still no sign of him.

Keisha heard his voice coming from the basement "Bingo." She took off toward the basement steps and quietly crept down the dimly lit stairwell. When she reached the bottom step, she was greeted by the barrel of Tucker's gun. Keisha screamed, and they both jumped.

"Damn, Keisha, you scared the shit out of me," Tucker yelled. "You lucky I ain't one of them scared shooters, or your ass would have been a goner."

"I know. You scared me too," Keisha said, catching her breath.

"What are you doing here? I thought you was suppose to be going out of town liked I asked."

"I know, but I got classes that I'm trying to make up, Epiphany's still in the hospital, and I've been waiting to talk to you, so—"

"So what, Keisha? I told you to go for a reason. You must wanna end up in the hospital with Epiphany, or better yet, like Mali. Yo, this ain't shit to be playing with—and where my son at?" Tucker's voice was getting louder, and she could tell he was getting annoyed.

"Well, ahhh, I sent him with Loretta so he could see Nana, but it's only for two weeks," Keisha answered nervously.

"Oh, so you gon' be like your mom now, huh? Shipping off your responsibilities for somebody else to take care of, is that it?"

The happiness Keisha had felt when she first got home was now replaced by rage. *How could he doubt my parenting skills? He was the one running from his family, trying to ship me off.* His words cut her like a knife. She burst into tears.

"Tucker, how could you say that to me? I'm not like Loretta. I would never leave my son like that. I am trying my best to be a good mother, considering the kind of mother I had, but I'm doing it. You come and go as you please. It's me that's left with all the responsibility. I have a baby to take care of, and I'm trying to finish school. It's not easy."

"Keish, you right, its not easy, and maybe I shouldn't have said that. Matter of fact, I know I shouldn't have, but I still wish you would've went with them just to make sure my little man is good."

"I know, T, but they all promised to look after him, and if I had the slightest bit of doubt that Li'l T would not be properly taken care of, I would have never agreed to it.

"Loretta has come a long way from being the mother I knew growing up. She proved it during her visit. I see the joy in her eyes when she's with our son, and I honestly believe that she won't disappoint me this time."

"A'ight, Keish, I hope you're right."

At this point, Keisha no longer wanted to discuss him and her. It didn't seem like she mattered to Tucker anymore. He made it very clear to her every time they talked that his only concern was their son.

She stared at Tucker. His clear caramel skin was so beautiful, and his silky black hair waves looked like the ocean. She thought back to how fine he was when they first met. As the years passed, he had only gotten finer. She loved him deeply, with all her heart, and would do anything for a second chance. Unfortunately, the ball was in Tucker's court.

Keisha headed back upstairs to the kitchen, loaded the dishwasher, and decided to get dinner started. She figured that maybe a home-cooked meal might soften Tucker's mood, assuming it might have been a while since he had one. Usually, if it wasn't Keisha or Mom Dukes cooking, he wouldn't fuck with it.

Keisha made fried chicken, rice, and steamed broccoli. As soon as the aroma filled the air, Tucker came running.

"Damn, Keish, what's that you cooking?" he said as he rummaged through the pots.

"Help yourself, T. I'm gonna go take a shower and lay down."

"What, you not gon' eat?"

"Nah, I made that for you."

"Thanks. Good looking out." Tucker piled his plate with everything and went back to the basement.

After Keisha showered, she threw on a large T-shirt and hopped into bed. All types of thoughts ran through her mind—mainly the sex tape and how foolish it was for her to do what she had, not to mention doing it a second time.

After beating herself up over and over again, she thought about how ironic it was that outside of Epiphany, Shana, and her classmate, Simone, none of the girls at the party had contacted her to see how she was doing. What was even stranger was how Simone called her several times, but her other classmate, Lea, didn't—especially since she felt much closer to Lea. They had three classes together, and Lea hadn't even bothered to see why Keisha hadn't been to school in weeks. It all just seemed a bit suspect to Keisha, and the more she thought about it, the more her fingers started to point at Lea, who put the whole shindig together.

Still, how would she get to the bottom of it all? That question boggled her mind until finally, she fell asleep.

About an hour into Keisha's sleep, Tucker came into the bedroom. He turned on the night light and watched her.

Damn, Keish, why you had to do me like this? I love you so much. You just don't know how bad you hurt me, girl, he thought.

Keisha was looking real good to him as she lay on her stomach. The covers were down by her feet, where she had kicked them, and from the way her T-shirt rested on her ass, Tucker could tell she wasn't wearing any panties. His dick started to get real hard. He didn't know if he wanted to get back with her, but he knew he wanted her now.

He took off his jeans and slowly crawled into bed behind her. Placing his fingers between her legs, he began to finger fuck her slowly, just the way she liked it.

Keisha started to moan and move to the rhythm of Tucker's fingers as her juices flowed heavily. She was so horny it felt like she was going to explode.

Turning over, she whispered, "Please fuck me, T. I want you so bad."

Tucker wanted to fuck her just as bad, but first he leaned over and grabbed a condom from the pocket of his jeans. When Keisha realized that he was putting on a condom, she got offended, because for one, she was on birth control and two, in the seven years they were together, he had never worn one before. The fact that he felt the need to wear one now made her wonder, which one of them he felt the need to protect. Her mind started telling her no, but her body was still screaming a strong yes that she couldn't ignore.

Tucker started out with slow, deep strokes as he kissed her neck and breasts. It had been a while since the two made love to each other, and they had both forgotten how good they felt to one another. Tucker then started to pound her pussy once he located Keisha's spot. He always could tell when he was hitting it by the way her pussy would start to pulsate on the tip of his dick.

Keisha knew that once she threw it back and tightened her vagina muscles, it would be a wrap for Tucker. As they both began to cum, Keisha felt like she had died and gone to paradise. She saw the sun, the moon, the mountains, and the rivers. It was heaven, just like Az Yet once sang, but before she knew it, the lovemaking was over and Tucker had rolled over, turning his back toward her as he drifted off to sleep.

Keisha smiled as she snuggled up close, burying her head into his back. She was happy just to have him next to her again and hoped that maybe, just maybe, tonight was the start of a clean slate and he was ready to forgive her, come home, and put all this mess behind them. She closed her eyes and dozed back off to sleep with high hopes.

Chapter 62

C-God was in Virginia, staying with his Puerto Rican mami, Marisa. He had met her about four years ago. She was one of his out-of-town pieces. Marisa was a bit of a big girl, but she had a real pretty face. She had three bad-ass kids. She also had a large appetite for the nose candy (cocaine), and she was a real freak-a-leak, as Petey Pueblo would say, once she got her hands on some.

C-God didn't quite hit rock bottom until he found out about his parents. That was the shit that took him over the edge. At this point, the large amounts of cocaine he was sniffing no longer numbed him, so he started free-basing it. He went from pulling in 50 G's a week to losing his right-hand man, having the feds on his ass, and now his parents were dead. All that sent him into a rage of fury. He couldn't even pay his last respects at their funeral, because the undercovers had it surrounded in hopes of his arrival. That hurt the most.

C-God broke down and cried like a bitch because he could no longer endure the pain he was feeling. He called Tanya, his newest baby momma, and asked her if she would pay her respects for him. Tanya agreed, even though she had never met his parents. She figured that with C-God being the youngest of four, he had to have shared a close relationship with his parents. She sympathized with him deeply. Tanya knew that some shit went down, but she didn't know any details, and she also knew not pry. Before saying good-bye, C-God promised to try to meet up with her soon to explain everything. Not once did he mention their son.

Chapter 63

The news about Malikai really devastated Epiphany. As far as her memory was concerned, she thought they had never stopped seeing each other. She recalled the weird dream she'd had when she was in the hospital. Over and over, she questioned its meaning. Was Mali saying good-bye?

On top of that, Epiphany had to get used to living with her parents again, something she hadn't done since she was eighteen, which was almost five years ago. It hadn't even been a full week yet, and already they were driving her up the walls with the questions: "Epee are you okay? Do you have your pump? Where are you going?"

"If you guys would have paid this much attention to me growing up, I could've avoided a lot of trouble," she'd constantly say. Her dad wasn't that bad, but Epiphany could barely pee in peace without her mom breathing down her back.

The only time she did manage to get some peace was when Tiara left for church; that is, after she failed to convince Epiphany to tag along. Epiphany could not believe how involved her mom really was with the church thing. She was still giving Jay the cold shoulder for his determination to find C-God. Jay was beginning to think she had another man, because he always thought church was only on Sundays, whereas his wife was faithfully attending every Sunday, Wednesday, and Friday evening service. It got to the point where he would smell her panties once she took them off, just to make sure they didn't have a sex or latex scent.

"Alone at last." Epiphany sighed with relief. It was one of those evenings when Tiara had church and Jay happened to be out in the streets. Epiphany hadn't fully recovered yet, but she needed to go back to her place, in search of some answers.

She grabbed her cell phone and car keys, and out the door she went.

Once she reached her apartment, she spotted a FOR RENT sign in the window. She got out of the car and attempted to use her key, but it didn't work. She walked around to the side of the two family house and peeked through the her bedroom window. It was empty.

"Where the fuck is my shit?" she screamed as she walked back to her car. Epiphany grabbed her cell phone and dialed the number on the FOR RENT sign.

"Hello?" a man answered.

"Yes, is this Mr. Raymond?" She was obviously aggravated.

"Ahhh, yeah. Who am I speaking with?" Mr. Raymond responded.

"This is Epiphany Wright. I was renting your first floor apartment over here off of Guy R. Brewer Avenue, and I need to know where my stuff is."

"Well, young lady, I don't know where your stuff is, but I do know that a gentleman claiming to be your father paid me the remaining balance of your lease and took your belongings with him."

"Oh, okay then. Thanks." Epiphany hit the END CALL button on her phone. She sat parked in front of the house, staring off into space, when suddenly a quick vision came to her. She saw Malikai's truck pull up in front of her apartment; then he was sitting on her couch. What Epiphany saw next caused her to have an asthma attack. She saw herself standing in front of Mali, pointing her gun at him, and in one last flash, the gun went off.

Wheezing and gasping for air, she searched the car for her asthma pump, but only found a brown paper bag instead. With tears pouring down her face, she quickly placed the bag over her mouth then inhaled and exhaled until she gained control of her breathing.

"Oh my God, I killed him," she whispered.

Epiphany replayed Mali's murder in her mind for days, but it just didn't make sense to her. *If I killed Malikai, then who shot me? Was it in self-defense?* The same two questions kept popping up in her head. She couldn't eat or sleep since her revelation. She needed answers. If her father was the last one in her apartment, she felt it was time to ask him some questions.

"Daddy, listen. I really need to talk to you."

"What's up, Epee?" Jay Wright responded.

"Are the police trying to find out what really happened?"

"I doubt it. As far as they're concerned, your friend is just one less nigga they got to worry about. The truth will surface sooner or later, and when it does, I'll take care of it. Meanwhile, don't stress yourself out, Epee."

"Daddy, you don't understand. I need to know what happened," Epiphany said, slightly raising her voice.

"Epee, look, I don't know what to tell you. I tried to warn you about the company you was keeping, but you didn't want to hear it."

"Daddy, did anything look suspicious in my apartment, like my locks? Were they broken or anything?"

"No, besides the blood-stained couch and a busted-up stereo, nothing was out of place."

"My gun, Daddy, the nine you gave me—was it still in my closet?" Epiphany continued to question.

"Nah, I ain't see no gun."

"Do you think the police found it?" Epiphany asked.

"Hell no! You kidding me? If so, they would've had a field day prosecuting you, especially since you're my daughter," Jay Wright said, checking his Rolex for the time.

"Epee, look, I have to go and take care of something. You gon be a'ight?"

"Yeah, I'm cool," Epiphany answered. She was disappointed. Her father's answers weren't much help.

Chapter 64

"I feel so stupid. I can't believe Tucker just fucked me and left without saying a word, like I'm some whore off the street or something."

It was day two since they hit skins, and still no Tucker in sight, not even a courtesy call. Keisha tried reaching him on his cell, but after leaving several messages, she gave up. At that moment, there was only one word to describe how Keisha was feeling: played.

If this is Tucker's way of making me feel like shit on the bottom of his shoe, well, damn it, he's done it.

Tears began to run down her face, and the feeling of loneliness came over her.

Maybe he's seeing someone else, she thought. *All the signs are right in my face: he won't answer my calls; he can't be living out of a hotel all this time; and he fucked me with a condom, I guess to keep from bringing my scent home to his new girl.*

"That has to be it!" Keisha cried out. Her assumptions made everything seem all too clear.

She got out of bed and started packing all of Tucker's belongings.

"If you want to be with somebody else, that's fine, but you won't do it here," she screamed out while throwing all his things into garbage bags. "I'm done with the apologies and making an ass out of myself over and over again."

Keisha struggled as she dragged the bags down the steps and left them by the front door. Then she dialed Tucker, who, of course, didn't answer.

"Tucker, this is Keisha, and since you haven't bothered to return any of my calls, don't. Just come and get your stuff. It's already packed and waiting by the door, so the hard part is over. Good-bye." Keisha exhaled as she plopped down to the floor and new tears began to fall, replacing the dry ones.

She took a moment to collect her thoughts, but all she kept asking herself was, *Damn, how could I be so stupid? Why did I do it? I know he's not coming back.*

Still holding the phone in her hand, she decided to call and check on her son.

Chapter 65

Shana was tight about having to pay Smitty that kind of hush money. Besides, she was starting to wonder if it was even worth it. K.C. didn't even bring his black ass home last night, and yet she was paying his right-hand man a cut of the money she made.

Shana wanted to get her mind off the stress in her life. She needed to throw on her "fuck him" dress, head to the club, get her drink on, dance, and just have some fun for a change. She called Keisha to see if she was down. Clubbing was something Keisha hadn't done in years, so it might help her get her mind off Tucker.

"Hello?" Keisha picked up after the fifth ring.

"Damn, Keish, I was about to hang the fuck up. What you doing?"

"Nothing, girl. Just finished surfing the net for a job and waiting for Tucker to come and get his things."

"Job? What you talking about? Tucker's moving out?"

"He needs to. I packed all his stuff and told him to come get it, so that means I'm going to need a job so I won't go through the money I've been saving."

"Shit is that bad, huh?"

"Yep. I'm only fooling myself thinking he'll take me back. It's obvious he don't want to be with me anymore, so I might as well face it."

"Did he say that?"

"No, but his actions say it. I can't even be mad at him, because if he did what I did, I probably wouldn't want him neither."

"Keish, you know what your problem is? You need to stop feeling sorry for yourself and get out the house and have some fun. Fuck that nigga. Let's go out and get our club on or something, girl. Do you for a change."

"I don't know," she said hesitantly.

"Keisha, what you mean, you don't know? The baby ain't there and neither is Tucker, so come on. Let's have some fun. Please!" Shana said, putting the beg on.

Keisha sat on that thought a few moments longer. It was time to get out, have a little fun, and focus on doing her.

"All right, I'm down. Let me see if Epiphany wants to come too."

"Epiphany! Do you think she's well enough to go to a club?" Shana asked.

"Yeah, she's good. It'll be like old times, just the three of us."

"Cool. I'll check back with you around ten o'clock."

"Just come over."

Keisha hung up with Shana and dialed Epiphany.

"Praise the Lord," answered Mrs. Wright.

"Ahhhh, hello?" said Keisha.

"Yes, who would you like to speak to?"

"Mrs. Wright."

"Yes."

"Oh, hi. Is Epiphany there? It's Keisha."

"Hi, sweetie. Hold for a moment, okay? Epiphany, Keisha's on the phone," she yelled.

"Hello?" said Epiphany, picking up the phone.

"Hey, girl, what's up?" Keisha asked.

"Girl, my moms is driving me nuts."

"Why? What's wrong?"

"She done went Christian crazy. Every five minutes she's talking about God or trying to get me to go to church with her. She even bought me a bible, and get this: She plays church music all fucking day now."

"Well, what does your father say?" Keisha asked.

"What can he say? She ain't even speaking to him, for whatever reason. I'm guessing it has something to do with her new-found religion.

"And that's not even the half of it. She told me that the name Epiphany meant some type of celebration for Christ."

"What?" Keisha questioned in disbelief.

"Yes, girl, that's it for me. I have to get the hell out of here. She's too much for me. I'll never get my memory back living here." Epiphany laughed.

"I got an idea. Why don't you come stay with me?" Keisha suggested.

"Are you serious? What about Tucker?"

"I packed his stuff, girl," Keisha said in a disappointed tone and sucked her teeth before continuing. "Besides, it ain't like he's ever here anyway, so he might as well take his belongings with him, right? Anyway, don't worry about him. Just come on, okay?"

"Check you out, finally putting your foot down. Even though you did wait until you fucked up to do it, but at least you doing it. Anyway, we'll talk about it when I get there."

"No, we'll talk about it tomorrow, 'cause me, you, and Shana hanging out tonight."

"Oh, for real. I'm with that. I'll see you in a minute then."

Chapter 66

Epiphany was so anxious to move out of her parents' house that she didn't put much thought into her decision to move in with Keisha. All she knew was she wanted out and wasn't quite ready to get a place of her own just yet. Epiphany also knew that even though she was grown, her mom would make a big deal about her leaving, so she decided that easing her way out would be her best move.

I'll just pack enough for a few nights, tell them I'm chilling with Keisha for a few days, and then gradually get the rest of my things, Epiphany thought as she plotted out her plan.

She packed fast and told her parents it was only for a few nights. Tiara was uneasy about her spending the night out so soon after what had happened and bearing in mind her condition, just as Epiphany had expected her to her to be. She already had her, "I'm twenty-two, soon to be twenty-three, which means I'm not asking permission. I'm just letting you guys know where I'll be" speech prepared.

"Baby she is grown. Besides it's only for a couple of nights." Jay Wright assured Tiara that Epiphany would be fine.

It was a done deal. Epiphany was out the door and in her car as soon as she said her rushed good-byes. She turned on the radio and blasted Hot 97 all the way to Keisha's house.

Keisha rushed to the door, kicking Tucker's bags further to the side to make room for Epiphany to enter.

"Hey, girl!" she screamed, full of excitement as they rocked side to side, hugging each other tightly.

"Thanks, Keish, for letting me chill here."

"Girl, please! Don't even mention it. You know you're like a sister to me, so cut it out and get in here. Shana should be here around ten."

"Damn, what's all this?" Epiphany asked, referring to the bags by the door.

"Tucker's stuff. What, you thought I was playing? I think it's really over between us, 'cause he don't act like he feeling me at all."

"Keish, he probably just wants to make you suffer for a little while, that's all."

"Oh, so I guess that's why he fucked me the other night, fell asleep with his back turned, and then got up and left and hasn't spoke to me since."

"Shit, at least you got some. I can't even remember the last time I had some dick. I just hope for your sake you put it on his ass and fucked him good, 'cause if you did, he ain't going nowhere." Epiphany laughed.

"You know I did, girl!" Keisha said, wondering if her sex was as good to him as his was to her. "Come on, let me take you to your room, 'cause we need to be getting ready."

Chapter 67

The trio was back together again. It had been a while since all three of the girls hit the club together, so of course they had to represent. Epiphany was dressed in an all-black halter top cat suit by Sean John (Not the Sean John hood shit you find in Monies or Macy's. This was P.Diddy's exclusive runway shit, only for the grown and sexy). She wore her hair straight back, and it flowed nicely down her back. She applied a glitter gloss to her lips, along with an earth tone eye shadow that complemented her slanted eyes. After all her last- minute primping, she slid her freshly pedicured feet into her Gucci sandals and was ready for whatever.

Keisha was dressed a little too conservatively for Epiphany's taste, in a knee-length Chanel skirt with a buttoned-up blouse by Donna Karan. Sister needed some serious help.

"Oh, hell no. You ain't going with me looking like that. We're going to a club, not a fucking job interview," Epiphany snapped.

"I know, but I don't have nothing else to wear," Keisha whined.

Epiphany dug down in her bag and pulled out a fitted little dress by BCBG. "Here. Put this on," she said, throwing it at Keisha.

The dress was a little too short and sexy for Keisha, but she didn't want to hear Epiphany's plain Jane jokes, so she decided to just roll with it. Epiphany took care of her hair and makeup, and Keisha threw on some stiletto mid-calf boots from Aldo to at least hide some of her legs.

Shana arrived at a quarter past ten. She was looking cute as well, wearing a black-and-white sheer shirt that hung off her right shoulder, black stretch boot cut pants, and a pair of heels. She wasn't really into all that name brand shit. To her it was the person that made the clothes, not the other way around. So, while chicks were out there trying to keep up with the Joneses, spending three or four hundred for an outfit, Shana's cost about eighty bucks, and she still looked good.

Epiphany was glad that both of her girls finally had their own rides now, but she got a little jealous when Keisha volunteered to be the designated driver with her brand new, fully loaded XS with spinners.

"Keisha, when did you get this?" she asked.

"Oh, Tucker bought it, but he gave it to me right before all the drama started. Why? You like it?"

"Yeah, it's a'ight, but he should've got you the silver one though."

Shana rolled her eyes, noticing Epiphany's hateration, but she kept quiet about it, because she was determined to have a good time tonight.

The girls made it to Club Suede around midnight. They headed straight for the bar. The club was kind of empty at first, but it didn't take long to fill up with all kinds of people—black, white, Asian, you name it and they were up in there partying it up.

Suede was also a well-known hangout spot for the baller/celebrities. That particular night, P. Diddy and his entourage were up in there, along with Cameron Diaz and Justin Timberlake, who danced the night away in the VIP section.

Epiphany, of course being the diva she only knew how to be, wanted nothing less than VIP status, plus she wanted Diddy to notice her and how good she looked in his Sean John design. She started by making eye contact with one of the big bouncers in front the velvet ropes. His arms were folded, and he didn't seem to pay her much attention.

She walked over to him and bluntly asked, "Ahhh, can you let me and my girls through, please?"

Without even looking down at her, he replied, "Nah, shorty, I can't."

"Come on. I said *please*. I'll give you my number," Epiphany said with a flirtatious smile.

He gave her a dirty look. Disappointed and bothered by the bouncer's rejection, Epiphany stormed off and headed back over to Shana and Keisha, who stood holding their drinks, waiting patiently for her to signal them over to VIP.

"That muthafucka got to be gay," she yelled out to them over the loud music.

"Or maybe you lost your touch." Shana laughed at her snide remark.

"Never that." Epiphany didn't find the humor at all.

"Oh, come on, you guys. Let's just have some fun." Keisha was the mediator as always.

"Yeah, let's." Shana rolled her eyes.

"Keisha, just give me my drink. You and her go have fun. I'ma go stand over there," Epiphany said, pointing toward the VIP section.

"You sure?" asked Keisha.

"Yessss, go," Epiphany yelled as she headed back over to the ropes. She was certain she'd get up in VIP.

The DJ was putting it down with the music. The fellas were hawking the females like vultures. It didn't take long for Keisha and Shana to find dance partners.

Epiphany sipped on her drink and checked out the scene carefully. Suddenly, she felt a tap on her shoulder. Slowly, she turned to her left, and there stood a six-foot-four, nicely built, caramel brown brother with light eyes.

"What's your name, shorty?" he asked with a killer smile. Jackpot bells went off in Epiphany's head when she looked down and saw he was standing on the other side of the ropes in VIP, where she needed to be. She smiled at him, damn near showing all her pearly whites.

"Epiphany."

"Epiphany?" he repeated.

"Uh-huh."

"That's nice. It's different."

Epiphany smiled again, moving seductively to the music and taking a sip from her glass.

"What you drinking?"

"A mimosa," she replied in a sexy but girlish kind of tone.

"Oh, word. So why don't you come chill with me and have another one?"

She smiled some more. "Okay."

"Yo, dude, let shorty through," he said to the bouncer.

Epiphany gave the bouncer a mean "you should've let me through the first time" look as he shook his head and reluctantly unhooked the rope to let her through. She walked over to her new friend's table, and he introduced her to four of his boys and two girls that looked like video hoes with all their assets hanging out.

"Okay, I know their names, but I don't know yours," she said. He gave her a dumbfounded look, like she was supposed to know who he was.

"That's 'cause you ain't ask."

"I'm asking you now," Epiphany replied.

"Wild."

"Wild what?"

"No, that's my name," he said.

"Oh, okay!"

The two hit it off so well that she forgot all about the celebs in VIP and her girls. Wild entertained her with his conversation, jokes, and plenty of Veuve Clicquot mimosa refills.

Epiphany didn't find him all that attractive. As a matter of fact, on a scale of one to ten, she'd rate him a flat five, but deep pockets and a free-hearted spirit could easily put him in the eight spot, especially if the dick was good. A big nigga like him had to be equipped with a get-up-in-ya-guts size dick, meaning twelve inches or more.

She learned that he was a music producer and owned his own company called Wild One Productions, with quite a few hits under his belt. Epiphany felt kind of bad for not knowing who he was from the jump. She loved the limelight niggas: Jay Z, 50 Cent, and P. Diddy, but she couldn't give a fuck about the behind-the-scenes nigga laying the tracks—until now.

"Epiphany!" Keisha was standing next to the security guard.

"Yo, is that your friend calling you?" Wild asked.

Epiphany turned around and noticed Keisha signaling her to come over.

"Yeah, that's one of them," she said, getting up to see what Keisha wanted.

"Nah, hold up a minute." Wild pulled Epiphany back down in the seat. "Yo, homes," he called out to the bouncer. "Let her through."

"Sorry, man, I can't let no more through right now," the bouncer replied.

"That's all right. Let me just go see what she wants, okay?" Epiphany said to Wild as she got up and walked over to Keisha.

"What's up, girl?"

"Nothing, but we're ready to go."

"Already?" Epiphany said, looking down at her diamond face Rolie, which only read three a.m.

"Yeah, I'm tired, and I think Shana had too much to drink."

Epiphany sucked her teeth and let out a hard sigh. "Okay, just give me five minutes."

"All right. We'll be waiting by the exit."

Epiphany walked back over to Wild with an agitated look on her face.

"What's up?" he asked.

"Nothing. I should've drove my own car, that's all, but since I didn't, I have to go."

"Ahhh, come on. You can't be serious. Our vibe is too good for you to go now."

"Yeah, but my girls are ready now."

"So then let them go and I'll take you home."

The offer sounded good, but Epiphany didn't want to seem too thirsty. Besides, the last time she was with a guy, she ended up with a bullet in her chest, so it was best that she played it safe.

"Nah, I'm gonna go, but why don't you take my number?"

"Oh, no doubt. Hold up. Let me put it in my phone," Wild said pulling out his phone. "Okay now, what is it?"

Epiphany recited her number while he punched the keys on his phone and then repeated them back to her. "A'ight, sexy, I'ma holla at you."

Epiphany blushed as she said good night.

"Damn, these bitches get on my nerves," she mumbled under her breath, making her way to the exit.

Chapter 68

It was six in the morning when the all the yelling and screaming woke Epiphany up out of barely two hours of sleep. She hopped up out of bed, cracked the bedroom door, and stuck her head out to hear what the fuss was about. Being miss nosey, she wasn't satisfied with just the earshot she had on Keisha and Tucker's argument. She wanted to see what was going on as well. Epiphany tippy-toed over to the stairs and peeked down into the living room. She still wasn't able to get a clear view, but she could hear them better.

"Who told you to pack my stuff up, Keish?" Not giving her a chance to answer his question, he continued, "Look, just unpack my things and put everything back where it belongs." Tucker tried to rationalize without getting loud.

"I ain't unpacking nothing." Keisha said, shrugging her shoulders. "I want you to take it and go. Since you don't want to be with me anymore, leave."

"You got some fucking nerve." Tucker laughed, pausing in disbelief. "I don't believe you. You walk around here acting like I'm the bad guy, Keisha, but if I'm not mistaken, you're the one that went out and fucked some gay-ass stripper nigga. You're crazy if you think I'm leaving my house. You better be lucky I let you stay here."

"What! You can't make me leave. My name is on the deed too," Keisha said.

"I don't give a shit. My money paid for this right here, so act up if you want to, and word to my son, I'll burn this bitch down and neither one of us'll live in it. I ain't trying to hear all that shit about your name. The only reason why you still here is because of my little man. You played me, and ain't no way in hell I could forgive some shit like that."

This was the first time Tucker had ever spoken about how he felt about what she did. He had finally confirmed it—it was over.

The only reason he lets me stay is because of the baby, huh, Keisha said to herself.

Tucker still loved her, but there was no way he could get past what she did, not now anyway. It might have been different if he heard that she fucked around, but seeing her get fucked by another dude, especially a stripper, left tainted thoughts of her in his mind. Watching her cry made him feel bad, but in all reality, she had done it to herself.

"Tucker, I'm sorry, baby. Please tell me you still want me. Please say we can work this out." Keisha sobbed. "I'll do anything. I love you so much. You're the only man I ever loved and will ever love. I can't live without you." Keisha poured her heart out to Tucker as he sat on the couch with his head down, trying to take everything she was saying into consideration.

There was a moment of silence between the two. While Keisha waited for Tucker to say something, he was at a loss for words. Part of him wanted to push his pride to the side and wrap his arms around her waist, hold her tight, tell her how much he loved her, and tell her, "Yes, I forgive you." The other part of him wanted to wrap his hands around her neck, squeeze the dear life out of her, and express the hate he felt toward her for playing him like she had.

Meanwhile, while Epiphany continued to get her ear hustle on at the head of the steps, she too waited impatiently for one of the two to respond. Her heart went out to Tucker as she watched him closely and imagined what her life might have been like if she had gotten with him instead of Mali. Tucker was fine, and she envied the kind of relationship Keisha had with him.

They were exclusive, and he adored her, so she couldn't understand why Keisha, or anyone else for that matter, would jeopardize perfection to get dicked down by some cornball with muscles. Even though she couldn't remember exactly what happened, she knew without a doubt that her strong influence on Keisha could have prevented her from making such a big mistake.

Still looking down at the hardwood floor, Tucker shook his head and finally broke his silence.

"Keish, I can't . . . can't fuck with you like that. You can stay here if you want, as long as you want. Just be a good mother to my son. That's all I ask. I'll still pay the bills, take care of my son, and do what I gotta do. But this is my house, and I'll come and go as I please, so don't be bringing no niggas up in here. You got that?"

Keisha didn't answer. She just stood in front of him with her arms folded, tapping her feet while the tears continuously rolled down her face.

"Go get you some rest. You can put my stuff back when you wake up." Tucker got up and walked out the front door.

"Keisha?" Epiphany called out as she stepped down to the middle of the stairs, where she saw Keisha balled up on the couch, crying.

Keisha didn't answer.

Chapter 69

When Shana got home, K.C. was in the bed ,knocked out sleeping. The eight apple martinis she'd had at the club had her stumbling all over bedroom while trying to undress. Easing herself into bed, she stared at K.C. with disgust while he slept. Considering he had chosen not to come home the night before, she was furious.

Hopping up out of bed, Shana was looking for a fight. Creeping over to K.C.'s side of the bed, where his pants rested on the floor, she kneeled down and checked his pockets in search of condoms or anything that might indicate that he was fucking around. Deep down inside she didn't want to believe that he was, but she wasn't about to sleep on him neither.

Shana then took his cell phone from its charger and headed to the bathroom with it. She closed the door and turned on the faucet to drown out the sound of the keys on the phone as she pushed them to check the call history of all his incoming and outgoing calls.

No incoming or outgoing calls all day. Bullshit. She found it ironic that no data appeared on the screen. From that, she assumed he was guilty of foul play. Shana stormed back to the bedroom and threw K.C.'s phone at him, scaring him up out of his sleep.

"Bitch, what the fuck is wrong with you?" he yelled.

"You, muthafucka, that's what. Where the fuck did you stay at last night?"

"Man, come on with all that bullshit. I tell you one thing: You throw something else at me like that again and watch me beat the shit out of you," K.C. threatened.

"Fuck you, nigga. You better go beat on the ho you was with last night. And why the fuck you erase all the calls off your phone, you sneaky bastard?"

K.C. jumped up and grabbed Shana by her throat, pulling her down to the bed. "You nosy, drunk-ass bitch, keep your hands off my shit! The only reason I did that was to see if your sneaky ass be snooping through my shit."

Shana struggled on the bed as she pulled at his hands, hoping to get him to loosen the tight grip he had around her neck. "Get the fuck off of me," she cried.

"You gon' shut the fuck up, right?" K.C. asked before he let her go, noticing how red her face had turned, along with the tears that were streaming down the sides of her face. He released her and started to laugh. "I bet you'll stay out my shit now, won't you?" K.C. said.

"K.C., just leave me alone," Shana whispered, massaging her neck.

"Ahhh, come here," he said, pulling her toward him, "I'm sorry, but you did hit me first." K.C. pleaded his case as he began to fondle Shana's breast.

"K.C., stop it."

"What the fuck you mean, stop it? This is mine right here." He grabbed in between her legs. "Right?" Looking dead in her face, he waited for the correct answer to come out of her mouth.

"Yeah, but—"

"A'ight then. Ain't no buts."

"K.C., for real, all jokes aside, are you fucking around on me?"

"Yo, why you bugging the fuck out with all this bullshit?" K.C. said, shaking his head, but still avoiding her question.

"I knew you was. You can't even answer the fucking question," Shana said, pushing his arms off of her so she could pull herself up.

"Sha, where you think you going? I ain't fucking no other bitch. Stop tripping and chill out, a'ight?"

"Yeah, a'ight." Shana was still not convinced, but she knew it was a no-win situation.

"Good. Now, here. Taste daddy. Make a nigga feel good since you woke me up," he said, wiggling his hardness from side to side.

***

Later that afternoon, Shana was still sleeping when K.C. came in the bedroom, already dressed and smelling like weed. He tugged roughly on her shoulder.

"Yo, Sha, wake up. Come on, get up and fix me and the fellas something to eat."

"Stop. Come on, no. I'm tired," Shana barked, pulling the covers up over her head.

"Yo, get up and feed a nigga. That's my word, yo, you slipping on your wifely duties. You don't do shit around this muthafucka. Get up!" he yelled, snatching the covers off of her.

"You get on my fucking nerves." Shana sucked her teeth, put on her sweats, and headed for the kitchen.

"I don't give a fuck. After you feed me, you can leave. And yo, I don't eat no pork."

Shana didn't bother to respond. He knew damn well that she didn't fuck with swine no more. K.C. was no doubt an asshole, but part of his performance was for the benefit of his boys, Smitty and some new jack nigga named Ness, who were sitting in her living room. They seemed to find his disrespect toward her entertaining.

Shana was still paying Smitty and still trying to figure out how to get out of that situation. She couldn't stand him, and K.C. was on her shit list too. She didn't know shit about this new cat Ness, except he was paid, and rumor had it he was the one that ran C-God out of town. One thing was for certain: Her vibes never lied, and if he hung with those two, he was up to no good as well.

Chapter 70

"Keisha, I know you ain't gon' keep moping around here like it's the end of the fucking world. You got to get it together, girl. Come on, get up. Your hanging out with me tonight," Epiphany said.

"No, I'm really not up for it."

"Keisha, how long are you gonna sit here feeling so damn sorry for yourself that you can't even get up and go wash your ass? You need to get up, take a nice hot bath, and come on out and have some fun. You don't even have to worry about finding anything to wear 'cause I already took care of that at the mall earlier, so come on."

"Epiphany, where are we supposed to be going?"

"Out!"

"Out where?"

"To Lotus." Epiphany started pulling the covers off of Keisha.

"On a Monday night?"

"Yeah, girl, that's the night it be jumping. And damn, do it matter? You act like you got a job to be at in the morning or something. What's with all the questions anyway? You ain't got shit to do but sit up in here and be crazy depressed. You might as well get used to going out and meeting people. I'm pretty sure Tucker's doing it."

"I guess you're right. Shoot, let me see that outfit," Keisha said, absorbing all of Epiphany's advice.

"That's my girl. Now go wash your stinking ass, 'cause we gon' party like it's your birthday." Epiphany started singing a verse from "In Da Club" by 50 Cent.

That night was just the beginning. Epiphany and Keisha were doing the club thing hard. Every night of the week there was something popping off in the "City that Never Sleeps," and those two were there.

Shana kicked it with them a few times, but like always, she was off doing her own thing. For Keisha, getting her party on was just what the doctor ordered. She couldn't remember the last time she had so much fun. She even arranged for her son to stay in Atlanta for at least two more weeks, and the more she got her club on, the less she thought about Tucker.

One night, they were out at this spot named Cream. Epiphany noticed these three guys at the bar buying Hennessy Privilege by the bottle.

Yeah, this is Privilege too, she thought, since they all seemed to be checking her out so hard. It got to a point were their stares started making her feel uncomfortable, like maybe they knew her or something. Then she saw Keisha walk over and talk to one of the guys.

Okay, now's the perfect time to go over and find out what's really good. Epiphany pranced over to the bar where they all were standing.

"Girl, I was looking all over for you," said Epiphany, putting her arm around Keisha.

"You was? Oh, I was in that damn bathroom on that long-ass line waiting to pee. Anyway, you remember K.C., right?" asked Keisha.

"His face looks familiar, but I can't really recall where I know him from."

"Girl, this is Shana's man. You don't remember him?" Keisha questioned.

Epiphany rolled her eyes and gave Keisha the "Hello, stupid, that's what amnesia means" look.

"Oh, damn. Sorry, girl. I forgot all about that," Keisha said, realizing what that look meant.

"Hi, K.C. I'm sure Shana told you about my little accident, right?"

"Yeah, she ran that by me. How you making out though?" K.C. questioned.

"I'm okay. Thanks for asking," Epiphany answered.

Meanwhile, Smitty and Ness kept their backs turned to avoid any chances of her remembering them. Although they had already been aware of Epiphany's memory loss, they didn't want to take any chances.

"Yo, B, that bitch really don't remember us," Ness whispered with a boyish giggle.

"Man, you believe that shit?" said Smitty, not easily buying into that amnesia act.

"Nah, that bitch don't remember! She got more than a good look at me to recognize who the fuck I am, plus that weak-ass nigga C said my name. She badder than a muthafucka, though."

"Yeah, I used to fuck with her. The pussy good, too. Word up, I can definitely vouch for that shit," said Smitty with a laugh. "Shit, matter of fact, nigga, I can drink to that," he added.

"Yo, you a funny muthafucka." Ness laughed.

"Where's Shana?" Keisha asked K.C.

"I don't know. She was home when I left. I'm surprised she ain't with y'all."

"So, K.C., who's your friends? 'Cause they were staring me down when I was standing over there by myself. Now I'm over here and they act like they're to scared to turn around and say hello," Epiphany said, being as blunt and bold as always.

"Oh, those my niggas. They ain't never scared. Right, fellas? Tell this pretty lady y'all ain't scared," said K.C.

"Nah, shorty, ain't nobody scared over here. We just over here talking business, you know. A'ight, love, nothing personal." Ness turned to face her while Smitty kept his back toward her.

"A'ight. Well, come on, Keish. Let's not keep the boys from discussing man shit. Later, K.C." Epiphany grabbed Keisha's arm and began to pull her away.

"Okay, take care, K.C.," Keisha said as she was being whisked away.

"You see, that's exactly why I couldn't fuck with that bitch. That mouth of hers is off the chain." Smitty fronted to his boys like it was his choice and not his actions that caused her not to fuck with him.

***

"Girl, why you do that? That guy was kinda cute," Keisha said, referring to Ness.

"Please, no he wasn't. Girl, I got to teach you how to separate the fakes from the real ballers. That was a fake one," Epiphany said, rolling her eyes.

"Ooh, come on, E, there's the cameraman. Let's go take a picture," Keisha said.

"Whew! Look at you pretty ladies," said the camera-man as he snapped several pictures of the girls. "Okay ladies," he continued, "log on to allnightclubs.com tomorrow afternoon and look for your photos."

"Oh, so they're gonna be online?" asked Epiphany.

"Yes, ma'am, every picture I take is posted at that Web site," answered the cameraman.

"Cool," replied Keisha.

"Come on, Keish. Ain't nothing really happening in here. Let's bounce," Epiphany said as she sucked her teeth to express her disappointment with the club's crowd.

On the way out, they spotted K.C. in the corner, kissing some hood rat–looking bitch.

"Hold up, E, ain't that K.C. over there, all on that girl like that?" asked Keisha.

"Oooooh, yes the fuck it is," Epiphany confirmed.

"Uh-uh, I'm going over to say something," said Keisha.

"No, don't. I got a better idea. Wait right here." Epiphany walked back over to the photographer.

"Excuse me. How good is the zoom on your camera?"

"It's excellent. Why?" answered the cameraman.

"I got fifty bucks for you if you could zoom in on the guy over there in the corner with that girl and snap a picture for me, but you got to put it on the Web."

"No problem," agreed the cameraman as he took the crisp fifty-dollar bill and slide it into his side pocket, zoomed in on the target, and snapped a perfect shot.

"Thanks," Epiphany said as she walked back toward Keisha, wearing a devious grin.

"Damn, E, you still scandalous." Keisha laughed.

"Yep! A picture *is* worth a thousand words."

The girls left the club and headed home. Fortunately for them, the night had turned out to be eventful after all.

Chapter 71

"Please don't hurt me," Epiphany cried out as she laid balled up in a fetal position, trying to shield herself from the kicks and punches that were landing one after another, bruising and paining her body. Suddenly it stopped, but Epiphany was too scared to hold up her head to see what was going on.

"Damn, son, you fucking that ho up." An unrecognizable male's voice laughed. More than one person was present.

There was a moment of silence, and just as Epiphany began to slightly lift her head to see what was going on and who was doing it, the telephone rang, waking her from the horrible nightmare. She rolled over on her back, relieved that it was all just a bad dream.

"Keisha, answer your phone." Epiphany realized she was in Keisha's guest bedroom. "Damn it. Hello?" Epiphany grabbed the receiver with an irritated tone.

"Yeah, what took you so long to answer the phone?" Tucker asked.

"What? Who is this?" Epiphany snapped, not realizing that it could only be Tucker calling.

"Who is this?" Tucker snapped back.

"Listen, you called here; therefore you need to announce yourself, or I'm hanging up."

"Bitch, that's my phone you answering. Now get my son's mother on the phone," Tucker said angrily.

"Oops! Sorry, Tucker, I didn't know it was you. This is Epiphany," she said, not knowing that she had just added fuel to Tucker's fire. He despised her.

"Yeah, yeah, yeah, just call Keish to the phone."

"Hey, T, I know you're sore about what happened to Mali, but you're not the only one feeling the pain of his death, you know."

"Call Keish to the fucking phone."

"I already tried that before I picked up, so obviously she
ain't here, and hopefully I won't forget to let her know you
called. Bye, now." Epiphany grew furious from his response
and hung up the phone.

Getting up, she headed to Keisha's bedroom. Since the door
was slightly open, Epiphany peeked in before entering.

"Keisha, wake up. Get up, girl," Epiphany said loudly as she
plopped down on what used to be Tucker's side of the bed.

"What?" replied Keisha, frowning up her face when the
scent of her morning breath mixed with last night's alcohol
hit her nose.

"Tucker just called for you."

"He did? What did he say?"

"Well, first off, he wasn't too thrilled with me answering his
phone," Epiphany admitted.

"Why? What did you say?" asked Keisha.

"I was trying to be nice, but he was the one acting all nasty,
so I told him you wasn't here."

"Girl, it's eight o'clock in the morning. You know what he
gon' think," said Keisha.

"And so what? Let him think it. I'm telling you, if you start
acting like you moved on, trust me, he'll be back."

"You think so?"

"Yes, I do. Trust me when I tell you. If I don't know nothing else, I know niggas. I'm telling you, I could write a book
on their asses. They may come in all shapes, sizes, and colors,
but they all think the same. Girl, please believe me." If there
was one thing that Epiphany didn't lose, it was her confidence.

"Seriously, Keish, does Tucker think I killed Malikai?"

"No, but he does think that maybe you had something to do
with it," answered Keisha.

"And what do you think, Keisha?"

"Come on, girl. Me and you go way back, like pimps and
Cadillacs." Keisha laughed, covering her mouth with her
sheets.

"I know that, but you still ain't answer the question,"
Epiphany continued.

"No, Epiphany, I don't think you had anything to do with Malikai getting murdered." Keisha stopped laughing. She realized that her friend was really worried.

"Good, because even though I don't remember what happened, I know in my heart I didn't have anything to do with that." Tears began to puddle up in her eyes.

"I know, and that's exactly what I told T, so don't even worry about it, girl. He's just bitter right now because he wasn't able to save Mali, that's all." Keisha sat up and put her arm around Epiphany.

"Before the phone woke me up, I was having this terrible dream, but I don't think it was just a dream. I think maybe it really happened.

"What was it about?"

"I really don't want to get into details right now, but just as I was about to see their faces, the phone rang and I woke up."

"Do you think your memory is trying to come back?"

"I don't know, but I hope so," said Epiphany just as the phone rang again, breaking her train of thought. "You better answer it this time, 'cause I'm sure it's Tucker calling you back," said Epiphany as she got up to leave the room.

"Hello?" Keisha answered.

"What's up, girly?" said the cheery voice on the other end of the line.

"Um, who is this?"

"It's Lea, girl!"

"Oh, hey, Lea. I ain't heard from you in a while."

"I know, girl. I've been so tied up with finals and all that, but I've been meaning to call you for a while now. Why haven't you been to class? You busy planning that wedding of yours?"

"No, the wedding is off," answered Keisha.

"Why? What's up with that? You guys are still going to get married, right?" Lea questioned.

"Lea, don't act like you don't know about the tape."

"What tape?"

"Come on, Lea. Don't you think it's a little ironic that you begged me to have that party and those strippers? *'Oh, come on, Keisha, you can go to the club anytime. This might be the last time you see some dicks slinging in your face.'*

Remember that? Then all of a sudden a video tape from that night shows up on my fucking doorstep." Keisha's voice was getting louder.

"Keisha, I can't believe that you would think that I would do something like that." Lea was taken aback by Keisha's accusation.

"Okay, so if you didn't set me up, why haven't you called me until now?"

"I told you why—school. Besides, Simone told me she spoke to you and things were cool with you."

"Whatever, Lea, school has never stopped you from calling me before."

"Keisha, if you really wanna get technical, most of our conversations took place in school. I never really called you at home in the first place, except for once or twice to talk about your wedding. But you know what? It's sad that out of everybody there that night you would accuse me. What about the other girls? Simone, helped me put the whole thing together. Or how about the girl that came with you? What about your friend Epiphany? She was the last one to leave the room."

"Well, Epiphany wouldn't do that to me. Neither would Shana and Simone. Come on. She doesn't even seem like the type that would do something like that."

"Oh, and I would?"

"Well, at first I didn't think you would, but the room was in your name; therefore, you had time to set up a camcorder before anybody got there."

"Oh, is that right? Well, you know what, Keisha? I'm not going to sit here and try to defend myself any longer. If you think I did it, fine. But I certainly didn't force you in the other room and make you have sex with that guy, now, did I?" Keisha was speechless. "Yeah, that's what I thought," Lea said sarcastically before hanging up the phone.

If that wasn't enough drama for one morning, soon after she hung up with Lea, Tucker came barging into her bedroom.

"Keish, what the fuck is that bitch doing in my house, huh? What is it with you? You think I'm that nigga, don't you?

That's what it is, huh? Just some muthafucka that you could all run over, right? I guess 'cause I ain't knock some sense into you yet. Are you testing me? Fuck me, right? You ain't got no fucking respect for me, do you?"

"What are you talking about?" Keisha said, playing the stupid role when she knew exactly why he was upset. That only made Tucker more furious, so furious that he snapped and slapped the shit out of her.

She let out a horrifying cry. Tucker had never put his hands on her before, nor had she ever expected him to.

"Yeah, you know what I'm talking about now, don't you? Where the fuck is my son at, huh? He was supposed to come home yesterday. I called your moms and she told me some bogus bullshit about you needing two more weeks. Two more weeks for what, Keisha? To hop your ass in and out the clubs? Yeah, I heard. So that's what you wanna do, huh, club hop?"

Still stunned from being slapped, Keisha didn't answer. Her face was beginning to swell. She sat there massaging her cheek with one hand, soothing the stinging and wiping her tears away with the other hand.

"All you do is cry, Keisha. I don't care about those fucking tears of yours. I've been trying to be cool throughout everything, but no, you stay pushing my fucking buttons. Damn, Keish, how much is a nigga supposed to take from you?" Tucker was fed up with Keisha's bull, and in his heart, he was beginning to feel like she really had no respect for him anymore. She didn't appreciate him or anything he did for her, so as far as he was concerned, it was time to let her go, move on, and put an end to the 'Tucker and Keisha" chapter of his life for good.

"Keish, you got to go!" Tucker realized that was the best and only decision to make.

"What? What do you mean?"

"I mean I'm not taking care of you no more. My son is my responsibility, not you."

"Wait a minute. My name is on this house too. How you just gon' put me out like that, T? I'm your son's mother. Where are we supposed to go?" Keisha pleaded.

"Keisha, I told you before, I'm not trying to hear all that. This is my house. I pay all the bills. Your name don't mean shit, so stop it. It's not gonna fly, and if you feel differently, take me to court. Okay! Now, yes, you are my son's mother, and I will take care of all my little man's needs—there's no questions about that—but you got two more weeks to yourself. I suggest you spend them looking for a place to stay."

Keisha wasn't gonna fight it anymore. Time and time again, Tucker had made it clear that it was over between them. She packed some of her things, and as she was about to leave, he asked for her keys. She removed them slowly from her keychain and threw them on the bed.

"Hold up. I'ma need the keys to the truck too," he added, taking it to the extreme. Keisha cut her eyes at him. *I hate you,* she thought as she tossed the whole keychain onto the bed and stormed off.

"Thank you," Tucker said sarcastically.

Meanwhile, just when Tucker asked Keisha for the keys, Epiphany felt her ears had heard enough. She eased down the stairs, grabbed her bags, and decided it would be best if she sat outside in her car and waited for Keisha. She didn't wanna be the next one to get slapped.

Chapter 72

C-God was slowly fading away, getting high whenever he could. Money was starting to get tight. Marisa lost her job at the grocery store and made her bills become his problem. C-God wasn't supplying her with any more coke, so she jumped on the band wagon and started sucking on the glass pipe with him. In Marisa's mind, it was only for a little while, just until she lost some weight, but if only she knew, dropping the weight would be the easy part. The addiction had a hell of a price to pay, and her children were the first to suffer. Why? Because getting high became more important to her than their needs. Most of the time she stayed locked up in her bedroom for hours with C-God, smoking crack while the kids' knocks for food, help with the homework, or just some quality time went ignored. Her children hated C-God and blamed him for their mother's neglect.

Reggie still communicated with C-God from time to time, to see how he was doing. Although he chose to roll with Ness for money purposes, he still had love for the nigga C. C-God understood that it wasn't about him. He knew Reggie had a lot on his plate, trying to take care of his grandmother, who he loved dearly, and hustling daily through rain, sleet, and snow to get up the dough to take care of her bills and pay the live-in nurse.

Reg kept C-God informed about what was going on and the moves niggas was making in the hood. He was the eyes and ears on the street that C-God no longer had. His information was priceless.

C-God was surprised when Reg called and told him how his baby moms Latrice went out.

"Yo, son, they played Latrice," said Reggie.

"Who?"

"That nigga Ness, man. Out in front of the projects the other day, he had her sucking on a dog's dick for that crack. Shit, in front of everybody, too, just 'cause she was short a dollar. Yo, C, I tried to stop her, but she wanted them drugs bad."

C-God was quiet. He flashed back to how fly Latrice used to be and that smart mouth of hers. All the ballers had tried to get at her back in the day, but she chose C-God when he ain't have a pot to piss in or a window to throw it out of, and he loved her for that; that was, until he started getting money and the gold diggers took notice. His excuse for moving on to the next chick was Latrice's jealousy and crazed antics after giving birth to their first child.

Reminiscing made C-God think about all his baby mommas. To let him tell it, all of them were some bugged-out bitches. Latrice and Sherri had lost custody of his kids, Lori and Jasmine, because of their crack addictions. Andrea married some Wall Street cat, who adopted C-God's seven-year-old daughter, Atria, and moved them out to the Hamptons. Kim had a good paying city job, but was always trying to hit him up for money for their son, Corey, who was seven also.

Then Yolonda's weed-smoking, welfare-collecting ass did nothing but get her fuck on with different niggas and threatened C with child support orders every chance she got. Sad to say, out of all of them, she was the one that had C-God open. He had made her his wifey before finding out how whorish she really was, and to this day, he still questioned if he was the father of her daughters, Kameechie and Yaya.

Last, but not least, there was Tanya. She was a good girl, smart and educated. C-God never had no problems with her. She was still young, so she did what she was told, and she had a strong, supportive family. They all took good care of his son.

"Yo, C, you there?" Reggie wasn't certain C was still on the phone. He had been silent for a minute.

"Yeah, I'm here. Anyway, fuck Latrice. Tanya's the only one out all them bitches that I give a fuck about. That's why I need you to check up on her from time to time and make sure she's good, a'ight? Do that for me until I get on my feet."

"Not a problem," Reggie said.

"Oh, and one more thing: Any word on Epiphany, you know the chick I was fucking with?" C-God asked.

"Yeah, I know who you talking about. I hear she a'ight. As a matter of fact, her pops came through the projects a couple of times looking for you."

"Word? I know what that's about, but it wasn't me. I'm glad she a'ight, though. Anyway, thanks. Good looking out, fam."

"It's nothing. I'ma holla at you later, a'ight?" said Reg.

"A'ight, man."

Chapter 73

Shana was so upset after Epiphany and Keisha called to tell her about K.C.'s behavior at the club the other night. Keisha had the proof, but didn't have access to a computer in order to print it out.

"What's wrong with your computer, Keish?" Shana questioned.

"Nothing. I'm staying with Epiphany for a while," answered Keisha.

"Shana, you can use my computer as soon as my pops gets my stuff out of storage." Epiphany offered.

"And when is that?"

"Probably next week, once he's done fixing up the basement for me and Keisha," Epiphany answered.

"Shit, I can't wait that long."

"So, what you gonna do, huh? Tell him we told you?" asked Epiphany.

"I don't know what I'm gonna do, but I know I ain't gon' be able to hold this shit in for a week," replied Shana.

"See, that's some bullshit. We look out for you and you gonna tell the nigga. If it was meant to go down like that, I wouldn't have paid the cameraman fifty dollars," Epiphany complained.

"Yo, I'll give you your fifty dollars back. That's not a problem," Shana said.

"You're right. The money ain't the problem. It's your fucking mouth," said Epiphany.

"Fuck you, Epiphany. Don't tell me shit next time," yelled Shana.

"Fuck you, too. I won't. Believe that."

"Come on, you guys. This ain't necessary—and Shana, Epiphany is right this time. It ain't cool for you to rat us out like that and have your man hating on us," Keisha explained.

"So what am I supposed to do, go out and buy a computer just so I can confront his ass?" Shana said sarcastically.

"No, we can go to Kinko's and use their Internet access," Keisha suggested.

"That'll work, but why didn't you suggest that in the first place?" Shana asked.

"Because I just thought about it while you and Epiphany were going at it. Now, can you two apologize, please?" said Keisha.

"I'm sorry, E," Shana said nonchalantly.

"Whatever. Just get me my fifty bucks," said Epiphany, still wanting to hold a grudge.

"Yo, Keish, you see what I mean? Fuck that bi—"

Before she could finish, Keisha took the phone off speaker and picked up the receiver, while Shana continued to express how she felt about Epiphany.

"Shana, just come and get me, all right? I don't have my car," said Keisha, changing the subject and calming Shana down.

"A'ight, I'm on my way," said Shana.

When Shana arrived, she called Keisha on her cell to let her know she was out front.

"Hey, E, I'll be back. Shana's out front," Keisha said.

"Yeah, a'ight. Get my money from that bitch, please," Epiphany replied.

"Uh-huh." Keisha walked out, shaking her head, not able to understand why the two of them just couldn't get along.

Once Keisha left, Epiphany went outside and sat on the stoop of her parents' house, which was something she hadn't done since she was a kid. It had to be about ninety degrees out. The sun was blazing. As she watched the kids on the corner running in and out of the fire hydrant, laughing, playing, and having a good time while trying to stay cool, she remembered some things. This time, it was clear.

She could recall taking a home pregnancy test and it being positive, the pain she felt from all his kicks and punches, but most importantly she could remember his face.

"It was C-God," she mumbled as her memory confirmed the beliefs of her father and Keisha.

Epiphany felt awful. It just didn't make sense to her at all, and there was still a lot of information missing.

Why did he try to kill me? she thought. *Was it because I found out I was pregnant? Or maybe it was Mali's baby. No, Keisha said I stopped seeing Malikai months ago. So maybe I wasn't really—*

The ring of her cell phone broke her heavy train of thought. It was someone calling from a 323 area code.

Where the fuck is 323?

"Hello?" Epiphany answered.

"What up, beautiful?" said the man's voice.

"You got the beautiful part right, but who is this?" she responded.

"Damn, ma, you forgot about me already, huh? It's Wild. How you doing?"

"Oh, hey, I'm good. I thought you forgot about me."

"Nah, never that. I just been tied up out here in L.A., trying to blaze some tracks, that's all."

"Oh, so when you coming back to NY?"

"I'm flying in tonight, late night, but I was hoping we could get together sometime tomorrow."

"Well, call me tomorrow and I'll let you know." Epiphany didn't want to seem as anxious as she really was.

"Oh, you'll let me know, huh? Why you can't just say yeah now?"

"Because I'm gonna be kind of busy tomorrow. I don't wanna commit to anything now and then have to disappoint you later. You know what I'm saying? It's called having consideration," Epiphany said with sarcasm.

"I'll see you tomorrow, early, so we could spend all day and night together. A'ight, shorty?" Wild disregarded her weak excuse.

His confidence turned her on and brought a smile to her face. "Yeah, okay. I'll see you tomorrow. Bye"

Wild's call had completely taken her mind off of her revelations—well, maybe not completely, but Epiphany was starting to feel like the more she remembered about her past and its horrid details, the less she wanted to remember.

Maybe it's best to just put it all behind me. Besides, no one has seen or heard from C-God anyway.

Chapter 74

Once Shana dropped Keisha back off at Epiphany's parents' house, she went home and waited impatiently for K.C. to get his ass home. She sat on the couch, staring at the glossy Kodak print of him all over some high yellow bitch who looked like she might have been cute if she didn't suffer from a severe case of acne. She was ticked off, but the funny thing about the whole situation was that she already had a gut feeling that he was fucking around on her. If that wasn't enough evidence, her suffering from dick deprivation should have been another clue. It seemed like the only time he wanted to fuck her was when she wanted to argue about his bullshit behavior. Shana wasn't happy. K.C. was obviously doing him, the bitch in the photo, and whoever else he was out there screwing, but it certainly wasn't her.

I can't believe I'm still paying that muthafucka Smitty. For what? To keep a dumb little secret from a nigga that don't even want to be kept.

Just as that thought ran through Shana's mind, she heard K.C.'s keys rattling at the door. Quickly, she laid the photo down right in front of her on the coffee table, just to see how long it would take him to notice it.

When he walked in, he wasn't alone. Smitty trailed in right behind him. Instantly, her attitude got worse. Sucking her teeth, she snatched up the picture, not wanting Smitty all up in their business, although he most likely knew way more dirt than she could ever imagine.

"What up, Sha?" K.C. said as he placed his car keys and cell phone down on the coffee table, right in the same spot as the photo.

"I need to talk to you, but I see you got your shadow with you," Shana said, giving K.C. the head movement and eye-rolling treatment.

"Well, hello to you to, Sha," Smitty said to further aggravate her.

Shana just rolled her eyes again and waited for K.C.'s response.

"Yeah, so can't it wait?" K.C. asked.

"No, it can't fucking wait. I'm tired of being put on hold for this muthafucka," she said, pointing at Smitty. "So either you excuse him, or I'll say what the fuck I gotta say right in front of him."

"Yo, Smitty, you see what the fuck I gotta deal with all the time? Yo, I'm telling you, a nigga be trying to keep from fucking a bitch up," K.C. said, feeling like Shana was trying to punk him in front of his boy. His nose began to flare, and he balled his fist tightly, trying to compose his anger.

"Yeah, nigga, I feel you, but yo, I'm out. You need to get that shit under wraps, dawg, 'cause word up, she stay with an attitude." Smitty added his two cents as usual.

"I'ma handle this, but just hit me later," K.C. said.

"Who the fuck is this bitch, huh?" Shana raised her voice as soon as he shut the door behind Smitty. Waving the photo in K.C.'s face, she demanded an answer. "Yeah, muthafucka you busted."

K.C. looked closely at the picture and laughed. "Where you get that from? I don't know who she is, and that ain't me."

"You'se a lying ass. So, that's how you gon' go out, huh? You can't even be a man and admit the shit you do. Who is she, K.C.?"

"Yo, I'm out, man, because you be bugging the fuck out, and I'm telling you, you gon' make me fuck you up." K.C. reached for his car keys on the table.

Shana made a quick dash for the keys, along with his cell phone, and hauled ass to the bedroom, locking the door behind her.

"Now, muthafucka, you wanna play games? Let's play games. You ain't going no-fucking-where. I got your phone and your key, so if you want your shit back, you better start confessing, nigga," Shana yelled from the other side of the door while trying to catch her breath from that Olympic sprint she'd just made.

"Bitch, don't fuck with me. Open the door and give me my shit," K.C. shouted as he tried to kick down the door. "Yo, wait 'til I open this door, Shana. I'ma—" K.C. had to catch his breath. "Yo, I think you be wanting a nigga to fuck you up. You like that shit, huh? Open this fucking door!"

Shana ignored his threats and continued to question the girl's identity, while he stood on the other side of the bedroom door, trying to figure out a way to pick the lock or bust through it. Inside, she prayed hard that the door would not give way.

"Let me see . . . Kiana. Who the fuck is Kiana? Latrell, Meeka, Valerie . . ." Shana called out each female's name as she scrolled down and deleted them out of his phone, one by one. "Just tell me who this chick in the picture is. I see you've been real busy lately, but where was all these hoes at when your ass was locked up, huh? I can't do this shit no more, K.C.!" Shana screamed.

"Ahhh, come on, Sha." K.C. showed a little compassion for her feelings. "Listen, Sha, them bitches don't mean shit to me, a'ight. I'll admit, occasionally I might fuck around on you, but that shit don't mean that I don't love you. You just need to understand that I was married to this drug game shit, the streets, and everything in it, long before you, and on the real, those are the only things I know how to be committed to. The streets ain't never going nowhere, and 'cause of that, a nigga like me gon' always get paper."

"K.C., what does all of that have to do with you fucking around on me?"

"Sha, didn't I just say I don't give a fuck about those bitches? They just hoes that come along with the game. I made you my wife, but you need to accept me for the nigga I am and the fucked-up shit I do, because at the end of the day, I'm coming home to you. Yeah, I fucked up the other night, but I was out all night handling business. Sha, you held me down when I was fucked up, so I ain't gon' never play you. Now open the door."

"K.C., I'm not gonna open the door until you tell me who this girl is."

"Yo, are you hearing what I said to you? She ain't nobody, Sha, so stop dwelling on that ho and open the door. Come on, yo, I ain't gonna do nothing to you. I just wanna chill with you, a'ight? Open the door."

Shana unlocked the door and slowly backed away from it, just in case he came in swinging. Fortunately for Shana, K.C. had already gotten over being mad thirty minutes ago. Besides, the number one rule in the players manual is to always treat the one you love better than the hoes you fuck. He knew that in order to keep the peace, he had to take care of home first, and he hadn't been holding down that part. So, for the rest of the evening, he did some serious making up, in hopes that Shana would get off his back for a while.

Chapter 75

"Yo, how I get to you?" Wild said as soon a Epiphany picked up her cell phone.

"Well, hello to you, too," Epiphany said as she glanced over at the clock, which read 9:00 a.m.

"Oh, my bad. Hello, pretty. Now how do I get to you once I hit Queens?"

Epiphany smiled, liking his persistence, and gave him directions.

"A'ight, I should be there in like forty-five minutes, and bring a few things, just in case I decide to kidnap you for a couple of days."

"Okay, I'll see you when you get here." After ending the call, Epiphany excitedly jumped out of bed to search through her many clothes for the right outfits to pack. She decided to wear her hot pink Roberto Cavalli sundress, along with her Prada sandals and matching purse. She packed three other cute outfits that showed expensive taste, class, and style, because by no means did she want him to think she was anything less than fabulous.

Keisha was awakened by the noise Epiphany made as she rushed to get herself together.

"Girl, where you going?" she asked.

"Oh, remember the guy that I was chillin' with at Suede, the producer I told you about?"

"Yeah," Keisha said.

"Well, I'll be with him for a couple of days," answered Epiphany.

"I hear that. Have fun. I got me a date tonight too," boasted Keisha.

"Get out! You mean to tell me that you finally decided to move on? With who?"

"With this guy I met at Kinko's yesterday with Shana."

"He works in Kinko's?" Epiphany said, not even trying to hide her disgust.

"No, he repairs computers for Kinko's. Anyway, I don't care where he works, just as long as he works, because I think I'm done with drug dealers."

"I hear that. To each his own. Anyway, what's his name?"

"His name is Rob. He's a cutie."

"Well, good for you, Keish. You need to get out and have some fun, make sure that nigga spends his paycheck. Let me go shower before Wild gets here." Epiphany was happy for her friend but abruptly ended their conversation, running to the bathroom to freshen up.

Wild pulled in front of Epiphany's parents' crib and phoned her to come outside. When she reached the front door, she fell in love with his sparkling silver Hummer—not the affordable Hummer H2. This was the real deal.

"What's up, sexy? Don't I get a kiss?" asked Wild as he held the car door open for her.

"Nah, I don't kiss on the first date." Epiphany laughed.

"I respect that."

"Good." Epiphany played it cool, but in her mind she was screaming, *Fuck a kiss! I'm gonna fuck the shit out of this nigga.*

Once they crossed over the George Washington Bridge heading toward Route 4, Wild phoned his cook and told him to start preparing breakfast for two.

"You like omelets?" he asked.

"Yeah, they're all right," Epiphany answered.

"Well, my chef Idris makes some banging-ass omelets. You'll love 'em."

Twenty minutes later, they pulled up to a tall black gate that Wild opened with a little remote. Epiphany was still trying to get over the fact that he had a chef when he pulled into a four car garage next to a convertible black Bentley.

This is so beautiful, she thought as she looked around the grounds. He got out of the driver's side and rushed over to open the car door for her again. He was being the perfect gentleman. His $2.5 million, eight-bedroom house was located in ultra chic Englewood Cliffs, New Jersey, and came equipped with an in-ground swimming pool, sauna, a huge patio, and a basketball court. Indoors were a gym, a small movie theater, a recording studio, and a game room.

Epiphany had to admit that this was far more impressive than any nice car or house she'd ever seen in her life. This was the type of lifestyle she felt she was born to live. She was tired of dealing with the small-time hustlers in the hood, who were satisfied with the minimum—a little bit of jewelry, a hot ride, fifty grand stashed in an old sneaker box, and a laced-out apartment in the projects, thinking life is sweet. She wanted to live like a celebrity, and if she played her cards right, Mr. Producer Man could be her ticket out of the ghetto.

He escorted her straight to the kitchen for the best breakfast she had ever had. After breakfast, Wild gave Epiphany a personal tour.

This house is definitely made for MTV Cribs, she thought as they entered the master bedroom. It had a brick fireplace, a king size bed with plush feathered pillows, and a matching cream-colored comforter. The bathroom was all marble, with an oval-shaped Jacuzzi and attached shower. His walk-in closet was bigger than the bedroom in Epiphany's old apartment, and being the fashion fanatic that she was, she couldn't help but take a look inside. According to her, you could tell a lot about a person from his or her style of dress.

She couldn't help but hum the tune "Why Don't We Fall in Love" by Amerie. Why not? He had everything she wanted.

Chapter 76

Ness, Smitty, and K.C. were doing the damn thing, making money in the hood. Since other niggas had no real weight in the streets, it was easy. Lately, however, problems were occurring in their own circle.

Smitty had started to feel like Ness was getting beside himself on some real control shit. He kept quiet for a minute, letting the nigga run wild with it, and assumed that maybe it was just a power trip. Ness had never been in a position to call the shots. Smitty decided to let him have his fun before he'd pump his brakes—only Ness was on some Nino Brown–type shit. All of a sudden, the streets were his. He made all the decisions, gave the orders, handled most of the money, and was reckless with his mouth and his decisions.

Now a real troublemaker, he created unnecessary drama with this kid named Righteous from Lefrak City. Ness had an altercation with him at a traffic light one day, 'cause he felt dude disrespected him by cutting in front of him without using his signal.

The truth was, Righteous had shit locked down on his side of Queens, selling top quality cocaine for fifty bucks a pop. The cokeheads loved him, and the crackheads preferred to buy his shit and cook it up themselves, because they got more for their money. Word was spreading around Queens about dude's product and price, and Ness wasn't happy about that. He ain't want nobody getting money in Southside Jamaica, but him. Eventually, Righteous would be a problem.

Ness arranged to meet up with Smitty and K.C. in Ajax Park to discuss how they should handle their competition. When Smitty and K.C. arrived, Ness was on the empty court with his shirt off, shooting hoops.

"Yo, what up, my niggas?" Ness greeted them with a pound.

"Ain't shit," Smitty responded.

"Chilling," answered K.C.

"Yo, Smit, how's shit moving over there by you?" Ness asked.

"Yo, son, shit's been a'ight. Why? What up?"

"Word. What about by you, K?" Ness questioned.

"Everything's straight where I'm at, dawg," K.C. answered.

"Yo, what's up with that kid Righteous? Y'all heard of that nigga?" Ness was still shooting the ball around.

"Yeah, I met dude when I was up north. He's a cool nigga," K.C. said.

"Um, what he do time for?" Ness inquired.

"He caught a one-to-three for some bullshit," K.C. said.

"Well, that nigga should've stayed locked the fuck up, 'cause I don't like him."

"Come on, man. Ain't no need to get caught up in no bull-shit over some nonsense. We don't need that type of heat right now," said Smitty.

"Smit, man, what's up with you? You been on some real sucker shit lately."

"'Cause, man, you be on some bullshit. You getting real loose with the words *I* and *my*. This shit ain't yours alone, nigga. You need to leave all that unnecessary drama alone and try to stay focused on what we doing, dawg."

Smitty couldn't believe that Ness was coming at them like that.

"Unnecessary drama? What the fuck you talking about? That muthafucka just came home and already he trying to interfere with *my* fucking money. Shit ain't going down like that. I ain't gon' let a muthafucka move in on me. Just like I did with that nigga C, niggas gon' know that I ain't that dude. I'ma make an example out of any nigga that tries to step up." Ness sounded like a madman.

"Yo, dawg, just leave that shit alone." K.C. just wanted to drop it already.

"Quite naturally you gon' say that. Nigga, you just fucking stood here and said you was cool with dude, so I ain't even fucking with you right now!"

"Yo, me and that nigga ain't tight. I ain't say I'll break bread with 'im. You're bugging. I could see if that nigga Righteous was trying to get at you, but you hating on the man for trying to eat. What he got going ain't even putting no dents in our pockets, dawg!" K.C. responded.

"Well, I still ain't feeling kid, yo, and I ain't gonna wait until he become a problem. You'se Smitty's man, dawg, so why is you even talking to me anyway, huh?" K.C. didn't feed into Ness's cocky-ass bullshit. He just shook his head, thinking, *This nigga done really bugged the fuck out.*

"Yo, I'm out," Ness said, throwing his shirt back on as he headed toward his Range Rover.

"Fuck y'all pussy-ass niggas," he mumbled, hopping inside his truck.

Everything Smitty and K.C. had said went in one ear and out the other.

The high from the purple haze made him feel like the baddest nigga alive, with murder on the brain. He turned down his radio and slowly crept down the streets of Lefrak housing, approaching the area where Righteous usually hung out.

Ness didn't really know the nigga's description, as far as his height and weight. Their beef took place while they both were driving, and he vaguely remembered his facial features, but that wasn't going to stop his plans. He parked his truck and waited.

"Yo, shorty, c'mere," Ness called out to a young boy around sixteen as he walked past. Ness noticed the kid's hesitation. "C'mere. I ain't gon' do shit to you. For real, I just wanna ask you something."

Not sure whether he could trust Ness's word, the boy slowly walked over toward the truck. His palms started to sweat, and his heart pounded rapidly.

"Yo, li'l man, you scared? I told you I ain't gon' fuck with you. I just want you to do something for me, a'ight?" asked Ness.

The boy slowly nodded his head.

"You talk, little nigga?" Ness asked sarcastically.

This time, the boy answered, "Yeah."

"A'ight, good. That's better. Yo, you know Righteous?"

The boy nodded his head again instead of opening his mouth, making Ness so angry that he started to yell at the kid.

"Yo, man, I thought you said you could fucking talk?"

"I c–can," stuttered the frightened boy.

"Then answer me, nigga, and stop shaking your fucking head. Now yes or no, do you know him?"

"Uh-huh."

"Is he out here right now?"

"Yeah."

"A'ight then, without pointing, where?"

"He across the street in front of the bodega on the corner."

"A'ight, what he got on?" Ness asked.

"I think he got on a green-and-white shirt and some jeans," said the boy.

"You think, or you sure?"

"I'm sure," answered the boy.

"A'ight, good lookin' out. Here." Ness handed the boy five twenty-dollar bills and left him with words of advice, "Toughen up, shorty. Learn how to open your fucking mouth and speak, a'ight?"

The boy didn't answer. He just clutched the bills and took off running, wanting no part of any mess that Ness was up to.

Slowly, Ness drove up to the bodega, and sure enough, he spotted Righteous wearing a green-and-white Celtics jersey, standing in front of the store, hugged up on some chick.

Ness got out of his truck and walked up on him. "Yo, what up, nigga?"

"What up? I know you, dawg?" Righteous slightly pushed his girl to the side. It didn't dawn on him that Ness was the guy from the traffic light. That was some minor bullshit he had brushed off, but Ness didn't look at it that way.

"Nah, son, you don't know me, but we bumped heads a few days ago. I came to tell you that you can't pump that shit you selling around here no more."

"What? Who the fuck is you, dawg? This me over here, nigga. I own Lefrak. I gotta give it to you, you a bold-ass bastard." Righteous was taking Ness for some little clown-ass nigga.

"Oh, word. I'm funny, huh?" Ness quickly pulled out his .38 and unloaded four bullets into dude's chest.

Since their conversation never got loud, no one anticipated any kind of beef, so when the shots rang, the few cats that was around scattered instead of coming to Righteous' defense.

"Yeah, nigga. I'll be funny, but how 'bout that was your last laugh?" asked Ness, calmly pointing his smoking gun at the frantic girl who had been with Righteous.

"Shut the fuck up, bitch!" He silenced her with one to the head and hopped back in his truck, speeding off.

Chapter 77

Keisha kept watching the clock, anticipating her date with Rob. It seemed like time moved extra slow, just because she looked forward to finally moving on.

It had been almost two weeks since Tucker kicked her out, and he hadn't even tried to contact her yet. However, he had managed to call Loretta at least two times a day to check up on their son. Keisha started to get jealous when Loretta would say he called, so her calls slowly started to decrease. She hated the fact that Tucker cared about their son more than he cared about her, when for seven years she was his number one. Now she felt invisible. It wasn't that she didn't love her son, because she did with all her heart, but she felt the three of them were *supposed* to be a family.

Keisha wanted a reason to hate Tucker. She started to blame him for what she felt she missed out on—her teenage years. That didn't work. Regardless of how bad she tried to paint the picture, she couldn't ignore the fact that Tucker never put restrictions on her and was only guilty of taking care of her and providing a comfortable life for both of them. She had a good man, and she hated herself more and more for cheating.

Out of spite, Keisha felt it would be best if her son stayed in Atlanta with her mother. *If Tucker can't find it in his heart to forgive me, so we could raise our son together, then he'll never see him again.*

Rob was in front of the house beeping his horn at exactly eight o'clock on the dot. Mrs. Wright rushed over to the window to see who was in front of her house, blowing his horn like a darn fool, when Keisha came running toward the door.

"Is that for you, Keisha?" she asked.

"Yeah, I think so."

"I should hope not, 'cause a real man would get out the car and ring the bell," Mrs. Wright said.

"I'm sorry, Mrs. T. Maybe he isn't sure which house to come to," Keisha said as she went out the door.

"Hey, Rob." Keisha was wearing a big smile once she got in his car.

"What's up, baby?" he responded.

She giggled and then answered, "Nothing."

"So, where you wanna go?"

"Wherever you wanna go."

"Well, I was thinking we could make this a Blockbuster night."

"Blockbuster night, huh? Well, I haven't been out in a long time, so what kind of date is that?" she asked.

"That's you, me, and a movie from Blockbuster at my crib."

That ain't no real date, she thought, but if his company could help take her mind off Tucker, then why not?

"Okay," she replied.

Rob's studio apartment looked like a real bachelor's pad—no sense of style, everything was black or gray, and he didn't appear to be a neat person, especially, since he had to push a pile of dirty clothes off the bed for Keisha to have a seat.

"Okay, which movie do you want to see: *The Italian Job* or *Unfaithful?*"

There was no way Keisha was gonna sit and watch a movie about a woman cheating on her man, so she selected *The Italian Job.* Rob popped in the DVD, pressed play, and before the previews could finish, he was all over Keisha. He started to kiss on her neck as he ran his hand slowly between her closed thighs.

Keisha let out a soft moan and slightly opened her legs, giving him the okay to continue. Rob climbed on top of her and started to rubbed the erection that bulged from his jeans up against her as their tongues intertwined.

Winding her hips in a circular motion, Keisha moaned louder as her panties started to get wet. Rob unfastened her bra and encircled her perky B cups into his hand as he softly sucked and gently bit her nipples.

"Oooh, yes," she moaned as her pussy throbbed for his dick.

Rob raised up for a moment to take off his pants, and Keisha removed hers also. He turned off the TV, putting them in complete darkness, and slid inside of her raw.

"Yeah, baby, you feel that? Damn, your pussy good," Rob said as he fucked her.

Keisha lay there in silence. She didn't feel a thing. It had felt better when they had their clothes on. Out of curiosity, she reached her hand down between her legs to see if he was really inside her.

"Uh-huh, baby, what you doing? I'm about to cum," he said as his breathing got heavy.

"Wait a minute. You don't have a condom on. Uh-uh, get off of me!" she yelled, pushing him off just as his body started to jerk and his thick cream erupted all over her pubic hair.

"Damn." He took a deep breath, and his little dick slowly started to go limp.

Damn, was right, Keisha thought. Disappointed and dissatisfied, what was she gonna do? She couldn't take the pussy back, so she decided to make the best of it and at least try to get some rest next to a warm body for the rest of the night. She snuggled up close to Rob and closed her eyes.

Minutes later, he nudged her shoulder. "Come on. You ready? Let me take you home."

Chapter 78

Shana was experiencing a burning and itching sensation in her pussy. It was the worst kind of discomfort that she had ever felt in her Iife. *I swear if K.C. gave me something, I'll kill his ass*, she thought.

Even though she had started making him wear condoms ever since he admitted to sleeping around on her, all types of disgusting thoughts crossed her mind.

What if he gave me something I can't get rid of, like herpes, or maybe even AIDS?

Shana loved K.C., and through all his wrongdoing, she was still trying to hold on, but if he had given her some kind of sexually transmitted disease, she would never be able to forgive him. Sure, he fucked around, but she dealt with it as long as he respected her enough to at least use protection.

She kept her discomfort from K.C. and held out from sex for a couple of days, hoping it would go away, but it didn't. She didn't know which was worse: fighting off K.C., or trying to soothe the irritation with every coochie cream Duane Reade, CVS, and Rite Aid carried.

Finally, she couldn't take it anymore, so she went to the clinic to find out what was wrong. Going to the department of health was embarrassing, especially since it was located on Jamaica Avenue, and everybody hung out on the Ave, so the chances of not being seen were slim.

Shana paced back in forth in front of the building for about ten minutes before she went inside, but that was the easy part. The hard part was not running into a familiar face while inside the waiting room, because more than likely if you were there, it was to treat an STD of some kind.

She quickly scanned the room as she walked over to the front desk to get a number and fill out a questionnaire. She was relieved when she didn't recognize any of the faces.

The wait was about an hour before her number was called. Inside the office, the doctor handed her a few STD brochures and asked her all types of questions regarding her sexual history before asking her the nature of her visit. After explaining her discomfort, the doctor told Shana to get undressed and lie back on the table.

Shana was so uncomfortable. She was twenty-three, married, and this was her first GYN checkup ever. The doctor told her to relax and talked her through the examination. In minutes it was over, and Shana was told to get dressed and return to the waiting room until the nurse called her for blood and urine samples.

As she walked down the hallway, reading the information the doctor had given her, someone called out her name.

"Shana!"

Shana's heart dropped when she heard the familiar voice. She looked up and recognized Chasity, dressed in one of those two-piece blue hospital uniforms, as if she worked there.

Fuck, Shana thought. Out of all people and all the places in the world, why did she have to run into her in here?

"Girl, what are you doing in here?" Chasity said as if everything was cool between them.

Shana rolled her eyes and refused to speak at first. Even if they were cool, she thought, *That's the last question I want to be asked right now.*

"Listen, Shana, I know you're probably still mad at me, and I don't blame you if you are, but I just want to say I'm sorry for the way I acted. I was just a little hurt, you know. Besides, I put dancing and all that other bullshit behind me ever since Scar was killed."

"Scar is dead? What happened?" Shana asked.

"I don't really know what happened. I wasn't at the club that night. Supposedly she left with some guy who, for whatever reason, nobody was able to identify and was later found butt-ass naked in a dumpster not far from the club, with a slit throat," said Chasity, getting teary-eyed.

"This happened at Honey's?"

"Yeah, about a month ago."

"Wow, I'm surprised I didn't hear about that," Shana said.

"I'm not. Don't nobody care. To them she's just another trick, but to me she was a good friend. You know, I actually have custody of her daughter, Starlavee, now. She's six."

"Oh, okay. I'm sure you'll take good care of her," Shana said.

"Yeah, me and my boyfriend are raising her together."

"Boyfriend?" Shana was surprised. She couldn't believe her ears.

"Yes, I have a man now. He's much easier to handle than . . . you know." She laughed.

Before Shana could respond, her number was called again. "Oh, hey, that's me. I gotta go, but you take care. And Chasity, thanks for apologizing." Shana walked into the nurse's office feeling like fifty pounds had just been lifted off her chest.

The nurse took her blood first, then handed her a cup and asked her to go to the bathroom and bring back some urine. Once she brought the urine sample back, the nurse gave her a pregnancy test, and in minutes, a negative result came back. Unfortunately, her discharge sample came back positive for Chlamydia. The nurse told her that it was a sexually transmitted disease, but the good news was it was curable. She gave Shana an antibiotic injection and informed her that it would take up to five days for her blood work to come back from the lab confirming whether she had any other STDs.

It took a lot to break through Shana's thick skin, but she had just reached her limit with the bullshit. With tears streaming down her face, she wasn't gonna take it no more. She lost herself a long time ago, fucking with K.C., but loving him was no longer worth her dignity. She put up with his ass whippings, his verbal abuse, and even his cheating. K.C. owed her more than this, because she had always been there for him. Being that down-ass bitch wasn't cute no more.

Chapter 79

Epiphany was enjoying her time with Wild so much that she didn't want it to end. In twenty-four hours they had already managed to do so much. He had bought her a Burberry bikini to swim in, amongst other things they had picked up during their shopping trip. They also played video games and spent half the night talking. Her stay felt more like a mini-vacation away from the hood, and it made her realize just how much she was ready for some changes in her life. Being with Wild was a different experience for her. He wasn't the cutest nigga, but he had the means to expose her to a whole new world, not to mention the other qualities she required: money, money, and more money!

Wild grew up on the rough streets of Newark, New Jersey, doing the norm—stealing cars, robbing niggas, and hustling. Even though he was fortunate to make it out of the hood, Epiphany admired the fact that he was still street, unlike some niggas who were quick to switch to that Hollywood shit. He also had other characteristics that she admired, like his confidence, sense of humor, and of course, his big feet and hands (assuming the myth was true).

Wild was feeling Epiphany's personality, which she worked to the fullest. He felt comfortable around her. She didn't appear to be fake, like most of the bitches he came across during his success. Plus, she could relate to his struggles, and to top it off, he found her absolutely gorgeous.

Sitting in the studio, smoking weed, Wild entertained Epiphany with crazy stories about the music industry. Quite often, he found himself staring at Epiphany. To him, her beauty was such a natural one that it made a nigga weak at the knees.

Epiphany was having a lot of fun with him, but all this fun was making her horny. She wanted him bad, and felt as though she would die from lack of dick if he didn't make a move soon.

She wasn't used to being around a guy for more than ten minutes that didn't try to fuck her. Wild was in the entertainment business, so Epiphany had already assumed that he wouldn't be pressed for pussy, since all types of chicks probably came at him. One thing was certain from his hard-on in the bed last night: he was definitely attracted to her. Still and all, Epiphany wanted to maintain a respectable "Take home to Momma" type of image, so she fell back on initiating sex of any kind.

Wild sat in his plush leather chair, staring at Epiphany; then out of nowhere, he pulled her closer to him and started to fondle her body as though he had read her mind. Epiphany straddled her legs across his lap and stuck her tongue in his mouth, for their first real kiss.

Damn, he can kiss, she thought as his tongue motion flowed with hers perfectly.

Wild started to undress her right there in the studio. He went to unbutton her shirt but noticed some resistance every time he made an attempt to remove it.

She didn't want him to go there, but she didn't say anything. Instead, she just redirected his focus by getting down on her knees and releasing his manhood.

Thank God the myth does apply. She opened her mouth and took in as much of his thickness as she possibly could. He was so big that she could only fit half of his dick in her mouth. Just like any pro, Epiphany was up for the challenge. She was determined to taste every inch of him, licking down the sides of his stiffness as he moaned and she lubricated his dick with her saliva, stroking her small hands up and down the base.

Wild couldn't take it any longer. He wanted to feel inside her walls. "Ahhh, man, wait! I want some pussy, 'cause I know it's good." Lifting himself up just enough to pull a condom from his back pocket, he passed it to her and smiled.

Epiphany stood up and unfastened her Seven jeans. Stepping out of them, she slowly rolled the magnum down on his horse-sized dick and was ready to ride.

"Wait. Let me see you play with yourself." Wild prolonged insertion as his way of teasing her.

Epiphany smiled. She knew the game and played it well as she leaned back on the mixing board and started to lick on her fingers until they were shiny from her saliva. Then, cocking her legs up, she slid two of her fingers inside of herself and began to move them in and out of her pussy.

"Ummmmmm," she moaned as her pussy became drenched with juice. Withdrawing her fingers from inside of her, she inserted them in his mouth. Wild sucked on them like they were Popsicles and then dove in head first between her legs for more.

"Ooooh, I wanna cum." Epiphany breathed heavily.

"Don't cum yet. I want you to sit on my dick and cum."

Without holding back, Epiphany mounted his manhood and slowly stroked him, not quite ready to endure the pain it would've cause if she slammed down on it right away. Once her pussy walls adjusted to his fullness, it was on and popping. She worked it, popping her pussy, bouncing up and down on his dick like a wild woman, until they both exploded.

Chapter 80

Tucker was having a hard time getting used to being without Keisha, but he knew moving on was the right thing for him to do. Besides, Leanne was a nice girl with a good head on her shoulders, and she somewhat remind him of Keisha.

He had met her two years ealier, when she came down to North Carolina with her cousin, Josae, one of Mali's jumpoffs. The two hit it off and maintained a platonic relationship for a while, until one day Leanne invited him over to her house because she needed to talk. When he got there, she tried to seduce him. Tucker found the whole situation flattering, but at that time, his heart belonged to Keisha, which he explained from the beginning. Embarrassed and rejected, Leanne felt it was best if they ended the friendship, and he agreed.

News of Malikai's death had brought her back into his life. Everything was falling apart for Tucker. Leanne saw an opportunity and went for it. She became the shoulder he needed to lean on, gave him moral support, and made him a priority in her life.

Her support kept Tucker sane, and for that he was grateful. So, when she arrived at his front door with her bags, he welcomed her with open arms, although he still felt he needed time to get over Keisha. Leanne moved in and wasted no time "de-Keishanizing" the place, getting rid of everything that had Keisha's name or face on it. The bedroom was repainted, the bathroom and kitchen redecorated, and every picture of Keisha was boxed up.

Tucker wasn't really happy with the sudden changes she made or her taste, but he understood her reasons. She wanted to help him take his mind off the past by all means.

There was one thing she couldn't erase: his son. Tucker missed his little man so much, and without him around, every day was very hard for him. His biggest fear was not being able to be a part of his son's life, and to keep that from happening, Tucker knew he had to make peace with Keisha. Little man's first birthday was a week away, and Tucker wanted him home for the celebration.

He picked up the phone and dialed Keisha's cell phone.

"Hello." She answered on the second ring.

"Hey, Keish, how's everything?" he asked.

"How do you think?" she answer snidely.

"Look, Keish, I ain't call to fight with you, okay? I just wanted to know how you was doing and when was our son coming home?"

"I don't know when I'm bringing my son home. I'm homeless, remember?"

"Yeah, well, you know his birthday's next week?"

"I know. I'm the one that had him."

"Keisha, cut out all the sarcasm, a'ight. Are you gonna bring him home or not?"

"That's all you care about, huh?"

"Keisha, he's my son."

"Well, you know what, Tucker? When you gave up on me, you gave up him. So if you're not calling me to come back home, then he's not coming home either."

"Yo, Keish, what's wrong with you? It's been over a month since he's been gone. He probably don't even remember us. You think you're getting back at me with your bullshit, but you're punishing him too. I never thought you could be such a fucked-up person, Keisha, but I swear to you, if you think you're gonna use my son against me or even try to keep him from me, I will fucking kill you. Do you hear me?"

"Is that a threat, Tucker? You're gonna fucking kill me, huh? Well, come on, muthafucka. Kill me, 'cause you ain't never gon' see your son again. We're a package deal, sweetie, so if I ain't got you, then you ain't got a son. You got that? Besides, I heard you got a new girl. Tell her to give you a fucking son and leave mines alone!" Keisha screamed right before she slammed down the phone.

Tucker was hot with Keisha. He tried calling her back, but she wouldn't answer her phone. He buried his head in his hands, thinking how Keisha must have really lost her mind if she thought he was gonna go for her bullshit.

"Baby, are you okay?" asked Leanne after overhearing his conversation with Keisha.

Tucker let out a hard sigh as he lifted his head. "Nah, she's trying to keep me from my son now."

"What! Baby, you can't let her do that to you. You're his father, and you have just as much rights as she does. What you need to do is just go get him," Leanne suggested.

"I just don't know why she had to go and fuck up everything," said Tucker.

"Well, baby, everything happens for a reason, and at least you found out her true colors before you two got married. Now, are you gonna sit here and regret what you can't change, or are we gonna go get your son?" She ran her fingers through Tucker's hair and secretly hated the fact that he still had feelings for Keisha.

"What would I do without you?" Tucker stood up and gave her a tight hug. "Come on. Let's go get my little man."

Chapter 81

Epiphany woke up and instantly went into a funk after overhearing Wild booking a flight for L.A. leaving that night. Her little vacation with him was over before she was ready for it to be. She wondered if he would ever call her again and hoped that her time spent with him wasn't a complete waste, because yes, she had a great time, but she wasn't doing it for nothing. Epiphany wanted to be rescued from the hood by a wealthy knight in platinum armor and live glamorously and happily ever after. That was the ghetto fairytale she was hoping for.

"Good morning, beautiful," Wild said as he plopped down next to her on the bed. Right off the bat, he sensed a bit of attitude by the way she twisted up her lips and cut her eyes at him. "What up? You okay?" he asked.

"Yeah, I'm okay," she lied.

"You don't seem okay, so tell me what's wrong."

"Nothing. I just overheard you making travel plans, and I guess I wasn't ready for it to be over with us," Epiphany said.

"Oh, so it's over between us?" Wild questioned.

"I don't know. You tell me," she answered.

"Nah, as long as you don't want it to be over, it ain't."

"And what do you want?" Epiphany asked.

"Well, first I wanna know why you won't let me kiss on your tits."

"Wild, come on. Be serious!"

"I *am* serious. I wanna know why every time we had sex, you did everything to deter me from seeing them." He thought that maybe she had gotten a bad boob job or something of that nature.

Epiphany's eyes started to tear up. He was right. She did stop him from removing her shirt every time they had sex, but it wasn't because of her tits. It was because of the ugly scar she was hiding. She really didn't know how she was gonna to explain it. Slowly removing her shirt, she thought of an explanation.

"What happened to you?" he questioned in shock.

Epiphany revealed the ugly scar from not only the bullet, but the lung surgery after the shooting.

"I was in an abusive relationship, and when I tried to leave him, he tried to kill me," Epiphany said.

"Damn, ma, I'm sorry to hear that. Where's his punk ass at now?"

"I don't know," Epiphany answered.

"What you mean, you don't know? Come on. For some sucker shit like that, he should be under the fucking jail."

"I know, but it didn't turn out that way. Believe me, I wish it did, because maybe then the nightmares would stop and I wouldn't have to worry about him coming back for me one day. But you know, with you I feel safe, I haven't even thought about it." Her tears continued to fall.

Epiphany had over-dramatized her story to gain his sympathy, and it worked. Wild had seen a lot of crazy shit go down in his hood when it came to a man and his girl, so Epiphany's story wasn't far fetched. He could understand a nigga not wanting to let her go, because she was absolutely gorgeous, but what she did for him was more mental than physical. He'd fucked plenty of pretty girls with good pussy, but with Epiphany, he felt a connection that was real, and that made him want to hold on to her.

"Listen, Epiphany, I'm feeling you like crazy, and if you feel like I feel and it ain't about the money, then maybe something serious could pop off. I'll be in L.A. for a couple of weeks, but when I get back, I'm trying to see what's good, a'ight?" He leaned down and kissed her ugly scar.

Epiphany didn't say a word. She just looked in his eyes and hoped her tearful emotions would say it all. In her mind, she was screaming, *I got his ass!* All she could think about was a life filled with the finer things, like shopping sprees, VIP status, trips around the world, and maybe even a career in acting.

Chapter 82

C-God lost himself completely as his addiction started to control his mind, body, and soul. His body started to take on the form of a true fiend, as well as his habits. His money was spent, his jewelry sold, and the only other thing he possessed that held any value, his Cadillac Escalade, was dogged out by the local street corner dealers, who he let drive it more than him in exchange for crack.

Marisa lost her kids to the system due to her neglect, and she started selling pussy to any nigga that would provide her and C with their next hit. C-God started asking Reggie to wire him money on the regular, until Reggie just started ignoring his calls.

Tanya had no idea that he was cracked out, so she would send him a couple of dollars whenever she could, until she started to suspect something was up. It got to the point where he would call at all times of the day, wanting her to go to a MoneyGram. He'd make up all kinds of excuses for why he couldn't see her. Eventually she washed her hands of him.

C-God was smoked out, and all he had was his memories of when he was getting paper. He would tell his story to any young hustler in VA who was willing to listen to him talk about what he used to have, how one of his own betrayed him, shaming him and his family's name.

Niggas didn't believe or respect him at first. They would clown him and his stories.

"Ahh, go 'head with that shit, nigga. You ain't nothing but a crackhead," they would say. It wasn't until he started to drop some valuable knowledge, rules to the game that could be beneficial to one's progression, that they really paid attention and respected the shit he was saying.

One particular nigga named Alpo, a lightweight in the game, had enough hunger to be a heavyweight and took a liking to C-God. He could tell C knew exactly what he was talking about concerning this drug shit. Even though he was a fallen soldier, Alpo still admired the position he once held. During a two-year bid in prison, he became real familiar with the reputation of the infamous Hinderson brothers from some stories cats told. C-God also took a liking to Alpo because he reminded him of himself eight years ago at the ripe age of twenty-two. He saw a similar hunger in him and felt, given the right type of guidance, Alpo would not only be official, but he could be what C-God tried to be—unstoppable.

Chapter 83

On the way home, Shana rehearsed her "I'm leaving you" speech over and over again. It was gonna be hard to face K.C. without trying to claw his fucking eyes out, but at this point, it was whatever, she thought.

Her cell phone started ringing, but no number registered on the screen. She debated for a moment on whether she should answer it.

"Hello?" she finally answered.

"Yo, Cream, they got me locked up," said Raina.

"What?" Shana had been caught off guard.

"Yo, it's me, Raina. They raided Honey's last night. I had your shit on me and got locked the fuck up. I'm at the Queens House, so ante up and get me out of here. My bail is five thousand."

"A'ight, I got you," Shana said nonchalantly.

Damn, what next?

"I hope so, because if you have me in here too long, I'ma start talking." Raina hung up before Shana could respond.

When Shana walked in the apartment, K.C. was on the phone, but her anger toward him was now diverted toward getting that bitch Raina out of jail. She cut her eyes at him as hard as she could to let him know they had beef, while passing him to get to the bedroom.

"Yo, Smitty, my chick stay mad at me, dawg," K.C. said, noticing her attitude.

Shana slammed the bedroom door. She despised Smitty's ass too. Plopping down on the foot of the bed, she tossed her car keys to the side and just sat for a moment, thinking about Raina's threat to snitch her out. The more she contemplated, the more she realized that Raina ain't have nothing on her but her stage name. She didn't know her real name, and if she did, she didn't know her full name, or where she lived, or anything about her connect. She was no longer worried.

If I was a complete bitch, I'd let her ass hang, Shana thought, getting up and walking over to the closet for her stash. She could still hear K.C. on the phone with Smitty, but she didn't pay their conversation any mind, until she heard Epiphany's name being mentioned. Pressing her ear up against the door, she eavesdropped on what K.C. was saying.

"Who, Epiphany? Nah, I don't think she got it back. If so, don't you think she would've had the police all over Ness's ass for that shit? What? I think so. Come on, man, the nigga tried to kill her. Yo, that's your boy. Nah, I can't even fuck with him like that no more. Yeah, he be bugging the fuck out, and I know that nigga is responsible for what happened to Righteous and his girl. Yo, you still asking about that bitch? Yo, man, let it go. Nah, Shana ain't gon' hook that shit up. She can't stand ya ass. Besides, Shana don't even fuck with her like that no more, and what's up with you and my sister? Yeah, you right. Trina is a crazy bitch. But yo, what's up with that money? Nah, I got mine ready, nigga. I'm waiting on yours."

From the sound of it, Shana assumed Ness was the one responsible for Epiphany's brush with death. *That dude Ness rubbed me the wrong way just by looking at him. Damn, he probably did Mali too. And what the fuck is up with Smitty wanting to get with Epiphany? That ain't happening. He's not even in her league. When I met him the first time, he claimed he already fucked her and couldn't stand her, so what's really good? Today is definitely just one of those days.*

Shana directed her attention back to her stash in the closet. Pulling down the Timberland shoebox, she notice it felt extremely light. Shana opened the box and instantly she noticed the dent in her savings. What used to be 42 G's was now only two thousand dollars.

Shana threw the shoebox on the floor, dug in the back of the closet, pulled out one of those metal baseball bats, and stormed out into the living room.

"Where that fuck is my money at, huh?" she screamed.

"Whoa, whoa! Yo, nigga, I'ma hit you back." K.C. quickly hung up the phone "Yo, Sha, chill the fuck out!" he yelled, making a move to grab the bat. Shana stepped back and swung with all her strength, hitting his arm.

"Don't fuck with me, K.C. Where the fuck is my money, you dirty-dick nigga?"

"Yo, what the hell is wrong with you, Sha?"

Shana positioned herself to slug his ass again.

"Yo, chill! Don't hit me no more!" he ordered as if he was in any position to make demands.

"K.C., I swear on everything I love, if you don't give me my money right now, I'm gonna take this fucking bat and try to kill you with it."

"Sha, listen. I just need a couple of weeks. Let me make this move with Smitty and I promise you, I'll give you back double. Come on, ma. Put the bat down. Just grind with me, please, so I can get this paper, a'ight? Come on, Sha, you know I got you. Clyde can't shine without Bonnie."

Shana did the math. Double meant eighty grand. She weighed out her options.

Raina's bail or a forty-thousand dollar profit. Fuck Raina, she thought, lowering the bat.

"See, that's why I love you, girl." K.C. let out a hard sigh of relief.

Shana turned up her lips and gave him a "Whatever, nigga" look.

"Well, if you love me like that then go get your dirty dick cured and stop fucking them nasty-ass hoes." She walked back in the bedroom, slamming and locking the door behind her. Shana lay on the bed, trying hard to understand how and why she loved K.C.'s grimey ass so much.

Chapter 84

Epiphany's mother was glad that she was home and still in one piece, considering that she hadn't heard from her in days. Really, she wanted to talk to Epiphany about Keisha's recent behavior, thinking maybe she could talk some sense into her friend. Lord knows she had tried. Keisha was like a daughter to her, and she couldn't sit back and watch her live recklessly.

"Epee, I need to talk to you." Mrs. Wright was obviously worried.

"Ma, before you start, I'm sorry I didn't call, but I was fine," Epiphany answered defensively.

"I can see that now, but you know what? I'm not gonna go there with you. I wanna talk about Keisha."

"What about Keisha? Is she here?"

"Shhh. She's downstairs."

"Okay, well, what happened?"

"Epee, I'm worried about her. She been running out of here with a different guy every night for the past four days, and you know that ain't like her."

"Ma, she's just trying to get her mind off of Tucker, that's all. It's not that big of a deal." Epiphany tried to justify Keisha's behavior.

"Well, I tried talking to her, and I'm telling you, she's not herself. She hasn't even mentioned her son."

"Ma, I'm sure she's fine, but if you want, I'll talk to her. Don't worry about Li'l Tucker. He's with her mom in Atlanta. I'm going downstairs now," Epiphany whined.

"I'll tell you this: You girls need to accept Christ in your life and stop running around here taking things for granted. Your father's trying to."

"Yeah, yeah, yeah. Where's Daddy at anyway?" Epiphany asked, heading down the basement steps.

"He went to see his brother. Your Uncle Ramel got arrested. Mm-hmm, the feds finally caught up with him."

"Wow, that's too bad," Epiphany said sarcastically.

"What's up, E? It's about time you came home, girl." Keisha excitedly sat up on her futon bed, anticipating the 411 on Epiphany's new friend.

"Hey, I know. Believe me, it wasn't by choice, and it ain't for long. Wild's gonna take me up out of the hood," Epiphany said with a smile.

"Are you serious? So what happened? He must have a lot of money, 'cause I ain't seen you smile like that since your father bought you that Beamer."

"Keish, he has everything I want in a man: a lot of money, a huge house, good dick, no kids, and he's not cheap at all. So, girl, you know I made it my business to put it on his ass, right? 'Cause shit, a bitch is trying to get a one way ticket out of Southside, okaaay!"

"That's good. I'm so happy for you." Keisha was a little envious. She once had everything she wanted in a man, too, and she missed the feeling.

"Anyway, enough about me. How was your date with that guy?" Epiphany asked.

"Which one?" Keisha answered.

"Well, damn, Keish, go on and brush your shoulders off. I'm scared of you." Epiphany laughed.

"Don't be, because my pimp game sucks." Keisha sighed.

"Well, what happened to the computer fix-it guy?"

"Oh my gosh, E, his apartment was a dump, his ding-a-ling was the size of my son's, and now he has the audacity to avoid my calls."

"The dick was trash and you're still calling him? Why?"

"I don't know."

"Well, did he at least take you out and spend some money?"

"Out? Out for him was a movie in his junky-ass one-room apartment."

"Keish, I know you been out of the loop for a minute, but did you not learn anything from me? If you're gonna give it up, get something out of it, okay?"

"I know. I had sex with three guys in the last four days, and none of them made me cum. It's like I'm going from bad to worse," Keisha confessed.

"Three guys? From where, Keisha?"

"Blackplanet.com."

"Are you crazy, Keisha?"

"No, I'm just lonely."

"So why don't you call to see how T's doing?"

"For what? He hates me."

"Keish, I'm talking about your son. When was the last time you called to check on him, and when is he coming home?" Not waiting for Keisha's response, Epiphany handed her the phone.

"I don't know, E. Maybe in a couple of days or so. I just haven't been feeling like a mom ever since Tucker left me. It's almost like I had a baby for him, and now that he's gone, I don't want my son anymore. I guess I should at least call." Keisha hesitantly dialed her mom's number.

Epiphany knew Keisha was hurting inside, but she couldn't believe what was coming out of her mouth, and she chose not to comment.

"Hello?" answered one of Keisha's sisters.

"Hi, this is Keisha. Who's this?"

"Hey, girl, this Kelly."

"What up, Kells? How's my son doing?"

"He ain't here."

"What? Then where is he?"

"I don't know. Didn't you send Tucker here to get him?"

"No, I didn't. Where is Loretta at?"

"She ain't here. Tucker took the baby two days ago. He said you told him to come pick him up," said Kelly.

"Well, I didn't. I have to go. Bye!" Keisha hung up and immediately started dialing Tucker's cell phone, then the house phone, but got no answer.

"What happened, Keish? Is Li'l T okay?" Epiphany asked.

"I don't know. He's not there. He's with Tucker," she answered.

"Tucker went to ATL and got him and you didn't know anything about it?"

"No, I didn't, and I can't understand why Loretta would let Tucker just take him like that without consulting with me first. Now Tucker's not answering his phone." Keisha took a moment to think. "Epiphany, do you think he's trying to take my son from me?"

"I don't know, but maybe you need to just go over there and see what's up. You could take my car, unless you want me to go with you."

"No, you don't have to, but thanks," Keisha said as she took Epiphany's car keys.

When she arrived at what used to be her home, Tucker's car, along with a light blue Honda Accord, was parked in the driveway. Keisha got out of the car and walked up the steps. She could see the that lights were on through the front window, and she proceeded to repeatedly press the bell, causing it to sing an annoying tune. Her heart pounded as she impatiently waited all of two minutes.

If I have to start breaking windows around this mutha-fucka, I'll do it. My presence is gonna be felt, she thought. She prepared herself to take it there if she had to.

Just as Keisha stepped down off the steps in search of a nice size rock with some weight to it, Tucker answered the door in a sweat, looking like he was getting his workout on. He was wearing a pair of Calvin Klein drawstring pajama pants, with no shirt and scratches on his chest.

"What do you want?" An annoyed Tucker watched her search the grass.

Keisha looked up and saw him at the door. "I came to get my son!"

"Keisha, I'ma take care of him from now on. You shipped him off and forgot about him, remember that? It took you two fucking days to find out I had him? Just continue to do you. My little man is straight right here with me."

"I don't care if took me five days. I came to get my son and I'm not leaving without him."

"Keisha, just go, a'ight!"

"No, I'm not gonna just go. What the fuck were you doing anyway, and whose car is that? I know your not stupid enough to have some bitch around my son."

"Whatever, Keish. Good-bye." Tucker went back inside the house and slammed the door.

"Tucker, you better give me my fucking son, or I swear you'll be sorry!" Keisha screamed, but Tucker didn't come back to the door. "Oh, so you want me to take it there, huh?"

Keisha walked across the front lawn, once again searching for a rock. She couldn't find a rock but spotted some bricks that were stacked next to the fence in the front lawn. Loosening three bricks from the soil, she slammed one into the windshield of the Honda, then the passenger's side window of Tucker's 745. The third brick she threw crashed right through the center of the front window of the house, setting off both car alarms and the ADT system.

Keisha was turning into some crazed madwoman, screaming vulgar obscenities and throwing a raging tantrum in the front of the house. She wanted her son, but what really set her off was the assumption that Tucker had a girl inside the house with him.

Tucker was furious. His tolerance had just exceeded its limit. Baby momma or no baby momma, he was gonna beat that ass.

Running out of the house, Tucker charged right at Keisha and tackled her. Releasing all the anger and pain he was holding in, he literally tried to strangle the life out of Keisha.

The upper class neighborhood they lived in wasn't used to such disturbances, so instantly many of their neighbors peeked from their windows to see what the commotion was about. Some even called police, but not one of them came over and tried to get Tucker off of her.

Leanne ran out of the house and tried to pull him off of Keisha, but he was so worked up that he shoved her so hard she went flying across the grass. It was the sound of his son's cry that caused him to free Keisha from his choke hold.

Breathing heavily, Tucker got off of her and rushed over to the door to calm and console his son.

Keisha's eyes were bloodshot and watery as she coughed and wheezed, trying to catch her breath. Once she gained control of her breathing, she heard a recognizable female's voice.

"Baby, are you okay?" Lea's face fit the voice, and seeing her set Keisha off again. She jumped up from the ground and attacked her from behind. Grabbing Lea by her long, frizzy, half-black/half-white mixed hair, she tossed her to the ground and ferociously punched her face.

It happened so fast that Tucker couldn't come to her rescue right away. He was holding his son. Running in the house, Tucker secured Li'l T safely in his stroller and came back out to her rescue, but by the time he made it back out front, the police had arrived and already controlled the situation.

After the police questioned the three of them, all fingers pointed to Keisha as the villain. Tucker decided not to press charges, but Lea did, so Keisha was hauled off to jail and charged with aggravated assault, disruptive behavior, and disturbing the peace.

Chapter 85

Shana stared at the ceiling half of the night, tossing and turning. Raina's threats, her STD results, K.C.'s infidelity, and her money investment with him, were all way too much to grasp. Through it all, one thing troubled her the most—K.C.'s phone conversation earlier. Despite felling that Epiphany was a complete bitch who worked every nerve in her body—plus, she had enough problems of her own not to get involved in someone else's—she knew her conscience would only eat away at her if she kept quiet about it. Not only did she feel Epiphany had every right to know what really went down, she also felt, without a doubt, that Ness should pay for his actions.

Shana glanced at the clock on the nightstand, which read 12:45 a.m. She got out of the bed, still fully dressed from earlier. Without turning on the lights, she felt around the bed for her car keys, which were still at the foot of the bed where she had left them.

She unlocked and slowly opened the bedroom door,. Peeking out, she saw K.C. asleep on the couch, with the TV watching him.

Thank God, she thought. The last thing she wanted to hear was his mouth.

Shana left the house, went for a drive, and ended up in front of Epiphany's house. She called her on her cell.

"Hello?" Epiphany answered, half asleep.

"What's up, E? I need to holla at you about something."

"Who's this?"

"It's Shana. Come outside."

"Shana, I'm sleeping."

"E, C-God ain't do it."

"What?" Epiphany's voice got louder.

"C-God ain't the one that shot you, but since you sleeping, fuck it."

"No, wait. I'm coming." Epiphany was awake now. She hung up, hopped out of bed, threw on some sweats and slippers, and headed out the side door.

Opening Shana's passenger-side door, she got in, eagerly anticipating what she had to say.

"What's going on, Shana?"

"Listen, I know who shot you. I don't know him like that, but he be with K.C. and this guy name Smitty."

"Well, who is he, and how is he linked to me?"

"His name is Ness. He used to run with C-God."

"So, how do you know he's the one that shot me?" asked Epiphany.

"Look, that's not important. I just know, okay?"

"What about Malikai? Is he the one that killed him too?"

"More than likely, but listen, his boy Smitty is feeling you hard, so I was thinking maybe you should fuck with the nigga just to manipulate the situation, try to turn him against Ness. That way he could take care of him for you," Shana suggested.

"I don't know. I think I should just put all this behind me. I mean, what's done is done. Besides, I'm trying to get up out of here anyway."

"What! Come on. I know you ain't trying to let that nigga get away with this bullshit, Epiphany. The muthafucka left you for dead, and you wanna put that behind you?"

"Shana, I almost died, and that shit scares me. I ain't trying get caught up in some bullshit with the same muthafucka that tried to kill me. And anyway, what's it to you? You act like you're the one with the vendetta."

"What? I'm trying to look out for you, but if you don't feel like your life is worth getting payback, fuck it then! Have a good night." Shana turned the tables on Epiphany. Of course she had her motives, but she couldn't disclose that.

"Yeah, whatever." Epiphany slammed the car door behind her and headed back to the house. Inside, she glanced over at Keisha's empty bed and briefly wondered where she could be at that time of night. Sitting up on her bed, she thought about what Shana said and the dream she'd had at Keisha's house. There were two male voices present the night she was shot.

Epiphany sat in the dark, deep in her thoughts, for more than twenty minutes, when suddenly the sounds of Prince's "Do Me Baby," Mali and her laughing, and the moment she froze from shock when she saw the bullet pierce through his skull flashed in her mind. She could remember the splattered blood mixed with pieces of Mali's brain sprinkling all over her, and the way her body trembled as she stood still in fear, watching his body slump over to the side.

C-God ordered the trigger man he called Ness to search her crib. She could feel the enormous amount of pain she had experienced that night all over again as her tears began to fall. Epiphany rehashed everything that had taken place that night, from the verbal to the physical abuse she was subjected to, and the reason it all took place. She remembered all the horrific details that led her to squeeze the trigger of her nine with the intent to kill C-God. It was Ness who entered the room and blasted off his .38 in C's defense, hitting her in the chest and sending her into a state of unconsciousness.

Chapter 86

Keisha cried the whole ride over to central booking. She couldn't believe Lea had actually played her like that.

How long has she known him? Keisha wondered. Putting two and two together, she realized how well Lea smoothly played everything off. She made it seem like she only liked Spanish guys, and she always claimed to have a man. She'd say anything to cover up the fact that she was a jealous, man-stealing, backstabbing bitch.

Keisha felt like such an idiot for letting her guard down and befriending Lea. She told her personal things about her and Tucker's sex life: his dick size, how he was always away from home, and even about her alter ego, BAPS, that she used in the dirty online chat rooms. She had to admit she had set herself up for the kill, played right into Lea's hands. She had agreed to inviting strippers that night, when in her heart she was dead set against whole the idea.

By the time Keisha finished getting processed, it was too late to stand before a judge. Although it was late, she decided to use her one phone call to call Mrs. Wright, she was certain she'd reach her. She explained her situation to Mrs. Wright and told her that she wouldn't know anything further regarding her release until the morning, which meant she had to spend the night in the bullpen.

Keisha had never experienced such filth in her life, locked up with prostitutes, drug addicts, boosters, and God only knew what else. It was a tight squeeze in the overcrowded cell. With one dingy stall in the corner, the men in the other cell directly across could see everything. The idea of having to stay in a place like this turned her stomach. There was one long wooden bench up against the wall that was so full, women were stretched out in the remaining three corners and all over the floor. With no place to rest, she thought she'd be standing in that one spot for the remainder of the night.

"Here, honey, come sit next to Big Doris," a woman said, patting a small space next to her on the bench. Detecting Keisha's hesitation, she continued, "Come, honey, I ain't gon' bite you. Shit, I got daughters your age."

That made Keisha feel a little more at ease. Hopefully Big Doris wasn't on no lesbo shit. She proceeded toward her.

"Thanks," Keisha said, sitting down.

"No problem, honey. What you in here for?" Big Doris asked. "Ahhh, I had a fight with this backstabbing bitch that stole my man." Keisha was still bitter.

All of a sudden, she noticed all the track marks and sores on every visible part of Big Doris's body.

"Honey, you are too much of a good-looking girl to be fighting over some damn man. And I'ma tell you just like I tell my own girls: If you got to fight over a man, then he ain't yours. Now look—you in here, and he's probably with that heifer."

Keisha explained to Big Doris that the situation was much deeper, because they had a child together. Big Doris told her she understood and advised that if a situation calls for her to move on, then that's what she should do. Keisha revealed how Lea had betrayed her, and that's when Big Doris changed her tune.

"You should beat that bitch with a bat every time you see the ho!"

Keisha was enjoying her conversation with Big Doris. She had a great sense of humor, plus she knew a lot of shit about life. Talking to her made the hours go by a little faster, despite the fact that she would nod off for at least thirty seconds in between each sentence and pick at the nasty scabs on her arm and neck, exposing the tendencies of a true dopefiend.

Finally, morning came and Keisha's name was called to stand before the judge. As soon as she entered the courtroom, she spotted Mrs. Wright seated, hopefully waiting to take her home. No doubt she was happy to see her, but she was also expecting Tucker to be present as well. Unfortunately, that didn't happen, and she couldn't hold back her tears from the pain she was feeling. The judge released her on her own recognizance and scheduled her to appear back in court in three weeks.

Chapter 87

C-God continued to school his new student, Alpo, about the hustling game. Even though C-God was still getting high as a kite, the two became kind of close. Alpo looked at him as somewhat of a mentor, while C-God viewed Alpo as his prodigy. He had heart, will, and a hunger that could take him far.

C-God wanted to help him prosper, but he needed something done for him first. Alpo was down for C-God's vengeful plan. He ran the necessary questions by Alpo: Had he ever caught a body before, and was he afraid to? C wanted to personally see to it that Ness suffered. He also needed to know that if Alpo had to pull the trigger, he wouldn't bitch up.

Alpo assured him that he had his back. All C-God had to do was say when and how he wanted the shit to go down. C-God had mapped out the whole thing weeks ago. All he had to do was get a hold of Reggie, who was still ducking C-God's calls, even though he left messages that it wasn't about money but rather another very important matter.

Reg figured he had somehow gotten word that he and Tanya were in a relationship, and he wasn't ready to face C with that yet. Once again, he'd betrayed C-God, this time falling in love with one of his baby mothers, and he didn't know how he was going to explain that. C-God had asked him to look after her, and now they were living together.

In order for his plan to be carried out, C-God was willing to ignore Reggie's shitting on him. He needed him as an inside connect and felt Reggie owned him that much.

Chapter 88

Epiphany had replayed that deadly night over and over again in her head for the last couple of days. It was clear now that Ness was the one responsible for Malikai's death and her being shot.

Because she was so focused on nothing but her newfound recollection, Wild's phone calls were the only thing that made her feel better. He would phone her whenever he got a break from the music, just to let her know she was in his thoughts. Their relationship was quickly growing strong, and he made it clear that he wanted to take things to the next level by asking her to come live with him.

Epiphany wasted no time giving him her answer. she excitingly blurted out "Yes!" without putting any thought into it. She didn't care whether it was too soon or if it would even work out. Love had nothing to do with it. All she wanted was to leave the hood and to live her life in a rich man's world.

As much as her gut was telling her to move on and put her past behind her, though, she just couldn't until Ness paid for what he had done to her and Malikai. After putting as much thought into it as she possibly could, she phoned Shana.

"What's up?" Shana answered, recognizing Epiphany's number from the caller ID.

"Shana, listen. I've been thinking about what you said and you're right. That son of a bitch has to pay for trying to take my life away."

"So what, you ready to fuck with Smitty?" Shana questioned.

"Yeah, if he's the one that could help me."

"Hell yeah, he's the one, plus he got it bad for you, E. All you gotta do is get the nigga open, and I'm telling you he'll probably do what whatever you want him to."

"But if Ness is his boy, how am I gonna get him to get at 'im for me?" Epiphany asked.

"Come on, E. Good pussy can make a nigga do anything. This is me you talking to, and I know you know how to put it down for your crown. Just manipulate the shit out of his ass and make him think you feeling him like that, then set him up for the kill."

"A'ight, I got you."

"Cool. I'ma set it up, so expect his call, a'ight?"

"Okay!" Ending the call, Epiphany felt jitters. She was a little nervous about the plan.

It has to work, she thought, *because nobody fucks over Epiphany Janee Wright and gets away with it.*

Shana wasted no time getting on it. As soon as she got off the phone with Epiphany, she phoned Smitty and made arrangements to meet with him at IHOP for breakfast. He agreed. Shana got up, showered, and dressed. On her way out the door, she glanced over and rolled her eyes, disgusted with K.C. He was on the couch, where he'd been sleeping for the past couple of nights, since she began her silent treatment.

When she got in her car, she turned on her cell phone and retrieved the six messages that were waiting for her.

Message one: *"Yeah, bitch, I see you trying to front on me, huh? A'ight, ho, I'ma see you!"*

Message two: *"Yo, Cream, I see your sheisty ass really ain't trying to get me outta here, huh? Watch your back, bitch!"*

Message three: *"Shana Scott, how 'bout this: You can ignore my calls all you want, but my peoples will be seeing you, a'ight!"*

Messages four, five, and six were pretty much the same. Raina went from calling her Cream to her government name and admitted she knew who her man was and where they lived. Now Shana was starting to fret.

She pulled up to the IHOP, went inside, and was seated. Of course, Smitty had her waiting for over thirty minutes, and when he arrived, he walked in like he had all the time in the world.

Look at this character, she thought, pissed off.

"Sha-money, what up, girl?" Smitty smiled as he slid into the booth next to her.

"What's up? Why you always gotta keep a bitch waiting, huh?"

"Yo, what's up? Oh, wait. Let me order some food first. A nigga starving." Smitty looked at the menu, disregarding her attitude and her question.

The two ordered breakfast before Shana began to conduct business.

"Listen, I know you heard that the police ran up in Honey's and shut shit down, right?" Shana asked.

"Nah, when this happened?"

Shana knew he was lying, but she didn't call him on it. She just continued on about Raina getting caught up in the sweep.

"A'ight, so why is you telling me?" Smitty questioned.

"I'm telling you 'cause the bitch is locked the fuck up and she's making threats to snitch me out. Her bail is five G's and I ain't got it, and if I ain't got that, then you know I ain't got the money to keep paying your fucking ass for that bullshit you got on me. Don't you think we played this game long enough? Me and K.C. ain't working out, but I'm willing to do you a favor if you could front me the money for Raina's bail, and after I pay you back, we're even."

Smitty laughed at her.

"What kind of favor you gon' do for me that's gonna cost me five G's? That shit sounds funnier than a muthafucka!" he said. "Anyway, what's up with your E connect? Honey's ain't the only strip joint you could sell them shits at."

"I know that, but my connect ain't fucking with me no more. The last time I went to check him he told me that that was my last play, 'cause he was giving it up and moving to Vegas," Shana lied. Truth be told, she didn't want to do it anymore, but she knew if she told Smitty that, his greed would get in the way.

She no longer cared about him telling K.C. about Chasity. Besides, Chasity had a man now. But she knew that Smitty would dig up some more dirt to hold against her, because he was that kind of nigga. She wanted all debts settled.

"Oh, word. So if that stripper bitch ain't get knocked, you still would've been ass out, huh?" Smitty asked.

"Yeah, I guess, but at least I would've had the dough she made for the week. Anyway, that's neither here nor there. Do we got a deal or not?" Shana questioned.

"Yo, I ain't hear no deal. What I'm giving you five G's for, and why you ain't ask my man K.C.?"

"'Cause he's the reason I ain't got it! Remember y'all little investment? Don't worry. As soon as I get my cut from him, I give you my word, I'll give it back to you.

"You feeling my homegirl Epiphany, right? I could hook that up for you—you know, wash my back and I'll wash yours."

"Get the fuck out of here." He laughed. "You want me to pay you for that? Yo, she already tried that. And I'ma tell you like I told her: The kid don't pay for no pussy. A'ight, yo!"

"I'm not asking you to pay for nothing. Are you listening? I said loan! C'mon, Smitty, one good deed deserves another. You been hitting my pockets hard. There's gotta be a reason why you wanted me to hook you and Epiphany up, so what is it? You already hit it, so why don't you just step to her again?"

"Yo, shit went sour between us, that's all."

"So she don't remember shit about you," Shana said.

"For real, that shit's really true about her losing her memory?"

"Yeah."

"No bullshitting?"

"Nah, no bullshit, so that means whatever happened between y'all don't even matter. You got a clean slate, homie," Shana assured him.

"So shit, I could holla at her myself then," Smitty responded.

"Yeah, you could, but she kind of leery about fucking with around-the-way niggas now. I'll let her know shit is cool and you'se my nigga, so she might rock with you."

"It's like that, with just your word. K.C. told me y'all ain't rock like that no more."

"He don't know what the fuck he be talking about. First off, the nigga stay too busy fucking other bitches to know who I'm cool with. Epiphany is my girl. We been cool for over ten years. You trying to holla at her or what?"

"Well, I don't know what you talking about as far as my man with other girls, but yeah, I'm trying to swing with that." Smitty tried his best to cover up for K.C.

"A'ight, cool." Shana ignored his bald-faced lie. "So, when you gon' give me the money?" she continued.

"When you hook that up!"

"Come on, Smitty. Don't fucking try to play me."

"Yo, I'm not. I'm trying to get at her," Smitty said.

"Then when you give me the money, I'll call her, so you could do that."

"What, you don't trust me?"

Shana didn't answer. She just gave him a look. that said, *Nigga, that's an understatement.*

"A'ight, a'ight." He got the message. "I'll have it for you later on today. When I call, you be ready to meet up, a'ight?" Smitty got up from the table and left, leaving her stuck with the bill.

Shana just shook her head. *What a desperate, thirsty muthafucka.*

Chapter 89

It took everything Mrs. Wright had in her to convince Keisha not to go back over to Tucker's house and confront Lea. She told Keisha that she needed to cool out for a couple of days, then take the police over there to get her son. Keisha agreed, but the thought of her son being around another women ate away at her. Blocking her number, she called the house.

The phone rang three times before Lea answered.

"Hello."

Keisha fumed with anger when she heard that bitch answer the phone, but she tried hard to keep her composure, because she didn't want to get hung up on.

"Can I please speak to Tucker?" she asked, grinding her teeth and breathing heavy.

Lea wasn't going to hang up, because she wanted the opportunity to rub her shit in Keisha's face.

"Do you mean my Tucker, or your little rugrat?"

"What did you just say, bitch?" Keisha yelled.

"You heard what I said, Keisha. Are you calling for my man, or that fucking little brat of yours?" Lea taunted.

"I know Tucker must not be there, because if he heard you talking about our son like that—that's right, I repeat, *our son*—your ass would be out of there so fast, bitch."

"Oh, you think so? You know what, Keisha? You're such a stupid-ass little ho. You fell right into my trap, dummy. I set the whole thing up. You ever wonder why you got tipsy so fast, huh? I spiked your drink and you got laid. The Damager's a male prostitute, a gigolo. It only cost me three hundred dollars to destroy your perfect little relationship."

"You fucking bitch! Why would you do that to me? What did I ever do to you besides trust you as my friend?" Keisha couldn't control the sadness in her voice.

"Honestly, Keisha, it had nothing to do with you. I met Tucker way before I even knew who you were. I liked him, but he told me that he had a girl that he loved, so he couldn't get down like that. At first I was pissed off. I felt rejected and I let it go. Then fate would have it, I ended up going to the same college and becoming friends with you.

"Funny thing is, I didn't even realize who you were when you started yapping your gums about how good Tucker was and the lavish wedding you were planning. That is, until you showed me his picture.

"I wanted to tell you I knew him, but then you started complaining about all the problems you were having with him. That was the break I needed. And you know what, Keisha? You were right. The sex is *incredible.*"

Keisha was appalled, enraged, and speechless. She sat lifeless, listening to Lea humiliate her.

Tucker walked in, and Lea switched it up, quick fast. "Oh, honey, you're just in time. Keisha's on the phone. Here, let me take li'l man so you two can talk, okay, baby? No, honey, talk to her for li'l man's sake. You have to."

Tucker must have refused to talk to her, 'cause all she heard next was the dial tone. From that point on, Keisha realized she was up against a real live one, and she needed to get her son ASAP.

She cried on Mrs. Wright's shoulder for half the night. She needed all the motherly love and moral support she could get, since she was holding a grudge and refused to speak to her own mother after she had allowed Tucker to take her son.

After Keisha explained the whole scenario to Epiphany's mom, Mrs. Wright suggested Keisha get a police escort to help her retrieve her son. The next morning, she did just that, but Tucker had a surprise for her. He handed the officer court papers. He had already filed for temporary custody of their son, citing abandonment on Keisha's part.

"Well, ma'am, there's nothing I can do," the officer said.

Tucker had already shut the door in their faces. Keisha wondered how she had ever loved him. With the police standing right there, she couldn't black out. That would definitely land her back behind bars.

Having no other choice, she went home and cried her heart out to Tiara.

"The Lord would never put more on you than you could bear." Mrs. Wright sat on the bed next to Keisha with a box of Kleenex and her Bible. "Maybe He was just a little unhappy with your behavior, and this is just His way of getting your attention."

God, why are you doing this to me? I have nothing, no one. Keisha would rather be dead than to live without her son.

Chapter 90

Smitty kept his word. Two hours after he left her at breakfast, they met up and he had the 5 G's for Shana.

Surprised that he really came through, Shana was even more shocked that he was going so hard at the chance to fuck with Epiphany again. If she knew that was what it took to get Raina out of jail and keep his ass off her back, she would've hooked him up a long time ago.

It was time to keep her end of the bargain. She dialed Epiphany, but after a few rings, her voice mail picked up. Shana ended the call and dialed her back again, still ending up with her voicemail.

Smitty was starting to get a little uptight, thinking that Shana was trying to pull a fast one on him.

"Yo, Sha, this is some bullshit. Just forget it, a'ight. Gimme my shit back, yo!"

"Yo, nigga, pump your brakes. Damn, I already told her you feeling her, so just take her number and holla at her later!"

"Nah, fuck that. That wasn't the plan. You supposed to hook that shit up in front of me."

"Well, I can't do shit if she don't answer, right?"

"Yo, that's why I'm saying fuck it. Just gimme my loot back."

"Wait, I'm a keep trying until I get her then."

"Nah, yo, I ain't got all fucking day!"

"Smitty, here, just leave a message. I promise she'll call you back," Shana said, passing him her cell phone, while it was ringing Epiphany's phone.

"Huh, what up, ma? This Smitty. Holla back, a'ight love." He left his phone number on the message too.

"Now, was that hard?" Shana asked.

"Nah, but shorty better holla back or else me and you gon' have a serious beef, word up!" Smitty threatened.

"Trust me, she'll call. Damn, what the fuck she did that got you so strung the fuck out, nigga?" Shana was curious because Smitty was acting a little too desperate and nervous.

"Yo, she ain't do shit," Smitty answered hostilely.

"Whatever, nigga, just hold on tight to your phone, so you don't miss her call. Oh, and here's her cell number just in case."

"A'ight, stop talking shit and hurry up and get Raina out 'fore she bust that ass." Smitty laughed, taking the piece of paper from Shana.

Shana ignored his snide remark, but that's exactly what she was on her way to do—post Raina's bail and be out. As she started up her car and pulled off, she tried dialing Epiphany again just to see if she'd answer, and this time she did.

"Hello?"

"Oh, now you answer," Shana said sarcastically.

"Girl, I'm sorry, I was on the phone with my boo, and the shit he was talking was sounding too good to be put on hold. But anyway, what's good?" Epiphany said.

"Well, damn, I'm glad my life didn't depend on you answering your phone, and what's good is the same shit we already talked about, unless your boo got you having a change of heart."

"You know what, Shana? I'm in a good mood right now, so I'm not even gonna entertain your smart ass, a'ight?"

"Yeah, okay. Just check your message and hit that nigga back!" Shana demanded and abruptly ended the call.

Ooooh, I can't stand that bitch. Epiphany retrieved Smitty's message and phoned him.

"Yo, who this?" Smitty wasn't familiar with the number.

"Who you been expecting?" Epiphany said in a sensual tone.

"Yo, don't play games. Who this?" Smitty asked again. Even though he assumed it was Epiphany, he ain't want to seem like he was beasting.

"Damn, my feelings is hurt. I thought you was waiting on my call."

"C'mon, ma, you know I been waiting to talk to you. What up, though?"

"I don't know. My girl Shana told me that you was checking for me."

"Yeah, you don't remember me?" Smitty questioned.

"From where?"

"I don't know, around I guess. But yo, that's neither here nor there. I'm trying to see you, ma."

"Not a problem."

"Cool. I'ma call you later at this number when I'm ready to scoop you, a'ight."

"No doubt. See you then!"

Chapter 91

All Shana did was post Raina's bail. She didn't care how the girl got home, or if she even had money to get home. As far as she was concerned, her part was done.

Shana was actually relieved now that she felt she and Smitty had resolved their issues, and once she paid him back, she would no longer be in debt to him. The Chasity drama was dead, and with Raina bailed out, all the skeletons in her closet were gone.

"Yo, Sha, this bullshit gotta stop between us," K.C. said as soon as she walked in the apartment.

"Stop what, K.C.? Your lying or your cheating?"

"Come on, baby, how long you trying to be mad at a nigga?"

"K.C., you know what? Right now you better be glad all I'm doing is giving you the silent treatment, 'cause I could go out and get me a nigga that knows how to treat a bitch. Instead, I stay stuck like glue to your muthafucking ass, and what do you do? Nothing but talk shit, lie, and bring fucking diseases home."

"Disease? Yo, what you mean, disease? Ain't nothing wrong with my dick." Since K.C. had no symptoms, he had no idea what she was talking about.

"Oh, nigga, you ain't go get your dick checked yet? That's right, disease, muthafucka. You know, the shit you get when you out in the streets fucking nasty hoes with no condom," Shana sarcastically yelled.

"Yo, I don't know what you talking about. I supposedly gave you something? What I give you, huh?" K.C. didn't have a clue.

"Nigga, you gave me Chlamydia from being out there with other bitches. Play stupid if you want to, but you better hope my other tests come back negative."

"Yo, I ain't never heard of that, but if I did, I'm sorry. I ain't fucked around on you in a minute, though. Sometimes I think something's wrong with me, like maybe I got the same shit that Halle Berry's man got. I don't know why I be fucking other bitches—I just do. I'ma go get my shit checked out, so can you stop being mad at me, please."

K.C. always had a way with words, and as much as Shana didn't want to fall victim to his bullshit, she couldn't help it. She suffered from a sickness called love. She just loved him. She didn't know why, but she did. He was always able to break her down, and love was stronger than pride. Shana forgave him, but only on one condition: Her tests had to come back negative.

Chapter 92

On his way to meet up with Epiphany, Smitty couldn't help but feel a little nervous about fucking with her again, especially after the way he dogged her the first time. It was like she had some kind of hex on him, because even after getting stomped out in public by C-God and Mike over her, he still sort of obsessed over her. Honestly, he regretted forcing himself on her and wanted another chance with her.

Epiphany wasn't comfortable with Smitty picking her up from her parents' home, so she arranged for him to meet her at this cozy little Cuban restaurant on Queens Boulevard. She waited for him to arrive, so they could go in and be seated together.

The dimly lit restaurant was small but always packed. The tables were so close together that it almost felt like people were sitting on top of each other, but for some reason, no one seemed to mind.

There was a long period of silence between the two. Epiphany stared at Smitty often. Her intent looks made him a little apprehensive, but she couldn't help it, because something about him seemed all too familiar.

"I'm sorry I keep looking at you so hard, but there's something about you—I just don't know what it is," Epiphany said, breaking the silence first.

"Stop trying to figure it out and let's just have a good time. We could start by ordering some drinks." Rudely, he flagged down the waiter. Epiphany ordered an apple martini, and since Smitty was feeling the guilt eat away at him, he ordered a Grey Goose mixed with Hennessy and a splash of cranberry juice to help mellow him out.

The alcohol did ease the tension a bit, as the two began to converse a little more. Smitty complimented everything from

Epiphany's hairstyle to her shoes and also ran a few dry jokes by her. Epiphany chilled on the hard looks and pretended to find his jokes funny.

After dinner, Smitty wasn't ready to call it a night just yet, so he suggested that she follow him to this little bar on Linden called Deja Vu. All Epiphany could think about was getting home in time for her midnight call from Wild. She tried to refuse but ended up giving in to his pleas and agreed to go and have one drink.

As they took a seat at the bar, Epiphany glanced around to check out the spot. She could tell it had a nice vibe to it, and since the crowd looked to be a mature one, there wasn't a lot of rowdiness. The bartender was very friendly as she took their drink orders, and Smitty went on to boast to Epiphany about a popular book the bartender wrote entitled *Sheisty*. Epiphany didn't find that to be all that impressive, but she did like the way the girl made her apple martini strong.

One drink ended up turning into three as they both started to unwind around each another. Epiphany had to admit that his jokes got better, and so did her liking for him (after the alcohol kicked in, of course). Smitty was doing his best to keep her entertained, hoping that his jokes mixed with the strong-ass drinks would land him up in the pussy again, only this time not by force. Unfortunately for him, that thought was more of a pipe dream, 'cause yeah, he might have been given a second crack at her, but the game was still the same as far as Epiphany was concerned. Her goodies stayed in the jar until a nice amount of money had been spent. It was gonna cost him a little more than a meal and some drinks to taste her cookie.

As soon as eleven-thirty hit, Epiphany decided to call it a night. Leaning over, she planted a soft kiss on his lips.

"Good night."

Damn, he thought, caught a little off guard as the softness of her lips and the whiff of her scent made his dick rise.

"You leaving me already?" Smitty questioned with disappointment.

"Yeah, I have to go. I finally recognize where I know you from though," Epiphany said.

"What?" Smitty responded tensely as his heart began to pound.

"Yeah, I remember you now, from Club Cream a while back. You were at the bar with K.C. and some other guy."

"Oh, yeah. Okay, right . . . right!" Smitty answered as he let out a deep sigh of relief. He didn't know how he was gonna fuck with Epiphany without the torture of worrying about when, or if, she would ever remember how much she really hated him and why.

As Epiphany left, Smitty waited for a few moments and then secretly followed her to her home for the hell of it.

Chapter 93

A couple weeks passed, and things were all good between Shana and K.C., especially since her test results came back negative. She even escorted him to the clinic to get tested. Since K.C. knew he was running around fucking everything in sight, he took it a step further and agreed to be tested for HIV. Shana still refused to take an HIV test, because she felt that since his results came back negative, then she was negative, and HIV was as simple as that.

Shana was also able to relax more without the static from Raina. Maybe Raina wasn't upset about having to stay in jail a couple of days and was just happy to be home, so she decided to let it go. K.C. and Smitty were still handling their business, and money would soon be straight for them.

Now Smitty was all caught up in Epiphany; therefore K.C. and his friendship turned into more of just a business partnership. Of course, Shana was happy about that, because that meant K.C. ran the streets less and spent more time with her. They were finally starting to connect. They laid up for most of the day watching movies, making love, getting high, and even talking about one day having kids. It all seemed too good to be true, because in the three years that she'd been with him, all they ever seemed to do was fight, fuss, and fuck. Sure, he claimed to love her, but this was the first time since his bid that she actually felt his love for her.

She felt the time was right to clear her conscience and pull all her skeletons out of the closet. She told him that she and C-God had had more than just a business relationship, but it was brief. She then went on to drop what she thought was going to be a bomb—her sexual experience with Chasity. To her surprise, K.C. already knew. He said he had gotten the word on all that when he was locked up.

"How?" Shana questioned, anxious to know the answer and hoping it wasn't Smitty that told.

"Yo, don't worry about it. Just know in jail a nigga hear everything!"

"Well, was you mad when you heard?"

"What I'ma be mad for? Baby girl, you was holding a nigga down, so how I'ma knock your hustle? The shit about you fucking with that bitch, man, I knew as soon as daddy came home that shit was gon' be a wrap!" K.C. said.

For the first time in a long time, Shana was able to exhale. She was glad to know that she didn't have to stress over none of her secrets anymore, but she also was mad that Smitty put a twenty-thousand dollar dent in her pocket for nothing.

K.C. caught Shana gazing off into a deep thought.

"Yo, is there something else you gotta tell me?"

"Nah, that's it." Shana smiled and snapped out of her trance.

"A'ight then, climb up on daddy's dick and give me some of that pussy," K.C. ordered.

Shana was more than happy to obey his order. Just as she was about to lay it down, there was a hard knock at the door.

"Who the fuck is that knocking like they crazy? Oh, boy, I bet it's Smitty's stupid ass," Shana said, slightly raising her voice as if her high was just blown. She got up out of bed and threw on something to go see.

Swinging open the door, expecting to see Smitty, she was surprised to find four policemen standing there. Her heart dropped. She knew it would be only a matter of time before she was busted.

"Shana Marie Scott, you're under arrest for the intent to sell and distribute drugs. You have the right to remain silent. . . ." The arresting officer read her rights, handcuffed her, and hauled her off to jail.

Chapter 94

Keisha was working hard to get her life in order. She was granted weekly unsupervised visits with her son until her court date for custody. After enrolling back in school part-time, she got a job at a real estate office, working for commission. Lastly, she left Blackplanet.com alone. Everything was starting to come together once she became a believer in Christ.

Going to church and reading the Bible with Mrs. Wright had helped Keisha develop a better understanding about what it meant to believe in God. She'd learned to stop blaming the Lord for her bad decisions and mess-ups, because "Although He is the Almighty," her pastor would say, "sin is your choice."

Changes didn't happen overnight, so when thoughts of killing Lea surfaced in her mind every so often, she just prayed for strength. Keisha refrained from having any kind of contact with Tucker, at least until the court hearing came. Momma D's house was the location for the baby's drop off and pick up. That way they never had to cross each other's paths.

When she was lonely and missed him, she'd press *67 before dialing his cell, just to hear him say hello. Oddly enough, she felt he was doing the same, because she had gotten quite a few crank calls herself. It was over between them, and she was almost ready to move on.

Keisha had made amends with Loretta and started calling her Ma. The two of them talked on the phone every day, sometimes twice a day, establishing a tight-knit relationship, discussing any and everything on their minds. Loretta's discussions were mainly about her mistakes and Keisha's younger sisters.

Keely, only sixteen, wasn't going to school and hanging out 'til all times of the night with the local thugs. Kelly was a breath of fresh air, attending Clark University and doing exceedingly well. Keisha would always be her mother's pride and joy, her firstborn, her lovechild, and she expressed that love to her every chance she got. Keisha had to admit she loved feeling her mother's love and how blessed she was to have a second mom in Mrs. Wright.

Keisha's improvement made Mrs. Wright proud. Keisha gave Mrs. Wright hope that her own daughter, Epiphany, would make a change in her life as well.

Chapter 95

Tucker was finally adjusted to Lea being around. She was loving, caring, and very helpful with his little man, and he appreciated that more than anything else. Following his mother's death, every woman his father would bring home despised him and didn't want the responsibility of caring for another woman's child, which led to abuse. His father's need for women was much stronger than his need to be a dad, so he allowed the hateful behavior from them to go on without saying a word.

Lea was such a good woman to him and his son that he decided to take their relationship a step further with a three-carat, emerald cut diamond and a marriage proposal. Yes, he was ready to take it there, but he didn't want a big blow-out wedding like the one he and Keisha were planning. No, this time he wanted it to be simple without her feeling cheated, so he planned to take her to Montego Bay, Jamaica, to tie the knot.

Sometimes he wondered if maybe he should've just married Keisha. Things might have turned out differently, and she would have been his wife. No matter how hard he tried to front, he missed what she was to him, and deep down inside, the love he had for her was still there. Clearly too much had happened to turn back.

Tucker phoned his boys down South to tell them the latest.

"Hey, what's up, cuz? You all right, dawg ?" Peewee recognized the New York number.

"Yo, I'm chilling, Pee. How you?"

"Man, shit is all gravy thanks to you."

"Where my nigga Cornell at?"

"Ay, T, man, since that nigga done got a little paper in his pocket, he stay fucking around with these scandalous-ass broads down here, man. I'm try'na get this paper, dawg!"

"I hear that! But listen, man, don't let no bullshit come between y'all niggas. You know what I'm saying?"

"Nah, dawg, never that. That nigga just a little off track. That's all it is. We good. But what up with that faggot-ass dude C-God, man? He surface yet?"

"Nah, he still hiding. But yo, I just called to let y'all niggas know, your boy gon' go 'head and jump the fucking broom!"

"Ay, T, man, that's what's up! Congrats on that, dawg. Make your baby momma your wife, cousin."

Tucker hadn't been in touch with Pee and Cornell in weeks.

"Nah, not me and Keish, dawg. Her name's Leanne," Tucker said realizing how awkward the conversation just became.

"Ay, dawg, I ain't even gon' touch that, but whatever happened musta been fucked up, 'cause, dawg, you was in *love* with Keisha."

"Yeah, man, I had to move on from that. This one's a nice one, though."

"Congratulations on that then, cuz. How Li'l Man doing?"

"He's good. Ay, that's them coming in now. Listen, tell Corn to holla at me, and y'all niggas stay tight. I'ma kick it with you soon, a'ight?" Tucker hung up the phone in a hurry so he could build up the nerve to pop the question.

Lea returned from the park with Li'l Man in her arms. As soon as he saw his daddy, the baby started squirming, crying, and fighting to get away from her. As soon as she put him down, he ran over and clutched onto Tucker like he was afraid of Lea.

"What's wrong with him?" Tucker picked up his son.

"I don't know. Maybe something scared him at the park."

Lea's excuse didn't sit well with Tucker. He never thought that Lea would do anything to hurt his son. Playing it safe, he chose to hold off on asking the question for a little while.

Chapter 96

Epiphany was spending a lot of time with Smitty. If she was still interested in niggas making small-time figures, he could've actually won her heart. He accommodated her need to be spoiled, but she wasn't trying to get caught up with him and lose focus on the plan. He was friends with the nigga that tried to kill her, and more than likely, he knew about it.

Epiphany didn't know what it would take to persuade him to kill Ness for her, but she decided it was time to let Smitty sample her goodies when she overheard a discussion he was having with K.C., concerning some conflict with Ness. She knew he was ready to sever ties with him. Their beef would be the beginning of Ness's end.

Smitty started to develop strong feelings for Epiphany; however, he was growing impatient and tired of doing all the wining, dining, and spending for nothing. He never was that type of nigga to kick out cash for ass, but he was splurging like crazy, and even though he had already hit it once, he was thirsty to find out what it tasted like.

Damn I guess you should never say never, but fuck it. I'm just gonna throw it out there and ask for some. Smitty picked up the phone and called to confirm their date.

"Hey, boo," Epiphany answered.

"What up, ma? We still on for the night?"

"Oh, no question. Why? Where you want me to meet you at this time?"

"Yo, why you always gotta meet me? Why I can't just come pick you up?"

"Because."

"Because what? You don't trust me?"

"Smitty, it ain't about that. You know what happened. I just don't want to bring no bullshit to my parents' house."

"Yeah, a' ight, yo. I guess I gotta respect that. So meet me at the Holiday Inn at nine o'clock, a'ight."

"Ooooh, so does that mean I should bring something sexy to wear?" Epiphany said, giving him all the assurance he needed.

Before he could respond, her other line beeped. It was Wild. She rushed him off. "Nine o'clock is good. I gotta take this call. Bye." Epiphany switched over to Wild.

"Damn, I miss you, baby," she said seductively.

"For real? I miss you too. I miss you so much I followed you today." Epiphany's heart pounded rapidly.

"S–stop playing, baby!" she stuttered.

"Yeah, I'm playing, but you saving that stuff for me, right?"

"Oh, no doubt, daddy. This pussy belongs to only the wild one. When you coming for it?" she teased.

"As a matter of fact, I'ma be back in town tomorrow afternoon. So what's up? You packing your bags or what?"

"Hell yeah. I can't wait."

"A'ight, sweet sugar panties, I'll pick you up soon as I touch down around noon."

"Okay, baby, as soon as you touch down," Epiphany repeated.

"I got you," said Wild as he hung up the phone.

Chapter 97

K.C. rushed down to the precinct to see what was up with Shana. The arresting officers wouldn't disclose any information other than that she was being brought up on felony charges. He took that little bit of info for what it was worth and immediately called his lawyer, Mr. Loboski, to explain the situation and ask if he'd take her case. His attorney agreed.

K.C. considered calling Shana's mom, Ms. Pat, but she hated him and would definitely use this situation as an opportunity to badger him. That was the last thing he needed right now, especially since he had nothing to do with this mess Shana had gotten herself into. The only thing left for him to do was go home and wait by the phone for Shana to call him.

After hours of interrogation, name calling, and harsh threats, Shana managed to hold her head. She wasn't confessing to nothing. The police had some solid evidence against her. Not only did Raina drop dime, but her supplier's perverted ways finally caught up with him, and he sang like a bird when the feds nabbed him. Apparently, an underage girl accused him of drugging her and then trying to have his way with her. Raina also told the police that he was a big-time drug dealer, which they already suspected.

Shana was not only concerned about her ties with her supplier, but the police confiscated several security tapes from his house, some with her on them. Still, Shana refused to talk. The only words she had for them were: "Can I make my phone call now?"

Chapter 98

C-God gave up on trying to get in touch with Reggie by phone. It was time to head back to the Big Apple and find his ass. C had already let shit ride long enough.

Alpo was his number one supporter, and he really wanted C-God to stop getting high, get himself together, and take back what was rightfully his. Of course C-God loved the sound of that, so he was trying hard to stay clean, at least while handling business.

They rented a utility van, loaded it up with rope, duct tape, guns, Alpo's dog Venom, and Hassan, one of the few ride or die niggas from VA. Being back in New York made C-God realize how much he had missed it, but with the death of his parents, the end of his reign and everything else the city represented—greed, murder, and betrayal—he vowed to never live there again.

Before hitting the hood, C-God stopped by the cemetery to ask his mom and pop for forgiveness. He was sorry for all the misery that he had caused them; their blood, sweat, tears, and death. Next to his parents' plots were his brothers, Paul a.k.a "Pop" and Russell a.k.a "Black Russ" Hinderson. Dead for years, they never saw their baby brother's rise to the top. C-God wasn't religious, but he knew they had to be watching over him, and he asked that they guide him through his mission and make sure he kept it straight gangsta.

Having made his peace with the family, it was time for revenge. Next stop, the hood!

After scouting out the project and all of his former spots, there was no sign of Reggie. C-God had no choice but to go by the nigga's crib. He carefully got out of the van, checking his surroundings, and instructed Alpo and his boy to do the same. He walked up to the front door and rang the bell.

"Tanya, you back already?" Reggie's elderly grandmother asked as she slowly approached the door.

C was confused. *Did she just say Tanya?* Still focused on finding Reggie, he didn't dwell on it.

"Nah, Mrs. Mattie, it's C. Is Reggie home?"

"C who? Naw, he ain't home."

C-God didn't respond. He returned to the van, parked it two houses away, and waited. Minutes later, Tanya drove up with his son, a bag full of groceries, and a pot belly, looking about three or four months pregnant. C-God shook his head in disgust and pulled off, realizing that was probably the reason why Reggie was avoiding him. To be honest about it, he knew he could never be what Tanya needed, even if he tried. He wouldn't have been mad if they, especially Reg, came to him with the truth instead of being sneaky.

But fuck it. What's done is done, he thought.

Taking one more loop around the area, they decided to stop and get a quick bite to eat at the Philly Cheesesteak spot on Linden Boulevard. While C-God sat in the van, waiting for Alpo and Hassan to come out of the restaurant, a pearly white Range Rover blasting "Lean Back" pulled up right in front of him. What do you know? Fuck finding Reggie, out jumped the head nigga in charge, Ness, who headed for the store next door to the eatery.

C-God smiled. His brothers up in ghetto heaven must've been listening.

"Yo, God, what the fuck you smiling at, man?" Alpo asked as he and Hassan got back in the van.

"Yo, guess who just hopped the fuck out that truck, right in fucking front of me?" C-God asked.

"Get the fuck out of here. You sure that's that nigga?" Alpo questioned.

"Hell yeah, that's that muthafucka Ness. He in the store right now."

"Yo, Hassan, gimme my shit."

Hassan handed Alpo his gun.

"Yo, I'ma go hop in that muthafucka's backseat, a'ight! Ay, C-God, pull up in front of the nigga's truck. I'll make sure he follows you." Alpo pulled his black hoodie over his head, crept up to Ness's car, opened the back door, climbed in, and waited for him.

Chapter 99

Epiphany arrived at the Holiday Inn at 9:05 p.m. She pulled into a vacant parking spot and took a couple of minutes to apply a little more gloss to her already shiny lips in her rearview mirror. Before getting out of the car, she clutched down on the bottom of her Fendi bag to make sure she had her .22. She made it a priority to never leave the house without it after her near death experience. Normally, she would have had her nine, but it never turned up after that night. For her, having some protection was better than none at all. She would say, "A .22 might not kill a muthafucka, but it will definitely complicate their intentions to harm me."

Covering all areas, she was ready for whatever and had her game face on as she pranced toward the hotel entrance, where she found Smitty waiting. Inside their room, Epiphany wasted no time getting down to business. Opening her little overnight bag, she pulled out something more appropriate for the occasion. She suggested Smitty order a bottle of champagne from room service, preferably Veuve Clicquot, while she showered and slipped into something sexy for him.

Smitty liked the idea of her slipping into something sexy. The hood rats he used to fuck with considered a matching bra and panties something sexy, if he was lucky.

The champagne arrived just before Epiphany opened the steamy bathroom door. She was smelling so fresh and so clean, like cucumber melon, in her red lace Victoria's Secret lingerie number. Smitty was mesmerized. As he held two glasses of bubbly, the bulge in his boxers was starting to show, and he wondered if she tasted as good as she smelled.

Seductively, she walked over to him, removed both glasses from his hands, and one by one took both of them straight to the head. Epiphany placed the empty glasses down, pushed him onto the bed, and slowly climbed on top of him, gliding her tongue across his chest.

Smitty's eagerness wouldn't allow him to just lie there and enjoy her foreplay. He wanted Epiphany—now. Flipping her over, he ripped her panties off and aggressively started licking her pussy.

Epiphany squirmed from discomfort as he licked and sucked on her with such brute force. She tried to move his head from between her legs, only Smitty continued like some kind wild beast in a trance, pinning her legs down to the bed and ignoring her screams for him to stop.

His behavior struck a chord. Suddenly, Epiphany flashed back to why she hated him in the first place. She remembered him raping her. In a panic, she began to gasp for air. Hysterical, she punched him repeatedly, finally getting him to stop.

She jumped up from the bed, grabbed her purse, and ran in the bathroom. Locking the door behind her, she quickly dumped out her bag, searching for her asthma pump. Calming down after a few minutes, she sat on the bathroom floor, holding her gun in her hand.

Meanwhile, Smitty stood on the other side of the door, begging for her forgiveness.

"I'm sorry, baby. I don't know what got into me. Please give me another chance. I really care about you, Epiphany. Come out. We'll just lay down. No sex. I promise."

It was too late. Epiphany wanted to shoot him through the door, but as badly as she wanted to kill him, she knew she had to see Ness suffer first. She put her gun away, pushed her feelings to the side, opened the door, and lay in Smitty's arms, awake for the rest of the night.

Chapter 100

"Shut the fuck up. Keep your eyes on the fucking road and let's follow that van, muthafucka." With Alpo's piece pointed at his head, Ness had no other choice but to follow his orders.

C-God led them to an abandoned house way out in Far Rockaway, where the torture began. Ness, scared shitless, parked his Range behind the unmarked van in the driveway. Hassan hopped out the van with his Uzi ready to shoot and instructed Ness to get out slowly.

"Yo, what the fuck is going on, man? What the fuck y'all niggas want with me? Here, take the fucking truck and let a nigga go, yo. What, y'all niggas want money, too? Let me call my man, have him bring as much as y'all want."

Ness's pleas went ignored. The car keys and roll of hundreds he threw at his kidnappers lay right where they fell on the ground.

"Shut the fuck up, nigga! This ain't about no truck or no money, you rat bastard muthafucka." Hassan patted Ness down for weapons.

"Move it, you bitch-ass nigga. Get in the house," Alpo said.

"Hell no. If y'all niggas is gon' kill me, do it right the fuck here, 'cause I ain't going inside that house," Ness said boldly.

"What, muthafucka?" said Alpo and Hassan. They pushed him to the ground and started kicking and pistol whipping him.

"Nigga, ain't nobody giving your punk ass a choice," yelled Alpo.

Hassan grabbed Ness by his feet and started dragging him toward the house. Ness yelled out in agony from the burning sensation of his flesh ripping across the concrete.

Once inside the house, they stomped him out again and tied him to an old chair that a crackhead probably brought in to use.

Staring through half shut eyes into the faces of Alpo and Hassan, Ness tried to figure out where he might know them from, but neither one of them seemed familiar. He wondered if this was payback for murdering that kid Righteous, or maybe just some hating-ass niggas that heard about the paper he was getting. All of his questions were answered when C-God walked in.

"Well, well, well, what up, sheisty-ass nigga?" C-God taunted.

Ness didn't recognize C-God at first. Once a buff dude, crack had made him lose over fifty pounds. If Ness hadn't remembered C-God's voice, he might have never figured out who he was.

"Oh, shit. C, that's you, nigga? Look like you could use a meal or two. What the fuck you doing, getting high? Damn, nigga, I'm disappointed in you." Bloody, bruised, and facing death, Ness was still a smartass.

"Fuck you, muthafucka. You should've killed me when you had the chance, 'cause a nigga came back just for your punk ass.

"Yo, Alpo, bring your dog in, since this nigga got a thing for dogs!" C-God demanded. He planned on having Venom bite into Ness's flesh while he washed the wounds with ammonia.

"Nah, nigga, that's your baby moms," Ness said sarcastically, referring to C's baby mother sucking off a pit bull to get some free drugs.

C-God had been disrespected enough by this guy, but he couldn't believe that Ness had the balls to be tied up with nowhere to run out in Far-ass-Rockaway and he still continued to pop shit. C-God rushed Ness, jabbing his stun gun right into his chest.

"Tape his fucking mouth up," C ordered Hassan.

After a night filled with torture, C-God was ready to end it once and for all. For the grand finale, C-God, Alpo, and Hassan placed Ness in a barrel filled with lye and watched while he helplessly hollered and squirmed as his skin burned away.

Chapter 101

Keisha picked up her son bright and early from Momma D's house. She had a wonderful day planned and wanted to get an early start.

During their visit, she noticed bruises on his upper right arm, like someone had squeezed or punched him really hard. Furious, she began to further inspect his body, finding another identical bruise on his thigh.

Oh, hell no! Right away she knew Lea was abusing her son, and there was no way she would allow him to spend another second with that monster. Outraged, Keisha called Tucker's cell phone and went off on him as soon as he answered.

"Wait. Calm down a minute. I can't understand a word you're saying, Keisha."

"I *said,* have you seen these fucking bruises on our son? Tucker, he's not coming back to that house as long as that bitch is in it. She better hope to God I never see her."

"What are you talking about? What bruises?"

"On his body, Tucker! Listen to me. Lea's playing you like she played me. I thought she was my friend, but she set me up and confessed to it after she had me arrested."

"What?"

"Lea drugged me the night of my party and sent you that tape. She told me how she wanted to get with you and how you shut her down 'cause we were together.

"Anyway, what's done is done. I don't give a fuck about none of that anymore. She got you and that's fine, but Li'l Man is another story. If you don't keep her away from him, I swear before God, I'm gonna hurt her."

"Keish, are you still at Momma D's house?"

"No, I'm at Epiphany's."

"Well, can you please come outside? I'm on my way." Tucker remembered his son's behavior toward Leanne a couple of days ago.

***

As soon as Keisha stepped out the front door with her son, Tucker was pulling up in front of the house. Hopping out of the car, he ran straight to Li'l Man to see what Keisha was ranting about.

"Tucker, she did this," she said, pulling up the baby's sleeve. "I know she did this. When I called you after I got out of jail, she was real loose with her mouth. She asked if I was calling to speak to *'her man'* or my *'fucking rugrat brat.'* That's why I tried to come get him, but you pulled that custody stunt, and now look at his arm and his leg. I'm telling you, T, she wants to get rid of Li'l Man like she got rid of me. Just think, if Lea can drug me, pay a guy to have sex with me, tape it, and send it to you, there's no telling what else she's capable of." Keisha was hysterical.

Tucker listened without saying a word. Everything Keisha was saying made a lot of sense to him. It was ironic that Lea had come back into his life just as shit fell apart between him and Keisha.

If she sabotaged my relationship, then Keisha's right. What else . . .? Tucker couldn't even finish his thought. He looked at the marks on his son again and his blood boiled.

"Keisha, I'll be back, a'ight."

"Tucker, have you been listening to anything I just said?"

"Yeah, and I believe you." Tucker got back in his 745 and sped off.

When Tucker reached home, Leanne was in the kitchen trying her best to cook, but the burning smell that lingered throughout the house told a different story.

"Oh, hey, honey," Lea said excitedly when she spotted Tucker standing in the doorway of the kitchen.

Tucker gave her a fake smile. During his drive back to the house, his first thought was to fuck her up, but since Leanne liked to play games, he decided to play one on her.

"Ummm, smells interesting," he said.

"I know, honey. I wanted to make you some breakfast, but it didn't turn out so great. Maybe we should go and get some takeout again. I'm sorry," Leanne said in a disappointing tone.

"It's all good. Listen, let me kick it with you for a minute." Tucker took her by her hand and led her to the living room couch. "Leanne, I've been thinking about just letting Keisha go ahead and take full custody of Li'l Man. I know he's a handful, and with you in school and everything, I just don't feel it's fair to you to have to take care of my son when he's Keisha's responsibility." Tucker wanted to see where her head was at.

Leanne's face lit up without smiling. "Well, honey, you know Li'l Man is a handful, but I don't mind looking after him. However, I think he does need to be with his mother. He misses Keisha. That's why I think he doesn't like me."

"Yeah, maybe you're right, 'cause I know Li'l Man can make you wanna knock the shit out of him sometimes, right?" Tucker chuckled then got serious. "Right, Leanne?" he asked again, looking her dead in the eye.

"No, I would never do that," Lea answered nervously.

"You wouldn't? Are you sure about that?"

"Of course I'm sure. What are you getting at?"

"I'm getting at the fact that you're not the only one that knows how to set up a hidden camcorder. That's right. Don't look sick in the face now. I saw you! I got you on tape hitting my son," Tucker lied to get her to confess.

"Tucker, wait. Hear me out. I can explain that. I didn't even hit him hard. I was just teaching him some discipline."

"Just go upstairs, get your shit, and get the hell up out of my house. A'ight!" Tucker didn't want to hear her bullshit.

"Tucker, please, don't!" Leanne cried.

Tucker let out a hard sigh, jumped up, and yoked her up from the couch by her neck.

"Don't what? You violated when you put your hands on my son, and that shit you did to Keisha was foul. Either you gon' get your shit and go, or leave it for the trash, but you better decide quick, and trust me when I tell you this is me being nice!"

Leanne's eyes watered from the tight grip Tucker called "being nice." When he let her go, she was so shook that she left her all her belongings behind, grabbed her car keys, and got the fuck up out of there. She knew she could never be his number one.

Chapter 102

Epiphany thought about what had happened between her and Smitty the entire night. Allowing herself to be in his company again sickened her. She didn't feel comfortable playing this little game anymore. All type of thoughts started to cross her mind, mainly that maybe she was the one being played.

Smitty almost raped me a second time last night, and Ness tried to kill me. Shit, maybe they're scheming to finish me off.

Finally, thinking sensibly, Epiphany felt seeking revenge this way didn't seem so sweet or safe for her anymore, and it certainly wasn't worth losing her life over (for real this time).

She eased Smitty's arm from around her, got out of bed, and quietly put on her clothes. Before sneaking out, Epiphany gathered up all Smitty's belongings, including his cell phone, and took them with her. Inside her car, she emptied out his pockets: $180 in crumpled twenties, a Cartier watch, platinum chain with a diamond-studded Jesus head medallion, a wallet with nine crisp $100 bills, and his license.

Epiphany started up her car and pulled off. Reaching halfway home, she smiled to herself, thinking, *Payback is a bitch.*

She stopped at a gas station and tossed the useless possessions—his clothes, sneakers, empty wallet, and phone—in a dumpster.

Strolling in the house, Epiphany was so excited to see her godson and Keisha together. She picked him up and held him tightly, and he patted her softly on her back.

"Ooh, it's so good to see you, Li'l T. I can't believe how big he got, Keisha." Epiphany kissed his cheeks. This was the first time she had seen him since she'd been home from the hospital.

"I know. They were feeding my baby well in ATL." They laughed, and so did Li'l T. "E, I thank you for making me realize that my son is my life. So much has happened, and part of it was because of my stupidity. The other part, girl, you wouldn't believe it if I told you."

"What?" Epiphany asked.

"We'll talk later, but since you're finally home for a change, why don't you take us for a ride to get some breakfast?"

"Damn, I would love to, Keish, but I have to start packing."

"Packing what? Where you going? You just got home."

"Packing my shit, girl. I'm moving to Jersey with Wild."

"The music producer?"

"Mm-hmm, and by the way, where's my parents?"

"Damn, E. See, that goes to show that you ain't never home, 'cause you don't never know what's going on. Tiara and Jay went on a three-day Gospel cruise."

"Gospel cruise! Pops must've finally gave in," Epiphany said in shock.

"Yeah, church is not so bad, you know."

"Oh God, not you too, Keish?"

"Epiphany, don't knock getting saved until you try it. Can I use your car while you pack?"

Epiphany paused for a moment and wondered how her mom had managed to turn everybody holy.

"Unbelievable," she mumbled as she handed Keisha her car keys.

"Thanks. We won't be long." Keisha took Li'l Man from Epiphany's arms and headed out the door.

Epiphany rushed to the basement and started packing. Far in back of one of her drawers, she found some photos of herself, Keisha, and Shana from the old days, when their clique was inseparable.

Now Keisha's a mommy, Shana's married, and I'm finally getting out of Southside Jamaica. Deep down inside, she was going to miss her hood, but she vowed she'd never come back there to live.

The house phone rang. Epiphany thought about not answering it, but she assumed that it might be her parents calling, so she decided to pick up.

"Wright residence."

"You have a call from 'Ramel' at a correctional facility. To decline the call, please hang up. If you accept, dial five now," said the recording.

Epiphany rolled her eyes and hung up. A few minutes later, it rang again, and she accepted the call.

"Hello? What happened?" Ramel said, wondering why the phone cut off.

"Nothing happened," Epiphany said coldly.

"Epiphany!"

"Yeah."

"Oh, shit! What up, baby girl? I finally caught up with you. I been trying to holla at you for a while now, but you don't never be home. How's everything? You all right?" After Ramel had moved out of her parents' house years back, he and Epiphany did their best to avoid each other.

"I was until now!"

"Yo, listen, Epiphany. I'm sorry for that foul shit I put you through. Damn, you don't know how much that shit fucks with me every day, especially now that I got a little girl. I hate myself for that nasty shit. I know I violated you in the worst way, and you never told on me. As many times as you threatened to, you didn't. . . . Hello? you there?" Ramel was uncertain she was there because she had been so silent.

"I'm here." Tears started to run down her face.

"Oh, a'ight. Just making sure. But listen, that's my time. I just wanted you to know that I'm sorry. I love you, and please be careful out there on them streets. Oh, and between me and you, your pops and I searched hard looking for the nigga C-God. But don't worry. He'll surface one day, and word is out in all the jails, so if he get locked up, he's finished—dead just like the rest of his brothers," Ramel guaranteed her.

"Ramel, can you keep your eyes and ears open for this kid named Ness? He was the one that shot me. Oh, and a cat named Smitty. He was down with it too."

"Ness. Oh, word, he was the trigger man! I'm hearing a lotta bad shit about that kid. He done already signed his death certificate when he killed that cat from Lefrak. He won't be breathing too much longer, but the other cat, I got you. A'ight, baby girl, I gotta go. Please take care of yourself."

"I will, and thanks, *Uncle*."

Uncle Ramel smiled, because in his heart, he knew Epiphany's last words meant that she forgave him. She had stopped calling him Uncle years ago.

Chapter 103

Shana's heart sank when the fat cracker bastard denied her bail and adjourned her case for thirty days, suggesting that she utilize the time to adjust her attitude problem. She turned to her lawyer with a "do something" look, but Shana (coming up in the courtroom rolling her eyes and sucking her teeth before the judge) made it difficult to do anything.

As she was being escorted back to the cell, Shana turned to K.C. He shook his head in disappointment.

Damn, I knew her attitude was gon' get her in trouble one day.

As soon as he walked in the apartment, K.C. heard the phone ringing.

"Yo," K.C. answered, rushing over to the phone.

"Hey, K.C.," Shana said.

"Ain't no 'hey,' Shana. What the fuck was all that attitude about today? Don't you know fucking around with the judge like that, you only playing with your own freedom, dummy? You could have all the attitude you want with them fucking police, but you ain't never s'pose to fuck around with no judge. But I guess now you found that shit out the hard way, right?"

"Yeah, I guess you're right, but they had it in for me from the door, 'cause these cops in here already told me how it was gon' go down. That's why I had an attitude," Shana explained.

"Regardless, you don't fuck around with the nigga that holds your freedom card."

"Well, do you think he'll let me out on bail my next court date?"

"Yo, Sha, you disrespected a judge in his courtroom, so I don't know. He might make you wait it out until your sentencing."

"Damn, I fucked up!"

"Yeah, that you did."

"Well, I got to go now. I'll let you know my visitors schedule as soon as I know it, a'ight. I love you!"

"A'ight, Sha. I love ya ass too, and ay, keep your head up, baby girl. Shit'll be okay!"

Chapter 104

Smitty jumped up out of his sound sleep when the hotel phone rang to inform him that it was checkout time.

"Yo, ma, you wanna go get some breakfast?" Smitty thought Epiphany was in the bathroom, but when he didn't get a response, he got up out of the bed to find that she was gone and so were his things.

"Damn, that fucking bitch!" he yelled out, standing in just his boxers. He became even more vexed when he discovered that his cell phone was gone too. He needed to call K.C. so he could bring him some clothes, but he didn't know the number by heart.

He paced back and forth until he came up with an idea. He could call information and see if anyone named Shana Scott was listed. Luckily, she was, and the operator gave him two listings.

Please, somebody be home. His heart pounded, impatiently awaiting an answer.

"Hello?" K.C. answered.

"Yo, man, thank God you're home!"

"Smitty?"

"Yeah, man. Yo, I need you to bring me a pair of jeans and a shirt." Smitty looked around the room to see if his sneakers were gone too. "Oh, and some kicks too, man."

"Yo, nigga, what happened? Where you at?" K.C. questioned.

"Man, I'm at the Holiday Inn next to Kennedy Airport. Yo, that fucking bitch done robbed me for my shit and bounced on a nigga while I was sleeping. Thank God I valet parked, 'cause the bitch probably would've took my car keys too."

"Who?" K.C. laughed.

"Your fucking chick's homegirl. That bitch Epiphany." Smitty was real sour.

"Yo, man, didn't I tell your ass to leave that shit alone? Nigga, see, you don't listen." K.C. continued to laughed and rub it in.

"Nigga, that shit ain't funny, yo, and I bet Shana's trifling ass knew what the fuck was up all along. Where she at? 'Cause I need that bitch Epiphany's number again so I can get my shit back."

"Yo, nigga, Sha ain't have shit to do with that. Besides, she got her own shit to deal with, man. Five-o came, took my baby, and locked her ass up. She gotta do thirty days before she could even go back to court for a bail."

"Word, that's fucked up! But, man, you got her cell phone at the crib with you? 'Cause I need homegirl's number now. I'm ready to kill that bitch, man. She played me good, for real!"

"Yeah, I got it. Hold up." K.C. searched Shana's phone and recited both Epiphany's house and cell numbers to Smitty.

"Good looking out, nigga. I'm in room 234. Come see me!" Smitty hung up and immediately dialed Epiphany's cell.

Epiphany had just finished packing when she looked at the time and realized it was almost noon, which meant Wild should be out front shortly to pick her up. The closer it got to noon, the more excited she became.

Epiphany reached for her ringing cell phone in her purse and accidentally pulled out Smitty's chain, which she thought would be a nice gift for Wild. She grabbed her phone and noticed the screen read BLOCKED. Normally she didn't answer blocked calls, but she wasn't going to take any chances on missing Wild, so she answered.

"Hello?"

"Yo, why you play me like that? That was some fucked-up shit you did. You know that, right?" Smitty said.

"What? Nigga, get over it! What? You thought I wasn't gon' remember what you did to me? Well, the joke's on you, muthafucka. It was a game, nigga. You can't possibly be that dumb to think that I would fuck with you knowing that your boy is the nigga that shot me and killed my boyfriend—or maybe you are.

"'You act like your pussy is gold.' You remember saying that to me the night C-God and Mike stomped your punk-ass out? Well, you know what? It must be, because your stupid ass went hard for it this time. Unfortunately, you've been punked, muthafucka!" Epiphany was filled with vindication as she slammed down the hood of her phone.

Smitty was steaming mad. Epiphany might have thought this shit was over, but this time he was gonna see to it that she pushed up daisies.

Nobody gonna play me like that and live to tell it. He sat on the edge of the bed and waited for K.C. to bring him some clothes.

Chapter 105

Epiphany would have felt threatened if Smitty knew where she lived, but since he didn't, fuck him. Right after she hung up on Smitty, Wild called to say he was only fifteen minutes away, so she should be ready. For sure, Epiphany was ready—ready to put Southside Jamaica, Queens, and all its drama behind her. She wrote three notes for the people she loved.

> *Mommy,*
> *I'm happy to see that you found a home in the church. Try not to worry too much. I'll be fine. I love you, and I promise I'll stay in touch.*
>
> *Epee*

> *Daddy,*
> *You know you're my number one. I love you more than anything. I only hope I haven't disappointed you too much. I know you only want the best for me. Don't worry. I only want the best for me too! Try not to let the born again version of Mommy drive you to drink. I'm just playing. I'm glad she got you into church. I'll be in touch.*
>
> *Love always, Epee*

> *Hey Keish,*
> *I was hoping I'd get to see you before I left. I'm gonna miss you. You are my true friend, and just because we don't have the same blood running through our veins don't mean we ain't real sisters. Take care of my godson, and if you and Tucker don't get back together,*

don't worry. It's his loss. You gotta promise me you'll come visit me soon. Tell Shana I said bye. I love you!

Epiphany

P.S. Keep the car.

By the time Epiphany finished her last letter, her knight in shining armor was outside her house, waiting for his princess. She took one final look around the house and headed to the door, where Wild's driver met her at the top of the stairs to carry her bags. Off to Jersey they went.

Keisha pulled up at the house seconds later, just missing Epiphany. She got out of the car and opened the back door to take Li'l Man from his car seat.

"Hey, E, I'm back," she yelled once she opened the front door. When Epiphany didn't answer, she put her son down and noticed there were three folded pieces of paper on the kitchen table. One of them had her name on it. She read the letter and tears started to fall.

Keisha was going to miss Epiphany, and part of her knew she'd probably never see her friend again. Truth be told, Epiphany was good at starting over. Keisha could only hope that she wouldn't be forgotten.

She called Tucker, and he told her that he and Lea were over. He also apologized for being so fucked up toward her. He wanted to know if they could try to make their family work.

Keisha was hesitant for a moment, but more than anything in the world, she knew she wanted her family back together. She agreed, but only under certain circumstances.

"Tucker, we can try again, but not in that house, not after Lea lived in it. I want us to start fresh."

Tucker didn't see a problem with starting fresh at all. As a matter of fact, when he had gone to get Li'l Man from Atlanta, he loved it so much that he had purchased a six-bedroom house on the low in hopes that maybe one day they would be reunited. He didn't tell her that part yet. He figured he'd hold on to that bit of information and surprise her with it later.

"Whatever you want, Keish. I'm with you."

"Good. Now me and Li'l Man would like to take you out."

"Sounds good. I'll be there to pick you up in a half," Tucker said.

"No, we're coming to get you. Epiphany gave me her ride."

"Keish, I'm coming to get you. You don't need her car." After everything that had gone down, Tucker still disliked Epiphany.

"Tucker, stop it. We're leaving now. You don't have to ride in my new car. We'll switch when I get there. Okay, baby? It's not a big deal, all right!"

"A'ight, and Keisha, I want you to know that I never stopped loving you."

"Baby, I'm glad to hear that, because I still love you too. I'll see you when I get there!" Keisha said, smiling.

Smitty spotted Epiphany's car pulling out as he turned the corner. Driving his black Expedition at full speed through the block, he unloaded six shots from his nine through the driver's side window, hitting Keisha. Realizing all too late that he had shot the wrong girl, Smitty panicked and mashed down on the gas harder, losing control of the wheel, spinning across the street, and crashing into a telephone pole. The impact knocked him out.

A few of the neighbors had witnessed the whole incident and called the police right away. Mr. Swinton, one of Jay Wright's buddies that lived next door, ran over to the car when he heard the baby's frantic cries and removed him from the back seat. Mr. Swinton checked his body to make sure he wasn't hit, then told his wife to take him in the house, away from the gruesome scene. In minutes, the police and ambulance arrived, but unfortunately, Keisha was already dead.

Tucker called her cell phone several times, wondering what was taking her so long. Becoming a little worried, he told himself that he'd try one more time before he headed over to pick them up.

On his last try, a police officer answered Keisha's phone and informed him that there had been a tragic accident and he needed to come right away. Tucker's heart dropped. Hearing the word "tragic" he automatically started to think the worst.

Rushing over to Epiphany's house, he prayed to God, "Please, God, not another one. Don't take another person I love away from me."

As the ambulance carrying Smitty, who was in stable condition, pulled off, Tucker arrived at the scene and instantly broke down when he spotted Keisha's dead body lying on the ground next to the car door, covered with a bloody sheet, awaiting the coroner. It was heartbreaking to see him down on his knees, holding her body, crying out in so much pain.

"Keish! Come on, Keisha! Please don't leave me. I need you, baby!" he cried repeatedly. Tucker would have given anything to bring her back.

The Final Chapter

NEW BEGINNINGS

It had been a year since Keisha was laid to rest in a Georgia cemetery, and even though everyone had finally started to move on, she would always be missed and never forgotten.

Tucker and Li'l Man moved down to Atlanta, where they were trying to make the best out of the situation, day by day. They found peace in spending a lot of time with Keisha's mother, Loretta, her grandmother, and her sisters Kelly and Keely, who had since straightened up her act. On Sundays, besides having dinner together, they all visited Keisha's grave to bring fresh flowers. Tucker now counseled youth about the negatives of the street gangs and the drug game. Li'l Man was growing fast and looking more and more like his mom every day.

Shana served six months in jail and was released, but she deeply regretted not being able to say good-bye at Keisha's funeral. She felt partly responsible for what had happened. Because of her own selfish reasons, she had hooked Smitty up with Epiphany.

She and K.C. were still together, and things were good between them. Their little investment had turned out to have a bigger profit than expected. They were able to purchase a condo and open a bar/lounge spot in Queens called Life. It was doing well for them. Although the money was straight, K.C. still hustled. Old habits die hard. However, he did stop cheating and in four months he and Shana would be the proud parents of their first baby, Keisha Shamari Cright. A girl, of course!

Smitty was brought up on murder charges and sentenced fifteen-to-life, but only lived to serve one month of his time. Uncle Ramel remembered the name and kept his promise.

When Smitty was in Rikers, he had some of his people take care of him with a nice slit to the throat.

C-God stopped getting high and was back on the map in the never-ending drug game with his new partner Alpo. Together, couldn't nobody hold them down, as long as the feds didn't catch him.

Ness's remains were never found and only C-God, Alpo, Hassan, and the dog Venom knew why, and they were not telling.

Epiphany never made it to Keisha's funeral. She knew Tucker would blame her for Keisha's death, just like he did with Malikai, and she had to admit she blamed herself too. She felt she was supposed to die, not them. If she had never invited Mali over to her house that night, or gave Keisha her car, both of them would still have been alive. The guilt ate away at her. She truly loved both of them dearly and did manage to visit their graves when she could. Her parents sold their house shortly after Keisha's death and moved to a nice area out in East Hampton, Long Island, where her father, Jay Wright, and mother, Tiara, were both studying ministry and were devoted members of a new church.

Epiphany and Wild moved to L.A. and shortly after their relationship started to deteriorate. It lasted for three months. Apparently, she felt he was *too nice*. She needed drama in the relationship and since there was none, it got boring. Epiphany started hanging out at all the celebrity affairs and managed to meet the right people and get the exposure she wanted. It's not always what you know, but who you know. Being with Wild for that short period of time served its purpose. Epiphany was now living lovely in Burbank California. She dabbled in everything from modeling to dancing in videos, but her heart was in acting.

31901064305792